War over Earth

Earth

Talin Wars

Written by
Scott A. Cheeseman

Edited by
**Douglas Cheeseman
& Sean Bourke**

PublishAmerica
Baltimore

ISBN: 1-4241-8296-4
PUBLISHED BY PUBLISHAMERICA, LLLP
www.publishamerica.com
Baltimore

Printed in the United States of America

To Chris

Scott Cheeseman

Table of Contents

Chapter One
The Beginning

August 5, 2025. That is the day every person's life on earth changed forever. It all started with my friends dragging me to a basketball game between two local college teams. We were about an hour into the game, which to me seemed like an eternity, when a loud thunderous crack filled the stadium. Then, two baseball size fireballs ripped through the stadium roof and exploded on the basketball court knocking the players off their feet and igniting the wooden court. The roof ignited into a blaze of flames. A third loud thunderous crack and another fireball smashed through the now sagging remains of the stadium's roof, striking the stands. The crowd stampeded towards the exits as a fourth crack ricocheted through the embattled stadium announcing the arrival of another fireball. That got us to our feet and moving towards the closest exit.

The exits were full of people pushing and shoving each other. Some of the fans fell to the floor and a few seconds later got trampled. Fights soon broke out amongst the stadium employees and the fans. More fireballs ripped through the stadium and struck the exit across the court. With an explosion the exit was crushed, sending wood, concrete, and body parts of people flying across the stadium. One or two people were hit by stray wood and concrete. A group of women fighting suddenly screamed bloody murder as body parts rained down on top of them. Over the loud screams and numerous raised voices, I could just make out numerous crashes. Chunks of the stadium roof began to fall. Little by little, the holes in the stadium roof grew. The crowd in the stadium started to thin as the roof began to cave in. The fighting among the crowd stopped and the flow of the evacuation quickly sped up.

Seconds after my friends and I escaped, the stadium collapsed with a horrific moan. Finally outside, we saw something that you should only see in nightmares and gory movies. At that moment, I wished it was a nightmare. I still do because in nightmares, you would eventually wake up and realize it never happened; however, it wasn't a nightmare it was real. The sky was a mixture of colors, there was a small glimmer of the blue sky that had dominated the heavens not that long ago. A mixture of reds, oranges, and yellows streaked across the sky and the sky itself was being turned into many different shades of blacks, whites and grays melding together. The stadium parking lot was roaring in pain from the countless meteor strikes. Cars were exploding, people were falling to the ground in flames, and the ground was red with flames.

We knew if we stayed there in the open parking lot, we would certainly be done for, so we decided to make a run for our car. We ran across the parking lot zigzagging between parked cars and just barely dodging meteors as they hit the tar. We were only a few feet from our car when a meteor a little larger than a football flew over our heads, with a loud roar, and struck the right side of our car crushing its roof and our hopes into its body. We turned and ran away from our car. Moments later, our car exploded, erupting in flames metallic shrapnel was hurtled into the sky. The explosion's concussion forced us to the ground.

"Hey, you four, do you need a ride out of here? My car is right over there," said a man off to my left, standing behind a large oak tree, pointing to a van off to our right with his right hand.

"Yes we need a ride."

"Hurry, let's get to my van," the man said as he started to gather some local team souvenirs from the ground.

We reached the van; I turned and faced the man. He was hastily walking towards us dropping souvenirs as he ran, when a meteor broke through the large oak tree, striking the man on his left side. The meteor continued into the tar as the man fell forwards to the ground.

Mike, David, and I rushed over to his side, his left arm and half of his torso was missing. We turned him over. With his last ounces of strength, he told us to take his keys and to get ourselves out of danger. His head lowered, what was left of his body started to convulse due to shock, and with an exhale of his last breath, the man died. His blood covered the surrounding tar. Under the heat of the tar his blood quickly clotted. The smell of his burning blood filled the air. The smell and the sight of what was once a man made me want to vomit. I closed his eyes. I took a deep breath, closed my eyes, and tried to gather my thoughts before I looked in his remaining pockets for his keys. I was brought back to reality by the jingling of the man's keys. Mike had fished through the man's remaining pockets and retrieved the keys. Mike tossed me the keys to the van then we joined Crystal back at the van.

I used the dead man's keys to unlock the van's doors and then the four of us climbed into the van. I tossed David the key to the van and he got into the front seat and turned the car on. We sped out of the parking lot as fast as the van could go. As we left the parking lot, a meteor crashed inches from the back of the van. The back window shattered as dust and chucks of debris were thrown against the back of the van. Glass crashed in on Crystal's and my head, covering the back seat with glass. Crystal and I immediately and carefully began brushing the glass off us and the seat. A second later the right side of the van jumped into the air and slammed back down.

"Hold on, the road is going to get very bumpy," David yelled while driving.

I raised my head and looked out the windshield at the road. Craters and burnt corpses littered the road in front of us. My jaw couldn't help but drop, not from what lay in the road but what lay alongside it. The road was surrounded on both the left and right, by long rows of houses that had been hit by meteors. The homes were in a fiery blaze and there were large breaches varying in sizes in the many structures. The grass of the lawns had been ripped from the earth by numerous craters. The green grass was roaring with pain as fire spread quickly through the grass. People were running out of their homes covered in fire and collapsed on the ground. There was very little left of the many tarred driveways and the tar that remained was starting to bubble. The sky was dark red with black clouds of smoke floating into the air. What was once a clear blue sky filled with white clouds now was filled with the worst sight I have ever seen. There were still meteors streaking across the sky with red and orange tails of fire leaving orange ripples as they cut through the smoke filled sky.

Four people engulfed in flames ran towards the van and slammed into the sides of the van. The looks on their faces said everything they were feeling. I could see the physical and mental pain in their cries for help. After a second their cries went silent. I still can hear their cries for help. Their hands covered in blood left bloody streak marks on the windows as they fell to the ground. I looked up to the sky when a meteor flew over the van and crashed nearby. I then noticed that the meteors were starting to diminish. Then without warning the van came to a rather hasty stop throwing the four of us forward. I looked up again at the road. The windshield was shattered, the hood of the van was bent up and there was steam rising from the engine. We climbed out of the van and walked to its front. A telephone pole had just fallen which left David no time to stop. The telephone pole was too large for us to move and the van looked too damaged to drive. We looked at the road ahead of us. Unable to use the van we had no choice but to walk to our safety.

"Where should we go?" asked David.

"My parents' house is only a few blocks from here, we can go there to get out of the meteor storm. The fastest way to get to my parents' house from here is to go to the end of the road we are on and then take the second right turn. My parents' house is at the end of that road about a mile or two down. Hopefully we will be safe there for a while, that is if it's still standing."

"Let's stop standing around here in the wide open and get to your parents' house," Mike suggested.

We left the van parked in front of the telephone pole and started to walk down the road in front of us. The screams from the suffering people got louder as we walked our way down the road. Smoke from wrecked cars, burnt homes, and other buildings drifted across our path. The smoke darkened the path ahead of us turning the road before us even darker than before. My friends and I quickened our pace as the air got heavier with smoke. My lungs filled with smoke with every breath I drew, and my head started to feel lighter than normal. My eyes got heavy, my vision got blurry, and my lungs burnt from lack of oxygen. A minute later the smoke started to lessen and the air began to return.

Seconds later, we emerged from the cloud of smoke out of breath and gasping for air. Out of breath I collapsed to my knees, the ground under me was wet and softer than it should have been. I glanced down. My eyes had just barely focused on a boy's body lying under my knees all but his head was burnt. His blood had soaked through my jeans, soaking my knees in blood. Crystal screamed when she looked down at me. I looked up at her, her face was white, and tears were running down her face.

"Crystal, come on we need to continue," Mike said. "It's too dangerous to stay here."

"Crystal, he's right we need to go now!"

We continued to walk down the road again, when a large meteor streamed across the sky and struck the ground. The earth shook when the meteor hit the ground. Smoke and dust lifted into the air seconds later. We hastened our pace as meteors continued to streak across the smoke filled sky. Corpses rested on lawns, sidewalks, driveways, and on top of the street. The yards were roaring with fire, the pavement was broke and turned to dust. Crystal started running down the street. Mike, David, and I quickly ran to keep up with her. We passed the first right-hand turn within ten minutes of running. Out of breath we reached the second right turn. We stopped running for a minute to catch our breaths, moments later we began down Hermit Rd. which looked like hell had risen from the bowels of the earth.

Hermit Rd. was in an even worse condition than the previous street. Most of the road and the surrounding lawns had been turned to dirt with craters of various sizes embedded in the surfaces. There were large chunks of the road and chunks of burning lawns that had been raised up by meteor impacts. Trees that had grown on Hermit Rd. for decades were now engulfed in flames and other trees lay on the ground in an inferno of fire. Very few of the trees had been untouched by the storm and an even smaller number had been simply splintered into tiny pieces. Smoke from burning buildings, structures and from numerous fires along the road ascended into the smoky red and black rich sky. On occasion with the help from gusts of wind the smoke would cross our path. The smoke had the odor of sulfur and brimstone with a constant stench of death in the air.

A Volkswagen parked on the right side of the road was engulfed in an inferno of fire. Thick black smoke rose from the flames. I could feel the heat from the burning car as we walked past it on the left side of Hermit Rd. Five minutes later David and Mike stopped and lowered their heads. Crystal stopped next to Mike's left side a second later and she lowered her head. I hastened my pace. I came to a stop next to Crystal's left side and I lowered my head when I saw what was in front of us. Ahead of us only a foot from where we stood, a large crater spread across both sides of Hermit Rd. and most of the surrounding buildings.

I looked over to the left side of the crater before us. A sign half-burned under dirt and debris read firehouse #31. A few feet above the sign was part of a fire engine, the rest of it was on the edge of the crater. Thick black smoke was pouring out of the two fire engine parts, and rose into the sky. Lying next to the engine part in the crater was seven firefighters. Half of them were fully dressed in their firefighter gear. The rest of them were either partially dressed in their gear or dressed in normal street clothes. Those of them that were not in their gear were burnt to a crisp and completely unrecognizable, only a few patches of fabric were left unburned.

The wind changed direction, blowing the thick black smoke and a horrid smell of burnt hair and cooking flesh to our noses. I turned my head to my right immediately as the smoke brushed over my face and hair. The wind did not let up causing the air to dissipate and grow thin. Needing breath, I dropped to my knees, folded myself up, and took a deep breath of trapped air. My eyes widened when I saw what had been resting beneath my feet. A round black ball lay on the edge of the crater. I reached down to pick it up, and a human spine extended from its base. I looked closer at the ball hoping it wasn't what I thought it was. What I thought was a ball had turned out to be part of a corpse. Realizing this, I immediately dropped the human remains and jumped back, raising my head back into the cloud of black smoke. I lowered my head back down into the pocket of smoke free air, drew a breath, and yelled out into the cloud to find out if the others were all right. I got a reply from all three of them seconds later.

"Alex, Crystal and I are fine!" David yelled through the smoke.

"I'm fine too but short of breath. How about you, Alex, how are you doing," Mike yelled through the cloud of smoke as well.

"I'm okay. I have just made a new friend."

The smoke lessened as the wind changed its direction and the thick black cloud of smoke returned to rising into the sky. As the smoke cleared, Crystal, Mike and David came into focus. Mike was standing on his feet brushing the dirt off his clothes and mumbling to himself. David was helping Crystal to her feet, as she stood erect, gravel slid out from under her feet and rolled down into the crater. I watched the gravel slide down the crater's steep slope. As I followed the sliding gravel down into the crater's edge, I noticed things in the crater that I had not noticed before. Dozens of bodies rested on the wall of the crater buried under gravel and dirt. Cars varying in makes and models also lined the crater's wall buried not only by gravel and dirt but also by collapsed buildings. Fire was roaring out of most of the cars, buildings, and those that lay dead on the ground. The ground itself was steaming and I could see flickers of red light buried under the dirt. CLAPS! The ground beneath the fire truck gave way and the remainder of the fire truck slid down into the crater and crashed into its other half.

"Alex, do you know of another way to get to your parents' house from here?" Mike asked over the few screams that remained in the air.

"Yes there is another way but it could take a few hours for us to walk there."

"Can we walk around the crater?" Crystal asked the three of us.

"No there doesn't appear to be a way we can go around, those buildings have collapsed on the edge and formed a wall in the crater."

"From what I can see there is a small opening in the wall a few feet from the center of the crater, we may be able to get through," Mike finished.

"Do we have to go through the crater, can't we take the other path?" asked Crystal.

"No we can't, it will take too much time for us to go around and the more time we spend in the open the greater the risk to any one of us if not all of us."

Crystal nodded and the four of us carefully walked down the edge of the crater. As we descended into the crater we zigzagged to avoid obstacles, unearthed bodies and the many roaring fires. I could feel heat from the ground through my shoes. The heat on the bottom of my feet got hotter and hotter as we got closer to the core of the crater. My feet started to sweat, steam lifted from my shoes as the sweat started to soak through the sides of my shoes. I started to feel the heat on the rest of my body. Sweat started to run down my face, down my back, and down my sides. By the time we had finally reached the narrow passageway in the core of the craters my shirt was drenched in sweat.

There wasn't very much room. Only enough room for us to go through single file. David passed through the opening and waited for the rest of us to get through. Crystal was second to pass through the opening. David lowered his hand to Crystal and helped her through the threshold. I was third to pass through the opening shortly followed by Mike. Once Mike and I had gotten out of the narrow passage, the four of us started the hard climb up the steep slope. We started to zigzag up the obstacle filled slope. Gravel slid out from under our feet as we put our weight on the loose gravel of the slope. Numerous corpses were unearthed as gravel slid out from under Crystal's feet and slid down the slope.

We finally reached the crater's edge. Slowly, we climbed out and on to the other side of the road. Without any delay we continued towards my parents' house. We walked for a few minutes down the other half of Hermit Rd., when Mike stopped walking and looked up at the smoke filled, and fire-lit sky. I walked over to him, and asked why he had stopped walking and what it was he was looking at. Getting no response, I raised my head to the sky and looked in the direction he was. All I could see was a meteor or two every so often streak across the sky. I turned my head to the direction the storm had been coming from and looked up there was very few meteors falling through the entire sky. I turned back to Mike and I placed my hand on his shoulder. Mike did nothing but stare into the sky for a few more minutes. He raised his arms, put his hands to his face, wiped his eyes quickly, and looked back up at the sky.

"Mike. What else other than the meteor storm letting up could you have possibly see?"

"I don't know exactly what it was. What ever it was it moved very quickly through the sky leaving a ripple in the smoke," Mike said as he lowered his head back to its normal position.

"What was it?"

"Don't know," Mike answered.

"We should get going and get to my parents' house as fast as we can."

"Alex, you're right. Let's go," Mike said.

Mike and I started to walk down Hermit Rd., once again. David and Crystal had gotten some distances down Hermit Rd. Mike and I had to quicken our pace to catch up. Our feet sank into the ground as Mike and I ran. At times, Mike and I had to hop over debris that lay in our path. We caught up to Crystal and David after a few minutes of running, my legs and the soles of my feet sheared in pain and my breathing grew heavier by the time we reached the two of them. As we reached them Mike and I came to a slow jog, dirt lifted from the ground as we slowed down. Gasping for air, I pointed down the road and said, "Almost there just a mile and a half." David and Crystal turned around as the dirt kicked up by Mike and I hit the back of their legs.

"What are you guys doing, kicking dirt at us?" David asked, raising his voice.

"Sorry, we were catching up to you two and when we slowed down we accidentally kicked dirt into the air."

"Why did you guys have to catch up to us?" Crystal asked the two of us quickly.

"Mike thought he saw something in the sky other than the meteors."

"Mike, what do you think you saw?" David asked.

"I don't know." Mike was interrupted by a high-pitched whistle coming from behind Mike and me.

The whistling was followed by a very loud crash that sent the four of us to the ground, which knocked the air from my lungs. At the same time a cloud of dust with tremendous surge of wind was forced over us. Lying there under the dust cloud, I could hear the others gasping for air. My lungs burned, demanding a breath of air. I opened my mouth and I pulled the dust filled air into my lungs. What light there was from our surroundings dimmed and eventually was

15

extinguished. The dust and the lack of light darkened our surroundings, making it impossible to see the others and my surrounding. The force of the wind let up and some of the dust settled a few minutes later. Almost out of breath and beginning to grow lightheaded I got to my feet and struggled to reach the cloud's edge and the fresher air ahead of me.

The air still had trace amounts of dirt and dust in the air but my lungs felt some relief. My eyes watered as the clean air brushed against the dry whites of my eyes. The inside of my nose began to clog from the dust in the air. A minute later the dust that remained in the air settled down and the light from the devilish sky slowly returned. My eyes started to dry and my surroundings started to return to focus. I turned to see my three friends lying on the ground under a layer of dirt. Mike and David were barely moving but did breathe every so often. Crystal, on the other hand, was lying there face to the sky under a layer of dirt and she was not breathing.

I raced towards her and slid to her side, kicking up dirt in the air as I slid. I got to my knees and wiped the layer of dirt off her face and torso. I lightly slapped her face in hopes I would get a response, but had no success. I then began to perform CPR pumping on her chest and breathing into her lungs for her. After the first breath of air, I returned to pumping on her chest, counting up to five before I breathed into her lungs again. Six times, I pushed on her chest and six times I breathed into her lungs. After the seventh pump and seventh breath, I stood up knowing I had failed knowing she had died. As I got to my feet my eyes watered again but not from the air but from the loss of a good dear friend.

I started to walk over to Mike and David. They had gotten to their feet, caught their breaths, and had watched as I performed CPR on our friend Crystal. David had tears running down his face as I confirmed Crystal's death to them. Mike stood there gazed at the lifeless body of our friend and showed little signs of sadness. David walked over to her lifeless body. He kneeled down next to her and started to pull Crystal closer to him. Crystal's head suddenly jerked forward, her mouth opened, and she gasped for air. She quickly exhaled and drew another breath of air just as fast as she could. David lowered her back on to her back, and put his left hand around her head A few minutes later Crystal's breathing slowed down, back to a normal pace. She sat up, looked around at our surroundings, and then stared into David's face.

"Wwhat hhapped?" Crystal asked David while gasping for air.

"Later we need to get moving and get to Alex's parents' house."

"Yyyeeess, yyyoouu'rrreee rriigghhtt," Crystal said as she slowly regained her breath.

David stood up and extended his right hand out in front of Crystal. She reached for his hand and pulled on his arm. David pulled back and brought Crystal to her feet. Her breathing had returned by the time she had reached Mike and me. Once she had reached us, she could not help but ask Mike and me what happened to her. Without thinking we both blurted out what had happened to her.

"Crystal, you died."

"Alex had performed CPR but it had no effect." Mike stopped when he saw the expression on her face.

She was frozen. Her eyes were wide, and her face had turned from a rosy color to a ghostly white. A few tears ran down the side of her face. David put his arms around her shoulder and whispered into her left ear. The color very slowly returned to her face as David quietly spoke into her ear. She raised her hand and wiped the tears off the sides of her face. Her blue eyes shrank back to normal, and then she opened her mouth and spoke.

"Sorry, I'm okay now. We should get moving," Crystal said in a low and shaky voice.

"Sorry, Crystal, for upsetting you."

"Crystal, I'm sorry too. We didn't mean to get you upset," Mike said as he lowered his head.

"It's okay. I forgive you both, thank you for telling me the truth and, Alex, thanks for giving me CPR." Crystal finished speaking and started walking down Hermit Rd.

Mike, David, and I quickly followed her and we quickly caught up to Crystal. The four of us walked for a few minutes without any interruptions which brought us in sight of my parents' house. My parents' house was on the left-hand side of Hermit Rd. and was the tallest house on the block. From our distance I was just barely able to make out the color of the house. The sides were a dark white, the roof was a barely noticeable black, and the window frames and doorframes stood out from the sides of the house, mainly because they were colored black.

In front of us lay a path of destruction. Cars lay in the road and in driveways in balls of fiery parts. The road like the rest of the road on Hermit Rd. was in ruins. All of the lawns on both sides of Hermit Rd. were engulfed in fire. Both the hedges and the trees on either side of Hermit Rd. were also in a blaze of fire. Large meteors had struck about half of the homes on the left side of the road as a result, the homes had been leveled. The rest of the house on Hermit Rd. had received fewer meteor strikes.

We made our way down Hermit Rd. and stopped briefly in front of my parents' house. We walked up the driveway and up to the front door, I knocked on the front door, and as I knocked on the door. It slowly opened with a creak. I pushed the door open further. The inside was dark, and a thin cloud of smoke drifted out the house. I stepped in and made my way down the entrance hallway a few feet. Mike, David, and Crystal soon followed me into my parents' house. There was barely any light in the house but there was enough to see the silhouette of our surroundings.

"Mom, Dad, it's Alex. Are you home?"

No answer.

"Mr. and Miss Track, are you home, it is Alex's friend David?" David asked, yelling into the rest of the house.

But still no answer.

"Alex, Mike and I will look upstairs for your parents, would you look after Crystal while looking for your parents?" David asked.

"Yes I will keep my eyes on her while I'm looking for my parents."

David and Mike started to head up the staircase in the hall, while Crystal and I started to walk down the hallway. We started to look the first floor over. We went from room to room opening and closing each door as we went. We had checked most of the downstairs when I heard a noise from behind a door to my right. I opened the door and motioned for Crystal to follow me in. Crystal and I now were in a short dark hall. There was a noise and a white light coming from further down the hall. We walked down the hall. At the end of the hall was a partly opened doorway that had the light and noise coming from with in. Crystal and I looked into the room. There was a dozen or so shadowy figures huddled around a small battery operated TV.

I recognized the sounds coming from the battery powered TV. The mass of shadows were huddled around the TV watching a news bulletin. Crystal and I slowly entered the small living room, trying not to make any sound because we both wanted to hear what was going on. We crept close to the mass I was starting to make out some of their faces. My parents were sitting next to each other and on either side was one of their neighbors. To my parents' right were the Millers, no relation to the beer, and on my parents' left was Nemeke. There were two elderly couples also huddled around the small TV. Both of the couples were on the other side of my parents' neighbors. I had never seen either of the two elderly couples before that night. All of them had a horrified look on their faces and other than a slow and quiet sound of air getting pulled into their bodies none of them made any sound. They did not move at all other than the uncontrolled blinking that each of them had to make every few seconds.

Chapter Two
Preparation

"Hi, Crystal. Hi, Alex, are you two okay?" my mom said in a low and emotionless way.

"We're fine, Mom."

"Hi, Alex, ALEX! You're all right," my dad said as he broke out of the huddle and hugged me as hard as he could.

"ALEX, YOU'RE okay!" my mom said as she quickly broke from the huddle.

My mom quickly broke into tears as she wrapped her arms around my father and me.

"We heard that the stadium had been destroyed and the body count was high. The reporter also said that the chances of surviving the devastation to the stadium and the surrounding areas were next to impossible," my dad said as he joined my mom in tears.

"Crystal, did you and Alex find his parents down there?" Mike yelled from the second floor.

"Yes, Alex and I found them."

"Where are you guys?" David asked, yelling down to us.

"We're in the downstairs living room it's just past the kitchen on your right," my dad yelled towards the ceiling.

"We will join you guys as fast as we can," Mike yelled from above.

"Alex, how did you, Crystal, David, and Mike get from the stadium to our house without so much as a scratch on any of you?" my dad asked as he let me go and wiped the tears from his eyes.

I started to tell my dad, my mom and the other people in the room what the four of us had gone through in the past three hours. However, it did not take very long for David and Mike to find the living room. In fact I had just reached the down telephone pole when David and Mike busted into the room. There was barely enough light to see my parents let alone anything surrounding us. Both of them were breathing hard and they both had trouble forming words.

"Why didn't you call us as soon as you found your parents?" David asked while he gasped for air.

"We did not call you because Alex and I just found them ourselves," Crystal said as her voice raised to match David's tone and volume.

"Sorry I didn't know," David apologized to Crystal and then walked to the mass of people huddled around the TV and sat down in one of the vacant sets.

"Jeff, Lorain, and the rest of you have got to hear this. The reporter has new information on today's meteor storm," said Mrs. Nemeke.

Crystal, Mike, my parents, and I walked over to the mass of people surrounding the battery operated TV. They had spread out so there would be enough room for us to sit. The news anchor came back on to the broadcast and delivered some disturbing news.

"This is Alison Turckoz with channel ten news, we have some troubling news about the meteor storm. This is not a local event this storm has showered the entire earth with meteors. An uncountable number of meteors have hit everything south of the North Pole and north of the South Pole. The president has been moved to a safe location and will give a statement first thing in the morning at 8 a.m. sharp EST."

Alison Turckoz left the broadcast and a damage report came across the screen. Names of cities, states, countries, and nations that were either destroyed/nearly destroyed or were in the process of being destroyed. Every couple of seconds or so additional names of cities, states, and countries were added to the list.

"There is nothing for us to do at this time so we probably should get some sleep," my dad said, standing up.

"Someone should stay up in case there are any additional news or meteor strikes," Mike said as my dad walked over to the door.

"That's a good idea, Mike, but who will take the first watch?" my dad asked quickly.

"I was thinking myself and someone else would take the first watch," he said this while he looked at Crystal, David and, me.

"Mike, buddy pal, I would but I am extremely tired, I need to get my sleep," David said as he faked a yawn.

"I'm not tired. I will stay up and keep watch."

"I will stay up with you and Alex," said Crystal.

"Second thought I am not really that tired I will stay up," said David, changing his mind.

"No you said you were tired so you go to sleep while Alex, Mike, and I keep watch on things," Crystal said, at the same time looking right at David with a serious expression on her face.

"But I am not tired," David quickly said after Crystal had finished.

"Crystal's right. Three people will be more than enough for the first watch. Therefore, you, Lorain and I will take the second shift. It's ten now so at three in the morning we will relieve the three of you," my dad said as he looked at his watch.

"All right, Dad. You, Mom and David go and get some sleep."

"See you three in the morning. Good night," my dad said as he left.

Everyone other than Crystal, Mike, and I stood up and followed my dad out of the small living room. David was the only one other than Crystal, Mike, and I that did not leave the living room, David only left the living room after my dad had come back and forced him out. Then it was just the three of us in the living room for the next five hours. We mainly sat on the sofa in the back of the room and talked amongst ourselves. Mike, Crystal, and I would periodically stand up and leave the living room and returned with something to eat and drink from the kitchen. Mike or I would once every so often go and check on the others making sure they were all right. Crystal would stay in the living room toned on the battery powered TV and see what was going on in the world. The five hours passed rather slowly even though we were talking about the past hours and taking brief walks around the house to stretch our legs.

Three o'clock rolled up, by that time, we had talked about everything that had happened hours before. However, when it did finally turn three, David and my parents relieved us. Crystal, Mike, and I left the living room and climbed up the stairs to the second floor.

We entered the upstairs living room and split up. I took one of the couches in the living room, Crystal took the other one across from me, and Mike slept in the reclining chair. My eyes got heavy with exhaustion, my thoughts dwindled to nothing, and I fell asleep.

Later that morning I was woken by my mom. She was shaking me back and forth and was telling me to get up. I sat up and started to tell my mom that I had a horrible dream. However, before I had gotten too far into the dream my eyes focused and as I stared at my dad waking Crystal and David waking Mike it all rushed back to me. The dream I started to tell my mom about was no dream, it had happened and it had only happened yesterday. My mom stepped back and I got to my feet and stood next to her.

"What's up, Mom?" My mom did not say anything.

The room was still dark and I could barely make out my mom's face. She was wide-eyed and had a glimmer of tears in them. Shortly after I woke up, Crystal woke up and joined my mom and me. My dad, on the other hand, walked over to David and helped him wake Mike. Mike stood up and made a low almost unnoticeable moan. The three of them walked over to Crystal, my mom and me, once Mike had woken up a little more.

"It's almost eight in the morning the president will be making a statement shortly," my dad said as they reached Crystal, my mom and I.

"The rest are waiting in the downstairs living room we should go and join them downstairs," said my mom.

The six of us made our way out of the upstairs living room and descended the staircase. Then the six of us walked through the first floor until we reached the living room. Everyone that was there last night was huddled once again around the battery powered TV. We crossed the living room, took a spot around the TV, and looked upon the little TV screen. The image changed from the constant update screen and went into an image with news anchor Alison Turckoz on it. Her mouth moved but no sound came out, tiny letters flashed across the small screen: audio difficulties. Three minutes went by before there was any change in the audio. Anchor Alison Turckoz voice started to return, at first all you could hear was brief and broken words nothing that could be made out. Finally, five minutes after the news anchor came on, the audio returned to normal and the image had changed. Now displayed on the TV was a podium with the presidential seal on it.

"Without any farther delay, the president of the United States President Peter Clark," said a short man standing at the podium.

The short man turned and left the podium and a taller man stepped up to the podium.

"Good morning, as of yesterday the entire world was hit by a massive meteor storm and it doesn't look like it will let up for a few days. I have issued an immediate evacuation of all residents to safe locations under all major cities. For those citizens in lower populated areas, make their way to local hospitals, fire stations, and local police stations. At those locations military personal will lead them to the underground entrances closest to them. Thissssshhh massssshhiiiggg wwwilllll repeat eeevvveeerrr ccccoooopppppaaaallll hhhoooouuuuurrrrrrs," said President Clark as the battery powered TV went black and silent.

"The batteries must have died," said Mr. Millers quickly after the TV had died.

"You heard the president, we need to head for either the hospital, fire station, or the police station," said my dad.

"The fire station is much closer than either the hospital or the police station," said Mr. Millers.

"No we can't go there, the fire station has been destroyed, and the police station is too far to walk so the hospital is our only choice."

"We got to take food water and first aid with us."

"Lorain, could you go and make food for us," my dad said in a nervous and scared voice.

"Arian, could you go and help Lorain with the food and water," said Mr. Nemeke.

"I will help too," said Mrs. Mills.

"The rest of us will go and get anything else we might need," said my dad.

Everyone stood up and started to explore my parents' house looking for supplies. David and I went to the garage to get the first aid kit from my parents' two cars and anything else we might need. David opened the car door of my mom's car and took the first aid kit from under the driver's seat. While he was looking for the first aid kit, I was looking for any tools we may need. David then walked over to my dad's car, opened the driver's side door, and looked under the seat. Then he closed the driver's side door, walked to the passenger's side door, and opened it. He stuck his head in and pulled it out seconds later without the second first aid kit.

"Alex, where's your dad's first aid kit?"

"Sorry I forgot he likes to keep all his supplies in the trunk of his car."

David walked back over to the driver's side again and reopened the car door. He reached down, popped the truck of my dad's car, then walked back to the rear of the car, and opened it the rest of the way. He reached in and pulled out a cardboard box full of emergency supplies. By this time, I had found hammers and a couple of fire extinguishers on my dad's metal tool rack. David walked over and placed the cardboard box on my mom's car. I walked over to the front of my mom's car. David and I started to remove the supplies from the box. We removed blankets, candles, road salt, flares, a first aid kit, another fire extinguisher, and emergency water from the cardboard box and set them on my mom's car. We left the road salt in the garage and returned to the living room.

Some of the others had returned to the living room before David and me. Both of the elderly couples were sitting in the living room talking amongst themselves. A few minutes later my dad and Mr. Millers returned to the living room with their arms full of supplies. My dad was carrying an armful of flashlights and some boxes of batteries. Mr. Millers returned with some blankets and numerous book bags and duffel bags. A short time after Mr. Millers and my dad returned Mike and Mr. Nemeke entered the living room caring a blanket full of fire extinguishers and bottles. Crystal, Mrs. Millers, Mrs. Nemeke, and my mom were the last in the house to return to the living room. All four of them were carrying the food in sandwich bags on large metal trays. Everyone set the supplies in the middle of the room and sat down surrounding the supplies.

The two elderly couples came over and joined us around the pile of supplies. My dad reached down and started to count the number of book bags and duffel bags we had. Mr. Millers started to separate the fire extinguishers from the rest of the supplies. Mr. Nemeke took the flashlights and began to check each one, at the same time under his breath he was keeping count of all the flashlights that worked. Mike

SCOTT A. CHEESEMAN

and I started counting the number of blankets we have all gathered. Crystal and David started to check the medical supplies everyone had gathered from around the house.

"The four of us talked and decided to stay here in this house if that's okay with the Tracks. We are much older than you and the four of us will just slow you all down. Besides, we have lived our lives you all still have so much to see and do. Just leave some food and some supplies for us and get to the hospital before the military leave the area. However, my wife and I will help you all get ready to leave. So hand my wife and I some book bags and duffel bags and we will start loading them full of supplies," the old man said this while trying to keep a strong face on his shoulders.

His wife's face was trying to hold back the tears but one or two would occasionally squeeze through. The two of them sat there packing the book bags and duffel bags full of supplies that had been gathered. Two minutes later, the other couple stepped in and started loading the bags. It did not take long for the four of them to get all the bags that had been counted full of supplies. Each duffel bag was loaded with fire extinguisher, a blanket, and some of the water jugs my dad and Mr. Miller bought back with them. The backpacks were loaded with first aid kits that were found, some water, some of the food and additional blankets.

"How many full book bags and duffel bags do we have?" asked my dad.

"There are six book bags and eight duffel bags full of supplies," replied the first elderly man.

"There aren't that many of us, there is only ten of us that are leaving, and heading for the hospital," said Mrs. Nemeke.

"Are you four sure that you don't want to come with us and get to safety?" asked my dad bluntly.

"Yes we're sure that we want to stay," said the second old man.

"Okay, then let's decide who is getting the duffel bags and who gets the book bags," said my dad.

"Let's take five duffel bags and all of the book bags with us. How many working flashlights do we have?"

"We have seven working flashlights and two that don't work," replied Mr. Nemeke.

26

"Have you tried replacing the batteries in those two non working flashlights?" asked my dad.

"No I didn't know that we had spare batteries. Give them here and I will check those two flashlights now," said Mr. Nemeke.

"Which of the book bags has the medical supplies in them?" my dad asked the two elderly couples polity.

"These three have the most medical supplies," answered one of the elderly women.

"The rest of the backpacks have some of the more common supplies, like bandages and antibiotics," said the second woman.

"Could you give those three bags here?" asked my dad.

"Yes, here you go, Jeff," said the first elderly male as he handed the three bags to my dad.

My dad took the bags one by one and slapping a sticker on the back of them as he picked them up.

"Here, Alex, take one of the medical bags. If you don't mind, Fred, I would like you to have the second bag, and I will take the last medical bag," said my dad as he handed out the medical bags to me, and Mr. Miller.

My dad then walked around everyone stopping only when he reached the elderly couples. He quietly spoke with them and then he reached down and started to hand the rest of the backpacks to the others. Crystal, Mrs. Nemeke and my mom got the other three bags. My dad then lifted one of the duffel bags and handed it to Mike. He then reached down, picked up a second duffel bag, and handed it to David. Then he handed a third to Mr. Nemeke. Finally my dad returned to his set but not empty-handed, he returned with a fourth duffel bag. He then handed the third medical bag to Mrs. Miller.

"Sorry if I just forced them on you but I looked at my watch and realized what time it was. It's ten a.m.; we have to get moving in a few minutes. If you have to use the bathrooms I suggest you do it now because there is no telling when your next chance may be," said my dad.

My mom Mr. Miller and Mrs. Nemeke got up and left the room. I set my medical bag down, got up, and left the living room. I went upstairs, found the bathroom in the dark, and did what I needed to do. Once I finished in the bathroom, I descended the staircases and headed for the living room. Everyone was sitting with their bags on their backs or at arms length. I walked over, put on my medical bag, and sat down.

"If everyone is ready we need to get going," said my dad.

Everyone stood up and started to head for the door out of the living room. Then my mom stopped, turned to face the two elderly couples.

"Thank you and good luck. I hope you four will be okay by yourselves. I look forwarded to seeing you again," said my mom.

"We will be just fine go and get to the hospital already," said one of the two elderly wives.

Everyone gave their best wishes and left the living room. The ten of us made our way through the first floor with all of our supplies in hand and on our backs. My dad leading the way stopped in front of the front door for a few seconds, then opened the door, and stepped through. One by one, the rest of us followed my dad out of his house. For Crystal, Mike, David, and me, we were returning to the nightmarish sight that lay outside of my parents' house, the same nightmare we had fought through hours before.

The sky was still black from smoke and was still illuminated by the many fires that had broken out. The streets were quiet except for the sounds of a few other survivors walking down Hermit Rd. and the roar of many fires that had grown in intensity. Those people that were alive were walking down Hermit Rd. in the wrong direction. They were probably heading towards the firehouse. My dad stepped forward and yelled in the direction of the other survivors.

"If you're heading for the firehouse you're going the wrong way, the firehouse has been destroyed," yelled my dad.

The groups of people in earshot of my dad turned around and started heading in the correct direction. The groups that were too far from us, continued to walk down Hermit Rd towards the ruined fire house. My dad returned to our group and motioned for all of us to start moving with a jerk of his head. All ten of us walked down to the end of the driveway, turned left, and began our long walk to the hospital. Usually from my parents' house to the hospital it would only take thirty to forty minutes by car but on foot would have only taken us twice that if it wasn't for the obstacles in our way.

We walked down the rest of Hermit Rd. as quickly as we could, not stopping for anything. The main reason for our haste was due to the condition of the rest of Hermit Rd. Everything on the sides of the road were engulfed in a mix of yellows, reds, and orange fires. A thick black smoke was rising from all the engulfed surroundings. The air still had the stench of charred flesh also numerous odors given off by the meteors penetrating earth's atmospheres and crust. With every breath I took, I could smell a slight odor of the earth burning under our feet. The air was also hot and there were trace amounts of smoke in the air.

After twenty minutes of walking down the rest of Hermit Rd., we turned on to Olive Road. In order for us to get to the hospital we needed to cross the business side of town which meant, we had no choices but to walk down Olive Rd. On either side of Olive Road businesses were roaring with flames as the ragging roaring fire laid them to waste. However, not all of the businesses were in a blaze of fire, some still stood with holes in the walls. The road itself surprisingly wasn't in too bad of state. Other than a few craters in the road, it seemed to be in good walking condition.

We started to walk down Olive Road, my parents took the lead, Crystal, and I pulling up the rear. The Millers and Nemeke were ahead of Crystal and me. Mike and David were in between the Nemeke and my parents the two of them were spread out over the width of the road. About twenty feet or more, we heard a thunderous boom from above our heads. We all stopped dead immediately and look up. A meteor a few hundred feet away looked to be the size of a, beach volleyball, was speeding across the polluted sky. We hastened for a minute and then everyone started to run in opposite directions.

Crystal and I ran backwards instead of running forwards with the rest of the group. The volleyball size meteor struck right on top of Mr. and Mrs. Miller and knocked the Nemeke off their feet. Crystal and I soon after the impact were knocked off our feet and to our hands and knees. A large cloud of dust and dirt lifted into the air and covered most of the surroundings. Then a loud explosion sent a hot flash of air sweeping over our backs. I waited for a few seconds before I called out to Crystal mainly because I did not know where she was nor did I dare to draw a breath of the hot air. Then I could not take another second without fresh air in my lungs so I opened my mouth and exhaled and quickly drew air. Just as quickly as I drew air, I yelled to Crystal.

"Crystal; are you alright?" I said, standing up.

"I'm fine, Alex, and yourself?"

"I am also fine." I started to walk in her direction.

"Crystal, where are you?"

"I am just outside the dust cloud. Alex, where are you?"

"I am still in the cloud," I said as I started to see illumination from the surrounding fires.

"Hurry up and get out of there."

"I should be out of the cloud any second now."

Five seconds later, I started to make out the silhouette of Crystal's body. I emerged two seconds later from the dust cloud and then I walked over to Crystal's side turned to face the cloud. The dust cloud was too thick for me to see through to the other side. There was an orange glow in the cloud from one side of the road to the other side.

"Mom, dad; are you alive?"

"We're fine so is David and Mike, but the Nemeke and the Millers are all dead," yelled my dad through the cloud.

"Are you and Crystal okay, you're not hurt, are you?" asked my mom.

"We're fine, Mrs. Track."

"Alex, can you go around the crater?" asked my dad.

"Yes I think there is a way, but—"

"We will wait here, for you to go around."

"No, Dad, it's not safe to stay in one place for too long and besides there is no telling when the meteor storm could start up again. You mom Mike and David go ahead and get to the hospital. Crystal and I will meet you there as fast as we can get there."

"No, we will wait here."

"David, Mike will you get them to the hospital."

"Yes we will," said Mike.

"Alex, take good care of Crystal?" asked David.

"Okay I will see you guys later. Bye, Mom. Bye, Dad; see you at the hospital."

"Bye, Alex," said Mike.

"Bye, Crystal," said David.

Chapter Three
The Labyrinth

The dust settled revealing a wall of fire spreading from one side of the road to the other. The buildings on either side of the road quickly erupted with a roaring fire. We began looking around at the buildings for an alternate path to a corresponding road. A building on our right had an alley that from what I could see led to another road. The building on the left side of the alley was quickly engulfed in flames. We did not waste any time Crystal and I ran over to the alley and ran as fast as we could between the two buildings. Burning trash lay on the ground of the alleyway. We didn't pay any thought about the burning trash we ran through. Our main concern was to get through the alley.

We emerged from the alley with minor burns on our feet and some smoke in our lungs. We continued to run from the alleyway in until we reach the middle of the street. This road looked just like Olive Road did except there was no large wall of fire in front of us but there was a large building further down the road that lay from one side to the other. The building seemed to have fallen over when the last meteor struck Olive Road. We started to head towards the building on its side hoping that there was a way to get through. There was a small opening where two of the levels came together.

Crystal and I were however unable to reach the opening in time. About five to ten feet from the opening, the meteor storm picked up once again, and it came down hard. The sky quickly filled with balls of fire flying through the air. We could not stay in the opened for very long and we could not go into the opening in the collapsed building. We looked quickly at the buildings around us. Once on the corner of Buckley and Rosemary, I saw it, I saw our salvation.

On the corner of Buckley and Rosemary (the road we were on) a slightly old building stood undamaged by time and the storm. The front door was ajar and swinging in the gusts of wind. I pointed out to Crystal the slightly old building; she gave me a look and started to run in the direction of the building. We ran to the building the whole time glancing up in the direction of the meteors. The sky was littered with them. If I was still five or six, I would swear that all the stars in the nighttime sky were falling. Reaching the door, I slid on something slippery under my feet, quickly I grabbed the door to stop myself from falling. I looked down to my feet as I held the door open for Crystal.

Below my feet was a pool of blood, my eyes followed the blood to a body that lay next to the building. The body was charred beyond recognition. One of his arms was missing, and there were veins and arteries hanging from the shoulder bone. The body still had blood flowing out of it even though it had probably had been dead for a few hours by that time.

"Alex," Crystal called for me to get into the building.

"Coming."

I entered into the building and pulled the door closed behind me. The entrance was poorly lit. As I walked through I stumbled on my own two feet. At the end of the entrance was a photo of the building we were currently residing in. Below the photo was a small sign that said: "Bomb shelter since 1940-1960." To the right of the photo was a doorway that led to a room off to my left was a tapestry. I walked into find Crystal lying on a couch naked with her face in the air, her left arm across her chest and her right leg bent.

"Did you read the sign? We can stay here for a while to wait out the storm."

"Yes I read the sign."

I looked around the room at all the things to be seen in the room. It was in good condition considering the age of the structure. There was a little bit of damage to the widows but nothing seemed to be any threat to the structure. Crystal's clothes were laid across one of the armrests of a chair in the far corner. Crystal cleared her throat bringing my attention back to her; she was on her feet facing me with a look of desire across her face. Under the light of the room Crystal looked like an angel. Her skin glowed, her eyes twinkled, and her hair shined. She slowly but seductively walked across the room towards me. Inches away from each other, I could feel the warmth from her body. She reached out with both arms and removed my shirt. She then lustfully kissed me on the lips and rubbed her hands over my chest stopping at my pants.

Crystal unfastened my pants. Her right had moved under my boxers and gripped me. With her left hand she took hold of my left hand and guided me to the same couch that she had been lying on. Crystal released her grip, let go of my hand, and sat down on the couch and pulled off my pants. She lay back on the couch. She pulled me on top of her and she merged our two bodies. She was warm and tight; her skin smooth and soft; her breasts full and her nipples hard and perky. I started thrusting in and out. She matched me thrust for thrust. Her breathing grew heavy she released a lustful moan of pleasure. Her breathing grew even heavier, and even faster by the second. Then her moans lessened and grew quieter.

We reached the peek of our pleasure, and collapsed on the couch in a pile of sweaty pleasured flesh. We lay on the couch for forty-five minutes gathering our breath and strength. We shared a few kisses and then, dozed off to sleep. We were both woken by alarms blaring. I quickly got to my feet, quickly gathered up my clothes, and started to get dressed. Just as I was sliding, my right shoe backed on a meteor the size of a golf ball crashed through the wall across from us, striking a reclining chair, igniting the chair, and continued into the floor. Crystal snapped to her feet and made a dash for her clothes, she ran over to the corner of the room where her clothes where. A meteor slammed through on of the windows and landed on the couch that Crystal just left. The couch erupted in flames and very quickly spread to the walls of our shelter and then to other furniture in the room. Crystal and I grabbed whatever we could find, and tried to put out the fire. The fire spread regardless of our attempts to snuff it out. The room stated to fill with smoke. The fire had grown too fast for us and the air was growing thinner by the second.

Metal slabs slid down the windows crushing the glass as it dropped. A large metal slab closed off the doorway to the room. The room began to fill with smoke as the fire burned up the air and spread along the furniture even faster. I watched as Crystal fell to the floor. I dropped to my knees and crawled over to her. She was still breathing but was non responsive to me. The room was completely lit up by the orange glow of the deadly roaring fire. The smoke above us grew closer and closer to the floor. We were stuck and there didn't appear to be any way out. I could feel the pocket of air growing thin and I could feel my head floating at the same time growing heavier. My arms could no longer support my weight and I collapsed to the floor. The room was growing too hot. Everything grew dark and I suddenly felt a cold and wet sensation over my entire body. I opened my eyes briefly to see the bomb shelter taking action then I blacked out.

"Here's my favorite part of the story," said an unidentified source.

"Yup this is by far the best part of the story," said a second unidentified source.

"I thought I told you two to stay off the computer. If you are going on to the computer the least you could do is leave my files alone."

"Okay, okay, but this still is our favorite part," said an unidentified source.

"To any ships in range of this message this is Commander Shaurha of the Talin ship *Kento*, please help us! We have been hit by a severe meteor storm and we have taken heavy damage to all of our systems. Our outer hull is buckling on our port side. Most of the crew was lost in the meteor storm. Our communications engines and weapons are failing life support has already failed. I am attempting to land on a nearby inhabited planet. I am unable to change our landing site; we will be landing in the middle of a small town. The planet has taken heavy damage by the meteor shower. I...command to eject in...escape pods. I do not...have idea...who is still alive...how many. I am the only one left in...command and...am stuck here, I'm going...with...the ship. If I am luck...to...make surviving crew...meet...with...me at a...hopefully safe location."

My eyes opened as cold water showered my face and my body. I was alive and more importantly I could breathe. I stood up and looked around, two of the windows in the bomb shelter were open and letting air in. I turned to Crystal, she was on her side coughing and gasping for air. The fire was out, the smoke was clearing from the room, and the chair that had been engulfed in flames was black and smoking. A sound to my left caught my attention. The doorway that had closed to contain the fire was now open revealing a half burnt tapestry and a door behind it.

Once Crystal regained most of her breath, we wanted to get out of the bomb shelter as fast as we could. Crystal and I ran back to the entrance hall and proceeded down to the door. However, when I turned the handle to open the door the doorknob fell off and dropped to the floor. Due to the darkness of the entranceway, I was unable to see where the doorknob had rolled. Crystal and I had no choice but to look for another exit from this hell of a bomb shelter.

Crystal and I walked back down the entrance hallway and took a left through the newly discovered doorway. Right off to the right was a staircase that led down under the bomb shelter. The stairway was darker than the entrance we could not see anything in front of us. We climbed down the staircase very slowly taking extreme care with each step we took. Once or twice, the stairs felt like they would fall out from under the weight of our feet but luckily the staircase mostly held our full combined weight. As we descended the staircase, the air got cold and had a musky smell. A breeze of hot hellish air rushed over us as we reached the middle of the stair case. I thought I heard wood cracking. I stopped for a second heard nothing and continued. Suddenly some wood snapped. Then I heard Crystal scream. I turned, looked back, the stairs under Crystal had given out and her arms were pushing on both walls of the staircase stopping her from falling. I stepped back up a few steps, pulled her foot from the broken step, and helped her down the rest of the staircase. Finally at the bottom of the staircase, Crystal paused for a moment and took a deep breath of relief.

It was too dark to see anything, the only way to find our way around was to feel for the walls and search for a light switch, and hope the power was still on. Five minutes of looking for a light switch Crystal found one about five feet from the staircase. She flicked the switch and a small desk lamp came on which illuminated the room enough to find additional lights and turn them on. As each light was turned on Crystal and I could see more of the room we were standing in. Books were stacked on bookcases and the bookcases lay against every wall. In the center of the room was a large circular wood desk which was covered by a layer of dust. There was a desktop computer sitting next to the small desk lamp. There were two doors in the room one was at the opposite side from the staircases and the second was to the left of them.

Both of the doors were old, extremely dark, and ajar. Light from the other side of the door to the left of the staircase shined through the opening. Crystal and I walked to the first door on our left opened the door and looked inside. On the other side of the door was a long hall with a staircase at the end. Crystal and I walked to the end of the hall and started to climb up the staircase. The staircase ended and a large metal gate stood in front of us. There was enough room in between the bars to see outside of the bomb shelter. I pushed and pulled on the gate to open it, in order to get outside once again. With my last push the gate swung open and we both stepped out into an alleyway. Across from us was a large brick wall that had partly clasped. The top of the wall was lying on the edge of the bomb shelter.

We looked both ways for a path to get back on the main road. On our left, the alley went on for some distance. To our left a brick wall had started to crumble. There was nowhere to go on our left so Crystal led the way as she and I started down the narrow alley. We passed gate after gate and door after door but none of them would budge. Every so often, we had to walk over debris from collapsed walls. After fifteen, twenty minutes of walking we had to stop not due to exhaustion but because we were forced to. About five feet in front of us stood a high brick wall and to its left was a large metal gate. Crystal and I both walked over to the last door in the alleyway and begin to turn the handle and began to push and pull on the gate. This gate was locked and no matter how much we pushed and pulled the gate would not budge.

We turned around, began walking back down the narrow alleyway and back over the debris that covered some of the alley floor. We slid under the collapsed wall that was leaning on the bomb shelter. Crystal and I were in a bind, if we stayed in the bomb shelter it was only a matter of time before the walls fell. I opened the gate to the bomb shelter for Crystal, she stepped back into the hall of the bomb shelter, and I quickly followed. We walked back down the stairs and then back down the hall. We opened the old wooden door and passed through.

We walked over to the other partly open door and passed through the opening. A second hall was on the other side of the door. However, this hallway had five doors: two on the right, and two on the left side and the fifth door was at the end of the hall. The doors on our right were very old and looked very frail. The doors on our left looked rather new and very strong. The door across from us looked to be old but very sturdy and solid. We started walking down the hall stopping in front of the two doors closest to us. Crystal took the door on her left and I took the door on my right. I turned the handle, stepped into the room, and began searching the walls for a light switch, I was lucky to find one only after a brief search.

"Alex, we got a bedroom over her," Crystal yelled through the walls.

"This one is a supply room. There are shelves in here with loads of boxes on them."

I turned the light off and closed the door. Crystal was waiting in the hall for me to return. We shined our flashlights down the hall and walked to the other two doors. I opened the door on my side turned on the light and stepped in. A dresser stood across from me, a mattress lay on the floor to my right. On the opposite wall was a closed closet door. As I closed the bedroom door, I heard a toilet flush from across the hall followed by running water. Two minutes later Crystal came out of the room with a towel in her hands.

She threw the towel back into the bathroom and walked to the last door in the hall. We walked to the last door and Crystal opened the door. On the other side was a third staircase. We climbed up the staircase and stopped at the end. Above us was a metal gate that led outside. I pushed on the gate it opened a little into the air but, was unable to open the gate the rest of the way. I moved over a little to allow Crystal access to the gate and then the two of us began pushing the gate up. We were forced to step further up the staircase as we forced the metal gate open the remainder of the way.

The gate's doors slammed on the ground as we climbed out of the bomb shelter. As I rose from under ground, the air from the outside filled my lungs. All the odors in the air rushed into my lungs as I took deep breaths. The smell of the air made me want to vomit, in fact I almost did. To our left was a wall of fire and smoke making Buckley Road impassable. Therefore, Crystal and I turned on to Rosemary once again. The building that lay there from one side of the road to the other had collapsed in on itself a little. We looked around all the buildings except the bomb shelter and the collapsed building were engulfed in flames. The opening into the lying down building had grown in size.

Just then, fire began to crawl rapidly across a shiny trail on the road. A car that I had not noticed before was lying on its side and the glistening trail led right to it. I knew what the glistening trial was immediately; an old car that ran on gasoline had leaked gas on the road. I grabbed Crystal's arm and pulled her closer to the collapsed building. We had no choice but to go into the fallen structure. We were cut off from the bomb shelter and our only chance was to risk another unknown structure.

We entered the structure carefully making sure we weren't cut on the sharpened walls. The walls were formed by debris that had falling, forming caverns paths. Dozens of coals on the walls and around the ground lit each passageway. The air was slightly hotter in here than the air was outside. We started to sweat as we started to make our way through the first couple of passageways. The air was heavy and there were some bodies lying in the rubble of the paths we were passing through. There was a scream, it echoed from somewhere in the debris labyrinth. Crystal and I stopped moving tried to pinpoint the direction of the screams. Then there was no screaming so we continued to advance into the maze further.

Then we heard the screams again joined by a cry for help. The cry for help came from our right. Crystal and I shined our flashlights in the direction of the screams and the cries for help. We could see a narrow path in between two pieces of furniture. Crystal being smaller than I went through the narrow passageway first. I had to remove my medical bag from my back in order to get through. I handed the medical bag to Crystal and then followed her through. There was only enough space for Crystal and I to go single file. We used our flashlights to illuminate the walls of the passageway. Because of how small the passageway was the light from our flashlights mainly covered what was ahead of us. Crystal's flashlight lit up the tunnel ahead of us and mine lit up Crystal's back side. Then there was another scream coming from ahead of us, we were close only a few feet from the screams.

As we got even closer to the screams, I started to hear low whimpering. Crystal and I pressed on with only a few more feet to go and then we would be able to see the source of the screams. We turned a debris corner and as Crystal's flashlight hit the left wall, I caught a glimpse of what was on the other side. A young girl maybe seven or eight was kneeling next to a dog (German shepherd). The German shepherd was half buried by fallen debris. Crystal and I made our way around to the little girl and the dog. The little girl was crying into her right hand and she was petting her dog with her left.

"Someone, help!" She stopped when she heard our footsteps.

"Can you help us? Mangy and my mommy and daddy are stuck and I am too little to get them out please help," she said with tears running down her face.

"Calm down, we will help you and your dog."

"What is your name, little girl?"

"My…" sniff, sniff, "name is…" sniff, "Marissa and…" sniff, "I'm not a little girl! I'm eight and my daddy says I'm a big girl." As soon as Marissa finished she began to cry harder than she had been.

"It is okay, Marissa, your dog Maggie will be okay."

"It's not Maggie that I'm crying for it's my mommy and my daddy," Marissa cried while she pointed to two pairs of feet sticking out from under a pile of debris.

Crystal walked over to Marissa, wrapped her arms around her, giving her a hug. I walked past Marissa, crouched next to Maggie, and looked at Marissa's dog over the best I could. Maggie was pinned underneath two pieces of debris, luckily, from what I could see her skin had not been punctured. However, there was enough discomfort to cause Maggie to whine. I walked over to the debris that was pinning Maggie and began to lift the broken wall that pinned her. She let out a low whine as I lifted the wall off her hind legs. Little by little, I raised the falling debris off Maggie.

The German shepherd lay with nothing on top of her for a few seconds and then she got to her feet. Maggie slowly walked out from under the debris, limped over to Marissa, and licked the tears off her faces. I dropped the debris back down and walked over to Marissa's parents. Crystal joined me and the two of us lifted the wall off Marissa's parents and looked down at them. Marissa's mom and dad were both drawing breath but were not able to move. A steel beam was lying across their waist and the upper half of the legs.

"Mmmrrriisssa," she coughed, "coomme here," said Marissa's mom while she coughed up blood.

I looked over at Marissa. She had not heard her mother's request for her company. I walked over to Marissa after I moved the debris that had been resting on her parents.

"Marissa, um your parents are for right now still alive. Your mom asked for you to come to their side," I said hastily.

"Mommy and daddy are still alive," she said, crying.

"Yes for now your mom and dad are still alive."

Crying, Marissa stood up, quickly walked over to her mom's side, and then gave her mom a big hug. She then walked over to her dad and gave him a big hug. Her parents began to talk to Marissa in low voices. They were talking too low for Crystal and me to hear what they were saying. A few seconds later Marissa stood up and walked over to Crystal and me.

"My mommy and daddy want to talk to you two for a minute," Marissa said as tears ran down her face.

Crystal and I walked over to her dying parents and kneeled down next to them. Marissa's dad coughed and started to speak to us.

"Our daughter tells us that you Alex and Crystal helped free Maggie. Could my wife and I ask you to do two dying," he coughed, "parents a favor? Would you two look after Marissa after we die?" asked Marissa's dad.

"If there was someone else here instead of you two we would ask the same of them," said Marissa's mother as she coughed up more blood.

"Yes, Alex and I will look after Marissa when you pass away," said Crystal before I had a chance to say anything.

"Do you have a piece of paper and something to write with?" asked Marissa's dad.

"Why do you want paper and something to write with?"

"So if anyone asked you about why you two are taking care of someone else's daughter you have proof of why."

"Here you go, sir," Crystal said, handing the paper and a pen to him.

"My wife and I of sound mind hereby give full custody of or our eight-year-old daughter Marissa and our dog Maggie to Alex Track and Crystal Cocks," said Marissa's dad.

"Now all it needs is our signatures and it's finished."

Marissa's mom reached up, took the pen with her right hand from her husband, and signed her name: Jan Harris. Tears ran down her face as she signed the piece of paper. Mrs. Harris then handed the pen back to her husband. He quickly singed the paper: Mark Harris. Mr. Harris quickly handed the paper to Crystal. She did not waste any time in signing it. When she finished she handed the paper to me to sign. I looked down at the paper then I signed it.

"Marissa, could you come here, your parents want to talk to you again?" Crystal asked very politely.

Marissa walked over to the four of us and kneeled next to her dad.

"Yes, Mommy and Daddy, what do you want? Mommy, is you and Daddy going to be okay?"

"Sorry, Marissa, we're not going to be okay and we want you to go with Uncle Alex and Aunt Crystal. Your dad and I want you to take Maggie and go with them to safety," said Mrs. Harris.

"No I won't go; I want to stay here with you and Daddy," Marissa said, crying.

"Marissa, do as you're told and please go with Crystal and Alex," said Mr. Harris eagerly.

"Why can't I stay with you?"

"Because your dad and I are dying and our deaths are not something you need to see," said Marissa's mom.

"Crystal, Alex take Marissa and Maggie out of here and don't let her come back," said Mr. Harris.

"Okay, Mr. and Mrs. Harris."

I pocketed the piece of paper with our four signatures and walked away from them. Marissa's mom and dad said their goodbyes to a heavy crying Marissa. Crystal helped Marissa to her feet and brought her over to me. I picked up the medical bag that Crystal had set down ten minutes beforehand and walked over to Maggie. Crystal grabbed a hold of Marissa's forearm and guided her over to the passageway, Crystal and I had passed through. I grabbed Maggie by her collar and then the three of us turned to Mr. and Mrs. Harris and gave our goodbyes. I could hear Marissa's mom crying as we began to leave them. Just as we started to leave Marissa's parents, a loud explosion shook the earth. The passageway we were in started to collapse from the shaking of the earth.

"Commander Shaurha here, I got the communication working for the moment. I am about to enter the third planet from the solar light....TSHSHSHSHSHSHSH. This planet seems to have been hit rather hard by the meteor shower. Just about every structure here has fallen because of it. My engines are failing, I no longer can keep the *Kento* in flight. I have no choice but to make a crash landing on this planet. If I survive I will make further communication attempts."

After a few more passageways and a few dead ends, we saw the smoke filled sky and smelt the many odors that lay in the air. I passed control of Maggie back to Marissa and Crystal and I led Marissa and Maggie out of the maze. We walked closer to the maze exit, and stepped into the open air. As we stepped out of the debris maze formed by the collapsed building, the ground beneath Crystal's and my feet gave way. I could see Crystal as she and I slid down a steep slope. We were going too fast for us to try to stop.

Our feet as we tried to slow ourselves down were kicking up dust. The dust and dirt caused a cloud around my face. I closed my eyes to protect them from the dirt and dust. I hit something in the ground, which sent me into sliding back flips. The sliding flips slowed me down some but not enough to stop. Then I felt my head slam into something really harder, pain seared in my head.

"This is Commander Shaurha of the Talin ship *Kento*. I have survived the crash landing on this alien planet. The *Kento* has enough power to keep replaying this message for a few hours. I will set a safe rally point for the surviving crew to rendezvous with myself."

Thud, thud.

"Something has just slammed into the ship. I am going to go outside to see what hit the ship and to attempt at any repairs I can to the ship."

My head seared with pain. I opened my eyes, everything was dark, and I could not see anything. Then I felt my body being lifted off the ground by someone. I was then set back down on the ground after a few minutes. I still could not see anything around me, nor could I see the person that had moved me.

"Two natives of this planet appeared to have fallen down the crater the *Kento* had caused. The two natives slammed into the *Kento's* hall. They both appear to be injured and they do not appear to be conscious. I will attempt to treat their wounds with the med kit from the cockpit. Hopefully I will be able to treat their wounds."

"Commander. Commander Shaurha, you made it, I thought you had not survived."

"Zar, you survived how did you manage to pilot the escape pod?"

"It wasn't easy; I just pointed the pod to the surface and held on."

"So what do you have there, Commander?"

"These two must be natives of this planet?"

"I believe they need medical attention, see what you can do for them."

Chapter Four
The Introduction

"Ha, this is one of my favorite parts of Alex's book, this is where we are introduced," said roommate one.

"Ya, this is my favorite part of his book to," said roommate two.

"Hey, get off the computer, this is my book, go write your own. Now if you do not mind I would like to continue telling what happened. Okay?"

"All right go ahead and tell your story we will not interrupt again," said roommate two.

"Thank you, now leave my work alone! Now as I was saying the sky was still, ha I thought I told you two to get off."

"We're off we're off," said roommate two.

"Sorry those are my roommates. Now let us continue."

I heard two people talking only a few feet away. I could barely hear what the two of them were talking about due to the pain pounding through my head. I could hear two pairs of footsteps walking closer towards me. Once they had gotten closer, I could make out what the two were saying. I may have been able to hear them but I still could not see the source of the voices. I was too groggy to try and talk to either one of the two figures.

"Why do they look different?"

"My guess is that the natives appear different because of gender, but I can't be sure until I scan them with the w-19. Then I will know more about these people."

"Zar, run your scans while I check over what's left of the *Kento*."

"I will do my best to help them; however, their physiology may be different from ours."

I heard five different toned beeps coming from above my head. Then after a few seconds, the beeping grew quieter. After a few more second, the beeping faded completely. I felt my head being raised by one of the voice's owners a minute later I felt something cold on the back of my neck and then my vision started to return. However, my vision was still blurry. I sat up as my vision slowly began to return. All I could see was two large blurry black figures moving around before me. I could not see either of their faces or any details on them.

"Zar, what did you find out?"

"The results of my scans identifies this one as the male and this one as the female. The male has a severe head injury and the female has minor wounds. I have treated their wounds to the best that I can."

"Do you have a clue why the male woke before the female if the male had more severe wounds than the female?"

"My best guess is he has been aware this whole time and has been unable to respond due to his injuries."

The two glossy black figures walked back over to me and bent down putting their weight on their knees.

"Cccaaannn yyyooouuu uuunnndddeeerrr ssstttaaannnddd mmmeee," said the first figure slowly.

"Dddooo yyyooouuu uuunnndddeeerrr ssstttaaannnddd wwwhhhaaattt wwweee aaarrreee sssaaayyy?" asked the second figure slowly.

My eyes finally cleared up and the detail on their faces came into focus. Their bodies were large, bulky and they had large flexible pipes coming out of their heads. Their skin was covered in a thick glistening fluid of some kind. I could not see a nose, mouth, or any eyes. There were no facial features anywhere on their heads, their head was like nothing I had ever seen. I turned my head away from the two figures and looked for Crystal in the creator. She was lying flat on the ground in her back about four or five feet from the two figures and three feet from me.

I looked back towards the two figures. One of them had their hands to their head and was pushing some latches on the side of its head. The other figure was removing devices from its body and took a look upon them. The head of the first figure was removed, revealing a much smaller head which had noticeable features. The first figure was yellow and had tattoos on its face. There was thick hair like strains coming down from the top of its head which wrapped around its neck. It had two eyes positioned in about the same positioned as my eyes. There was a definitely distinguishable mouth in the lower middle of its face. From what I could see there was no noise on the figure's face. The figure then removed the rest of its suit and laid it on the ground. The figure was wearing a gray uniform with an insignia on its left shoulder. There were strange writings on the insignia.

I crawled over to Crystal, stopped, and kneeled next to her. She was showing very little movement other than her breathing. I started lightly slapping her face. This worked quite well. She flinched and then started to wake up. I stopped slapping her face and quietly started calling out her name. Her eyes opened and looked at me and slapped me across my check and then hugged me. The two aliens walked over to us and kneeled down in front of us. Crystal let out a scream when she saw the two aliens kneeled in front of us. The two aliens quickly got up and left us by ourselves. Crystal's screams grew quieter as the two aliens left us alone. Her face was once again white but this time it was from fear. Crystal stopped screaming, closed her eyes, took a deep breath, and reopened her eyes. She stood up took another deep breath and turned to face the two aliens.

Crystal walked in the direction of the two aliens and stopped a few feet from them. I stood up walked over to Crystal's side and looked at her face. Her checks had a little more color buried deep under her skin. From the exasperation on her face, I could tell that she wanted to say something, but she did not. Then I heard one of the aliens starting to talk. The words the alien spoke sounded very similar to our language except for a few exceptions. I could hear their conversation. There were only a few words that the two aliens spoke that I didn't recognize.

"What is the existent of the damage to the *Kento*?"

"Well the *Kento* will not be taking off any time in the future I also found out that our ship didn't crash because of the meteors. It had signs of weapons fire and I think that it might have been blasts from their weapons but I can't be sure."

"The only one that would know is Hamole. He's the only one that would know for sure. Hopefully he's alive. Have you heard any news about the royal family?"

"There hasn't been any communications from any of the survivors, if there are any other survivors."

"Zar, I will send a message to the other survivors to meet us here."

"Shaurha, we can't stay out in the open too much longer. It's too dangerous if that was their weapons fire and what about the natives?"

"They know this planet better than we do and you may have to treat their wounds again, so for the time being they have to come with us."

"Do you think they might know a safe place for us to set a rally point?"

"Then I guess we have no choice but to ask the two natives."

I managed to piece together their conversation, by replacing the unknown words with what fit the sentences. The two aliens stopped speaking and walked back over to us. I looked at Crystal again, her face had returned to the pale, white color it had been a few minutes before.

"We need your help. We need to get out of the open; to somewhere safe."

"There's an old bomb shelter not that far from here, but there's a few obstacles in the way. Along the edge of the crater there's a maze and on the other side of the maze the bomb shelter is only a few feet from the maze exit."

"Once we have gotten to the bomb shelter, I will send another rally point to the survivors, hopefully the royal family is alive and not badly hurt."

"What are you two called and where are you from?"

"Later, we do not have the time to ask or answer any more questions right now. We will answer everything you want to ask at the bomb shelter, okay?" asked the alien still in the spacesuit.

"Can, can we get going now there is a little girl that we have to look after?" Crystal said quickly and uneasily.

The alien with the helmet off nodded her head and the two began walking up the crater's wall in the direction of the maze. Crystal and I looked at each other briefly and then ran to catch up with the two aliens. We slowed down when we got close to them.

"Alex, we need to get in front of the two aliens. They might scare Marissa," said Crystal.

"Is it okay with you two if we take the lead only because Marissa might get a little scared of you two?"

"Go ahead, but I would like to speak with the male for a minute while we walk."

"Go ahead and get to Marissa. I will join you shortly when I can."

"Is this Marissa you speak of your offspring?" asked the alien still in the spacesuit.

"Yes she is an offspring, but no, Marissa is not our offspring. We do however have to look after her now."

"What do you mean now?"

"Marissa's parents gave her and their dog to us a little while ago because they were about to die and her parents wanted their daughter to live on and to be taken care of. They gave Marissa to us."

"Is Maggie the dog you referred to?"

"Yes she is."

"You can go now and join your mate's side."

"She's not my mate, she's my friend."

I left the two aliens and caught back up with Crystal. She was only a few feet from the entrance of the maze. Marissa and Maggie were nowhere to be seen. Crystal and I waited for the two aliens to catch up to us and then we went into the maze. The smells from the outside air disappeared and the sounds from outside were quieted from the maze walls. The air of the maze was still hot and dry and there was less light in the maze then there had been. Crystal and I turned, took out our flashlights, turned them on, and began to advance further into the maze.

Crystal and I led the two aliens deeper into the maze, avoiding the dead ends and the passageways that led away from the bomb shelter. Then after a minute of walking I heard Marissa crying to our left. I shined the beam of my flashlight against the left wall. There was a small opening in the wall not big enough for either of the aliens or me to fit through but possible Crystal could fit through.

"Crystal, you're going to have to go through and get Marissa and Maggie out of there."

"Do I have to go through, why can't you go and get Marissa and Maggie?"

"Because I am too big to get through you, on the other hand, should just make it through if you take your backpack off."

"Fine, I will go and get Marissa and Maggie out of there."

Crystal took her backpack off, got down on her hands and knees, and began to crawl through the small hole in the wall. The two aliens and I stood in the passageway for a few minutes. After five minutes or more, Marissa crawled out of the hole followed by Crystal and Maggie. Tears were running down Marissa's dirty faces and Maggie was covered in dust.

"I have already told Marissa about the aliens and she is okay with it. So can we go now?"

We continued through the maze until we finally found the exit to the labyrinth. I could smell the odors from the outside again. We quickly exited the maze. For Crystal and me, we returned to the burning street. Most of the fires had burned themselves to mere flickers of fire. The fires that still burned hot were far enough from us to give any problems to us. The bomb shelter was still standing although there were signs that a few meteors had passed through the concrete walls on the wall closest to us. We walked a little ways down and then cut across the road until we reach the upper level of the bomb shelter. The main entrance was closed with a large metal plate and two chucks of the wall. The alien still in the suit walked over to the entrance and tried too force the door to the bomb shelter open.

"There is another entrance to the lower level of the bomb shelter around the corner. That's where we exited the bomb shelter when we got trapped in there earlier."

"Show us."

"I will send another message to the survivors to go around the corner of the bomb shelter and everything else that they will need to know to meet up with us."

After the alien without the suit sent the message we walked around the corner and over to the bomb shelter door. A large chunk of debris had fallen on top of the gate. The two aliens walked over to the debris and lifted the chuck off the gate. We climbed down the stairs and entered the hall that led to the library. The alien still in its spacesuit walked over to the door to the library and opened it. Then the two aliens walked into the library separated from the rest of us and walked around the room. Then the second alien started to remove its suit and set the pieces on the computer desk.

After the alien had removed its suit, I could see differences between the two aliens. The second alien was a bluish gray and there were no tattoos on its face. This alien had similar features on their heads. The second alien had smaller hair-like tubes on its head. Its eyes were slightly bigger than the first alien and there was a distinguishable scar on the right side of its face. The second alien was wearing a similar uniform to the first alien, except the color was different. Then both of the aliens walked over to Marissa, Maggie, Crystal, and I and introduced themselves to us.

"My identity is Commander Shaurha."

"And my identity is Chief Medic Zar, and what are your identities?"

"My name is Crystal Cocks."

"My name is Alex Track and this is Marissa and her dog Maggie."

Once we had finished our introductions, I heard footsteps coming from the stairs in the hall behind us. Crystal, Marissa, and I turned our heads down the hall. Four sets of boots identical to the boots Zar had set on the table, stepped down the stairs. Once they descended the stairs, I could see what they looked like. Four more aliens walked down the stairs and proceeded into the library. Three of the aliens were carrying large suitcases one in each of their hands. They walked in, set the suitcases on the desk, opened them, and removed their contents.

Three of the aliens were wearing identical uniforms to each other but nothing like any of the other uniforms the other aliens were wearing. The fourth alien was wearing a uniform similar to the uniform Shaurha and Zar were wearing. Two of the four aliens looked very similar to Shaurha and the other two looked a lot like Zar except for their color and their personal features. The four of them started to set up computers that had been counseled in the six suitcases the three aliens brought with them.

"Alex, Crystal, Marissa, this is Chief Science Officer Whaloa of the Talin ship *Kento* and his two assistants. Sorry I do not know their identities. If you want to know their names you can ask them or Whaloa."

Crystal and Marissa walked over to a bench that had been lying on its side, behind the computer desk. Marissa sat down and started to pet Maggie rather fast and then Marissa gave Maggie a hug. Tears were still in her eyes and every now and then one or two tears would crawl out and run down her face. Just as Marissa was releasing Maggie from the hug, the sound of debris came from the stairs, seconds later footsteps followed in the hall's stairway. Seven injured Talins, eighteen Talin troops and two Talins in the same uniforms as Shaurha, Zar, and Whaloa descended the staircase and entered the room. The troops had Talin weapons in one hand and a briefcase in the other.

"Alex, can we tell our favorite part?" roommate two.
"Yeah let us tell some of your story?" asked roommate one.
"Why do you to want to tell this part of the story?"
"Because this is our favorite part," said roommate one.
"Okay just do not get carried away."

We saw an injured native lying outside of a building so we walked over and picked the native up. We pulled the wounded native through the maze and helped him out from the labyrinth. Out of the maze we found the building Shaurha had set as a relay point. Carrying the native, we walked around the building and found the staircases, right where Shaurha's transmission had indicated. Our muscles flexed as we both carried the injured native across the street and into the building. We climbed down the staircase and into the building. As we climbed down the stairs the native jerked around and with a release of air died. The hall in front of us was dark. There was debris on the stairs and on the ground blow the stairs. There were five more doors in the hallway, two on each side, and one right across from us. We walked towards the end of the hall and passed through the door. Just about everyone aboard the *Kento* was there plus three natives and a native animal.

"Wait a minute, that's not entirely how it happened."
"Yes it is," said roommate two.

"No, it is not."

"Now if you two do not mind I would like to tell the readers the truth."

"Please don't," said roommate one.

"Sorry got to," I responded.

Shaurha walked over to us and kneeled down next to us, and started to point at the different Talins to us.

"Alex, Crystal, Marissa, this is military expert Hamole and engineer Gupp. Among the injured were Gupp's two assistance, and the other three injured were Zar's medical assistance. The last two of the injured Talins are the *Kento* top pilots, Flito and Nozad. Well that's all of the groups from the escape pods except for pod four."

As Flito and Nozad entered the library they tripped over their own feet and fell face first on the bomb shelter floor. The two of them were skinny, not very tall and both of them were having trouble getting to their feet. When they finally got to their feet, they clumsily made their way over to the rest of the Talins. Zar walked over to the injured Talins, began to look at their wounds and treat them as he went. I walked over to Crystal, Marissa and Maggie and sat down next to them. There were too many people in the library so I decided to leave the library and go to one of the bedrooms for a while. Marissa Maggie and Crystal joined me after a few minutes later. Shaurha came in about five minutes later with one of their digital data pads in Shaurha's hand.

"I got some questions I would like to ask you three if you do not mind."

"Go ahead and ask your questions. I will answer anything you ask me."

"So will I," said Crystal.

"Me too," answered Marissa.

"I will try to answer any questions you three might have for me or any of the other Talins."

"Okay we will."

"Alex, Crystal, Marissa, where were you going when you two fell into the *Kento's* crater."

"We were on our way to the hospital to get evacuated to a much safer location by our government."

"Shaurha, why are you and the other Talins here on earth?" asked Crystal.

"That's difficult to answer. However, one reason we were in your solar system was that we were exploring the outer planets when we were hit by the meteor shower but that is not what caused the *Kento* to crash."

"If the *Kento* did not crash into the meteors then why did your ship crash on our planet?"

"The *Kento* was just not hit by meteors but by *Shadows* weapons fire."

"What do you mean Shadows weapons fire?"

"For the past one hundred years give or take my race the Talins and this Shadow race has been at war. We have no idea why they first attacked us but they have not changed the attack style in that length of time. You are not the first race that has been devastated by their meteor attacks. They do this so the targeted planet and any survivors are defenseless. Usually we Talins would come in at the last minute before the invasions and rescue as many survivors as we can before we have to retreat. But your race is in luck because if I and my crewmen can get a message to our home world or at least a Talin or allies vessel, we can prepare this planet for a war."

"So how do you and your shipmates plan on sending a message?"

"Whaloa and his associates are working on it right now. We need to get to the government you spoke of earlier and we need to get there as fast as we can. First, we need to let you three and the injured Talins rest, and then we will head for the hospital. Where is the hospital from here?"

"Back through the maze; straight past the *Kento* and a mile or two down in that direction."

"Get some rest we will be leaving in a few hours."

Shaurha stood up, pushed a few things on the data pad, and left the bedroom.

"Crystal, Marissa, you can have this bedroom. I will rest in the other bedroom further down the hall."

"Okay see you in a few hours, Alex."

Sniff...sniff...sniff. Marissa did not say anything she just sat there crying with tears running down her face.

53

I stood up got off the couch and left Crystal, Marissa, and Maggie in the first bedroom. I closed the bedroom door as I left, turned, and walked down the rest of the hall. I stopped at the bedroom on the right, opened the door, and stepped through. I threw the medical backpack on the floor next to the raggedy bed. I sat down on the raggedy bed and lay down on my back. I closed my eyes and I must have dozed off.

Chapter Five
The Blockade

"Hopefully my roommates won't interrupt me and interrupt my count of things. My roommates have a tendency to put themselves on a high pedestals when in reality their pedestal is the size of a grain of rice. However, they are good people and I should not go picking on them too much. I never know when I may need their help so it is best to be nice. Well that's enough of that so let's get back to the story."

I was woken up a few hours later by Commander Shaurha.

"Alex, we could use your help in the reading room shortly. We are having trouble accessing your network."

"Okay sure just give me a few minutes to wake up."

"Just do not take too much time, because time is something we do not have the luxury of wasting."

"I will be right out, Commander."

"You and your friends can just call me Shaurha."

"Command—I mean, Shaurha, why do some of the other Talins and you look different from some of the others?"

"That's simple those Talins that look like myself are female and those that look like Hamole and Gupp are the males of our race."

"How can I tell the difference between male and female?"

"The females of my species have larger crowns around their head," said Shaurha while she pointed to the hair-like horns surrounding her face.

"There is not enough time to answer any more questions at the present time, so if you would come with me now into the reading room and help Whaloa complete the interface to your network."

"Alright let's go and I will see what I can do to help you out."

Shaurha and I walked out of the bedroom I was in and walked to the end of the hall. The door into the library had been removed from its hinges, and set up against one of the hallway's walls. Through the doorway I could see the Talins walking around the library as though they had their heads cut off. Shaurha and I walked through the doorway into the library and moved towards the desk with the Talin computers.

The Talin computers were weird looking. They had three different color lights that would go on and off every few minutes. Gupp and Whaloa apparently had opened the desktop computer and had connected the Talin computers up to it. I stepped up to the computers and looked them over. I had no idea what I could do to help.

"Shaurha, what is the problem, why do you need my help?"

"We can't get access to your government's computers because we do not understand your writings or the symbols on the projection screen. We tried but we cannot make any sense of it," said Gupp from behind the desk.

"I do not understand anything about your computers but I can at least get you on to the net providing that it is still possible."

"What do you mean by net?"

"It's the main source of communications across the planet. The net or the Internet is the information highway that can allow everyone with a computer to be connected to each other."

"How do you plain on getting on to the Internet?"

"If the net is still running I should be able to log in from here by using my password," I said as I walked over to the desktop computer.

"We are in luck the net is still running; give me a minute and you should be able to do the rest without me."

I logged onto the Internet within minutes and motioned for Whaloa to take over. Whaloa and his assistants went to work on their Talin computers immediately.

"We are in, Shaurha, we will need only a few minutes more then we should be able to access their station on the orbital body."

"There is no station on the moon."

"There is a station on this moon you speak of. You and the rest of the civilians just do not know about it," said Shaurha.

"We are in. We have access to the station's computers, but there are some restrictions to what we can do."

"What are the restrictions?" asked Shaurha.

"We don't have accesses to their weapons or long range communications systems. We do have a compete visual of this planet, Commander."

"If that's all we can access then we might as well take a look at the surface. Whaloa, would you zoom in on our current location we need to know what is ahead of us?"

"The smoke in the sky is preventing me from getting a visual of our location but there appears to be a map of this area that I can access."

"Let's see."

I watched Shaurha and Whaloa work on the computer. The monitor showed the entire earth for a few minutes then it zoomed into an overhead view of the bomb shelter.

"Whaloa, zoom it out a few frames," said Shaurha.

"Okay, Commander," replied Whaloa as he pushed a few buttons on his computer.

"Alex, could you show us which structure is the hospital."

"Okay."

I walked closer to the monitor with the map of our current location and looked for a few seconds. I raised my hand and pointed to a large building on the map. The map then zoomed in on the hospital and gave distances between our location and the hospital's: 2.3 miles.

"Alex, do you know where the safe location you told me about is from the hospital?"

"I can't be sure but I think it is the military base on the outside of town."

"Show us where it is."

"I believe it is to the right of the hospital about two maybe three miles out of town. But other than that I do not know."

"Thank you, Alex, you can go back and wait with Crystal and Marissa for myself or one of the others to come and get you."

I got up, left the library, and walked back to the bedroom with Crystal, Marissa, and Maggie inside. I opened the door and walked in, Crystal and Marissa were asleep on the bed, and Maggie was lying on the floor next to the bed. The three of them had a peaceful look on their faces. I did not want to wake them up. I wanted to let them sleep in peace and quiet for as long as possible. I found a chair in the furthest corner from the bed, to sit in. Once I had gotten comfortable, I closed my eyes and started to doze off.

The two Talin pilots, Nozad and Flito, woke me up only minutes after falling asleep. Crystal and Marissa had already woken from their peaceful sleep and had left the bedroom. The two Talins left me alone once they saw my eyes open up. They left the room leaving me alone in the bedroom. I got to my feet, walked to the door, and exited the bedroom. I looked into the library, most of the Talins had left the room, and most of their supplies had been removed as well. I walked down to the second bedroom and retrieved my backpack. I exited the bedroom and walked into the library. Whaloa was packing up the last of the Talin computers and Gupp was taking a few books from the bookcases and stuffing them into one of the briefcases they had brought. I walked over to Gupp and looked at some of the books on the shelves.

"Excuse me, Gupp, what is going on and where is everyone?"

"We are getting ready to head to the military base and everyone is outside waiting for us to finish."

"Gupp, I am all set the computers are put away and I am going to go outside with the others."

"We're coming."

Gupp and I put the books we had in our hands into the briefcases and we followed Whaloa out of the bomb shelter. I looked down at my watch as we returned to the surface. The crystal lens on my watch had been shattered and the digital clock was no longer working. I took off my watch and threw it back into the bomb shelter. The twenty-one Talins were spread out in the street. Crystal, Marissa, and Maggie were by the bomb shelter door waiting for us to come out. Our surroundings were darker than they had been hours before due to the fires that had burnt themselves out. The air was heavy with smoke and the air was rather warm against my skin. Smoke was rising from our ruined surroundings making it hard to see past the ruined buildings. Red coals from burnt out fires were scattered in the path ahead giving an orange glow to the ground. Most of the ground surrounding the bomb shelter was turned to dust with chunks of road and buildings scattered in amongst the red coals.

All of the Talins started to gather at the edge of the bomb shelter. Crystal, Marissa, and I walked over to the group of Talins. Maggie followed Marissa as close as she could. The Talins were talking amongst themselves. They were talking about which way to go. It did not take long for them to come to a decision of which direction. They decided that going back through the maze would be the fastest route.

"Alright if you are all ready, we need to get through the maze as fast as we can," said Commander Shaurha.

The Talin troops went ahead of us and stopped in front of the outer wall of the maze. They speared out along the wall turned to face the rest of us and waited for us to catch up to them. The wall of the maze was black and there was smoke coming off the debris. They didn't have to wait very long, about five minutes then we joined them in front of the maze.

"Where is the entrance to the maze?" asked Gupp.

"It was right there, the maze must have collapsed in on itself," said Whaloa.

"Is there another why into the maze?" asked Shaurha.

"There has to be a why to get to the other side," said Gupp.

"Could we go around the maze? All the other routes are blocked from what you have all told me. The maze is our only option we have to find another way over the maze or a way to go through. So everyone speared out and looked the maze wall over for either option. Crystal, Marissa and Alex, you do not have to look for if you do not want to," ordered Commander Shaurha.

All of the Talins including the troops spread out along the maze wall and started to search the maze wall.

"Alex, should we look too?" asked Crystal.

"Yeah, I think we should help."

Crystal, Marissa and I walked over to the end of the maze wall on our right and began to look for a way to get in or go over the maze. I heard in my left ear Hamole talking loudly to Shaurha.

"Shaurha, I really think that blasting the wall with our rifles will work."

"They could do more harm than good, the concussion from the rifles could weaken the maze's structure even further than it already is."

"But the rifles might give us a path either in or over the maze."

"Sorry we just can't risk it, not yet."

"If we don't use the rifles we may not get past the maze."

"Using the rifles on the maze will be our last resort and only as our last resort. Now go and help the others look for a way past the maze."

Hamole turned and walked over to the maze wall and began looking for a path. I turned back to the maze wall that I had been looking at and went back to my own search. I used my hand to search the exterior of the maze wall. The wall was warm and very rough on the palm of my hands. Then the wall shifted and I could feel terrible pain as debris tore right through my right hand. I pulled my hands back from the wall and looked at both the palm of my hand and the back of my hand.

My hands were covered in dirt and there were large amounts of blood coming from the rip in my right hand. The pain in my hand did not subside even after I had removed my hand from the debris wall. I took my backpack off with my left hand and set it on the ground. Then I opened my backpack and took out the water that I had gotten at my parents' house. Very carefully I opened the bottle, and poured the cool water on my right hand. The water was very cold on my right hand, as the water washed the dirt and blood off. The pain in my right hand slowly faded and returned as the water dried. After the dirt and blood was washed away, I could see a large hole that went right through my right hand. Blood was pouring out both sides of my hand. The pain in my right hand faded and then returned as it had done before. I then poured the remaining water over my right hand to ease the pain for as long as I could.

"Alex, are you okay? What happened to your hand?" Crystal asked as she came running over to my side.

"I was searching the wall when some of the debris shifted and then I felt pain in my hand. I then got the bottle of water out of my backpack and washed the dirt and blood off my hand."

"You should go and talk to Zar and see if he can help you mend your hand."

"Why, isn't there anything we can do by ourselves?"

"We could try and doctor your hand but it would probably be better if you ask for his help."

"Let's see what we can do to doctor my hand. I do not want his help."

"Why don't you want to ask Zar for help?"

"Because I don't trust him."

"You do not trust them? Why not?"

"As far as we know they could be behind the meteor shower and they could just be using us to gain access to our government."

"Alex, you could be right but for now we have to trust them a little because we need their help to get to the military base."

"For now you're right. We do need their help."

"Alex, hand me your bag and I will see if there is anything we can fix your hand with in the medical supplies."

I handed the bag to Crystal with my left hand. She took it in her right hand. She set the bag on the ground, opened the bag, and began to take out the supplies in the bag including the medical supplies. She took out bandages, salve, ace bandages and rubbing alcohol from my bag.

"I don't think we have the supplies to doctor your hand. So, are you going to ask Zar for help? If you don't I will on your behalf."

"Looks like I do not have any choice, I will ask Zar for help."

Crystal started to put the medical supplies that she had removed from the backpack back into the pouch that they were originally stored. Crystal stood up and checked our surroundings passing right by us. Crystal stopped looking our surroundings over and just stared at me. I do not think she wanted to leave me alone.

"Alex, are you going to ask Zar for help now?" asked Crystal.

"Yes I will ask him for help once I have found him."

"Zar is over there looking at the left side of the maze wall," Crystal said as she pointed to Zar.

She turned, walked back over to the wall, and began to look it over again. I turned around to face the direction Crystal had pointed. I could just barely see Zar past all of the other Talins. He was searching the wall on the left side of the mazes. I walked past the other Talins and over to Zar. He was in the process of looking over the debris of a collapsed building that was next to the debris wall.

"Zar, could you doctor my right hand? I'm in a lot of pain. I would do it myself, but I don't have the proper medical equipment."

"I will take a look. How did this happen to your hand?"

"I was trying to remove some of the debris to make a path through the maze when the debris shifted and ripped through my hand."

"Do not worry. I will heal your right hand once I get X-17 and the X-30 out of my briefcase."

"I have alcohol to sanitize my hands and any instruments you can use."

"You do not have to use alcohol on your hand, the X-30 sanitizes your hand as the X-17 heals your hand."

Zar set his briefcase down on the ground, opened the briefcase, and took out two small devices. Zar took the X-17 and the X-30 and put the two devises together. Zar turned the two devises on and moved them over my right hand. A small stream of steam rose from my hand as Zar passed the two devices over the wound in my right hand. The pain in my hand lessened as the skin on the palm of my hand healed over. With Zar's left hand, he turned my right hand over and began to heal the back of my hand. The pain faded away as the hole in my hand healed up.

"Alex, how does your hand feel?"

"Much better, thanks for help."

"You're welcome, is there anything else I can help you with. If there is anything you need, just ask and I will help you."

"No there is nothing else I need and if there is—"

An explosion to my right cut me off in mid sentence. Zar and I leaned our heads to the sounds of the explosion. The center of the maze wall exploded out throwing small debris in multiple directions. The Talins in the debris path tried to dodge the projectiles but only half of them managed to avoid the debris, the rest of them were impaled by the debris and fell to the dusty ground. The maze wall roared in flames while the Talins hit the ground, which caused a cloud of dust to lift off of the ground. A few of the Talins had debris sticking out of them which had fire burning on the opposite end of the debris.

Zar dropped to his knees and quickly packed up his medical supplies and made a mad dash for the closest injured Talin. As he dropped to his knees, his medical case broke open, as the case hit the ground, and all of Zar's medical instruments within the case fell out. Zar reached for a few of them and began treating the Talin before him. The cuts on his arms slowly began to heal as Zar passed the medical instrument over the wounds. Zar stopped healing the Talin's arm and moved to his face. Like his arms, the skin on his face slowly healed. Zar packed up his supplies, ran to the next injured Talin, and began to treat her wounds.

Zar's assistants began to treat the remaining injured Talins. Each one of the assistants treated the Talin closest to them. Two of the assistants finished with their patient and moved on to the Talins with the debris stuck in them. Zar and the other assistant joined them shortly. I moved closer to Zar and the assistant that had been working on the Talin. The two of them worked on the impaled Talins for at least thirty minutes before they were able to remove the debris from the Talin's chest. A bluish blood squirted out of the chest wound as the debris was removed.

The Talin began to spasm as Zar and his assistant worked to stop the bleeding. The spasms stopped, Zar and his assistant spend up the treatment on their patient. After a minute they slowed down, started to pack up their instruments, and moved on to the other impaled Talin. Zar and his three assistants worked diligently to save the last impaled Talin. After five minutes, the four of them packed up their instruments and covered the two dead Talins with a metallic sheet. Zar stood up, walked over to Shaurha and Gupp, and began to talk to them. I moved in closer to hear what they were saying to each other.

"Commander Shaurha, we need to get moving we have to find them now," said Gupp.

"Sorry, Gupp, we can't go looking for them, we don't even know if they made it off the ship. Our first priority is to get to safety at the hospital and just in case they did get off the ship alive and survived the crash. I have left my homing beacon on telling them where we are and to rendezvous at the hospital's coordinates."

"Commander, what about the four injured Talins and the two dead Talins, what do we do about them? Do we have time to give them an honorable burial?"

"We don't have time to bury them, the most we can do is say a few words. As for the injured Talin get them to their feet and ready to move out. There will be time for them to rest later."

"Commander, how are we going to get to the hospital with this debris in our way?"

"That explosion has left a trail of debris that we might be able to stack other debris on top in order to make a ramp to the top of the debris."

"That might work, Commander. I will tell everyone to gather debris and bring it to the trail of debris."

"My assistants and I will tend to the injured Talins."

"We shall say a few words for the deceased after we have got the ramp made."

Commander Shaurha and Gupp walked over to the Talins that had been watching Zar and his assistants. Shaurha and Gupp spoke with the group of Talins for a few seconds and then they turned and walked over to Hamole. The group broke off and began to gather debris for the ramp. Zar walked over to the closest injured Talin and began to treat the rest of the Talins wounds while his assistants treated the other three injured Talins. Zar and his assistants had to move the four injured Talins to give a clear path for the Talins that were moving debris. It did not take long for the Talins to get the ramp finished. The ramp was sturdy enough to walk on, ten minutes after the Talins were ordered to build the ramp.

"Okay everyone gather around," said Shaurha.

"Before we go any farther we need to say good-bye to our fallen brethren in arms...I did not know Cadet Mallows or Cadet Sorrow personally, but I do know that they desired Hamole's unit. I also know that they felt, as we all feel, honored to be with such great Talins. They died in the services of our majesty and there is nothing that is more honorable and noble than that. As long as there are Talins living and walking they shall never be forgotten...If there is anyone else that wants to say a few words in their memory of Cadet Mallows and Cadet Sorrow now is the time to do it."

"Cadet Mallows finally achieved his dream in his last day. His dream was to be one of the first to walk on an alien planet. Cadet Sorrow was new to our team so, I had not had the chance to get to know him as some of you have. I just wish we had more time to honor them." Hamole finished by removing two patches from his uniform and placing one on Cadet Mallows' body and the other on cadet Sorrow's body.

"I'm sorry but that is all we can do now but once we have gotten to safety, we will have a second honor service. I know some of you want to say good-bye and say a few words, but there is no more time. Our job now is to finish or mission which will honor them and their families. Sorry if this sounds cruel but get your gear and get on top of that wall ASAP," Shaurha ordered as she placed a patch on Private Mallows' and Private Sorrow's bodies.

The Talins spread out again. Most of them walked over to a pile of briefcases, took one, and proceeded over to the ramp. Crystal walked over to Marissa who had been sitting on what was left of a curb hugging her dog Maggie. Crystal, Marissa, and Maggie then walked over in front of the ramp waiting for everyone to gather again. I saw no more reason for me to stand around by myself so I decided to join Crystal, Marissa, and her dog by the ramp. Zar, the four injured Talins, and his assistants joined us at the ramp.

Gupp and his assistants soon followed Zar and his party.

Shaurha and Hamole were still standing above Private Mallows and Private Sorrow's bodies. We watched as Shaurha and Hamole set fire to the two private's bodies. Both of the bodies caught on fire quite quickly. The fire rose from the fallen Talins in a circular ring. The fire was a mix of bright oranges yellows and, reds which gave our surroundings an orange glow. Shaurha and Hamole walked over to us and continued up the ramp behind Crystal, Marissa, her dog Maggie, and me.

"Okay, everyone, we don't have much time so let's get moving…and, everyone, be careful, we have no idea how sturdy the surface of the debris maze is," Shaurha said as she walked to the top of the maze.

"You heard the commander, let's move out with caution," said Hamole as she joined Shaurha at the top of the maze.

"Alex, you, Marissa, and Crystal, can go ahead of my assistants and me if you would like to," Gupp said as Zar and his assistants went up the ramp.

"Crystal, is that okay with you?"

"It's okay with me, Alex."

"Thank you, Gupp, we will."

Crystal, Marissa, and I walked up the debris ramp, soon followed by Gupp, his assistants and the rest of the Talins. The ramp was steep and felt as though it could crumble at any time. With everyone's collective weight the ramp began to fall apart. The debris that had been piled up fell out of place and landed on the ground below. Everyone hastened up their pace, the faster we climbed the ramp the more debris fell from its side. As the last Talin reached the top of the maze, the ramp collapsed sending the debris to the ground with a crash. There was a small ledge about three feet wide stretching from one side of the maze to the other side. Zar and his three assistants followed Shaurha and Hamole down the ledge. Crystal, Marissa, and I followed them across the ledge and joined Zar, his assistants, Shaurha, and Hamole at the far side. Gupp, his assistants, and the rest of the Talins spread out over the ledge. I began to look around at our surroundings. The maze roof did not look sturdy and looked very dangerous to cross.

Most of the roof was covered with debris, which was lit by orange coals and a few roaring fires. Amongst the coals and fires there appeared to be a path that looked like we could walk on it. The path was only a foot and a half wide and it was broken in spots. Deeper down the path, the path split up into two different paths, one to the right and the other to the left. Shaurha and Hamole talked amongst themselves for a few minutes. Then Hamole stepped out on to the path and slowly began walking across the maze. As he walked, he used his feet to check the path in front of him. Then when he reached where the path split up, he turned right and vanished behind a wall of debris. After a few minutes, Hamole walked back out from behind the debris wall and walked across to the left path. He walked a few feet on the left path before he vanished from my view. We waited for what seemed like an hour for him to return. Then Hamole reappeared on the left then made his way back over to Shaurha and talked with her for a few minutes. Then Hamole walked back on to the path, walked a few feet on the path then seconds later Shaurha joined him.

"Hamole has found a way across the maze roof. The paths are not very sturdy so only small groups, five to six at a time, five feet in between each group. Hamole, Zar, two of his assistants, and I will lead in the first group. Everyone, divide up into groups, those that are closest to the path will follow our group."

Zar and his assistants walked out on to the path and joined Shaurha and Hamole. Shaurha, Zar, two of Zar's assistants then turned and began to follow Hamole across the maze. Everyone began to divide into groups of five or six.

"Alex, Crystal, and Marissa, come on, let's go we're the closest group to the path," Gupp said from my right.

"Alright let's go."

The five of us stepped out on to the path led by Zar's remaining assistant. Zar, Shaurha, Hamole, and Zar's two assistants had just turned to the left when our group stepped on to the path.

Chapter Six
Kingdom for Hospital

"Excuse me, Alex, but she has requested your presence in the main hall."

"Do you know what she wants, Shaurha?"

"No I don't. Are you in the process of telling what has happened for everyone to read?"

"Yes I am, Shaurha. While I am in the main hall could you continue telling what happened?"

"Okay just let me see where you are...I see why you want me to continue for you."

"Alright see you later, Shaurha, be back as soon as I can."

"Hello, readers, while Alex is gone, I shall be continuing the account of events for you."

Hamole had just led Zar, two of his assistants, and myself around a small wall of rubble. Alex's group was a little more than five feet away from us. When I heard a loud, high-pitched scream from the other side of the rubble wall. Zar and his two assistants turned and began making their way around the rubble wall. I then heard Alex yell for help. Hamole and I quickly made our way around the rubble wall. One of Zar's assistants was on the right path looking down into the maze. Alex, Crystal, Marissa, Zar, and two of his assistants could not be seen. One of Zar's assistants popped their head up from where everyone was staring at. He spoke with Gupp for a few seconds before his head popped back down. Gupp spoke with his assistants briefly, and then he helped Alex out of the maze, while his assistants dropped on the other side of the path. I walked over to Zar's third assistant and looked down at what everyone was looking at.

Zar and his assistants were standing over Marissa and Crystal. Marissa was clenched in Crystal's arms tightly. Zar was having great trouble getting Crystal to let Marissa go. A few minutes later, they were able to break Crystal's clutch and get Marissa free. Zar told her to go over to Gupp and he would help her out of the maze. Marissa walked over to Gupp, she then reached up, and Gupp grabbed her arm and lifted her out of the maze. Marissa then ran over to Alex and looked down at Zar, Crystal, and two of Zar's assistants.

I looked back down at the commotion in the maze. Zar reached behind Crystal's head and slowly and carefully moved her head. Crystal's head was covered with small pieces of rubble and Zar's hand was covered in red blood. Zar opened one of the medical cases, took out one of the medical instruments housed within it, and began to pass it over Crystal's head. A trail of steam sprouted from Crystal's head as the medical instrument passed over her wound.

"Will these work, Master Gupp?" asked one of Gupp's assistants from within the maze.

"Yes that should do, now get your butts back up here, and let's get to work," said Gupp to his two assistants.

Gupp's two assistants handed Gupp two pipes and a rather dirty cloth that they had found in the debris maze. Gupp laid the pipes and the cloth on the path and then reached down at his assistant. Then with the help of Gupp, they climbed back up to the roof of the maze. They began to tie the cloth to the two pipes making a crude stretcher. Gupp then lowered himself down joining Zar and Crystal on the other side of the path.

"Zar, tell me when you need to move Crystal. I have a stretcher ready for her," Gupp said as his assistants handed him the stretcher.

"Thank you, Gupp. I will need the stretcher in a few minutes," replied Zar.

Zar and one of his assistants carefully turned Crystal over onto her left side. She was bleeding from numerous wounds on her legs and arms. Zar began treating Crystal's arms and legs with his medical instruments. More trails of steam extended from her wounds and vanished just as fast as they appeared. The flowing blood stopped as each wound was healed, leaving bloody uniforms and skin behind.

"Zar, will she be okay?" asked Alex with a concerned voice.

"Will she be okay?"

"Yes, Shaurha. Yes, Alex, she should be okay," replied Zar.

"What do you mean she should be okay, Zar?" asked Alex.

"Your physiology is different from ours so I can't be absolutely sure. Gupp, could you bring the stretcher closer? Don't go anywhere I will need your help getting Crystal out of here."

"Okay."

Gupp walked closer to Zar, Crystal, and the two medical assistants with the stretcher in his arms. He then set the stretcher down on the ground opened it up and the four of them lifted Crystal on to the crude stretcher. Then they walked towards the path with Crystal over their heads. When they reached the path's wall they handed Crystal and the stretcher to Gupp's two assistants. They pulled Crystal up on to the path with the help from Alex and Marissa.

"Master Gupp, Chief Physician Zar, and Commander Shaurha, if it's okay with you I would like to carry the human female the remainder of the way or until she wakes up?" asked one of Gupp's assistants.

"I would like to help too?" asked Zar's medial assistant still on the maze roof.

"It's okay with me if Zar and Gupp don't have a problem with it."

"I'm okay with it," said Zar.

"I as well, if you get tired just ask, and we can stop long enough for you to switch out," said Gupp.

I walked over to Hamole. He was still on the left path waiting for everyone to get moving. I turned to face everyone. Whaloa and most of the other Talins were still on the ledge waiting to move forward. I looked at Alex and Marissa. They had moved on to the left path to let Zar's assistant by.

"Alex, Marissa, why don't you come with Hamole and me. Don't worry about Crystal. She will be fine with those two."

The two of them did not say anything, they walked over to us and then waited. Hamole turned, then walked around the rubble pile. Then we quickly followed Hamole. The path got wider as we got closer to the end of the maze. By the time we got to the end of the path, it had grown to three feet in width and started to slide into the crater of the *Kento*. Hamole led us halfway down the slope of ruble, when he stopped and looked down.

"This is the end of the rubble so we are going to have to jump down from here. I will go first; then you can lower Marissa and possibly Alex to me," said Hamole before he jumped down into the crater.

"Could you come here, Marissa, so I can help you down from here?"

"Okay, Shaurha," replied Marissa.

Marissa walked over and sat down in front of me; she then raised her arms and nodded to me. I kneeled down, reached under her arms and slowly and carefully lowered her to Hamole. Hamole grabbed her around her waste kneeled down and released Marissa. Alex walked up and turned to face me then he bent down and climbed down the rubble. I turned and was about to climb down the rubble myself; when the two assistants caring Crystal joined me; followed by Zar, Gupp, and their remaining assistants.

"I will go first then you two can pass Crystal down to Hamole and me. Once you two are down you can go back to carrying Crystal if you wish to."

"Okay, Commander Shaurha," the two assistants said in unison.

"Hamole, I am going to need your help with Crystal once I have gotten down."

I did as Alex did and climbed down the rubble then Hamole joined me at the base of the rubble. Zar's assistant lowered Crystal and the stretcher to me. I waited a few seconds for them to give the okay. I then slowly started pulling on the pipes of the stretcher until I felt Hamole pulling also. Once she was completely off the rubble Hamole and I set Crystal on a chunk of road that lay flat in the crater. Zar, Gupp, their assistants, Whaloa, and all but two of the troops got out of the rubble without a problem. The two troops that were carrying Maggie needed help getting Maggie down from the rubble. Once everyone had traversed the path over the rubble maze and were back on the ground we started down into the crater, towards the *Kento*. She had received even more damage than when we crashed.

"Hamole, would you go ahead of us and take a look at our ship. See if you can find out what crashed our ship?"

With a nod he walked to the back of the group and returned with four troops. Hamole and four of his troops walked ahead of us then drew their rifles. They approached the *Kento* with caution. I think Hamole was expecting to get attacked by the Shadows. While Hamole and the four troops were investigating the *Kento's* crash the rest of us were waiting a little ways from our crashed ship. They walked around the biggest part of our ship and then walked back over to us.

"What did your scans tell you? What took down our ship?"

"The scans could not tell but from years of experience I know it was them," said Hamole.

"Are you sure it was them?"

"Without a doubt in my mind, it was them."

"Now more than ever do we need to get to that hospital and then the military base. Let's not waste time. Everyone, let's move."

Everyone stood up and then we continued to the hospital. It took us a few minutes to climb out the other side of the crater. The crater and the road ahead were littered with wreckage from the *Kento* and wreckage from our surroundings. We paused for a second on the crater's edge and then we kept going. After a few minutes of walking down the road a large building came into view. There was a large red H partly hanging on the buildings side. We had very little problems getting to the hospital. Most of the rubble on the road had been pushed to one side or the other. The hospital had received meager damage to its roof and about five of its upper levels. There were a few holes about the size of boulders in the middle of the wall with the entrance. Next to the hole was the large red H hanging from the wall. Smoke was pouring out of the top levels of the hospital and out of the scares in its visible side. There were large vehicles sitting around the outside of the hospital's walls. Some of the cars were on their sides and others were on their wheels. There were no humans in sight other than the smoking corpses around the hospital.

We reached the main entrance to the hospital. There was a small barricade that blocked off the road across from us. The hospital had two large glass doors that opened when you walked in front of it and two large windows on either side of the entrance. The glass in both of the windows and the glass in the doors had shattered and lay in shards on the ground. We entered the hospital; it was quiet, motionless, and there was a thin cloud of smoke in the air. A few flickering ceiling lights and a computer monitor on a desk across from the entrance lit the lobby.

"Shaurha, how are things going?"

"Fine, we just entered the hospital's lobby."

"Thanks for filling in while I was gone."

"It was no problem, so what did she want?"

"Nothing, she just wanted to talk and had a few questions for me."

"Alex, I have to get going later maybe we can have a few rounds in the combat simulator."

"That sounds like a good idea. Maybe in a few hours we will have a few rounds, will that do?"

"Okay, see you later, Alex."

"Bye, Shaurha."

The lobby was lit only by the sparks from broken ceiling lights and a computer monitor. Each spray of sparks gave a brief flash of light throughout the lobby. The brief flash of light illuminated everything in the hospital lobby. There were stretchers lying on the floor and along the walls. There were three seat chairs lying on their sides and backs. Across from the main doors was a front desk with piles of papers on the top. There were also papers scattered over the lobby floor. Some of the stacks on the floor were burning and others were blowing around from the wind coming from the outside. There was a small lamp hanging down the side of the desk. There was no light coming from the dangling lap.

Zar pointed to one of the lobby's three seat chairs. Zar's two remaining assistants walked over to the chair and set it on its legs. Zar then motioned to the Talins that were carrying Crystal. The two Talins walked over to Zar, his other two assistants and the three-seat chair. The two Talins set Crystal and her stretcher on the floor. Zar and one of his three assistants reached down to Crystal's shoulders and her feet. The two of them then lifted Crystal onto the three-seat chair. Zar then bent down to her head and began to look over her wounds once more.

Shaurha and Hamole started to give out orders to their fellow Talins. A dozen troops were ordered to go back outside and keep watch for the Shadows, any one from pod four, and any other human survivors. The rest of the troops were ordered to spread out through the hospital and look for survivors and any sign of the military. Gupp and his assistants branched out into the hospital so did two of Zar's assistants. Marissa walked over to an upright seat and sat down. She then hugged Maggie and began to pet her.

"Alex, could you come here?" asked Shaurha.

"Whaloa, could you join us?" asked Hamole.

I put my bag down next to the main door and walk over to where Shaurha and Hamole were standing. The two of them were over by the lobby desk looking at some of the papers on top. Seconds later Whaloa joined us at the lobby desk.

"What can I do for you two?"

"We are going to rest here for a little while then we will begin to walk the distance to the military base. For now, Alex, remain in the entrance where you are safe. Before you do, could you and Whaloa take a look at the computer. Maybe there is some mention of where everyone went. I am going to have a look around and will be back in a bit," said Shaurha.

"Commander Shaurha, wait, a few of the troops have found something outside you have to see," said Gupp, running from within the hospital.

Shaurha and Gupp left Hamole, Whaloa, and myself in the lobby and followed Gupp. Hamole then joined the troops in front of the hospital leaving the computer to the two of us. The monitor was on its side and projecting light, and the tower was on its side with the case taped on. The case was dented and had bloody handprints covering it. There were no cables for the monitor and the mini microphone wasn't on the desk.

Whaloa picked up the CPU tower, set it on the desk, and began to look it over. While he was busy I looked on the floor around the desk for the missing cables and the microphone. The cables weren't hard to find even in the poor lighting. I had the misfortune of tripping over the monitor cable. The microphone was much harder to find due to its size, color, and its location. The microphone was black and the size of a headphone speaker. The microphone was hiding against the right wall as you enter the hospital and sitting under a chair that had been knocked over.

"How are things going, Alex?"

"Hello, Shaurha, everything's fine."

"After I left you to your book a few days ago it got me thinking and I was hoping you could let me help some more, to fill in the gaps of what happened."

"That will help a lot and you're right there are things that I was not there for so I will ask everyone to help fill in the gaps. However, since you're here would you fill in one of those gaps now, if you have the time?"

"How far are we in the line of events?"

"We are still in the hospital."

"Still you have had five days to add on to what I added."

"I did it's just I have been busy and the writing has been slow."

"Sorry forgot she has requested your presence a lot...So what are you going to do while I am filling in the gaps of our story?"

"I have nothing to do so I am going to help in writing. That is if you do not mind, Shaurha. I will just add my two cents when you get stuck or when you need me to fill in gaps when you weren't there and I was."

"I will fill in the events that I was present for and you weren't then I will pass it back to you to fill in the rest."

"You can begin, Shaurha, whenever you want I will just sit back and listen."

"Okay."

While Alex, Whaloa, Hamole, and most of the others were in the lobby Gupp and I were on our way to see what they had found at one of the other entrances. It took us a few minutes to get there due to the hospital's state. Walls and levels had been falling in on the ground floor making it harder to navigate through. Structural problems weren't the only thing that we had to get around. There were hospital supplies, corpses, and hospital furniture laying on the ground and the hardest part was the thick cloud of smoke that filled the hospital's halls, probably caused by fires throughout the hospital.

"Shaurha, we're here," said Gupp.

In front of me was a large entrance that had partly caved in upon itself leaving a gap just barely big enough to get through. On the other side of the hospital were a large earth vehicle and a sheet of metal lay against the vehicle's side. The metal looked like it had been ripped from one of the escape pods. I could see that there were other vehicles outside lying on their sides and roofs. Gupp walked ahead of me and passed through the opening, turned and motioned for me to follow. I walked up to the gap in the entrance and stepped through. Gupp walked over to the large vehicle, looked back at the hospital and me. Then he walked along the length of all the vehicles. A few minutes later he returned with an angry look upon his face which in all the years I have worked with him is very unusual.

"They better have a good reason for leaving," said Gupp loudly.

"What is wrong, Gupp?"

"First look at what we have found," Gupp said, pointing to the sheet of metal and the large vehicle.

I walked closer and looked close at the metal, from close up I knew what it was instantly. On the metal there was part of a word and a number was visible. There was enough of the message to make out what it said. The message, even though most of it was gone, read: Kento Pod 4. The sheet of metal was from pod four which we had not heard from or seen.

"This is from pod four."

"I know I told my assistants to stay here and wait for us to return and they are nowhere to be seen."

"This is great but you said you had two things to show me."

"Yes I did, you're in front of it. From what the male told us the military base is too far for us to walk especially with all our supplies and equipment. Not to mention too far to carry the female human and it's probably too far for the male to walk. My assistants and I were thinking that with the help of everyone of us we could put this vehicle back on to its wheels. Then we make a few alterations to it and head to the military base."

"Go and get the others and ask Alex to help and don't bother going through the hospital, it looks like it might be easier to go around the hospital. I will join you all in a bit. I am going to look for your assistants and the others that journeyed into the hospital."

"What if Hamole refuses to let any of his troops help?"

"Remind him that the prince and princes may have been in pod four and the sooner we get to the military base the sooner we can find the two of them. If that does not work tell him it's an order from me."

"He won't like that at all."

"That's why he will help you."

"I will tell him, I will see you in a short bit, Commander Shaurha," Gupp said as he turned and walked down the length of the hospital's wall.

"You too, Gupp," I said as I turned to the partly caved in entrance.

I stepped through the opening in the partly collapsed entrance. As I stepped through the small opening, smoke rushed out of the hospital and over my face. The smoke filled my lungs introducing me to many different odors. The stench of death and sulfur was rich in the smoke. There were also many odors that were most foul. I reached into my uniform's pockets, took out my SD-006 (scanning devise 006) and scanned the air. My SD-006 sucked in a small amount of the air in the hospital, analyzed the elements compaction of the air.

The SD-006 then gave a reading of the air in the hospital. There were too many elements in the air for me to recall all of them. I do remember some of the elements and chemicals in the hospital's air. There was what humans called cyanide, a collection of radioactive elements, and a few explosive gases were present in the air. None of which were in high enough amounts to do harm to Talins, but I had no idea if Alex's, Crystal's or Marissa's systems could handle such large amounts of toxic elements and I did not want to risk their lives anymore than I had to. I continued farther into the hospital, keeping my mind and my eyes on my SD-006.

The further into the hospital I went, the hotter the air surrounding me got. The smoke grew too thick to see through and the higher the chemical elements got in the air. If I were to go any further the toxicity of the air could start affecting me. Then I heard something in amongst all of the roaring fires, a cough followed by wheezing. I walked deeper into the hospital following the wheezing to its owner. Too dark to see I could only rely on my instruments to guide me through the collapsing hospital. A few minutes of wandering in the dark I found the maker of the sounds but I still could not see their source.

"Come with me, I will get you out of here," I said to the source of the sounds.

No sound, just a hand grabbing my leg for help. I reached down and pulled him up and I could just make out the words "thank you" in a low whisper. I removed one of my instruments from my uniform and pushed it to his mouth. The dark made finding his mouth hard.

After a few tries of hitting his face I finally found his mouth. I heard the device activate and the contents within the device rush into his lungs. He choked on the air briefly then he accepted the fresh air. I began the journey back to the large vehicle and the piece of pod four with the man under my arm. He could barely walk which as you can imagine was not very easy for me to move him.

The journey back was long and not much happened so I will not bore you with the details.

We emerged around an hour later. I helped the man through the opening to the outside. I expected to see Hamole and the others waiting for me, but they were nowhere in sight. I set the man down and walked around the bus there was no one. I walked back to the man and looked him over, he had some burns on his hands face and legs, and there were a few cuts pushing through his burnt skin. I picked him back up and began to walk around the hospital. I could see why Gupp took me through the hospital instead of walking around as I was doing with the injured man.

The path around the hospital was long, filled with smoldering debris and numerous craters ranging in sizes. The smallest I could see was the size of my hand and the biggest I could see looked to be thirty feet in diameter. We started to ascend a small incline of debris when the man began to wake up. He started to fight me as he woke from his unconscious state. These obstacles proved to be very challenging to climb up with the extra resistance of the man. The breathing device I had given him fell to the ground. The man broke free and fell to the ground alongside my device. He slid a bit on the ground before he tried to stand up, as he tried to stand I could see his legs were shaking and a painful look rushed across his face.

He got to his feet and slowly walked to me, his legs still shook as he walked. Once or twice he almost lost his balance and fell back down. As he got closer to me, I reached out to assist him. Then his legs gave out on him and he fell into my arms, he tried to speak but his heavy breathing overpowered his words. I reached around his shoulders and hoisted him back to his feet then I lent him my shoulder to lean on while we walked to the others. With me supporting most of his weight, which was quite less than what I had been carrying, it made it much easier and faster to reach the others. With him supporting part of his own weight we reached the main entrance to the hospital within half of these humans' hours. The two of us were greeted by six of Hamole's troops. One of them walked over and helped me carry the injured man while the others walked around us with their rifles ready.

Chapter Seven
The Flood

As we walked through the main entrance his head lowered to face the ground and his feet went limp. Loud yelling brought my attention to the middle of the lobby. Gupp was yelling at Hamole, telling him that I told him to tell Hamole to get all the troops to help with the bus. Zar was still looking after Crystal's wounds and trying to ignore the commotion caused by Hamole and Gupp. Gupp's assistants had returned and now were helping Whaloa and his assistants at the desk terminal. Zar's assistants had not yet returned from their journey into the hospital. There were a few of Hamole's troops standing around the lobby looking bored and bothered. Alex was at the desk looking upon the terminal and Marissa was still crying on her pet dog.

The two of us carried the man over to one of the triple seated seats and we sat the man down. Zar took notice of the movement next to him, came over with his medical instruments, and began to work on his burns and cuts. I left Zar to treat the injured man's wounds. I walked over to Hamole and Gupp. As I approached them they immediately stopped arguing with each other. They turned and looked at me and Hamole was about to speak when Gupp cut him off.

"Commander, I have been trying to get Hamole to order his men over to the large vehicle and the fragment of pod four...But he refuses to follow the order you had me relay to him," Gupp said as he turned to face Hamole with anger plastered on his face.

Hamole then turned to face Gupp and began to speak.

"As I have told you, Gupp, the only Talin I take orders from is Shaurha and I do not take orders by relay!" Hamole said, raising his voice higher than Gupp's.

"At first I did not order you to have your men help, but when you said no I was told by Shaurha to relay the order."

"Gupp, Hamole, that is enough. Hamole, I order you and your men to follow Gupp around the outside of the hospital and help him with our transportation. And I do not want to hear a word from you until you have finished the task at hand. Now if you excuse me I have to check in with Whaloa and his team."

Hamole gave me a disgusted look, and then ordered his men out of the hospital. Gupp quickly followed Hamole and his men. I walked over to the lobby desk and walked around to join Whaloa in front of the terminal. Alex stood up, walked over to Crystal, and kneeled next to her. I bent down and looked upon the screen to see if they had made any progress.

"Hello, Commander," said Whaloa.

"Have you made any progress on the computer?"

"Yes, in fact, we have some good and some bad news. The bad is that since the only other pod that made it out of the *Kento* was pod four, and there is no mention of the king, queen or the prince, it appears that they are dead. It is possible that they ejected before we entered this planet's orbit but from here I just don't know."

"What about the good news?"

"The good news is that the princess is alive and is at the military base waiting for the rest of us to arrive. However, from what this reads they aren't going to remain there for too long."

"Good job, I want you, your colleagues, Gupp's assistants and Alex to go and help Gupp with our transport."

Whaloa stood up, walked over to Alex and spoke to him briefly. Alex walked over to Marissa and spoke to her, then Marissa, Maggie, Alex, and Whaloa made their way to the entrance. Then the rest of the Talins except for Zar and I followed them out of the hospital. I walked over to Zar. He was now working on the man's face. By now the man had regained consciousness once again and was staring at Zar as he was being treated. The man showed no sign of fear, no sign of anger, or hate. He just had a serious expression across his face. His eyes moved from Zar to me, once I realized that I was standing over him watching him while he was being treated. Zar finished healing the man, walked back over to Crystal, and scanned her from head to toe. The man jumped up off the seat and quickly moved over to where Crystal had been resting.

"Stop what you are doing to her, I'm a doctor let me take a look at her. Let me see what I can do," the man said as he touched Zar on the shoulder.

Zar stepped back to give the doctor room to look Crystal over.

"What kind of doctor are you and what's your name?" Zar asked as he walked over to me.

"My name is James and I work in the emergency room on the more severe cases. I am assuming that you two and the others are from the ship the *Kento* that I heard about?"

"Yes I'm the Commander and Zar is the ship's doctor and the personal doctor to the royal family. Since you know about us I'm assuming that you have seen other Talins."

"Yes before the military evacuated everyone else. There were six, two females. One looked very young by her size the other was quite a bit taller and looked to be tired, and the other four were all males; three of the males did not survive. The soul surviving male seemed very protective of the younger female. He would not let any of the military go near her. The military finally convinced the male to let them escort them to a safer location."

"The military base?"

"Yes I think so but I can't be sure."

"So how is Crystal doing?" Zar asked, stepping closer to James.

"She is fine just resting from the looks of it."

"If everyone was evacuated then why are you still here?"

"I got stuck behind a locked door and was left behind. When I finally got the door open everyone had gone."

"Commander, we have our transport ready and we are ready to head to the military base when you are ready," said Gupp as he entered the lobby through the outside entrance.

"We will join you and the others shortly."

"Okay, Commander," said Gupp and then he turned and left us alone.

"James, could you help Zar and I get Crystal to our transport, it's on the left side of the hospital."

"I think that is a grand idea. I'm coming with you if you don't mind, to help any way I can."

"Commander, we should get moving before too much longer."

"You right, Zar, let's get Crystal back on the stretcher. James, could you take her feet, I will carry the head of the stretcher. Just in case, Zar walk along our right side."

We were just about to leave the hospital when Zar's assistants came out of one of the corridors that led deeper into the hospital. The three of them had their arms full of medical supplies and bags of food. They saw that we were just about to leave and then they quickly joined us. We left the hospital and the six of us plus an unconscious Crystal made our way around the side of the hospital. We quickly made our way to the bus that Hamole and his sixteen remaining troops had rolled the vehicle over until it was on its wheels. Nozad and Flito were working on the bus with Whaloa's and Gupp's assistants. Alex was in the bus trying to explain to Gupp how the bus worked and how to drive it.

"To us the human technology was fairly primitive so we had a hard time understanding how it all worked. At this point I will turn his book back over to him because I have filled in his gap...Alex, it's all yours I shall leave you now."

"Thank you, Shaurha, I really appreciate what you did for me and all those that might read this."

"Alex, give me a ring if you need any more help with you book. I am honored you asked me to help. I am sure the others might feel the same way I do, well except Hamole he has never been one for words written or spoken."

"Thanks again for your help, and I will let you know if I need your help again."

"All right see, you later."

"Bye."

By the time Shaurha, Zar, James, and Zar's three assistants arrived with Crystal, we had managed to get the bus back on its wheels. As they loaded on to the bus I was in the process of explaining how to drive the bus to Gupp who was taking in every word I said with careful analysis. Gupp's assistants were adding metal plates to the sides the roof and the engine of the bus. Apparently they thought that there would be another meteor shower on our way to the military base. Hamole and his sixteen soldiers had circled the bus with their rifles at the ready. Whaloa and his assistants were loading all of their supplies on to the bus. Shaurha and Zar carried Crystal on to the bus and set her down on the back seat behind Marissa and Maggie. Shaurha walked up to the front of the bus where I was explaining how to drive the bus to Gupp. I stopped talking and waited for Shaurha to speak. After a minute she sat down on a seat and spoke.

"Gupp, how close is the bus to being ready to take us to the military base?"

"Hello, Shaurha, the bus should be ready to move in just a few minutes."

"That's good, let me know when everything and everyone is ready to move out, and then we shall quickly depart."

"Yes, Commander."

Shaurha left the bus. I watched her walk around the bus until she vanished from view. I went back to explaining how to drive the bus to Gupp. He would stop me after every couple of minutes, look around the outside of the bus and then ask for me to continue. After ten to twenty minutes Gupp stood up, excused himself and left the bus. He walked alongside the bus, spoke to those that had been working on the bus. He patted one of his assistants on the back then they walked back to the front of the bus and piled in.

Shortly after Gupp, Whaloa, their assistants, Shaurha, Hamole, and everyone else got in. Zar and James sat in the back of the bus near Crystal. Shaurha, Hamole, Gupp, and Whaloa sat as close to the front as they could. All of Hamole's men were sitting near the windows with their rifles in hand, and everyone else filled in the remaining seats. I had the privilege of driving the bus to the military base, since the only others there that knew how to drive the bus were Crystal and James and they were both occupied. I started the bus using a makeshift key that Gupp had installed awhile ago. The engine started and the bus moved forward.

It took me some doing to get the bus out of my former hometown. Roads were blocked by cars, collapsed buildings, fires that roared, and large craters that took up most of the road at times. A few times I had to drive through burning homes and damaged buildings. We ran into cars as we turned, and plowed down the many roads. The cars bounced off the bus's reinforced skin sending reddish gold sparks raining in our wake. Marissa screamed with each car and building I had to drive through. Our escape was slow. We left a path of debris leading out of my hometown. A loud roar came from behind the bus. I slammed on the brakes and stepped out of the bus. The hospital had collapsed and there was a big cloud of smoke and dust rose from the hospital's former location.

I got back into the bus and continued to drive us further out of town. This was a little bit easier to drive due to the fact that there was nothing but burning fields. Even with the craters in our path, because all I had to do was to go around the craters. Once or twice I had to go a long distance out of the way to get back in the direction we were heading. Inside the bus was very quiet compared to the roar of fire coming from outside the bus. There was a small conflict in the back of the bus between Zar and James about Crystal's condition.

Forty minutes went by. The roaring fires outside of the bus softened and heavy clouds of smoke soon covered earth's surface in front of us. A bright flash of violet light, from above us illuminated the black clouds forming above. Milliseconds later a tremendous clap of thunder broke the silence. A second later the sky was filled with dozens of lightning bolts that rained down on the earth. Thunder followed the lightning within milliseconds which caused the windows to rattle in their frames. An even brighter flash of violet light flashed as a bolt of lightning struck a car's length ahead of us. Rain began to fall, which started just as fast as the last lightning bolt flashed. The rain began to fall quickly and heavily which grew into a wall of rain that smashed down upon us with a sound like a billion rocks being dropped. The only other sound that could be heard was the tremendous claps of thunder forcing its way through the wall of rain. Lightning continued to flash causing the wall of rain to glow a brilliant, bright violet light. Between the wall of rain and the lightning, made it almost impossible to see where I was driving. By then I had slowed the bus down to a crawl.

The craters soon filled with water. The surface glazed over the craters forming a smooth sheet of water. Unable to see what was in front of us I had no choice but to stop the bus before I drove into a crater. We were fortunate that I stopped the bus when I did. The rain climbed up the sides of the bus and soon climbed above the doors and continued to rise. Water began pouring into the bus through the cracks in the windows and the doors. Marissa was in the back crying into Maggie's fur as the water poured into the bus. Gupp and his assistants got to their feet and spread out over the bus. Gupp had a device in his hand and was passing it over the cracks of the door. As he passed the device around the door, foam grew on the frame of the door stopping the water. After fifteen minutes, Gupp and his assistant stopped the flow of water into the bus. By that time a foot and a half of water had covered the floor of the bus. Outside the bus was a different story, surrounding the bus was about two additional feet of water, which was now very close to the top of the bus.

The sound of the rain stopped but I could hear thunder some distance away. Even though the rain had passed, we still had a river of water that surrounded us. The bus began to move slowly forward by the force of the newly formed river. Unable to do anything those that were standing slowly started to return to their seat when we were forced to sit back down by a sudden jolt of the water. The river grew faster, so did our speed, until we slammed into something hard which slammed us towards the left of the bus. The bus stopped moving and lay with its left side against a large structure. The roof of the bus was only a couple of feet lower than the structure's roof.

"Okay, everyone, we are going to climb up to that structure's roof," Shaurha said from behind me.

Gupp stood up and walked under one of the roofs emergency exit doors, and popped it off without any problem at all. Hamole joined Gupp underneath the opened hatch and motioned for Shaurha and me to go first. We stepped forward, they locked their hands together and lowered them so Shaurha or myself to step on. Shaurha stepped on to their locked hands, Gupp and Hamole raised Shaurha up to the opened hatch. She climbed through and lay on the roof with her hands hanging down into the bus.

"Alex, come on we have to get everyone out," Shaurha yelled into the bus.

I did not speak. I just moved my feet and stepped into Hamole's and Gupp's hands. I then felt my arm raise and my body soon followed. Shaurha grabbed my arm and lifted me the rest of the way out of the bus and onto the bus's roof. I walked a little closer to the edge of the bus. I faced the structure and hoisted myself up on to the roof. I sat down on the roof facing Shaurha and the bus and watched as Shaurha helped two troops out of the bus. Shaurha stood up, walked to the bus's edge, and climbed on to the roof. One of the troops lay down where Shaurha had lain and took over for Shaurha. The other troop followed Shaurha on to the structure. The troop at the first hatch reached in and helped Hamole and then helped Gupp out of the bus.

The second hatch was popped open and Whaloa climbed out followed by Nozad and Flito. Both Nozad and Flito joined me on the structure while Whaloa lay chest down on the bus. Then he reached in and was handed one of their computers and then some of the supplies we had gathered at the hospital. He stacked them close to the right side of the bus. One of his assistants was helped out of the first hatch. He walked to the stacked supplies and began to transfer them on to the structure. Whaloa continued to bring out the supplies and his assistant stacked them on to the roof. Then Whaloa stopped passing supplies and now was helping James out of the bus followed by Marissa. Next was Crystal and then Zar was helped out. Zar's assistant finished moving the supplies, turned and helped Zar with Crystal's motionless body. Zar and his assistant carried Crystal on to the roof and laid her down carefully.

The bus was then hit by something under the water. The force of the impact on the bus caused it to shift. The bus moved further along the structure, causing the bus's nose to get closer to the fast flowing river. Those on the bus looked up at the incoming river, I did the same. Debris varying in size was flowing down the river at a fast speed. Whaloa and the troop reached in and began pulling Hamole's troops out as fast as they could. Half the troops had been helped out when the bus was hit by a cluster of six logs. The bus inched forward, the nose of the bus only inches from the structure's edge. Once the bus stopped moving, the troops still on the bus quickly climbed into the structure.

The rest of troops soon followed their comrades. Maggie was lifted out by Whaloa and was carried to the roof by one of the troops. Then the bus was hit again by an unknown source causing the bus's nose to slide a foot out into the river. Whaloa pulled out one of his assistants then was about to reach back into the bus to help the next Talin out. When his assistant stopped him.

"Whaloa, you're an officer, you need to get to safety, I will get the rest of them out."

Whaloa did not like what his assistant said but did not argue. His assistant took his place and helped the troop at the first hatch evacuate the bus. All of Gupp's assistants and Whaloa's second assistant just made it to the roof. The bus was hit again just as one of Zar's remaining two assistants were helping out. The bus began to pick up speed as it was pushed further out into the raging river. One of Zar's assistants quickly ran and jumped to the roof. The remaining troop and Zar's last assistants ran toward the roof. Zar's assistants slipped on the bus's wet roof, went head first into the structure's wall and fell into the raging river. The soldier was just shy of the structure's roof by a few inches. His body hit the wall, his hands scrapping at the wet tin roof then was swept away.

Whaloa's assistants did not make an attempt to join as she just drifted down the river. She climbed down into the bus, closed the hatches as she was helpless to do anything else. The bus then drifted past some dead trees that some how were still rooted and standing. We were stuck. We had no way to get to the military base, if there was still a military base. The water was too fast and too dangerous to swim through and there was no other way to continue our quest. Time flew by so slowly that at times I just wanted to go for a swim just to ease my boredom.

I looked at my watch. Pointless it stopped working back at the bomb shelter and that's where I left it. I began to get sick of boredom so I began to look at all the Talins, Gupp, Whaloa and Hamole were in the middle of our party. James, Shaurha, Zar, and his assistants were on the left side taking care of Crystal. All of the other assistants were scattered among the troops on the roof. I then began to look at the Talins around me, mainly at the differences of their features. Quite a few of their faces were scarred and slightly disfigured. A couple of them had one of their eyes sown closed. A few had a scar that crossed their entire face, from their eyes down to their jawline. I continued looking around the roof; most of us were sitting on the tin just looking as miserable as possible. There was little room for anyone to really walk about so no one could get up and stretch their legs.

At that time I had no idea how much time had passed or how close the next storm was. All I could do was to sit and think. However, that proved pointless, my thoughts would not stay in one place, they would get bored of themselves and move on.

Sometime after we transferred to the structure I started hearing faint clapping over the roaring of the water. The clapping sound got louder and louder as time past; however, there was no sign of its source. Minutes passed and the sound stopped, got a little weaker, changed its direction to my right, and continued on. The clapping stopped again and then got softer and broke up, into multiple claps. Then they changed their direction again, and then they broke up and spread out over the river. A few minutes later five lights fell down over the ragging river. The lights spread over a thin layer of fog that quickly spread over the river's surface. They continued to advance up the river, the whole time scanning the fog covered river. As they advanced they continued to get further and further apart. A few of them finally got close enough to see the maker of the claps and the spot lights. Three helicopters came into full view and then the other two followed shortly after. Two small helicopters and three large helicopters were in the air looking at the river.

A minute later and the three larger choppers were advancing towards us. A few seconds later and the other two followed their three comrades in their advance upon us. The helicopters slowed as they passed overhead, they sped up once again and hovered in a circle around the structure. One broke away from the circle and moved over our heads, then hovered, then a rope was dropped down and a soldier repelled down the rope. Shaurha and Hamole walked over to where the rope came in contact with the roof and stood waiting for the soldier.

The soldier's feet hit the surface of the wet tin roof with a just barely noticeable ping. The soldier removed his helmet, paused then walked over to the middle of our party. The soldier began to speak to Gupp, Whaloa, and Hamole for a minute. Gupp then pointed in the direction of Crystal and James. Shaurha and Zar were walking through the other Talins to join Gupp, Whaloa, Hamole, and the solider. The solider walked towards Shaurha and Zar briefly then stopped. Shaurha and Zar joined the solider after a few seconds. The solider began to speak to Shaurha as soon as she reached him.

Then the solider broke from the conversation and walked over to the rope and gave it a tug. The rope began to get pulled up then the chopper broke its hovering position and joined its fellow choppers. A minute later and second helicopter that looked just like the first took the same hovering position. A few seconds later a rope ladder was dropped from the side of the helicopter. The ladder hit the roof with a splash, and then the solider walked over to it and held it as still as he could.

Shaurha motioned to the rest of the Talins to start climbing up the ladder. All of the Talins hesitated for a few moments, and then Hamole walked to the ladder, received a few words from the solider, and began to climb. Thirty seconds later and the Talins gathered around the ladder. Once Hamole reached the top of the ladder another solider pulled him in. One of Hamole's troops stepped on to the ladder and began to climb the ladder. Soon after one of Whaloa's assistants started climbing, followed by one of Gupp's assistants then another troop. I began to count as they climbed and boarded the helicopter. Troop after troop climbed the ladder and boarded the waiting helicopter.

At twelve the solider put his hand up and yelled to stop, and then he waved his hand over his head. The ladder began to rise into the helicopter's side. Then the chopper broke its hover and left the circle of helicopters. However, the space above us was not left unoccupied for very long. A third helicopter like the ones before it filled the void above us. Like its predecessor it hovered rather close to the first helicopter's position. The solider walked over to the rope ladder as he did before and grabbed the rope ladder.

The Talins gathered around the ladder again, half a dozen of Hamole's troops were the first ones to board the helicopter followed by Nozad, Gupp, Whaloa, one of Gupp's assistants, and the remaining two troops. Once again the solider told the waiting Talins to stop then he waved to the helicopter. Like the second helicopter the third one broke from its hovering position, then left the circle, and then vanished from view. Then the solider motioned for everyone else to move over to Crystal's and James's location. The solider followed us over to the left of the structure and spoke to the rest of us.

"This chopper, there," the solider said as he pointed to the helicopter resting at the edge of the structure, "is for the injured and all supplies you may have. I am going to ask you all to help load the helicopter, once that's done we will board the next helicopter and get out of here."

He walked over, picked up a few of the Talin computers and carried them to the helicopter. James and Zar picked up Crystal and moved her towards the helicopter. One of the soldiers in the chopper stepped out and helped Zar and James load Crystal on to the helicopter. Shaurha walked over to the pile of supplies, picked up hospital supplies and moved them to the helicopter. Marissa with Maggie's collar in hand walked towards the supplies and picked up a small bag of food and began to walk towards the chopper.

One more of the soldiers hopped off the chopper, walked towards Marissa, and spoke to her. The soldier then reached down to Maggie and picked her up. Then the soldier walked with Marissa to the chopper, he handed Maggie to one of the other soldiers and then helped Marissa on to the helicopter. I walked over to the supply pile that was slowly diminishing, pick up one of the Talin computers, and carried it to the helicopter. I handed it to the solider and told him about Marissa and the arrangement we had with her parents. He assured me that everything would be all right and that I should continue to help with the supplies. I turned away from the helicopter, walked back to the pile, and helped fill the helicopter.

Once the helicopter was loaded with all of the supplies, the soldiers it came with, and the new passengers the helicopter departed. Then another helicopter filled the void across from us. The soldier from the first helicopter directed us into the chopper. One by one we loaded into the chopper. Shaurha was first, next was Zar then James then myself then the remaining Talins and the soldier was last to board the chopper. The soldier put on a headset and spoke into the microphone. I was unable to hear what he was saying due to the roar of the chopper's rotors.

Chapter Eight
The Military Base

Within a few seconds the chopper rose and moved in the direction it originally came from. I looked out the window, the last chopper was following us on our right. I looked down at the earth's surface there were few trees standing, and a few ruined structures poked out of the water. The water was dark brown and was filled with debris. I watched as we quickly flew across the saturated earth. A short time later concrete emerged out of the river, a road rose from the water and climbed up a hill. We followed the road until the military base came into view off to our left. We broke from the road turned left and within a few minutes we landed on concrete, there were a few emergency personal waiting nearby.

The solider in the back climbed out of the chopper and motioned for us to follow him. We all piled out of the helicopter, the soldier began to walk towards a nearby hanger and we followed him. Then a loud whistle from above silenced the helicopter's roar. A meteor flew over our heads and plowed through a nearby building sending it into a blaze within seconds and throwing burning rubble into the air. Then a second meteor flew over our heads, across the base and struck the road, we had just crossed. Within a few minutes large turrets rose up from under the earth. The turrets turned towards the meteors, with a cloud of smoke the turrets lunched a missile at the meteors. With explosions the meteors broke apart and the pieces fell to the earth.

"Quickly, everyone, into the hanger now," yelled a soldier as he ran to the open the hanger's doors.

We listened to what the soldier said and followed him into the hanger. Four large military trucks with open canvas backs were parked lengthwise to the hanger. Marissa Hamole and all of the others had climbed into two of the trucks. We joined the others in the hanger and boarded one of the other trucks. I took a seat facing the hanger bay's doors. I looked through a crack in the canvas towards the helicopter when it erupted into flames as a meteor crashed through the side of the helicopter. A cloud of fire erupted from the helicopter sending parts of the helicopter everywhere. The explosion's concussion sent nearby soldiers to the concrete. A few of the soldiers had been stuck by burning debris which sent them to the ground. I watched until the hanger bay doors started to close, shortly after the doors closed the ground began to shake. The concrete around us began to rise and we began to descend into the earth's crust.

It began to get dark as we sank further into earth. Lights inside the truck came on lighting the inside and the outside of the trucks. Outside of the trucks was a large concrete wall that had a metal rail in the middle of it. We sank further and further down into the earth for what seemed like an hour. Then we came to a stop and the trucks we were in began to move forward. The concrete was replaced with a large open room with many vehicles parked on either side of the truck. We drove past tanks, jeeps, and other military vehicles. Then we came to a stop. The engine shut off and the driver's side doors opened and closed. The other two trucks pulled up on either side of us and the third pulled up a few feet behind us. The soldier that joined us from the helicopter stood up and spoke to us.

"Stay here I will go get Lt. Richardson. He will take you to General Ames."

The soldier stepped off the truck walked along the driver's side. A door opened in front of us and closed with a loud metal crashing sound. We were forced to wait in this large parking lot. Not much time had passed. The door ahead of us opened and many footsteps soon followed. Marines walked along our truck then split up, a few men and women walked to the back of each truck. Two men and one woman dressed in soldier gear walked to the back of our truck. The two men stood at each side of the truck and the female stood in the center.

"These two soldiers will help everyone out of this truck. Then you and the rest of your party will come with us to see General Ames."

I heard similar conversations coming from behind the other trucks. Everyone cleared out of the four trucks and walked single file past the front of the trucks. Crystal was now on a stretcher being carried by two Marines. Zar and James spoke to them briefly, and then followed. In front of the trucks a man stood in front of a large metal door with a rifle at the ready. He opened and held the door open as we passed through entering into a hallway. At the end of the hall another solder stood with his rifle ready. He opened the door behind him as Shaurha approached and he held it open for us. We found ourselves standing in a large room smaller than the garage, but bigger than the hanger bay.

We now stood in a room that had five walls, two on our left, one wall ahead of us, one to our right, and one wall behind us. The wall to our right had six doors. The wall ahead of us had at least five doors. The middle door was made out of metal and looked to be twice the size of the other doors. One of the walls to our left had three doors and the other on our left had a large mirror that stretched the length of the wall. The wall behind us that we had just passed through had one other door which was a large metal shutter towards the middle of the wall. The walls were made out of metal and had lights embedded in the metal. A side from the doors the walls where lined with black and brown crates and metal cylinders. There were support beams stretching from the floor to the ceiling. Each of the support beams were surrounded by additional carts and cylinders. Other than our party and the soldiers watching us the room was empty of life. The room was quiet, none of us had the energy to talk or to move very much, and the soldiers remained quiet.

A short bit of time had passed when the few minutes of quiet was broken. The third door on the wall in front of us opened, three men walked out and made their way over to our group. Their footsteps echoed throughout the room. Two of the men were dressed like soldiers and the third had an officer's uniform on. Shaurha and Hamole stepped forward and greeted the three men.

"Hello, my name is Lt. Richardson. General Ames wishes to speak to those that are in charge. The rest of you can follow the solders. They will get you registered then take you to the refuge room. There you can wait for the others to return, get something to eat, drink, and receive medical treatment and get some rest. A few of your solders can come with you and the rest of the soldiers can go with the others."

"We have a few questions that need to be answered, Lt. Richardson."

"Save all of your questions for General Ames. He knows more about our situation and the others like you than I do. Now if you would follow either the soldiers or me."

"Okay, Lt. Richardson, we will do as you ask," Shaurha said as she motioned to Zar, Whaloa, and Gupp.

Zar, Gupp and Whaloa stepped forward and joined Shaurha and Hamole in front of Lt. Richardson. "Follow me," said Lt. Richardson as he turned and started walking to the left.

"Everyone else follow us," one of the soldiers said, before they both turned to their left and started to walk towards the doors on our right.

"Come on don't just stand there follow us," the second soldier said while the two of them walked to our right. None of the Talins moved they just looked at each other. They looked like they had no idea what to do. James and one of the Talin soldiers stepped out from the crowd with Crystal still unconscious on a stretcher. Then a few more soldiers stepped out of the crowd with some of the Talin computers and some of our supplies. Then everyone else started to gather the supplies and the remaining computers, and followed the two soldiers to the right.

We continued through the third door of the six, into a small hall that was not that long or that wide. There was one other door in the hall. It was only thirty feet from the door we just passed through. We did not stop we continued through the second door. On the other side of the door was a much larger room than the room where we were greeted. This room was also very busy with life and very packed full of people. There were thousands of people walking and talking amongst themselves. Bunk beds stacked on top of one another lined the four walls of this room. The bunk beds were packed flush with the walls and the other beds had a ladder that stretched from the floor to the fourth bed. There was a break in the beds against the walls, where there was a break in the beds a door stood. I counted the number of doors. There were five doors in total.

"We need you all to go over to the second door on your right. You all have to be registered. Follow Mark to the registry desk."

"If you would follow me," said Mark.

We were led around the single beds in the center of the room. I could hear whispers coming from the occupants of the surrounding beds as we passed. We passed about fifty beds on both sides before we came to a stop and had to turn to our left then we continued on down the path. After turning to our left we passed fifteen more beds before we passed a door. Another twenty beds before we reached a second door. Mark stopped, walked over to the door, opened it, and held it open. I glanced down the remaining path that separated the beds. There still looked to be a lot of beds before the path veered off to the left again. I was the second to last to pass through the door. After I had passed through, Mark continued to hold the door open for a few seconds then he let the door go and followed through. We were in a much smaller room then the previous rooms. Like all the other rooms this one was the same color and was illuminated by the same kind of wall floor and ceiling lights. There were four large concrete support beams, a table, and a few chairs stood in between the beams further in the room. On the far wall was a metal door to our right there was large amounts of boxes filled with supplies.

"Okay let's get started and get you all registered and take inventory of what equipment and supplies you have. I will register the humans first since there are only four humans. If I could get you two to bring yourselves and the two ladies to the table we will begin registration."

I looked over to James and began to walk towards the table. James and the troops carrying Crystal followed behind me. Mark walked past the table, and passed through the metal door. He returned a short time later and in his hands he was carrying a small box and a pile of papers. He walked over to the table and set the tin box and papers down. Then he sat down in one of the chairs facing us.

"Print your full name, occupation, skills, hobbies, your age, height, and weight if you know them, date of birth, and past jobs of any kind if any."

"My name is Dr. James Lock. I was a brain surgeon at the community hospital until all this happened. I also have pediatric training and chemical lab training. I am thirty-five years old, I am six feet eight inches tall and I have no idea how much I weigh. I was born in September 16, 1990," James told Mark while Mark wrote down the information.

"What about you?"

"My name is Alex Track. I am twenty years old. I have no idea how tall I am or my weight. I do not remember what my occupation was. I do not know what jobs I have had. I do remember by birthday is June 3, 2000."

"You don't remember what jobs you have had, what about skills? Do you remember what you're good at?"

"No I don't, I did hit my head back in town and was treated by Zar, a Talin doctor."

"Very well, when you all go and get checked by our medical staff, I will have them look at your head. In fact, Dr. Lock could do it later. And what about her, do any of you know her name?"

"Crystal Cox. She is twenty, born April 28, 2000, and anything other than that you're going to have to ask either her or my other two friends, Mike Fisher and David Dryer. If they are here they would know."

"I will check the registration database after we finish. You're the last one, aren't you?"

"Yes, sir."

"What is your name?"

"My name is Marissa Harris and I am eight years old."

"And who is your friend?"

"She's my doggie, Maggie."

"Excuse me, Mark, could I speak with you for a minute."

"In a minute. Marissa, where are your parents?"

Marissa turned and began to cry.

"I am so sorry, Marissa."

"Excuse me, Mark."

"What is it, Alex?"

I handed him the piece of paper that Crystal and I were given by Marissa's parents. Mark read the note a few times then said he would be right back with the note that he was going to copy it and check for

Mike and David in the database. Before he left he handed out registration forms to the Talins and asked us to help them if they needed it. Mark stood up and passed through the metal door. The Talins looked at each other then at the forms handed to them. James and the soldier set Crystal down on the table which sent the tin box to the floor breaking it open, throwing pencils and pens all over the floor. I picked up a few of them and handed the pencils to the Talins. They looked at the pencils and then back at the form. A confusing look spread across their faces.

"Is there something wrong?"

"What are we supposed to do with these?"

"You are supposed to fill out the form with the pencil or pen."

The Talins began talking amongst themselves. Then they all one by one walked to the table and set the pens, pencils, and papers down on the table. I looked at the forms as they were placed down on the table, they were all still blank.

"We can't fill out the forms. Our written language is much more complex than any humans. Plus our race has not used the written word for nearly five hundred years. Our texts are strictly computerized. None of use knows how to write with pens or pencils," said Flito while he set the pen and the form I had given him onto the table then stepped aside.

The door across the table opened and in walked the other soldier that we had met earlier. He walked across the room and took a seat in one of the chairs at the table.

"Where did Mark run off to, there is no way he got everyone here registered already."

"He went to check if any of my friends and family made it here."

"What is your name?"

"Alex Track."

"Well since Mark is not here I guess I will have to register the Talins, could you and Alex take the two women over there and have a seat?" the soldier said, looking at James and pointing to a row of chairs sitting against the wall on the soldier's left.

James and I picked up Crystal and carried her over to the row of chairs then we set her down across three of the seats. Marissa soon followed with her dog in tow. She sat down in one of the chairs and began to pet Maggie's fur. Marissa had tears running down her face and fell to the concrete floor. James and I both took a seat on either side of Marissa and watched as the soldier asked for the first Talin to get registered. None of the Talins looked like they really wanted to be wasting time by getting registered especially the Talin troops. Then one of Zar's assistants stepped forward and began to talk to the soldier. Then a few minutes later Zar's assistant walked away and Nozad and Flito stepped up to the table, while the two of them spoke to the soldier some of the troops began making noises. Then Nozad turned to face the troops and made a loud roar like noise. Almost at once the troops quieted down and lined up behind Nozad and Flito.

Nozad and Flito finished their registration and joined Zar's assistant at the back of the Talin party. The door behind the table opened and out walked Mark with a few sheets of paper in his hands. He glanced over at the table and spotted the pile of filled out registration forms then looked around the room until he spotted James, Marissa, Crystal, and I. He walked past the table and made his way over to us while sporting a pleased look on his face.

"I have some good news and bad news. I looked up your names and your friends' names in the system. I found Marissa's aunt. Alex, your parents and your two friends are here. I also found Crystal's parents, but they did not make it. The rest are all here in this facility. I will take you to them after you have been checked out by the base doctors," Mark said with a partial smile on his face. "Alex, James, could you carry Crystal? And, Marissa, you can follow behind Alex and James. After a checkup I will take you to your aunt."

Mark walked to the door opposite the door he passed through not that long ago. James and I lifted Crystal off the row of chairs, walked across the room, and joined Mark at the door. Marissa slowly at first walked towards us still with a grasp on Maggie's collar. Mark opened the door and led us back to the room with the five walls. Shaurha and the others were talking to a few people in black suits. The men in suits stopped talking when we entered and tried to direct Shaurha and the others towards the wall with the long mirror stretching across it. Shaurha resisted their attempts once she noticed us entering the room without any of the other Talins. Hamole, Zar, Whaloa, and Gupp also noticed the absence of the others. The five of them departed from the suits and walked towards us.

They did not have a happy look on their faces for that matter they did not have an angry look. They had a sad look mounted on their faces. They looked as though they had lost someone or something very important. Their walk was slow, shaky and looked very weak. Their heads were lower than they had been when Mallow and Sorrow had died. Hamole sped up, leaving Shaurha and the others behind him. He quickly made his way over to us I could, hear him mumbling to himself before he spoke to us.

"Where are my troops and the others?" Hamole yelled as he stepped in front Mark.

"They are all being registered and you five have yet to be registered, if you haven't been already," Mark said.

"Hamole, like always you jump to the first thing that comes to your mind," Gupp said as he, Shaurha, Whaloa, and Zar hastily joined us at Hamole's side.

"Lt. Richardson, I was taking them to sector 5 because their friends and family are there, but first they needed to be seen by the base doctors. The med bay is where we were heading before we got stopped," said Mark.

"Private, you may proceed," said Lt. Richardson.

Mark gave a quick forward wave to us then began walking to our right and stopped at the fourth door on the wall. He turned the doorknob and pushed the door open. He then remained at the door holding it open. By this time my arms were getting tired and I could tell that James's arms were also getting tired. However, we had to push on for a little longer. I hadn't told Crystal this but I thought at that moment that she should lay off of the burgers for a while. We moved forward and walked through the opened door. The med bay was directly on the other side, dozens of beds and operating tables occupied by the wounded filled the room. The floor walls and the ceiling were all white excepted where blood covered the floor and some of the walls. Towards the back were many curtains drawn to a close and the room was lit by bright wall lamps and ceiling fixtures. The room was filled with moans and many screams from the wounded. In front of us was a reception desk with a nurse sitting behind it. The nurse wore large glasses, had a white nurse's uniform on, looked to be in her late forties, had blondish gray hair, and had brown eyes. She looked to be very tired and very worn out.

"Could I help you with anything? Oh hello, Mark. What can I do for you?" asked the nurse.

"The four of them need to be checked out by one of the doctors on call. Do you know if they can spare some time?" Mark replied.

"Stay here I will go and see if one of the doctors can spare some time, but I would not count on it," she said as she stood up and walked towards the closed curtains.

She pulled one of the curtains open and walked in closing the curtain behind her. The light coming from the lights caused shadows of her and another person. She moved from closed curtain to closed curtain asking doctor after doctor. She was heading towards the third to last doctor when she stopped moving and turned back to the fourth doctor. The two of them talked for a short time then she stuck her head out from behind the curtain and waved to us to come. Mark started to walk towards the nurse, having to pass many injured people. James and I started to follow Mark still with Crystal in tow when Maggie started to wine, James and I turned.

"Alex, I don't what to see a doctor," Marissa said, backing up to the door.

"Marissa, it is all right, it is just a checkup, there is nothing to be scared about. The doctor will not hurt you."

"I am not scared of the doctor. I just don't want to see him."

"Alright, for now you stay there. James and I have to take Crystal to see the doctor. Then I we will see about you not seeing the doctor."

"Okay, Alex, I will stay here until you come back."

"I will be back in a few minutes."

James and I turned around and began walking towards the curtain with the nurse behind it. I walked as fast as I could, nearly pulling the stretcher out of James's hands. On both of our sides people were bandaged from head to toe, others were bleeding and had limbs missing and skin burned off. Some of the tables and beds had bodies covered by white bloody sheets. The air around us had a familiar stench of burnt flesh, burnt hair, and death. I then realized why Marissa did not want to see the doctor, I didn't blame her. In fact I think Crystal was glad that she was unconscious for it all. I wish I had been. Those images still haunt me plus all the other images. James and I reached the curtain Mark then opened it from the other side and helped us with Crystal. The small room formed by the curtain was

101

empty aside from the four of us. The three of us set her down on a clean table, and just stood there waiting for the doctor to return.

The curtain was drawn back and a doctor stepped out in a long white doctor's lab coat. "Hello I am Doctor Emit." He was a little shorter than I was. He had a handle bar mustache and black hair. He was pushing a cart loaded full of medical supplies, all of which was packaged and clean. He moved slowly because of a limp to his right leg which made it hard for him to push the cart. He walked around Crystal stopping on her left and then pushed the cart as close to the table as it would go. Doctor Emit then took a small pen light out of his pocket, opened Crystal's eyes with one hand, and shined the light in her eyes. He then made a few marks on a piece of paper that had been lying under some of the supplies. He then checked Crystal's arms legs and ribs for any breaks, when the curtain to his left was opened. Zar walked through then closed the curtain behind him. Zar started to walk, stopped opposite of the doctor, the whole time the doctor's eyes fixed on Zar.

"Ah can I-I help y-you?" Doctor Emit asked, fumbling his words.

"No but I could help you with Alex, Crystal, James, and Marissa, the scared human child across the room."

"How could you do that?"

"I am a doctor from the Talin planet and I treated Alex, Crystal, and James with my medical instruments. Although your human physiology is different from my own, I was able to stabilize their conditions. There could be side affects from my treatment, hopefully the three of us can find and treat any conditions they may or may not have."

"Exactly what did you and the others like you do to these people?" asked Doctor Emit.

"As I said I tried to treat them and as I said your physiology is different so there could be side affects. None of the others did anything to them except try and help. Now if you would help there is not much time for further conversation."

"Fine, then what do you know of her condition, Zar?" asked Doctor Emit.

"As far as I can tell Alex is in good heath. Crystal fell on our way to the hospital and has been unconscious since. Other than a few scratches and being unconscious she is in perfect heath. James was easier to treat because he did not receive any trauma to his brain. James only suffered from serious smoke inhalation and chemical and fire burns across his body. I was able to treat his burns and most of the damage caused by the chemicals and smoke to his lungs."

"Actually, Zar, I don't remember very much about my past before the meteor storm started. I know of my parents when I was born, my age, my name, and my friends. I also remember how to drive, and I remember a few things about computers. Other than that I do not know very much else."

"Alex, this probably happened when you fell down into the crater that the *Kento* made. The treatment I gave you on your head apparently caused you long-term memory loss. I have no idea if it is forever or temporary. Even if you were Talin there is no way of knowing if your memory will come back. The brain is something my people have spent centuries trying to map out and understand. Only in the more recent years we have made quite a bit of progress."

"From what I can see Crystal is breathing, she has a pulse. She is probably in a deep sleep from the fall you told me about," Doctor Emit said, looking towards his notes. "As far as I can see none of you are in need of medical beds so you all can leave and since Crystal is not in a coma or dying, I see no reason she has to stay here," he said, looking up from his notes.

"What about Marissa, Doctor...Emit?" asked Zar.

"Who? Oh, that is right, the scared little girl. All right take me to her."

"Right this way, Doctor Emit," said Zar.

James and I picked up Crystal and then we all left the crowded curtain cubical and made our way back through the rows of injured people. Mark and Marissa were sitting on chairs against the wall on my right. The nurse had returned to her desk and was moving papers around. Eight other nurses were walking around the room now, hanging IVs, and other medicines. There were two janitors pushing mops around the room trying to clean the floors of all the blood. Mark stood up as we approached them.

"Hello, Doctor Emit, done with their checkups?" asked Mark.

"Yes none of them appear to be in danger and they don't appear to need any of my skills. I only have on last person to look at and that is Marissa."

"So you checked Crystal?" Mark asked.

"Yes and she is in no danger. She is just resting. From what I can see Marissa is fine. Marissa, do you feel any pain or discomfort?"

"No, Doctor."

"That is good, Marissa, you are in good heath, now all of your checkups are finished. Mark, you can take them to a refugee sector now."

"Let's go, everyone, to refugee sector 5 where your friends and family are," Mark said, opening the door.

"Alex, is it okay if I come with you?" asked Zar.

"It's fine with me."

We walked back to the five wall room and then we were escorted through one of the doors on the wall across from the garage doors. Running on adrenaline, Marissa, James, and I followed Mark through hallway after hallway. Both my arms felt like they weighed a hundred pounds each, and Crystal felt as if she weighed at least a ton. My legs were sore, my mind tired, and going black and I was fighting with myself to keep my eyes open. My stomach was growling and my mouth was dry. I had sweat running down my face, down my neck and my hair.

Mark opened a door ahead of us marked sector 5 in red paint and let us through the door. Sector 5 was packed full of tables in the center of the room and there were rows of bunk beds surrounding the room. People were sitting at the tables eating and drinking. Some people were sitting at the tables just talking to other people and some were just sitting looking very depressed. There were people lying down on their bunk beds tying to sleep. Others were crying into the blankets. The room was loud with crying, screaming and conversations. Like all the other rooms, this one was lit by the same kind of lights and the walls were white, and the floor was concrete. Across the room was a large kitchen that expanded the length of the wall. There was a line from one end going to the other end with people waiting to getting food and drinks.

Mark moved forward into sector 5. He turned to his left and walked. We walked forward, turned to our left and followed Mark in and out of rows of bunk beds. People at tables and people lying down on beds stopped what they were doing, their jaws dropped eyes widened, and a gasping noise came from their bodies at the sight of Zar. As we passed conversations broke out among some of the people and the topic was Zar. Mark stopped, took out a piece of paper from one of his pockets. He looked at the paper then he looked in between two of the rows, towards the wall then moved forward again. About five six rows later he stopped again and walked down in between two rows. We followed him down. The bunks were unoccupied and looked untouched.

"Take any bunk you like it doesn't really matter. You all stay here and I will go and find your loved ones for you," said Mark.

I was too tired to say a word. James and I set Crystal down on an empty bunk then Marissa sat down on a bunk and petted Maggie. James took a bunk then I took one, lay back, closed my eyes, and dozed off, to only have myself woken up by familiar voices. My mom and dad were standing on my left, next to my bunk, whispering my name and David and Mike were standing across from my parents. I sat up as best as I could with arms that felt like lead and a body and a mind that was very tired.

"Hi, Mom. Hi, Dad. Hi, David. Hi, Mike. How are you all?"

"We're fine, honey. What about you and Crystal?" my mom asked.

"Crystal is fine she is in a deep sleep. She should wake up any time. I, on the other hand, barely remember any of you from before the meteor storm."

"You're kidding, right? You're just playing a trick on us."

"Sorry but no."

"He is telling the truth. He was in an accident and he hit his head, when I treated his head wound there was a side affect probably caused by my medical equipment, mostly his long-term memory has been affected. As a result it appears that he has no memory of events leading to the day that the meteor shower started. His memory could return, but I can't promise it will," said Zar.

My parents turned around, faced Zar, and stared at him.

"Who are you?" asked my dad.

"Sorry my name is Zar from—" said Zar.

"You're from the planet Tallinea, right?" Mike said, interrupting Zar.

"How do you know of Tallinea?" asked Zar.

"David and I helped save three other Talins back at the hospital before the hospital was evacuated. One of the Talins seemed very protective of the younger looking Talin."

"That sounds like Ramus. He has always looked after the family's needs, and he's always been very serious about his job. The young Talin is probably Princess Paloween from the way Ramus is protecting her," Zar said, looking very sad.

"That's good right at least one of the royal family is alive."

"Yes that is good, but it would be better if they all were alive."

No one said anything for a while. None of us knew what to say to Zar. We just stared at his gloomy face for several minutes. Then the silence was broken by a woman being led by Mark.

"Hello, everyone, this is Marissa's aunt, Laura Harris. Miss Harris, this is Alex, his parents, his friends, and Crystal is the one sleeping on the bed," Mark said, pointing to each of us. "Alex and Crystal were the ones who saved Marissa, and were the last to see your brother and his wife alive. Their dying wish was for Alex and Crystal to take care of Marissa. They have a signed paper turning custody over to them," he said while he pulled out the paper signed by Marissa's parents.

"Where is Marissa? Is she okay?" Laura asked Mark.

"She is fine. She is extremely tired. She dozed off shortly after Alex did. She is sleeping against the wall with her arms wrapped around her dog," James said, turning his head to the wall.

"Thank you, Alex, for saving her and thank Crystal when she wakes up."

"You're welcome. Mark, can I have that?"

"Here you go, Alex."

"Laura, do not worry about Marissa's parents' last wish. They only made it because they did not know if you or any of their relatives were alive. So I will just tear that piece of paper up. Marissa is your niece and is your family. She needs you more than she needs Crystal or me," I said, tearing the paper in two.

"Thank…Thank you."

"Please take care of Marissa."

"I will look after her and I will raise her well."

"Her parents would probably like that."

"After Marissa wakes up I will fill her in on what has happened," said Laura while she walked to her sleeping niece and sat on an empty bed across from Marissa.

"Alex, honey, you need to rest especially after what you have been through."

"He will not have time to rest or eat anything for a little longer," said Zar.

"Why is that?" my dad asked, moving closer to Zar.

"Well due to Alex's and Crystal's condition they need to be monitored by myself and a one human doctor. Since Shaurha and all the other Talins including me are leaving to meet with your president very shortly. They need to be looked after by me, they have to come with us to Washington. James, I would like you to come with us to help with their treatment."

"Alex is not going anywhere but to bed," said my mom with a raised voice.

"Calm down, you four. You're going to come with us to help Alex and possibly Crystal regain their memory. Now if you all would follow Mark and me back to the five sided lobby we will soon depart."

We left sector 5 and slowly walked back to the lobby where the others had already gathered in front of the large mirror. We crossed the lobby and joined them against the wall. "Alex...Alex," David was calling me but I did not want to speak. I was in no mood to talk. Yes my parents and friends were alive, but I barely knew any of them. I barely knew Crystal and myself. All I wanted to do was go to sleep and wake up to everything right in the world. I did not pay attention to anything or anybody. I closed my eyes, laid my head on the mirror. After few seconds went by, the door to my left opened and out walked Lt. Richardson and a heavyset man. They walked along the mirror fitted wall and came to a rest in front of the mirror and us.

"Hello, those who don't know who I am, my name is General Ames. Now if you would follow Lt. Richardson and me, because we have a train to catch," said General Ames.

Lt. Richardson and General Ames started walking towards the large metal shutter door on the wall to my left. For some of us moving was getting hard and taxing. Regardless of how tired I was, I like the others slowly followed Gen. Ames and Lt. Richardson. The shutter opened as we approached, we were joined by a six armed soldiers.

We were led into the garage, turned to the left then walked the full length of the garage. We came to a stop in front of two extremely large doors. The door directly in front of us had a normal doorway cut out if it. Through the door I could see large machines about the size of the two extremely large doors.

"Right this way, everyone," said Gen. Ames.

Gen. Ames and Lt. Richardson passed through the opening in the massive doors. We quickly followed through single file. Once through I was in a brief state of shock, on my left and right were five massive robotic soldiers. They stood erect about seven stories off the ground give or take a story. They were armed with missiles and rockets across their bodies. Lasers were mounted to their shoulders and there were two large machine guns one on each arm. Standing in between each one of the giants stood a much smaller robotic suit of armor. There were three rows of ten. They stood only about ten to twelve feet high and had much smaller machine guns compared to the giants. Their fronts were open and looked as though a human operated it.

We continued into the room, a few of the smaller armored units were walking around the room housing a soldier in its chest. We walked to the end of the room, turned to the right and passed through another door. In front of us was a large gray train, there was one engine at each end of the train, six passenger cars and five flat beds two of which were loaded with supplies and raw materials. The station grew loud as the train cars separated from the flat beds. As the flat beds and the cars separated a loud hissing came from steam being released in between the two.

"Quickly, everyone, onto the first three cars, the other three are full of supplies and equipment," Gen. Ames said, walking to the train.

The engine connected to the passenger cars let out a loud howl and blew a cloud of steam into the air. We quickly boarded the train and took sets throughout the train. A few minutes after everyone was on board the train started to move and slowly picked up speed. I closed my eyes, tried to get comfortable and almost immediately I fell asleep.

Chapter Nine
The Assault Begins

I awoke to the screeching of the train coming to a stop and the loud howl from the engine. I opened my eyes. The car was dark, lit only by small flickers of light from the lights mounted in the tunnel. The door connecting the car to the engine opened and out walked five people. The small flickers of light highlighted their bodies and faces. Gen. Ames, Lt. Richardson, Shaurha, Gupp, and the train's conductor walked out of the door. They walked through the car, forced the doors on the left side of the car open, and exited the train. They split up. Two went towards the engine and the other three walked towards the last car.

The lights inside the car flickered on and off until they came to a stop poorly lighting the car. The train was lit. Most of the seats in the car were full and their occupants were looking around or outside the train. My parents, David, and Mike were nowhere to be seen. James and I were the only humans in this car. Hamole and his troops and a few of the other Talins filled the car's seats. Flito and Nozad were in the front of the car looking around their seats toward the back of the train. The rest of our party must have been in the other two cars.

The doors on the right and left of the car opened, Gupp, Shaurha, Gen. Ames, Lt. Richardson, and the conductor boarded the train once again. Shaurha and Gupp walked to the front of the car and sat in empty seats. Lt. Richardson, Gen. Ames and the conductor followed Shaurha and Gupp. They continued on past them, opened the car doors, and returned to the engine. A few minutes went by then the train started up again and quickly picked up speed. There was a small whine echoing throughout the train and the tunnel.

"Sorry about the stop. There was a small electrical surge which knocked out the train's computers. The problem has been solved, and once again we're en route to Washington. Feel free to get something to eat in the fourth car or go back to sleep." Gen. Ames's voice quieted and so did the whining.

I closed my eyes and tried to go back to sleep. The sounds of the train moving across the rails filled my head. The next thing I knew the train was slowly screeching to a halt. The train was still poorly lit; however, outside the train was brightly lit. The black walls of the tunnel were replaced with a cut out that looked like a train station. The screeching lessened as the train came to a stop. The doors opened on both sides of the train, followed by the door to the engine compartment, and Gen. Ames walked out.

"This is where we must depart. Lt. Richardson will take you to the conference room, and there, the president will join you," Gen. Ames's voice came over the intercom Gr. Ames's voice was then replaced by Lt. Richardson's.

"This is Lt. Richardson. Could everyone exit to the right, I will join you shortly."

Shaurha, Gupp, Hamole, James, the Talin troops, and I stood up and made our way to the exit on our right. We exited the train two at a time, and then made our way to the station's platform. The rest of our party unloaded mostly from the second car. David and Mike were the only ones that got off the third car. Zar and his assistant were carrying Crystal on a stretcher. My parents followed Zar and his assistant out of the train. We all gathered on the platform facing the train, after a few minutes, doors behind us opened. Dozens of people ran towards the remaining three train cars. Four of them boarded the train, the rest lined up facing the train, then a few seconds later boxes, crates, and black cases were handed to the people still on the platform. They then handed down the line until it reached the last two people. The last two people in the line took turns stacking the contents of the train. There was one line per car of people unloading the train.

"If everyone would follow me I will take you to the conference room now," Lt. Richardson said as he walked toward us from the train.

We followed Lt. Richardson through one of the two doors across from the train. He led us through two hallways, before we entered a large room. This room had nine doors. The far wall had two doors one at the base of a staircase and one door at the top of the staircase. At the top of the staircase there was a walkway leading to a door on the left wall. There were four twenty-foot plasma screen television screens about eight feet from the door on the left wall. Below the large televisions were dozens of monitors and computers in three rows. Many people were quickly moving from computer to computer. The monitors on the left wall displayed everything from orbital pictures of the earth's condition to the United States current military status. Others displayed neighboring countries military strengths.

Along the walls there were red emergency lights, fire extinguishers, and fire alarms. The ceiling was high, about ten feet higher than me. The walls were concrete. The whole room was lit by lights in the walls and florescent lights hanging from the ceiling. One of the monitors switched from a visual of earth to a map of the U.S.A. The map showed all of the underground bases constructed by the U.S.A.

"Come on there will be time to look around later; it's only a bit farther," Lt. Richardson said, walking across this room that looked like a command room.

He led us to the staircase across the room. He started to climb the stairs. He opened the door at the top and waved for us to follow him. Hamole was first then Gupp, Whaloa, Zar, then Shaurha, and the rest of us followed them up the stairs. We passed through the door and walked into a room with many pictures on the walls, a large wood oval table stood in the middle of the room surrounded by many leather chairs. There were large plants in the four corners of the room. The walls looked like they were wood or wood paneled. The room was lit by two chandler table lamps and numerous wall mounted lamps. The floor was covered with a white carpet with the president's seal under the table.

"Shaurha, Whaloa, Gupp, Hamole, Zar, take a seat around the table. The rest of you will have to sit on the floor in the back until the

111

meeting is finished. I must leave you now. I will go and inform the president and his staff of our arrival."

Lt. Richardson left the room. Shaurha, Gupp, Hamole, and Whaloa took seats around the oval table. Zar and James walked to the back of the room and set Crystal down on the floor. James sat down next to her and Zar took a seat at the table. Hamole's troops walked around the table and stood against the walls. The other Talins walked to the back of the room and found a place to sit. Nozad and Flito mumbled something as they took a seat on the floor. My parents, Mike, David, and I followed them and took a seat on the uncomfortable carpet. I was still partly tired so I decided to give my eyes a brief rest.

A short time past then I heard the doorknob turn. I opened my eyes as the door opened. Three more Talins walked across the threshold of the room. Two of the three looked like Shaurha and Whaloa in appearance, but not in height. The shorter of the two looked very young in appearance, and the other was older than she was but not as old as either Shaurha or Whaloa. The third Talin was larger than the two Talins and resembled Zar, Hamole, and Gupp, but was bigger than the three of them in height and width.

"Princes Paloween, it's great to see you alive. We heard about the rest of your family. We're very sorry for your loss. Your parents were strong, brave, and honorable. They will be missed for many years to come, your highness," said Shaurha.

"Thank you, Commander Shaurha, you're right, they will be missed for many years and I will do my best to honor them. Commander Shaurha, what has become of my brother?"

"Your highness, he was on one of the escape pods that ejected in this plant's orbit. We have no way of knowing if he survived. Once the rescue team has come there will be a search for him."

"Hopefully he is found alive."

The room went almost completely quiet. The only sound that could be heard was the sound of breathing. All of the Talins once again looked very depressed. Their chins were to their chests. They stayed like this for several minutes. I think it was ten or fifteen minutes before any of them changed their pose. Half of them raised their heads off their chests when the door we passed through opened.

Six men in black suits wearing sunglasses entered the room. Three of them walked to the opposite side of the room and stood against the wall. The other three did the same but one of them held the door open. The president and two females walked in. President Clark was wearing a gray suit. One of the females was wearing a black suit and the other female was wearing a black dress suit. She was carrying a pad of paper. The president sat down in the chair at the end of the table the two women sat down on either side of the president.

The door opened again and two men in military uniforms and one in a white lab coat entered the room, and then took their seats around the table. The two men in military uniforms sat down next to the two women and the one woman in the lab coat sat down on the right of one of the men dressed in military uniforms. The room was silent again, this time for a longer period of time. Everyone just stared at each other looking over their features. The quiet was broken by President Clark, moving back his seat. President Clark then walked behind his seat and pushed it back under the table. He stood behind his chair, his hands resting on his chair his head moved from Talin to Talin.

"First thing we need to do is introduce everyone. My name is President Peter Clark. The female on my right is the Secretary Melissa Mills. The man on Melissa's right is General James Reads. He has experience in most scientific fields, a few of which he is the leading scientist in the field. The female on my left is General Samantha Dawn. She deals in cultures, politics, and religions. Like Reads she is the leading scientist in her fields. The man on Samantha's left is Secretary of Defense Jack Whales. He specializes in strategies. The man on his left is Dr. Curtis Rees. He is leading in medicine."

Shaurha stood up out of her seat.

"President Clark, please allow me to introduce everyone from my race to you and your staff formally."

"Go ahead."

"I don't know if you have met Princes Paloween, head chef Ramus and Metallurgist Herban," she said, pointing to each one as she spoke their names.

Shaurha paused listening for a moment then continued through the rest of the Talins. However, I stopped listening once she had finished introducing Princes Paloween and the other two Talins. When Shaurha finished she sat back down in her seat and President Clark stood back up.

"Princes Paloween said that her family was exploring our solar system's outer planets, when the meteor storm that has devastated our planet battered your ship forcing you to abandon your ship in our orbit. I assume your ship crashed to earth. Then most of you met up with a few humans and now you're here. From what General Ames has told the Secretary of State; you all have been through a horrible couples of days, but there are a lot of things we need to talk about."

"The first thing you need to know, President Clark, is that our ship did not crash as a result of the meteor storm, our ship crashed as a result of another alien race," said Hamole.

"You were attacked by another alien species?" asked General Reads.

"We weren't attacked by them. Were we?" Princes Paloween asked.

"I am sad to say that your family has joined those that have been taken by the Shadows. Our scans of our former ship proved it. We were attacked by the Shadows."

"The Shadows, could you tell us about what they are?" asked General Dawn.

"We would if we knew more about them. The only things that we due know is that they have been attacking our home planet and dozens other planets. As far as we know our race is the only species that has stood up against the Shadows and has been able to defend our planet. All of the other species we Talins have had to come to the rescue for like what we will have to do for your species."

"What do you mean you are going to have to come to our rescue?" asked General Read.

"Your planet has already been attacked by the Shadows and you don't even know how. The Shadows' first attack is with debris from other planets they have conquered. Most of the time their first attacks is in the form of meteor storms. They batter the surface of the planets that they want, and then they move in after one of our weeks which, is ten of your days. They never seemed to care about the inhabitants on the planets. But as soon as we come to the rescue they attack our ships while we are trying to evacuate the remaining survivors. If we hadn't intervened after they conquered the planet they would start mining the planets for resources and the survivors would be beaten, murdered, or converted into them. Talins are the only race that we know of that has been able to defend our home planet from their first attack," said Shaurha.

"How is it that you are the only species that has been able to successfully defend against these attacks?" asked General Samantha Dawn.

"Our planet has been continuously bombarded by meteor storms throughout our recorded history. Over the past three millennia, we have had to fortify our buildings and more recently we have constructed an orbital defense system to destroy the meteors as they approach our planet. In the most recent century the storms have increased in intensity and have become more frequent. With the orbital defense grid in place the meteors were of little problem. This did not make the Shadows very happy with us. They haven't directly attacked us with ships, only their meteor storms. We believe that they don't want to fight a losing battle."

"What happened?" President Clark was interrupted by loud screaming.

Everyone turned towards the source of the screaming. Crystal was now sitting up with a horrified look on her face. Her hair was soaked and sticking to her face, she looked around the room, pulled her hair from her face and said she was sorry for interrupting. Zar and James stood up and moved towards Crystal. Zar asked her a few questions then James asked her some questions. They asked her if she knew whom she was, what happened to her, her age, and if she knew the two of them. She answered all the questions correctly then asked them a few questions. Crystal mainly wanted to know where she was and how she got here.

After Zar and James got Crystal up to speed they returned to their seats and the meeting resumed. Shaurha then apologized and introduced everyone to President Clark and his staff. The meeting went on for hours. The main topic of conversation was what we were going to do to prepare for the invasion. Hamole and Gupp had a few ideas on how to upgrade our weapons, fighters, and land forces. Shaurha and the president agreed to evacuate the United States, inform the other nations of the pending invasion and have them start the evacuation preparations and prepare for the invasion. After hours of discussion the president stood up, walked to the right side of the room, turned, then he walked to the left side of the room and back before he spoke.

"We have been talking for hours we should end the meeting and start the preparations."

Everyone around the table stood up. The president spoke to Secretary Melissa Mills. Then he and all but Secretary Mills left the room soon followed by the Secret Service, Melissa Mills walked to the door then spoke.

"Could everyone please follow me? Some barracks have been prepared for you."

The room was semi quiet, the sound of footsteps and breathing surrounded the room. Melissa opened the door she was standing in front of, and walked through. Shaurha, Gupp, all the other Talins, and the rest of us followed behind. We passed through the door and back down the stairs. The president was standing at one of the computer terminals. The Secretary of Defense was on the computer terminal next to President Clark. Earth was displayed on the monitors along the back wall. After a few seconds a bunch of numbers scrolled across the screen.

"Shaurha, will you come over here for a few minutes?" asked President Clark.

Shaurha left our group and walked towards President Clark. The two of them talked loud enough so everyone in the room could hear what they were saying. President Clark asked Shaurha for help sending a SOS signal to the Talin's home planet. Whaloa joined President Clark and Shaurha at the terminal after a minute or two the monitors displayed a blue planet that had three metal rings around the planet. The monitors changed and a Talin's face was now being displayed. This Talin's face shared much of the same characteristics that Hamole had.

"Hello, Commander Shaurha, what has happened? You are not transmitting from the *Kento*?"

"Hello, old friend. We were attacked by the Shadows and crashed on planet earth. I have some bad news. It doesn't appear that the King Ralon, Queen Faraly, and Prince Palarise made it off of the *Kento*."

"What of Princes Paloween, is she alive?"

"Yes she is alive."

"That's good at least one of the royal family is still alive."

"What do you mean?"

"We were attacked a day ago and a ship managed to get through our orbital defense grid and they deliberately crashed into the palace. Her uncle and aunt did not survive the explosion, in fact no one survived. All that remains of the royal family is Princes Paloween. All of her family has been killed by the Shadows…A ship will be dispatched to rescue Princess Paloween and all of the *Kento* survivors immediately."

"Thank you, my good friend, but we need more than just a rescue ship we need a planet evacuation ship as well, and as many warships as possible. With Princess Paloween on this planet it is possible that they will launch a devastating force. We can not take a chance that Princes Paloween could be hurt. We need to evacuate these people as fast as possible. We are going to prepare these people for both a war and an evacuation."

"That's a good idea, and our fastest ship has been sent to take Paloween home and I am putting the order for ships to transit to your location. Keep Princes Paloween safe and good luck to you all."

The screen went blank and displayed the earth once again. Shaurha and Whaloa walked away from President Clark and rejoined us at the bottom of the staircase. Once they rejoined us we walked towards the wall on our left. We stopped at the sixth door from the staircase. Melissa turned open the door, and walked though, we quickly followed. We walked through one hallway then came to a stop in a second hallway. On our right and left was a decorated metal door across from us was a metal double door. Melissa walked down the hall, opened the door on our right and walked through. We followed her in. We now stood in a room that was elegantly decorated with ten cubical-like walls encasing beds along both the right and left walls. There was a door across from us and on either side of the door were two desks. There was a circular couch in the middle of the room that surrounded a large TV. There were bookcases filled with books to our direct right and left.

"Ten of you can take this room, and ten can take the room across the hall. There is a bathroom through the door ahead of us. There is a door across from that door in the bathroom that leads to another one of these rooms. The room across the hall is identical to this room, it has a door to another bathroom, and that leads to another bedroom. All the rooms on this base have a capacity of ten beds. Back through the hall and to the right, that door leads to a massive kitchen which connects to a dozen doors. The majority of the doors led to room clusters like this one. You may explore some of the base and in the morning someone will come to each one of these rooms. I will leave all of you now to do as you would like."

Melissa left the room through the door all of us just passed through. Some of the Talins spread out and started looking at the decorations and furnishings in the room. Mike and David walked around the room, split up and vanished behind two cubical walls. My parents left the room through the same door Melissa did. Shaurha, Gupp, Hamole, Zar, Whaloa, and Princess Paloween moved to the middle of the room, sat on the couch and talked. Nozad, Flito, Gupp's, Zar's, and Whaloa's assistants were investigating the desks in the back of the room. Hamole's troops stood at the two doors and a few stood in the middle of the room behind the couch. James and Crystal had vanished behind their own cubicles. I moved to the one of the cubicles in the back and set my bag down on the bed. A dresser stood against one of the cubicle's walls only a few feet from the bed. There was a light stand next to the head of the bed.

I opened one of the dresser drawers. Inside were some grayish blue uniforms. I picked up some of the uniforms, checked the size and then walked to the back of the room. I figured after being in the same clothes for almost four days, I was due for a change. I wasn't the only one; Crystal had the same idea that I had. As I headed to the door I saw Crystal following me with a uniform in her arms. One of the Talins by the door opened and held the door open for me.

The bathroom was huge, across from me was another door just like Melissa had said. On my right was row of stalls, next to them there was a partial wall that divided the room. Across from the stalls was a row of sinks and a row of mirrors above them. The floor was made of white ceramic tile and the walls were a pale gray tile with lights mounted in them. The ceiling was made of metal with two rows of florescent light fixtures going down the length of the bathroom. Everything on the left side of the bathroom was identical to the right side in every possible way.

I walked to the wall next to the stalls on the left side then walked behind the wall. There were ten enclosed standing showers on this side of the wall. Three on the wall in front of me, three across from those and four on the left wall. There was only a foot, to a foot and a half of space between the showers. Each one of the showers had two walls not including the bathroom wall, and curtains that were drawn back, showing the inside of the showers. There was a small bench inside the showers that rested next to the curtain which was just out of the reach of the shower spray. On the bathroom's right was a countertop full of packaged up soaps and shampoos. I walked over to the countertop, picked up soap and shampoo, and walked over to one of the showers. One of the bathroom doors opened on the other side of the wall as I set my uniform and the soaps down on the bench inside one of the showers.

A few seconds later, Crystal joined me on this side of the bathroom. She looked around, walked over, picked up soaps and a bottle of shampoo. Crystal walked right up to me and set her stuff down on the bench next to mine. She grabbed me by my shirt and pulled me into the shower with her. We discarded each others clothing and started to help each other have a satisfying shower. We finished our delightful shower after taking an hour to actually get clean. Crystal had a pleased look across, her face. I do not know if I had one across my face or not but I definitely felt like I should have had one. We watched each other put on the uniforms we had bought with us. She was stunning with her wet dirty blond hair hanging over her face. Her skin was silky smooth and bore a tan that she had to have gotten before all of this started. The droplets of water that still clinging onto her tanned skin shined in the light. After Crystal and I both were driest. We shared a passionate lustful kiss and returned to our room.

Most of the Talins had left the room. Zar, Nozad, Flito, and two of the Talin troops remained in the room. Mike and David were sitting in front of the TV in the middle of the room playing a video game. James was typing on one of the computers to Crystal's and my right side. Nozad and Flito were looking through a few books from the bookcases and Zar was walking around the room examining the decorations on the walls. Crystal looked at me, smiled, blew me a kiss and started walking to her cubical. I smiled and blew a kiss back and returned to my cubical. I set my dirty clothes on the floor picked up my bag and exited my cubical.

It had been sometime since the last time I had anything to eat and my stomach was letting me know exactly how it felt about it being empty. I walked past Mike and David and passed back through the door Melissa had led us through earlier. I turned to the right and passed through the door at the end of the hall. The cafeteria was huge compared to many of the other rooms I have seen. It looked like a few acres long and a few acres wide. Melissa was right the cafeteria did have many doors connecting to it. There were rows of tables pushing toward the middle of the room. In the center of the cafeteria a large kitchen spanned almost the width of the room. There were only two other people in the room, one was sitting at a table close to the kitchen and the other was working in the kitchen preparing food.

I walked down the path separating two rows of tables. The person that was sitting at a table began to come into focus as I approached. So did the person in the kitchen. After a minute of walking the person sitting came into complete focus, then the person in the kitchen came into focus shortly after. Princes Paloween was sitting at a table and a Talin called Ramus was busy in the kitchen. I walked past Princes Paloween and walked towards the kitchen. Ramus walked in front of me put his hands on a countertop.

"What would you like to eat?" asked Ramus with a loud tone.

I looked over Ramus's head and looked at a food menu. I chose something to eat, walked over to the table Princes Paloween was sitting at and sat across from her. Her head was resting in her hands. She was crying heavily into her hands. Next to her was a tray of food, barely eaten and a drink untouched. Princes Paloween was definitely the youngest Talin among the Talins on earth. In human years she looked ten or eleven years old. I ate a little of my food while I thought about what to say to Princes Paloween. A few words came to me. I swallowed a mouth full of food and spoke.

"I am sorry for your loss. The death of loved ones is a horrible thing to have to go through." *Stupid thing to say*, I thought when I finished.

She removed her hands from her face and looked at me, there were tears running down her face. She did not say anything she just stared at me with a very sad look across her face. She put her hands back up to her face and cried a little more. She whined then she spoke.

"Thank you, you're the only one that has talked to me since I found out about my family."

"You're welcome, sometimes distractions help get your mind off things. For at least a little while."

"What kind of distractions would get my mind off of the loss of my whole family?" she said, removing her hands from her face again and raised her voice.

"From the sound of your voice you are very angry at the Shadows. I saw Mike and David, my friends, playing a video game. Were you are able to kill holographic monsters. It might keep you distracted for a while and help you deal with your anger."

"I don't know maybe I will."

"If you decide to play you can find my friends and I in the room Melissa showed us, and again I am sorry for your loss."

I stood up and took my tray back over to the kitchen where Ramus had been not that long ago. I dumped the remaining contents of my tray out and set my tray down to be washed. As I turned to head back to the barracks Ramus grabbed me by the collar of my uniform and pulled me back up against the kitchen causing dishes to crash to the floor. He pulled me again until my feet were just barely touching the ground and I could feel his warm breath on my left ear.

"Listen very carefully you filthy little human. You will stay away from Princess Paloween if you know what is good for you."

"Or what?"

"Well for starters you won't have to worry about the Shadows killing you because I will do it for them."

"That's enough, Ramus, you let Alex go at once, and you leave him alone and that is an order."

"I am sorry, your highness, I will leave him alone, but if he tries to hurt you I will deal with him," Ramus said as he released me.

He left Princess Paloween and I and then walked away from us muttering to himself.

"Sorry he has always been protective of me and I would like to play that game. Maybe it will help me."

"Great, let's go."

We returned to the barracks and David and Mike were still playing on the game. Princess Paloween and I walked over to them and joined them in the game. Princess Paloween figured out how to play and got pretty good quick. She gave David, Mike, and me a run for our money. We continued playing the game for a few hours then Mike and David got tired of getting beat by Princess Paloween. A little while after that I quit but she continued in the main game by herself. She was doing well then she finally turned the game off after she had beaten the whole game without dying once. She had played the game for ten hours straight. She thanked me for getting her mind off of her problems and retired to her quarters.

I retired to my bed and went to sleep. I awoke to a red lit room and alarms blaring. I got dressed and made my way to the command room. People were running from door to door and moving about in between the computer stations. The monitors on the back wall turned on and displayed a huge spaceship.

"Target that ship and prepare to fire on my command," President Clark said to one of the men at one of the computers.

"Target locked and the station is ready to fire at your command," said a man at a computer next President Clark.

"Don't shoot. They are friendly, that is one of the hybrid ships that a few other races and my people have built. That is supposed to be the fastest model of spaceships in our whole fleet," said Shaurha as she and some of the other Talins rushed into the command room.

"May I contact that ship, President Clark?" asked Shaurha.

"By all means, go right ahead, Shaurha."

Shaurha walked over to the computer next to the president and typed on it briefly. After a minute or two six different alien species including one Talin were displayed on the monitors.

"Hello, Commander Shaurha, it is good to see you. How is Princess Paloween doing with the news of her parents?" asked the Talin on the monitor.

"Like anyone that has lost family."

"I see. We are preparing this ship to come down and take you and the Princess home."

"Thank you, but I have things to do down here."

"As you wish, Commander Shaurha."

The monitors returned to displaying the alien hybrid ship. It moved into earth's atmosphere. The ship glowed red and orange as fire showered the ship's hull. It was soon devoured by the black clouds that now filled earth's skies. A small ripple was left behind in the clouds were the ship entered.

"We need to go to the surface and help them unpack as soon as they land."

"What is it that needs unpacking?" I asked.

"We got to unpack weapons, ships, and raw materials. Since half of that ship is a massive factory which they will be leaving here we need to empty it of all the supplies before it is put into production?"

"That ship is a factory?" asked President Clark.

"Yes it is in fact almost all of our large ships have a detachable factory with them."

"General Reads and Secretary Whales, go round up as any people that can help and bring them to the hanger bay. Anyone in here that wants to go up and help unpack the ship may go with Melissa to the hanger bay," said President Clark.

Melissa stood up and walked towards the door along the wall with the staircase. A bunch of people including the Talins joined Melissa at the door. I quickly followed the others. We walked through hallway after hallway, these halls were larger than those I had seen previously and the doors were heavy steel doors. The halls were long about two thousand feet long and a few of the halls had a door either on the right or on the left but never on both. After five halls we reached the biggest room I had seen. This room put the cafeteria to shame. The ceiling was two massive doors that spanned the hanger bay. There were planes, tanks, and many of the robot giants throughout the hanger bay.

We walked along the hanger bays length for ten minutes or more until Melissa stopped in front of one of the hanger bay walls. Climbing up the wall was large gears and rails. They went up as far as the hanger bay doors. Attached to the floor was two large boxes that attached to the wall in front of us and to both the right and left walls, and there were two more boxes attached from the floor to both the right and left walls. The room grew loud with the conversations of many people talking. I turned around, anywhere from sixty to one hundred people were walking towards us. They were being led by General Reads and Secretary of Defense Jack Wales.

They walked next to us, came to a stop, and then waved in the air. The floor below us started to shake, moan, and screech. The noise grew louder and so did the shaking. There was a sudden jolt as the floor we were on broke away from the floor bellow us. We began to climb the out of earth's bowls. The elevator ride was long and slow. About halfway up, one of the hanger bay doors slid into the wall behind some of us. We rose from deep within the earth about what seamed like a mile. I looked down into the hanger bay. There were piles of raw material scattered about. People were hard at work, working on many different things. Then we rose past the second hanger bay doors which blocked my view of the inside of the bay.

The sky was just as black as it had been two days ago and the stench of death and the smell of numerous things that had burnt was still fresh in the air. The air was much cooler than it had been. To my right came a loud thunderous roar. Everyone turned. The ship was floating close to a hundred feet above the ground. It slowly lowered down to earth's surface and with a thunderous crash the ship landed. Steam or smoke jetted out from all over the ship's hull. There was loud grinding noise, and the front half of the ship separated from its large box end of the whole ship. Then a section of the front half turned up facing the sky at an angle. More steam was released from the ship as a large ramp extended from the middle of the ship and then dropped to the ground.

A large door opened above the ramp and four tiny ships (in comparison to their mother) were launched. The ships flew fast right towards us, and landed in a row, about two hundred feet from us. A door on the closest ship to us opened and two Talins and two other aliens of another species walked out. The four of them walked towards us. Shaurha, Hamole, and Gupp walked forward and greeted the four strangers. They talked briefly then the seven of them walked over to Melissa, General Reads, and Secretary of Defense Whales. The spoke briefly then Whale spoke into a radio and the three of them walk off of the left and on to the battered ground. Shaurha, Gupp, Hamole, and the four strangers stood on the ground next to the lift. One of the new aliens walked back and forth about thirty feet. At the end of the hanger doors was a long building that expanded the width of the hanger bay doors. In the middle of the building was a metal shutter door that opened a few minutes later and a jeep drove out of the building. Melissa, General Reads, and Whales walked a few feet ahead of us, and stood with their backs to the four ships.

"Could we have everyone quickly load up into the four ships as some of you know we do not have any time to waste?" asked General Reads.

Everyone loaded into three of the four ships. We lifted off and then began our task of unloading the hybrid ship. Later that day the president reactivated the draft; however, the majority of the people freely volunteered. The factory was up and running in a matter of hours. Modified weapons, modified tanks, planes, and personal armor were quickly put into production. After the president's decision about the draft, basic training, and flight training was underway. Just about everyone learned how to fly the hybrid planes that had been made. Towards the end of the day Princes Paloween and Ramus blasted off on their journey back to their home. Two days later I awoke to the alarms blaring again, six huge ships and one massive ship entered earth's orbit. Shaurha said that those were Talin ships, the massive ship was a *Colonizer*, and the six others were warships.

The *Colonizer* broke its orbit an hour after entering orbit and descended down through the black abyss of smoke. The whole facility shook as soon as the ship came within a few miles from us. The facility shook even more when the ship began to land. A short while after it landed the hanger bay doors were opened and the hole contents of the hanger bay was being used to transport the remaining civilians to the ship. At the same time hundreds of ships like the three we used a few days ago launched. Each one landed just long enough to pick up one human then they took off around the world to bring the survivors here. I finally got to look at the ship it was more than massive. So much so there is not a word to fit it. It was taller than building humans had created and it looked like it went on for miles. All along the ship's hull were many rows of orbs and at the base of the ship were long giant doors around two hundred feet tall and five hundred feet long. There were three other doors from what I could see, each equally apart going up the ship. Two were right across from each other and the third was set above the other two but in the center of the ship.

A battle plan was drawn up to the best that it could have been. Weapons and positions were assigned to everyone. There were ground forces, but the air forces had the most people in it mainly because the Shadows had to come through space and the sky. The Talins in orbit set up a defense position. They were going to engage the enemy first then anything that managed to pass them would be left to the modified fighters. By chance anything managed to break through both lines the ground forces would be in for a challenge. The alarms went off again during dinner everyone paused and waited then what we did not want to hear over the facility's com system was broadcast. We were told to get to our positions that our enemy had arrived in our solar system and they were on their way. We all stopped what we were doing Crystal, David, Mike, myself, and hundreds of people ran to the hanger bay.

Everyone got geared up and made their way to a fighter that had been assigned to them. Everyone climbed into our assigned plane, each plane fitted two people: one tail gunner, and the pilot in the front not only controlled the plane but also operated stationary guns. TV screens that surrounded the hanger bay turned on and displayed a battle underway, between the Talins and the Shadows. Three of the six Talin warships had been destroyed and two Shadow warships had been lay to ruin. The Shadows' ships were as black as the space that surrounded it all except a small blue light that glowed from within the Shadows' warships. There was only one Shadow warship left fighting plus hundreds of thousands of small reddish black ships firing upon Talin fighters and the remaining warships. There were many fighters exploding on both sides. There was too many in fact that there was no way to tell who was winning at that time.

A short time went by. The Shadows' warship blew up, and the explosion quickly stopped. Shortly after that the alarms ended and over the com systems we were told to stand down and to return to what ever it was we were doing. Just before the TV screens shut down the last image displayed was of the Talin fighters returning to the remaining warships. Those fighters that did not return to the warships entered earth's atmosphere and either burnt up on descent or docked with the *Colonizer*. David, Crystal, Mike, and I retired to our barracks. David and Mike returned to playing the video game, Crystal found a book to read and I decided to continue writing down everything that had happened over the past week. I had written a few pages of what happened before I called it quits and retired to my bed.

I would love to say that the battle that took place in orbit last night was the only battle that took place over earth but I can not. After that battle however the facility was put on high alert, the evacuation process quickened and all of our training was doubled and sped up. Then at noon the alarms were triggered, once again everyone was told to report to their stations and prepare for battle. Crystal and I stopped our training and ran to the hanger. We got geared up and went our separate ways. Crystal was a pilot for her fighter and I was a pilot for mine. David and Mike were gunners for separate fighters. We were then told to board our fighters and get into the air. The massive hanger bay doors opened, the pilots waited impatiently for the doors to lock open. A minute later the first wave of fighters rose out of the hanger bay and ascended into to the black sky.

David's and Mike's fighters took off soon followed by Crystal and me. The sky was still filled with thick black smoke that blackened the earth's surface in darkness. After I leveled my fighter out I saw exactly how many people had survived and how big the facility actually was. All of our forces were lit up ever so slightly just enough to see where our forces were. There were hundreds of hanger bays that had fighters rising from within. After the fighters had lunched the robot giants, the tanks, the people in the small robot armor, and tens of thousands of people rose from the earth using massive elevators. The number of fighters in the sky was in the hundreds of thousand and the land vehicles were in the thousands from what I could see.

We flew in the black sky for a while doing nothing but watching for the enemy. Then over the ship's com we were told that the enemy broke through the Talin fighters. Purplish red glowing objects appeared in the darkness of the sky, they moved quickly towards us. Then out of nowhere some of the purplish red objects exploded, then a large number of ships dropped in between the purplish objects and us. They moved closer to the objects and began firing on them. Over the fighters com we were told to attack the purplish red fighters. Some of our fighters moved forwarded and joined the Talins against the Shadows. Soon everyone was firing at the purplish red fighters, between the Talin and human fighters the Shadow fighters were easy pickings. As the last Shadow fighter was destroyed, cheering came over the intercom, followed by screaming then static. The cloud above us shined a brilliant purplish red, and then more Shadow fighters joined our skies. There were so many that no one could tell where one fighter began and another ended.

Chapter Ten
The Assault Rages On

The purplish red lights from the Shadow fighters grew brighter. Then they dropped down joining us, there were purplish red lights everywhere, they soon filled the sky, and immediately they fired upon both the Talins and our fighters. My gunner began firing at an enemy fighter I quickly followed in response, flew our craft, and began firing at any enemy I could. It was hard to tell where our fire was actually hitting. There were so many fighters in the air that the battle had to quickly spread out filling the black clouded sky. I spotted an enemy fighter. I moved in closer and began firing upon the Shadow fighter once we were in range. It quickly made a run for it taking off at incredible speed and tried to evade me. He was not fast enough and went out in a fiery explosion.

There were explosions everywhere. There was not a part in the sky that did not have fighter fire in it.

My gunner yelled at me to hull ass. Two fighters were moving towards us. I accelerated the fighter, and began maneuvering when our enemy started firing at us. My gunner was constantly firing the guns and kept yelling to the enemy to stop moving about and to stay still long enough for him to shoot them down. He screamed after a minute saying he got one of those fighters. This went on for a while, my gunner destroyed a few, and then I destroyed few. Then over the com we heard that the Shadow warships had lunched a large number of transport ships and they were heading for the surface. We and all other fighters were ordered to attack the transport ships and not to let them land. Shortly after we were ordered to destroy the transport ships I spotted a large red glow growing in intensity. A ship roughly the length of four buses, and as wide as two an a half buses pushed through the cloud. The ship was a large ruff cone shape that looked like it was made put holes in anything it wanted.

I moved in and began firing upon the transport ship which left two glowing rows of small blast marks from were I had shot it. However, there was very little damage to the transport ship. I pulled up and went for another pass. As I pulled up, my gunner fired upon the transport ship but still had no effect. Then we went for another shot, this time I fired the rockets on the transport ship, a hole was blown into the side of the transport, fire was blazing out its side and seconds later the ship started to spin erratically. Then the transport picked up speed, fell to the earth, and crashed into the ground. In a blaze of fire the enemy transport exploded. I looked around the sky for any other transport ships. Five ships were close to the surface. One of the transport ships was destroyed and the other four landed. I looked around the sky there was more transport ships descending from the sky and they were heading for earth. My gunner and I destroyed a few more fighters then moved into attack a nearby transport. I fired four more rockets at the transport and they were all intercepted by two enemy fighters. The two fighters blew up and their remains fell to earth. I started to come around for another pass when we were hit by enemy fire. Alarms began blaring and it got hard to control the fighter. There was fire pouring out of our plane's right side wing. I tried to keep the fighter leveled out but it was getting very hard to.

I yelled back to my gunner, "I can't keep the plane in the air for much longer." His reply was that we were going to have to eject and glide down to the surface. I agreed and started to prep the ship for ejection and looked for a good place to eject. I found the best place to eject. I aimed our ship at a transport and accelerated the plane. We waited until we were close to the transport then ejected. Our ship crashed into the enemy transport causing a huge explosion. We were in a small capsule that had small wings a small engine and had the same turret in the back for the gunner. We descended to the earth very quickly. At the speed we were going it was extremely hard to keep the capsule from rolling over and going into a spin. There was intense turbulence from the speed and the wind outside. The turret started firing and then we were hit hard. The turret ended and wind was rushing around the cabin. I yelled back to my gunner but there was no response.

The left wing broke off and the capsule started so go into a spin, and I lost complete control. I could see the ground was coming up very quickly. I pulled back on the joy stick. The capsule's nose leveled out a little and then I slammed into some ruins. My head was bouncing around like crazy then the capsule slammed to a stop. The glass of the capsule was shattered and fell on top of me. I looked around. I was surrounded by ruins and the darkness. I climbed out of the capsule looked back at my gunner he was bleeding across his hole body and there was no sign of life. I tried my radio; however, it had been damaged by the crash and no longer worked. There was nothing more I could do at the capsule so I gathered my modified automatic sniper rifle then left the capsule.

I figured that I would have a better chance of reaching one of the hangers I saw then I would if I stayed and waited for a rescue. I started walking in the direction I thought my friends and I had launched. My weapon was at the ready just in case if I ran into any problems. The streets were deserted there were craters all over the place, buildings were black and they were completely in ruins. There was very little movement only the dust getting kicked up from the wind and from me walking. I walked down a deserted road. The sounds of the battle over my head and around me flowed through the air. I continued walking for close to twenty minutes, then I heard some weapons fire from close by. Two men ran out from a side road about hundred feet or two ahead of me. They turned left and ran in the same direction I was heading. They came to a stop turned completely around and ran towards me. They were being chased by a large black dog, like creature. I flipped a switch up on my gun, took aim through my sniper scope, and fired.

My gun had a real powerful kick, my shoulder hurt. It felt like my shoulder was hit by a pile of bricks. I looked up and saw two of the black dogs lying on the ground not moving an inch. I walked slowly towards them. As I went I switched my gun back into an automatic just in case either one of the creatures made an aggressive move. I was not the only one, the two men had heard the shot and saw the two creatures on the ground and slowly walked out of the ruins. They slowly walked towards me, never moving their eyes from the two creatures and from the road they had come from. I moved closer to the creatures there was a hole through the first one's side and the other had its head blown clear off. There was no blood. My shot sealed the inside of the wounds completely. I looked over at the two men they were in shock yet they looked happy not being chased by the two creatures.

"Hi. I'm Jeff Murray. How the hell did you do that?"

"Alex. This is a modified sniper rifle with one hell of a shot and kick. It doubles as an automatic rifle and it has been enhanced by alien weapons."

"My name is Stan Eden. What brings you to this little piece of the world?"

"I crashed my ship. What about you? Did you crash?"

"We were separated from our platoon; we have no idea if any of them survived the attack," said Stan.

"Our platoon was heading back to base when we were attacked. Three of us were forced away from our platoon. Then we were hunted by those things. We lost Henry a ways back," said Jeff.

"Do you guys have any weapons?"

"We have only our side arms, but they are not very effective," said Jeff.

"Stay close and we will head towards the base and hopefully we will find your platoon."

We started walking down the road, Jeff and Stan had their side arms drawn and ready to fire. We walked for a while. We could not see anything in the area. Like before there was no sound in the area except the battles that was still going on overhead and surrounding us. One of the Shadows' transport ships cashed down. The earth shook and second later dust came rolling out from a few of the side streets. There was a loud howl in the air, which drowned out the battles. That was followed by a loud roaring noise that got louder as seconds past. Stan and Jeff turned white and took off in a mad run down the street. I waited a few seconds then followed their lead, we ran as fast as we could. I could just make out the sound of scraping and taping hiding under the loud roaring. A few seconds later and the streets behind us erupted with the Shadow creatures.

I turned and started firing upon the enemy. Orange bolts of fire flew out of my automatic rifle. The bolts hit two of the creatures. After they were shot, they fell to the ground, and were trampled by the other creatures. The remaining hounds continued after us, not giving a care about the trampled hounds. I turned back around and returned to running. I didn't do as much damage as I had hoped. The hounds were closing in only a few feet behind us. I heard smacking sounds from behind then the road lit up briefly and went dark again. There was a rumble off to our right joined by someone telling us to get out of the road. We complied. We ran in between two buildings. There was a loud bang and the road lit up with a bright explosion of fire. The hounds were thrown past us, down the remaining road. The rumbling started back up, and the sound of debris being crushed joined in. Then rumbling stopped, and the sound of metal creaking replaced the rumbling.

"It is safe to come out for now, so make it fast!"

Stan, Jeff, and I left the small opening and returned to the street. On my right was a pile of life less smoldering hounds on my left was a large tank and a hand full of people, about six or seven people in sight. One of the seven people was on top of the tank with a gun drawn. The ruined building in front of the tank had fallen to the ground, and the ruined building behind the tank was completely leveled and converted to dust. The other six people were standing around the tank with weapons resting in their hands.

"What are you boys doing out here by yourselves, where is your platoon?"

"We were attacked and as far as Stan and I know they are all dead," said Jeff.

"The two of us were forced away from the others, and then our lives were saved by Alex."

"Alex, what about you?"

"I was shot down, and my gunner was killed. I saw Stan and Jeff being chased and killed the two hounds chasing them."

"You guys are welcome to come with us. We have been ordered to return to base and help defend it. You can call me Surge."

"That sounds like the best idea I have heard to day," Stan said, climbing on to the tank.

Jeff and I took Surge's offer and joined Stan on the tank. Surge ordered everyone to the tank. One by one the six soldiers climbed on to the tank. The six of them joined Stan, Jeff, and I on the right side of the tank. I looked down the road past more soldiers sitting left side of the tank. There was a much bigger pile of hounds than the one on the opposite side. The tank started to move through the ruined building ahead of us. The rubble broke under the weight of the tank. Rocks and dust got kicked up as the tank pushed straight through battered walls and rubble. We traveled for a while everyone on the tank kept watch looking around the tank for any signs of movement. Some of us were looking up into the dark sky, at the flashes of light above. Most sounds were drowned out by the tanks treads crushing debris.

We saw many transports crash down to earth. Our tank picked up a little speed. We had to change our direction a few times to go around transport ships. The darkness was soon replaced with the red glow from all of the transport ships that now sat on earth's surface. We turned on to a road and pushed on. Surge apparently did not want to make any unnecessary sounds. After about forty minutes we reached a clearing. As far as I could see there was a building like the one I had seen a few days ago in the middle of the clearing. We pushed forward into the clearing. As we got closer a hand full of tanks rose from the earth along with hundreds of soldiers and a few of the robot giants. We picked up speed. One of the soldiers, towards the back of the tank yelled into the tank. I looked back to see what he was screaming about. After a minute I saw the ruins pouring out countless hounds. The soldiers on the back of the tank stood up and started firing back at the mass of hounds.

"Everyone, get your heads down," said someone inside the tank.

The tank's barrel moved to its left. Everyone on the tank had to shift his or her positions to allow the barrel to face backwards. The barrel stopped, after a few seconds the soldiers returned to firing. Then a few seconds later the tank fired, causing an explosion in the path of the hounds, throwing some of the hounds back into the mass of black. The soldier's weapons fire just barely reached the mass, causing little damage. I stood up, flipped the switch on my gun up again, and looked through the sniper scope. There were hundreds of the hounds running in rows behind each other. I took aim at one and fired. The kick from the shot hurt, but I shrugged it off. I continued to fire, the blasts from my gun took out three at a time. However, with each shot the gap was filled, and those I hit fell to the ground and like before vanished under the feet of the mob of hounds. Out of my right ear I heard Surge yell out of the tank.

"Whoever did that keep it up?" asked Surge.

Just as I was firing, rockets flew overhead and hit the mob. I pulled away from my scope and looked back. We had reached the cavalry, and they started firing upon the mob. The giants fired huge laser bolts from its hand, and then fired rockets from their shoulders. The bolts carved a line all the way back to the ruins. The rockets took out a small portion of the mob, with large explosions. A few of the Shadow fighters dropped down and purposely crashed into one of the giants. The giant burst into flames and fell backwards to the ground, then exploded. More purplish red fighters dropped down and headed for the giants. Some were shot down by both the giants and a few of our fighters. The rest pulled up and engaged our fighters as close to the giants as they could.

There were too many for us to hold them back for very long. We kept having to move closer and closer to the bunker. The last giants fell to earth by the intense concentration of the Shadows' weapons fire. One fell by losing its balance and got over run by the hounds. The crew was lost while trying to escape the self-destruction of the giant. This explosion blew a large hole in the mob. The Shadows quickly filled the gap. We still had no choice but to fall back to the base. We reached the base the metal shutter door was open and turrets mounted on the base started firing at the mob. Surge ordered everyone to abandon the tanks and the heavy armament, mainly the tanks. No one hesitated, the tanks were abandoned, and everyone ran to the bunker. However, there were too many people there. The soldiers already in the bunker started to direct people to the stairs and the huge elevator.

The tanks continued to fire at the mob. A few were hit by the Shadows fighter's fire but weren't destroyed at least not right away it took a few runs of the fighters. Then they changed their attack pattern and started to attack the bunker. Dirt and dust fell from the bunker's roof with each hit it took. The tanks plus the turrets held the mob back but was not able to extinguish the threat. Stan, Jeff, and I were directed to the elevator. The bunker shook, debris flew over the shutter bay doors and into the mob. The elevator started descending into the earth. Shortly after we started descending back into the earth's bowls; dust and small bits of debris fell over our heads. We continued down, the sounds of the outside dimmed to a silence.

We reached the bottom, the doors opened and we stepped out of the elevator. Sitting along the walls of a hall that was big enough for a tank to pass through were black cases. One of the cases was lying on its side with ammo lying on the floor. The floor was drenched in blood and there were foot prints crossing the floor. There were four doors on the other side of the elevator, and two on the right, and two across from them. We walked forward through the room the blood on the floor caused some of us to slip on the floor. Then from behind us the elevator shaft collapsed and the elevator floor was pushed back down by the debris covering it. The door was opened by someone on the opposite side and the people ahead of me passed through the door. Jeff, Stan, and I walked through the door. There was chaos everywhere people in beds bleeding and armed men directing us. There were five doors to this room one in front of us the one we passed through and three around the room.

We were directed along a bloody path to a door at the opposite side of the room. I was a little surprised that none of us were asked for our guns. We reached the door which was being held open for us. The room before us was a medical facility. There were people lying on the floor, tables, and beds dead. Doctors were looking over as many people as they could and as fast as they could but they were overwhelmed. One by one we were seen and allowed to leave. It was my turn. One of the doctors asked me a few questions, like if I had been in physical contact with the Shadows, and if I had any wounds that needed to be looked at. I said no to his first question and told him about my shoulder. He said that I would live and said I could go. He gave me a piece of paper to give to the guard outside.

I walked past Stan and Jeff and left the medical facility. I handed the paper to the guard. Then the doors opened across the hall in front of the blood path. Dozens of people started pushing and shoving to get through the metal shutters. Quite a few of them were limping and bleeding over the floor. They quickly made their way to the medical facility. I stepped out of the way to let them through the door. The guard allowed me to leave. I walked past him and started to walk towards my barracks halfway there it hit me I was in the wrong base for my bed. I had no idea what to do so I walked back over to the guard and asked him if there was something I could help with. He told me that the base was being evacuated and was being prepared for self-destruct.

He told me if I wanted I could go find the train station and help load the train with supplies. He pointed towards a door across the hall, then I left and walked across the hall with my rifle on my back. I opened the door and walked into a hall that had crates stacked up to the ceiling along both walls. There was a small path in between the walls of crates leading to another door. The door opposite me opened, a few soldiers walked out, removed a few crates, and walked back through the door. I walked forward, picked up one of the crates and followed the soldiers through the door. The station was busy with hundreds of people walking back and forth, loading the train's cars full of supplies. I walked toward the train. A man standing in front of the train pointed me to a flat bed car that was being stacked full of black crates. I handed the crate to a soldier on the train, walked back to the hall, and retrieved more crates.

We finished loading the train, and then it pulled out of the station. Four jeeps pulled up into the stations, then the soldiers driving the jeeps climbed out, then helped load the jeeps up. The supplies had to be handed down to the jeep's drivers because the station platform was higher than the jeeps were. The drivers got back into their jeeps, drove down the tunnel, and vanished into the darkness. Alarms went off the station turned red, and there was a wine over the intercom then a man spoke.

"Everyone with a weapon report to the lobby and set up defenses because the enemy is digging their way down. They have used the elevator shaft and the staircases. The self-destruct for this base has been set up for remote detonation. After being remotely triggered there will be a five minute window before the base completely explodes. I will join everyone in the lobby that is going to be there. Everyone else evacuate this facility by the train station, soldiers will direct everyone further," said the man over the com system.

The com went silent. Some of the people in the station jumped down to the train tracks and started running down the tunnel. Others passed through the doors connecting the station to the rest of the base. I paused for a minute then followed a few soldiers out of the station. We walked back to the room I had been in before. Jeff, Stan, and Surge along with a hand full of people were setting up guns around three doors in the room. Dozens of people were stacking ammo crates behind blockades made up of filing cabinets and desks. Every person had rifles, shotguns and other firearms. There were about two dozen people at each door and those that weren't setting up defenses were being ordered into their positions. Everyone was facing the door that led to the elevator and the staircases that had led to the surface. There were small gray pouches surrounding the door, each one of the pouches had wires sticking out.

A man stood near one of the doors with a remote in his and a rifle in the other. Rumbling started behind the door leading up to the surface, the rumbling grew louder by the second. The commotion subsided, the room grew quiet, and the rumbling stopped. The rumbling was replaced with the sounds of the enemies scraping the walls, howls of anger, and their moans of pain. There was a loud crack at the metal shutter door at the same time a dent was put into the shutter. A second later and there was a second crack. The dent was pushed further out. Then again and the shutter was almost pushed completely off the wall. A second later, the shutter, and a large portioning of the wall fell to the ground. A cloud of dust settled, the hall before us was black, the lights no longer shined in the hall.

The hall erupted with the enemy. Creatures resembling bugs walked along the walls, creatures that looked like a ball rolled across the floor. The hounds were pushing the balls creatures out of the hall. Behind the hounds was a creature standing on two legs, it had two arms, there didn't appear to be ahead on the creature. The Shadows pushed forward into the room they started to spread out, the man holding the remote said fire. Just about everyone with a weapon fired at the enemy. Weapons fire crossed the room and struck the Shadow creatures, and then the man holding the remote yelled to take cover. Everyone ducked, there was an explosion surrounding the Shadows. Dust filled the room, dimming the light in the room and the temperature of the room grew from the sudden outbreak of fire. The room was quiet not a sound was made for a while as the dust settled. Then the room echoed with the countless howls, moaning and the scraping of the Shadow creatures.

The dust settled and what remained was a pile of Shadow creatures lying on the ground, without warning the Shadows pushed back into the room. Everyone started firing on the enemy, the hounds, the bugs and the ball creatures made a mad dash at us. Those standing on two legs stood still, raised their right arms and black projectiles fired from their right arms. The projectiles flew across the room and hit one of the guns on the middle of the barrel, and hit two soldiers. One of the soldiers was hit in the face; the other was hit on his chest. The gun dissolved into a pool of gray slush, and the soldier hit in the face fell to the ground screaming until his head caved in. The other soldier screamed just as loud, he fell to the ground and most of his torso dissolved in a pool of black blood.

There were too many to hold back, the Shadows just pushed through our weapons fire. They grew too close to one of the doors. The soldiers guarding the door made a run for it. They ran through the door they had been guarding. The Shadows broke through the blockades in their way. Then the ball creatures started to burrow through the door and the walls surrounding the door. The door collapsed and some of the Shadows pushed against each other to get through. A few seconds later there was an explosion, the Shadow creatures that had passed through the door were flung across the room in a blaze of fire. The hall was engulfed in flames, the Shadows steered clear of the fire. They pushed forward again, the creatures on two legs continued to fire at us. More people fell to the ground and died like the two soldiers before them.

Our numbers were diminishing. We had no choice but to abandon the lobby. The man with the remote yelled to everyone to fall back to the station and escape through the train tunnel. We turned and passed through and ran down the hall. After we reached the station the halls behind us exploded; everyone paused and waited. It was almost completely silent. All that I could hear was soft roar of fire and the breathing of everyone in the station.

"We're going to need at least five minutes to escape the explosion of this facility. I am setting the self-destruct of this facility for eight minutes no more than eight minutes and no less. Hopefully the last explosion was enough because I do not want to blow up this facility."

He pushed four buttons on his remote and stood staring at the three battered doors of the station. There was still nothing. No sound came from behind the battered doors. Stan and Jeff were standing close to the tunnel. They looked as though they were ready to jump down to the rails. The three doors fell to the ground, the halls were completely caved, and there was no way around the ruble. Some of the rubble started to shift, the rubble fell to the ground; many of the black ball creatures pushed through the rubble causing the rubble to cave in behind them. They turned around and started to dig back through the debris, as they dug they left what I thought looked like a large mine shaft. Everyone started moving closer to the tunnel.

"Everyone, into the tunnels now," said Surge.

Everyone jumped down to the tracks, and started running into the darkness of the tunnel. Surge, a few soldiers, and I stayed behind, with our guns aimed at the three mining tunnels being dug. About a minute went by and the tunnels filled with the hounds and creatures on two legs. We started to fire upon the enemy when we were told to retreat. Then over the intercom came a female voice saying we had only five and a half minutes till base destruction. We looked at each other then ran into the darkness of the tunnel. The voice went into a countdown from five minutes and twenty-seven seconds until base destruction. After about a minute of running into the tunnel, the tunnel had small lights just barely illuminating the tracks and the tunnel. Two minutes and fifteen seconds left and the sounds of the Shadow creatures echoed from behind.

I looked behind me. What light there was had been drowned out by the blackness of the enemy. I was starting to get winded, my pace slowed down, and I looked back again and started to fire into the mob of creatures. I hoped I could slow them down just a little. I was not the only one. A few of the soldiers had slowed down and were firing at the mob as well. The tunnel flashed with every shot from our weapons. One minute left, our pace had slowed considerably; we were all breathing heavy and our attempt to slow the enemy was not working very well. We continued into the tunnel. I could no longer hear the countdown over the sound of our weapons and the sound generated by the enemy. All of the sounds were quickly drowned out with a loud bang. The tunnel behind our enemy lit up with an orange glow. The soldiers and I turned and ran as fast as we could into the poorly lit tunnel.

From behind came a roar and the countless moans of dying creatures. The temperature increased, the air grew hot and dry, and the stench of death rushed through the tunnel. I could feel the hot air sweep over me. I was then forced to the ground by the concussion of the blast. I turned on to my left side, as a cloud of fire rushed just above me. I could feel the heat of the flames above my skin. The tunnel vanished; all I could see was the brightest oranges, yellows and reds that I have every seen. The way the fire moved and swirled above my face was deadly destructive and yet it had a certain beauty to it.

Chapter Eleven
The Assault Continues

The bright colors of the fire disappeared just as fast as they appeared. The temperature of the air remained the same for several minutes. I looked around one of the soldiers was pitch-black; his skin was smoldering and he was standing straight up not moving an inch. The smell of burnt flesh was strong and potent in the air. The fire vanished from the tunnel. The lights returned the tunnel to its dim glow. I stood up and looked around then focused on the black soldier. Smoke was rising from his body. Suddenly one of his arms dropped to the ground and broke into ash. The soldier's legs gave out. The rest of him fell to the ground and shattered. I heard a howl and a moan from within the tunnel. The next thing I knew I was shoved to the ground by a surviving hound. It bit into my right arm and pulled hard, just about the time I thought my arm was going to be torn off, the hound was knocked off of me by a second hound.

My arm burned with pain from the bite, I grabbed my arm and applied pressure above the bite. The two hounds howled, wined, and moaned as they fought against each other. In the near darkness I could not see exactly what was happening between them. The sounds that they were making were loud, and filled the tunnel. With my left hand I picked up my rifle, I turned on the small flashlight attached to it. I pointed my gun at the commotion a few feet on my left, the two hounds looked different. One of the hounds was red and looked like it was burned, the other was half black and the other half was red like the first one. The black was surrounding his head and his front feet. The two hounds were biting and clawing each other, both of their blood mixed on the ground.

The half black and half red hound kicked the red hound off of it. It looked around then spotted me and started walking towards me. It was hit from its side by a bolt of fire that looked like it came from a gun like the one in my hands. The hound was thrown off its feet and with a thud slammed to the ground. It lay on the ground motionless with a hole in its side. The burned hound got to its feet and walked back and forth then slowly approached me. It walked over to my right side and licked my face. It made no aggressive movement towards any of the soldiers or me. Three flashlights turned on, the light moved from the dead hound, to me, and then focused on the red hound. The beams of light grew brighter as the soldiers moved closer to the burnt hound and myself. One of the soldiers moved his flashlight a way from the hound and shined the light on me.

"Are you all right, Alex?" Hamole asked, standing above me.

"No I was bit by that hound," I said, pointing to the dead hound.

"Where were you bit?"

"My right arm."

"Show me your arm."

I extended my arm. Hamole moved the light from his flashlight to my arm. He moved the light up from my hand towards my shoulder. He stopped past my elbow and looked closely at my arm. He took a piece of cloth and wrapped it around the bite and tightened it above where the bite was. Pain shot up into my arm, it felt like someone stabbed a knife into my shoulder. Hamole then bent down, took hold of my left arm, and pulled me to my feet. Once on my feet Hamole walked over to where the burnt hound was and talked to the soldiers. They looked like they disapproved of what Hamole said but did not say anything to him. They moved closer to the hound. They had their weapons aimed at its head. Two soldiers came out of the darkness of the tunnel; in between them was a large metal cage. They moved towards the hound. One of the two soldiers moved behind the hound. The cage was put in front of the hound, the soldier behind the mutt moved forward forcing the mutt into the cage.

The cage door was closed. The four soldiers picked up the cage by its corners and walked into the darkness. Hamole, the remaining soldiers, and I walked further into the tunnel. After thirty minutes of walking we reached the train station of another facility. The train and jeeps that went into the darkness of the tunnel were nowhere to be seen. The supplies that were loaded on to them had been removed and now rested on the platform of the train station. The four soldiers carrying the occupied cage were being helped by other soldiers. The crates were being moved out of the station, by both Talins and humans. We climbed on to the platform and walked through one of the doors connecting the station to the facility. Like the facility I had just left, the floors were covered in blood and the walls were lined with crates.

A few hallways later, Hamole and I returned to the command room we had been in a day ago. The floor was covered in papers and the computers had been removed from their positions. I left Hamole and returned to my barracks. There was barely anything left in the room, a few books were left on the floor, and a bed had been abandoned. I left the room and returned to the command room, President Clark was standing next to Hamole, and the two of them were talking amongst themselves. I walked forward and joined the two of them at one of the former computer stations.

"Hamole, how much time do we have left before we have to abandon this facility?"

"It won't take them long to dig their way here."

"We have no choice but to start evacuation of everyone and retreat to the Freedom. There is one major problem, Hamole, there are too many people to evacuate and we do not have enough time to evacuate everyone. After this facility has been evacuated I will give the order to activate the self-destruct of the facility. Anyone left in the facility will have very little time to escape to the surface. There may only be twenty minutes from the time the alarm goes off before the base explodes. There should be just enough time to reach the surface, only if the elevator in the hanger is used. Once the explosions start there is a very small chance that someone could escape."

"From the way you are talking, Mr. President, you want me and a butch of soldiers to buy enough time to complete the evacuation."

"You are correct, Hamole."

"We will do what we can, Mr. President."

President Clark left the command room. Hamole turned, faced me, and looked at my arm.

"How is your arm? Think you can fire your weapon?"

"My arm hurts; however, it's nothing I can't handle, why?"

"I'm sure you overheard President Clark and me talking."

"Yes I did."

Hamole walked across the command room, over to the door Hamole and I passed though a short time ago. He paused in front of the door, turned, and stood staring at me. He then waved for me to follow him. I ran across the command room, my arm hurt with every step I took, I reached Hamole a few seconds later. The two of us passed through the door and made our way back to the train station. On our way back to the station President Clark came over the intercom.

"Every capable person report to the armory. There you are going to be given a firearm. Once you have been armed report to the train station for further orders. All parents or guardians and children, members of the base staff will direct everyone to the hanger bay. Everyone will then proceed to the back of hanger bay where you will wait for staff to take you to the surface. Once on the surface you will proceeds to the Freedom a large Talin *Colonizer* ship, then you will board the ship. All of the injured will be evacuated from this base anyone that can help with the evacuation of the injured, please help."

The president's voice left the intercom his voice was replaced by the alarms. We reached the train stations. People were running around blockades that had been set up along the edge of the train station. Manned guns were being placed on the barricades and ammunition cases were being placed by the guns. Explosives were being placed around the train station, on the train tracks, on the support beams and around the doors. A few minutes passed, the doors of the station opened and dozens of people holding firearms ran out. A few soldiers directed the people to line up facing the train tracks a lot of them took positions behind the barricades. Others were very close the doors. Most of the people were dressed as pedestrians. Hamole and I took positions behind one of the barricades, closest to the train tracks. Hamole then handed me a rifle identical to the rifle I had before.

I looked my rifle over; it already had been converted into sniper rifle mode. I set it on the barricades, aimed the barrel down into the black abyss of the tunnel that we had ran out of a short time ago. Hamole also aimed his rifle's barrel towards the never ending darkness of the tunnel. The station soon crammed full of people, armed with rifles, handguns, machine guns, and explosives. There was nothing to do but wait, wait for the screams the howls of creatures. Creatures I had seen a short time ago, creatures that forced their way through a base, and have come to kill everyone in their paths. The train station was mostly quiet; the only thing that could be heard was the alarms in the background and the infinite breathing from the dozens of people in the station. The air was heavy and warm enough to cause sweat to force its way down my face and arms. My right arm burned with pain from the sweat soaking my bandage wound.

A new sound (a moan of sorts) forced its way into the train station. It quickly drowned out the sound of breathing and made strides to overcome the alarm's screeching. The moaning overcame the alarms. The tunnel then erupted with the many forms of the enemy. No words were spoken; or rather no words could be heard. The air passed the barricades, quickly filled with our weapons fire. The tunnel lit up as our shots zoomed into it, striking anything in its path. Our enemy pushed their way out of the tunnel and filled the depression of where the rails were. Creatures fell from our shots, those that remained continued over the fallen. Loud howls and screams forced their way through the sound of the creatures' movement, their sources being the trampled enemies.

Once the railway had been completely filled by the hounds, the bugs, the balls, and the human-like creatures, they turned their attention to us, a band of people defending our planet. As our shots continued to hit their marks the creatures started moving on to the platform. They were only a few feet from Hamole and me now. At this distance I could plainly see their faces and how ugly they were. Boy, were they ugly. I felt pressure on my shoulder Hamole's hand was now on my shoulder. He pulled me back away from our enemy. Everyone in the station was retreating through the doors. Hamole and I returned to the command room, the door leading to the hanger bay was ajar.

Hamole and I ran across the former command room, Hamole paused at the door and looked back across the room. The alarms went quiet and a computerized voice replaced them. "Five minutes until the base self-destruct, all personnel evacuate this facility, now!" The message ended and began repeating every few seconds. The hall across from Hamole and I erupted with the creatures, they poured into the command room, and they quickly spread out into the former command room. Hamole turned and started in through the door I quickly followed him through the door. We ran through hallway after hallway as fast as our bodies would allow.

Hamole triggered an explosion after every hallway we passed through. Each time an explosion was triggered dust and coals were propelled past my ears and into my hair. "Three minutes until the base self-destruct personnel evacuate this facility, now!" Like before the message ended and started repeating. We reached the hanger bay a few seconds later, the hanger bay was in shambles and nearly empty. Across from us was a group of people on the elevator, they had already started to climb to the surface. There were two modified fighters left in the hanger bay, one was twenty feet away from us. The second was farther in the hanger bay and it was lying on its cockpit. "One minute until base destruction." The message ended. We ran toward the closer of the two fighters.

"Alex, you fly us out of here," Hamole said while he climbed into the copilot's seat.

I said nothing, as I climbed into the pilot seat and buckled my ass in. I quickly turned the fighter's systems on and skipped the preflight check. The countdown ended, and a deadly explosion which came from every direction replaced the countdown. The hanger bay started to come down around us, steel rafters, and concrete chunks from the walls fell to the ground. Fire forced its way out of the walls and floor igniting fuel tanks at the opposite end of the hanger bay. The bay erupted with a cloud of orange yellow and green flames. Dust and metal debris fell on top of us and rolled off the glass of the cockpit.

I engaged our engines. We were quickly flung into the air, towards the large metal hanger bay doors. The opening left between the doors grew smaller and smaller, as we approached. There was no time to react. We passed through the small opening with the sounds of nails being dragged over a chalk board. We had collided with the doors, and for a brief moment the doors embraced us, then we were let go, then we immediately went into a spin, as we shot out of the ground and into the black sky. The cockpit immediately went bright red, alarms began blaring. The fighter continued to spin; the controls grew stiff and unwilling to move an inch.

My right arm erupted in pain as I poured all the strength my combined arms could give to force the fighter to come out of the nauseating spin. We spun higher into the sky; both my arms grew numb, from the prolonged vibrations forced upon me by the fighter. We reached the peak of our ascent and began to make our free fall to the surface. Giving it all I had, I pulled us out of our spin, in time to pull our asses out of certain death. We rushed across the surface of earth leaving smoke and waves of dust, behind us. After a few seconds we began dipping to the right.

"Alex, we just lost most of our right wing."

I glanced out to my right sure enough our right wing was gone only a small portion remained. Fuel was pouring out, of what remained of the right wing. A computerized female voice replaced the alarms, and filled my ears. "Damage to right wing severe, complete fuel loses imminent, land immediately to avoid crashing." The message repeated itself a few times then quit and was replaced with a second message. "Power failure in ten minutes." The two different messages began repeating. Struggling with the controls I forced the fighter to turn in the direction of the Talin *Colonizer*. "Power failure and fuel lose imminent pilots eject now."

Hamole and I began the necessary steps to eject from the fighter. We finished preparations, I pulled the eject lever and nothing happened. "Unable to eject, damage to cockpit critical, land for repair." The message repeated once more then stopped. We had only one option left, head for the *Colonizer* and land in one of the hanger bays. I turned the controls left as hard as possible, my arm flared with pain, and the fighter reluctantly turned. The fighter and I fought over ever inch of progress we made. Off to our left and about a thousand feet bellow us the *Colonizer* lay in wait. The controls locked now we could only turn to the left. With no other options I had no choice but to circle the awaiting ship as we descended from the blackened sky.

We circled the *Colonizer* and slowly growing closer to its hull for three minutes. In these three minutes the cockpit was mostly quiet the faint gasp for air broke the silence every few seconds. At the end of the near silence the message came back on "Five minutes to fuel depletion six minutes to power failure, pilots eject now or land."

"No shit, you stupid ass machine."

A minute left until fuel loss and we were just coming around the ship's right side. At our current angle we were going to crash into the ship's hull in a matter of seconds. I put every ounce of strength and as much of my body weight as I could against the controls. We made a fast and sharp jerk to the right our left wing dug into the hall of the *Colonizer* making grinding sound and sending sparks flying from the scrape. The controls shook even harder than before; my arms were growing more numb with every passing second. "Complete fuel depletion in five, four, three, two, one, zero. Thank you for flying today, please have a peaceful and painless death." I forced the controls to the left once more, until we were face to face with the massive mass of metal, called the *Colonizer*. Once we were heading right at one of the lower hanger bays, I pulled up on the controls with all my might to give us a little falling distance.

"Hamole, we are going in as fast as we can. If you can radio the *Colonizer* and have the lower hanger bay on the left cleared out in the next two minutes. Tell them we have no power no fuel and we can't eject."

Hamole wasted no time getting his hands on the radio. Within seconds of my first comment he had the radio on and broadcasting. I flipped the necessary switches to ignite the engines. I hoped there was enough fuel left to give us a burst of speed before the power failed. The engines moaned and with a quick sprint of speed we lunged forward and then the engines stopped. The lights inside and outside the fighter went out. The controls grew stiff and the cockpit was once again as quiet as it could have been. I could see the hanger bay growing closer and closer to us and we started to come out of our angle and slowly leveled out.

We slammed on the edge of the hanger bay doors, we were lifted a few feet into the air. A second later we slammed hard on the hanger bay floor. We continued into the hanger bay sparks rained into the air as our left wing dug deep and left wide gashes into the floor. The left wing broke clean off, sending us into a spin. The hanger bay went a blur; the sound of metal scraping upon metal lessened, and was overwhelmed with the sounds of things slamming on the outside of our fighter. I could hear voices from somewhere outside, in the hanger bay. With a sudden jerk forward we came to a complete stop, the fogginess remained for a few seconds then subsided. Most of the sounds outside stopped. The voices quickly grew louder.

Twenty Talins and a half dozen other alien species circled us, they were carrying large equipment in their arms, a few had cases similar to the one Zar carried. One of the Talins walked closer towards us, moved to the back of the cockpit, taped on the glass.

"Admiral Hamole, we will have you two out shortly."

Six Talins and a few other aliens moved forward, they turned on their equipment and brought their equipment closer to the fighter. The outside of the cockpit glowed with a bright orange, and the equipment made a sizzling sound, as the equipment cut the cockpit's seal. After a few minutes they turned off their equipment and stepped back. Two Talins stepped up, with what looked like a two-foot long crowbar in their hands, and shoved the bar into the cut. The two Talins were joined by six additional Talins and four other aliens. Both the crowbars suddenly grew out about two additional feet in length. The twelve of them took places on either side six on either side of us and started to push down on the now four, foot crowbars.

Both the bars bent as their combined body weight was applied to the bar. A crack formed at the base of the cockpit. The crack grew as more Talins joined their comrades in pushing down on the bar. Slowly the cockpit separated from the fighter, and after a few minutes, the cockpit sprang free. One of the Talins walked over to us and opened the cockpit the remainder of the way. The Talin reached into the cockpit, took my right hand, and assisted me out of the fighter. Once out of the fighter I was guided away by one of the other alien species. I was brought over to a group of four Talins that stood behind a table covered with medical supplies, supplies identical to the ones Zar and his assistants used.

One of the Talins walked around the table, took hold of my right arm, and raised it to the table. The remaining three Talins behind the table picked up a medical device with X-17 engraved on its side. He passed the X-17 medical device over my arm a few times. My arm burned as the device passed. After the fifth pass over my wound the

Talin stopped and looked closer at my wound. The Talin raised his head, walked around the table, and spoke to the other Talins. Hamole joined me on my left side in front of the table for a few seconds then moved behind the table and spoke to the four Talins. After a few minutes of talking to the four Talins, Hamole and one of the four walked around the table, stopping just ahead of me.

"Would you come with us to the medical level, Alex, to receive treatment for your arm?" asked Hamole.

"Why do I have to go to the medical level; can't my arm be treated here?"

"No the treatment devices here are not powerful enough to heal such a large wound like you've got," replied the Talin standing beside Hamole.

"Alright, seeing, I have no other choice I will come with you to the medical level."

Hamole led the way across the now busy hanger bay. Talins and the other alien species were hard at work cleaning up the floor of the bay. Just after we passed the second fighter I crashed a large claw dropped down from the ceiling and dug into the fighter. The fighter was then lifted off the floor and into the air. The claw pulled the fighter through a door at the top of the wall. Once the fighter had disappeared, the wall began to open as the wall separated into two extremely large doors the sound of metal grinding echoed throughout the hanger bay. After a few minutes we reached a door on the left side of the *Colonizer*. The door opened for us as we approached; we walked through the opened door and entered a hallway. The color of the walls in the hallway was a reddish brown with yellow trim along the ceiling and along the floor. Doors lined both walls; each door was separated by what looked like ten feet of wall. The floor was smooth and reflected the light the ceiling mounted lights provided.

We turned left and started walking down, a hall that appeared to have no end. We passed eleven doors before Hamole and the other Talin stopped walking. We turned again to our left. We now stood in front of two large metal doors. Across the two doors was a sign that said lift. Hamole reached out and pushed a few buttons on a panel next to the door on our right. After almost ten minutes the two doors opened and we entered a twelve by twelve foot cubical room.

Hamole and the other Talin walked over to one of the lift's clear walls and grabbed a rail that ran across the lift. The lift's shaft had two lights mounted to the metal beams and one light in each corner. Either Hamole or the other Talin yelled Medical level into the room. After a few seconds the lift doors closed and with a jerk. We began to move deeper into the *Colonizer*. The lift quickly picked up speed almost making me lose my footing. The lights blurred together forming a sold white line of light, on the shaft as we moved deeper into the *Colonizer*. After a few minutes we began to slow, the lights of the shaft became more independent by the passing second.

We slowed to a stop; the lift paused. The shaft was filled with a loud sound of metal moving. I looked up at the source of the sound; above two large metal doors were opening up. Both the doors slid into the walls revealing a shaft going straight up. After a few more seconds we started up the shaft, and with a jerk we sped up faster, faster than before. This time I did lose my footing and fell back against one of the lift's walls.

I'm not a hundred percent sure. I could have imagined it, but I could have sworn that either Hamole or the other Talin chuckled as I fell back into the wall. It is hard to remember every detail of what happened, especially things that are not important as it has been some time.

The lift's speed leveled out. After five minutes the lift began to slow. After a few more minutes we came to a stop. The loud sound of metal moving returned, now below us. The sound of moving metal stopped; then the lift opened into a hallway. Hamole, the other Talin, and I left the lift. The doors to the lift closed behind me. The three of us then turned left and started walking down the hall. This hall looked almost identical to the other hallway. The doors were much closer together, only four feet of wall in between each door. We walked to the end of the hallway. The other Talin turned to his left and passed through the last door in the hall. Hamole and I followed shortly after. The room was full of injured humans and Talins laying on beds and medical tables. Numerous Talins and two other alien species were moving from one injured person to another.

The walls of the room and the ceiling were a pale white. The floor was solid metal that would have reflected everything, if it weren't for the blood that covered the floor. In between some of the beds there were gray desks with a see through monitor hovering above the desk's surface. The Talin that accompanied Hamole and I up here walked through the mass of people and disappeared through a door towards the back of the medical bay. Hamole and I stood in the entrance of the medical bay for what felt like a half-hour before the Talin returned accompanied by Zar and a female Talin.

"Alex, would you come with us, there isn't much time?" asked Zar as he stopped in front of Hamole and me.

"What do you mean there is not much time?"

"I mean I have a lot of things to do and every second counts," replied Zar.

"Okay."

Zar, Hamole, the other Talin, and I walked through the chaos and through the door Zar had exited moments before. I was now in a room with two beds in the center of the room. All but the wall off to my left had black shelves and black countertops resting tight to the walls. The floor was a pinkish white with traces of blood in the cracks of the metal floor. The walls were white, aside from a few bloody handprints left on the wall to my left. Across from me was a second door.

"Alex, would you please sit on the bed?" asked Zar.

I walked over to the bed and sat down on its surface. Zar stepped forward, raised my arm and stared at my wound. Hamole walked to my left side and the other Talin walked to my right side. Zar released my arm, walked past Hamole, stopping in front of the shelves. He opened the cabinet door, removed some medical instruments, and walked back past Hamole. As he approached a small metal slab rose from the floor and folded out into a small table. Zar set the instruments down on the table; he picked up one of the instruments.

"Alex, this will help with the pain in your arm."

He moved the instrument above the black line above my wound and pushed against my skin. I felt a brief pinch followed by the pain in my arm fading. After a few minutes I began to get lightheaded, very tired and my vision grew blurry.

"My head, what did you give me?"

"I am sorry, Alex, we need you unconscious when we treat your arm," said Hamole.

"WH-what wh-why!" My speech grew sluggish and incomplete.

I tried to get up and fight my way free but the drugs were kicking in, and Hamole and the other Talin had their hands pressed down on my shoulders. Everything grew dark and quiet, my head was light, and the pressure being forced onto me had grown.

I awoke in a battlefield, my arm was healed and weapons fire flew overhead. I was on my back looking into a black sky with hundreds upon thousands of ships firing at one another. There were numerous explosions going off all around and from above. I rolled over on to a dead Talin. I then quickly looked at my surroundings. I was in a crater nearly filled with dead Talins. I moved towards the edge of the crater and peered over the ridge. I was in a mountain range that once had what looked like a forest that had been present.

The forest had been cleared all but a few broken trees and rows of stumps. Talins and another alien species that resembled the Talins and a third species unlike any of the species I had seen were at war with one another. The three of them were hard at war with one another; neither of the species had taken sides. The dirt ground was covered in two different colors of blood: a dark red and a bright green.

There were numerous large tanks (three different designs) that surrounded the battlefield. They did not move nor did they fire into the battlefields. They remained still with their guns fixed on the other tanks. The battlefield went quiet, and then a brilliant bright light from above blanketed the battlefield. Everything went dark, the sounds of screams echoed through the dark. The battlefield returned. There were now only two species left. The third species, the one that I had not seen before was lying on the ground burnt to a crisp and motionless. The second species was twice the size of the dead species and was covered in black tar identical to the Shadow creatures.

Neither the Talins nor the species that looked a lot like them were to be seen. All fighting including the fighting above stopped, ships from the third species fell out of the sky. All the other ships had changed course and now headed away from the battle. Shadows on the ground were in a dead run for the stationary tanks. The battlefield cleared out, and then the tanks started to move in many directions.

The ground started to shake; my ears were filled with the sound of ground being crushed. There was nothing close enough to be making the crushing sound. The sound continued to grow louder and louder. The ground's shaking grew stronger with every passing second. I looked behind me, a tank was passing over the crater and me. The light from the outside went black; a hatch on the under side of the tank opened and a Shadow creature stepped out. I raised my hand. I didn't want to but I was no longer in control of my body. The Shadow creature reached down, grasped my arm, and pulled me to my feet. I moved forward. I did not want to go into the tank. I was no longer in control of my legs or my body.

Chapter Twelve
A Debt Paid (Part 1)

I awoke in a small room with a killer headache. I looked around. The room was decorated in the same fashion as the halls had been. To my right was a knee high metal dresser with two drawers marked by two red buttons. I reached to push the button of the top drawer and fell short by an arm's length. I raised my right arm to look at the palm of my hand. Nothing had changed. My right arm had been removed. I was hit by a wall of emotions. I was pissed at Hamole and Zar for what they had took from me, I felt betrayed and I wanted to know why they had lied. I stood up and moved to the only door in the room. There was no doorknob, no keypad on the wall and the door did not open when I approached.

I punched at the door with my right hand; then I corrected my actions and punched the door with my left. I wanted out of the room and find out why Zar removed my arm. I continued to punch at the door until my left hand started to hurt; then I returned to the bed and sat down on the edge facing the dresser. I reached across to the buttons on the top dresser drawer and pushed one of the buttons. The drawer slid out of the dresser. In the dresser's left side was some medical supplies and there was Talin clothes on the right side. I rummaged through the clothes and the medical supplies for a minute, before I closed the drawer. I lay back on the bed and stared at the ceiling, I began to worry about Crystal, David, Mike, and my parents; I hadn't seen them in a while.

I closed my eyes and tried to fall back to sleep. The door slid into one of the walls. A dark pink female Talin, younger than Shaurha but older than Queen Paloween, walked through the door. Once she had cleared the doorway the door returned, back to its original position. She wore a bright white lab coat that was much too large for her size. The lab coat was a few inches above her feet. Her arms were folded across her chest, which pressed dark folded clothes against her white lab coat. A few of her hair-like tubes rested over her shoulders and disappeared under her folded arms. The rest of her hair stretched down her back, stopping only inches from her waist.

"Good morning, Alex, you must have been quite tired. You have been asleep for eleven hours."

"Who are you?"

"My name is Mallowon. I am one of this ship's doctors."

"I want to speak with Zar."

"He is quite busy, dealing with all the wounded. I will tell him you wish to speak with him."

"Maybe you can answer the question I have for him."

"What is your question?" Mallowon said as she moved closer.

"Why was my arm amputated?"

"He did not tell you?"

"No in fact he did not tell me that it was being done."

"That's not like him," she said as she set the clothes on the dresser. "Your arm was infected with an extremely bad virus when your arm was bit by one of those hounds. The virus had already spread throughout your body; however, the worst part of the virus which was still in your arm is fatal. The worst part of the virus in other species has moved throughout their whole body in a matter of hours. Your species however apparently takes longer for it to spread. If your arm was left you would have been dead within a week."

"Why was the door locked?"

"Hamole and Zar felt it best for you to remain here until you had a chance to speak with either of them. When one of them gets a chance I will have them come and speak with you. For right now you can come with me to the rec room. In the rec room you can use one of the computers, read a book, or try one of our games."

"It beats this tiny room."

"That is true. When you have had enough of the rec room, return here to your room on medical level 2, room A-16. Do not forget your room number," Mallowon said as she moved towards the door, the door opened and then she passed through.

I got off the bed and followed her into the hall. She had turned to her left and was walking down the hall.

"How many rooms are there on this level?"

"There are 1000 rooms on this medical level. The floor above and below are both for medical purposes only. The floor below and the floor above have 1500 bedrooms a piece. This floor is where the labs and the rec rooms are and that's why there are fewer rooms."

She stopped, turned to her right and passed through a double sliding door. I followed her through the doors, the rec room was much larger than my room and larger than the medical lab Hamole falsely led me to. There were two other double sliding doors; one across from us, and the other was on the wall to my right. The wall to my left had a single door in the center of it. Along the corner of the wall across from us and the wall to my left was five desks with no chairs and resting on the desks surfaces were Talin computers.

Off to our left was a couple of blue couches; the larger of the two couches faced the wall behind us, and the smaller couch faced the wall off to our left. There was a path about three feet wide in between the two couches. Up against the walls were metal bookcases with grey data pads on the shelves. What looked like two multilevel games of chess and some weird sculptures were in the center of the room. The corner off to my right had large screens stretching from the ceiling to the floor. A Talin was standing in front of one of the screens moving about in no particular way. I started to walk towards the corner, when Mallowon grabbed me by my left shoulder and pulled me back.

"Don't ever cross the line on the floor when it is lit red, if you had you could have caused injury to all players in the game and yourself! The only way to enter the game is when the game first starts or when a new player interrupts the original player and requests entry. For now I think the virtual reality may be too much for you to handle. You can go do what ever you want just stay away from the virtual game. If you need any help with something come and ask me."

I wasn't happy being told what I could and could not do; however,

I had no choice in the matter. She left my side and walked over to a flat table and she pushed down on its surface. Seconds later a plastic slab rose from the floor and folded out into a seat, then folded out once more giving the seat a back. She sat down and pushed on the table once more. A second later, four board levels rose out of the table. After the levels stopped moving two sets of game pieces formed on all four of the levels. One set of game pieces formed in front of Mallowon and a second set formed across from her. She pushed on the surface of the table with one finger for a minute; then one of the pieces advanced forward starting the game.

I watched her play the game for a bit before I decided to go over to one of the computers and have a look at what the Talin computers had to offer. I walked across the rec room over to one of the computers along the wall. I looked down at the surface of the desk. There did not appear to be any buttons on the surface nor any place that hid one. The desk was a dark wood with a shine that reflected my face. For a minute I didn't recognize the person who was staring back at me. I didn't remember what my face looked like at first but it was familiar to me. I began staring at myself looking at my face taking in every detail of how I looked.

"Alex, are you all right do you need any help?"

"I'm fine. I was just trying to figure out how to raise one of those chairs."

"Give me a minute and I will be over there to lend you a hand."

"How very funny," I said under my breath.

She pushed on the table once more before she stood up, left her game, and walked over to me.

"What is the problem? Is the chairs activation button not working?"

"What activation button? I do not see one anywhere."

"This is going to be fun, apparently humans can't see as many colors as Talins otherwise you would have no trouble activating the chair. If you wish to do something then you are going to have to ask a Talin for help until Whaloa and Gupp are able to solve the problem. I will inform everyone about this problem shortly. For now, was there something you wanted to do on one of the computers?"

"Is there a way to type on these computers; to put their thoughts into words?"

"I believe there is but I don't know what the program is called. Whaloa was up here earlier installing numerous human programs. He said to tell any humans that wanted to use one of earth's programs to tell the computer to open human programs. From there a list appears with everything he installed. He had shown me and a few others some of the programs he installed before he left. If you have any further problems let me know."

She pushed down on the desk and walked away. Seconds later a chair rose from the floor and folded out. As I sat down the computer on the desk in front of me turned on with a soft and subtle hum. A monitor rose from the desk and came to a stop in between the computer and me. The monitor turned on, the screen changed from black to white then displayed an insignia that was on all of the Talin uniforms and on the sides of the computers.

"What would you like to do?" asked the computer.

"Open human programs."

The computer's hum grew a little louder; and did nothing for a few minutes. Then a list filled the monitor with program after program; a few of the programs names looked familiar.

"To narrow your search what kind of programs are you looking for?" asked the computer.

"Document writing programs."

The screen went black, the computer hummed louder again for a few seconds then quieted as a new list was displayed on the monitor. The list was much shorter than the previous list. There were only eight programs forming the new list. Like before I recognized a few of the programs, only the first three.

"If you have found the program you were looking for, just call out its name to open it."

I did as the computer told me to do. The program opened to a white screen with a small blinking line at the top.

"This program has been enhanced with complete voice recognition software. If you wish you can talk instead of typing."

I stared at the screen ignoring the computer's last comment, and tried to figure out how and where to start. There was so much to tell and so much that I don't remember of my life up until the basketball game. I just began typing, just putting one or two sentences about the past few days on to the computer. After I had a page of just sentences,

I went through and started to arrange them as they happened and added to them as I went. After five hours on the computer I had six pages typed up. I had a few sentences dipping into the many things that had happened to my friends and me but not very much detail. I saved my document and a data pad ejected from the side of the computer. I took the data pad out the remainder of the way put in my left pocket and closed the program.

"Would you like to open another program?" asked the computer.

"No."

"Would you like to turn this computer off?"

"Yes."

The monitor returned to its black state then lowered into the desk. The computer hummed for a few minutes then stopped. I stood up and started walking away when the chair folded up and lowered back into the floor. The rec room was still pretty much deserted. Only Mallowon and I remained. She had finished her game, had moved over to one of the couches, and was reading one of the data pads from the shelves. She had stretched out on the smaller of the two couches with her left hand holding the data pad. Her hair lay off to her right side and coiled on the cushion under her. I walked into the cubical that the two couches made and sat down on the longer couch. Mallowon glanced up at me as I sat down across from her.

"You have finished with the computer; it is probably a good time for you to return to your room."

"Alright."

She got to her feet, put the data pad into the closet's shelves, and left the cubical. I stood up and followed her out of the cubical and we both walked over to the double door behind the smaller of the couches. The doors opened as we approached, allowing access to the hall. We turned to our left and walked back down the hall to my room. She opened the door and we both entered into the sardine can of a room. I walked over to my bed and sat down. She walked over and sat next to me. Her hair swayed as she sat and just barely touched the covers of the bed. My mind was uneasy partly because my mind was going over everything that had happened, partly because I did not know what had happened to my friends or my parents, and partly because I was still mad at Zar and Hamole.

"I will go see if Zar is free, I will be back shortly."

She stood up and left my room. I was once again left alone in a sardine can. I looked over the room again and came upon the clothes Mallowon had brought in earlier. I unfolded them and changed out of the clothes I had been wearing for the past day, day and a half. I retrieved my data pad from my old clothes and pocketed it again in my left side pocket. I set my dirty clothes on the dresser, climbed on top of my bed and lay back. I stared at the ceiling for a while just thinking about the past few days playing everything back in my head. I closed my eyes and my mind focused on the two episodes with Crystal and me. The picture of Crystal's beautiful body moving in rhythm under mine on one of the old couches in the bomb shelter came into mind. I pictured the expression on her face as our bodies merged and our spirits became one.

The sound of our coupling; her moans and screams of pleasure ringed in my mind as the event played out once again. The memory of the sensation of her soft and smooth skin coming in contact with mine sent a shiver throughout my body. Then a surge of exotic ecstasy rushed through us both which brought to close our coupling then we faded off to sleep. My mind moved forward to Crystal's and my second coupling of our bodies and souls. She undressed and pulled me into the shower and closed the curtain behind me. We locked lips as she quickly removed my clothes and tossed them outside the shower. She turned on the water and brought it to a comfortable temperature.

We moved under the water, she broke our kiss and grabbed some soap and began to lather her body up. With all the soapsuds clinging to her body only heightened her beauty. After she finished lathering, she wrapped her arms around my neck and hopped up wrapping her legs around my waist. We shared a few lustful kisses, and then we moved up against one of the showers walls furthering along our union. The suds washed away and the sound of water falling was overwhelmed with Crystal's moans and screams of pleasure. The expression of delight on her face was enhanced by her natural beauty and by the amplified effect of her body covered from head to toe in water. Her breasts slid up and down my chest with every motion we made. Soon her breathing grew faster; not that long after my breathing had caught up to hers, with a surge of pleasure our union started to come to an end.

I opened my eyes and at that moment I really began to worry about my friends, mostly Crystal. I sat up and tried to think about something else other than my friends and the events that happened in the past few days. I sat there trying not to think of anything or anyone. I just breathed slowly trying to calm myself down when the door opened. Zar walked in, walked over to my bed, and sat down on its edge.

"You probably have questions for me. So go ahead and ask."

"Alright, why did you lie to me?"

"I didn't have enough time nor was there enough time for me or anyone else to go into detail about your injury. We also didn't know how you would react so we decided not to tell you."

"Couldn't you have treated my wound without having to remove my arm?"

"When the substance covering the claws of those Shadow hounds is introduced into a bloodstream, the substance can cause a fatal or an even worse outcome. Some of the species that have been attacked have almost died immediately; other species have died as soon as their skin is broken. Species like mine will become one of the Shadows in a few hours depending on how much of the substance comes in contact with us and depending on where we are infected. There is barely any time for us to perform any surgeries like the one we performed on you. Luckily for you, your species appears to have a high resistance to the substance. An enough of a resistance for us to remove your infected arm without having the infection spread any further."

"You said that it moves through the bloodstream; doesn't that mean I still have some of the substance in my system?"

"Yes it does but due to your system's resistance, not enough of the substance got into your system; to neither turn you nor kill you. In fact it appears that the trace amounts in your body have had a positive effect on your system. The amount that is currently in your system not only helped your immune system hold off the rest of the substance but has also from the looks of things improved your immune system and your physical abilities."

"What do you mean?"

"From what Hamole told me and the Talins that were salvaging your fight. You were able to move the controls of your fight even though the controls and the turning thrusters on your fighter had locked up. The amount of turbulence Hamole reported implies that you were faced with great resistance and yet you forced your fighter to land in one of the lower hanger bays. From what Gupp has reported it was next to impossible for any normal person to fly a fighter that badly damaged. From the scans I have taken from other humans your increased strength and possibly an increase in your other abilities is abnormal in your species."

"Okay, then this substance will just pass through my system, or will it remain?"

"I have no clue. You're the first one of your species that has not been fatally wounded. The substance never had a chance to spread as far as it did with you in any of the other humans."

"Couldn't you have given me a shot or some medicine to defeat the substance?"

"As of yet there is no vaccine let alone a cure. We just have not had enough time to study how it kills or turns. As I said before the substance kills too fast; however, we have been able to learn a little about how come Talins and our cousins are turned so easily, I will get into that at another time. Do you have any other questions for me?"

"Yes I do, do you know if my friends and my parents made it and are okay."

"No I do not know but you and Mallowon can go down to the ground levels and find out while Gupp, Whaloa, and I prepare your replacement arm."

"What do you mean prepare?"

"You will see when you return, but for now follow me and you can go look for your friends and family. We first have to go and tell Mallowon that you're ready."

Zar stood up and walked over to the door, it slid open and Zar stepped out. I got to my feet and followed him out of my room. We walked past the elevator and came to a stop in front of the rec room's double sliding doors. The doors slid open and we walked across the rec room's threshold. The rec room was a little bit busier than it was a short time ago. There were a few Talins, one or two people from a few other species and a few humans spread around the room. Some were on the computers, others were playing the chess-like game, a hand full were playing in the virtual game and two Talins were laid out on the couches and were focused in reading their data pads. Mallowon once again was stretched out on the smaller couch reading a data pad.

"Excuse me, Mallowon, Alex is ready to go."

She stood up and pocketed the data pad she had been reading, walked around the smaller couch joining Zar and me. Zar turned and left the rec room, Mallowon and I soon followed. The three of us walked together until we reached the elevator and then Zar left us and continued down the hall. Mallowon reached up and placed her hand on the left side wall. After a minute the elevators double doors opened and we entered the lift. She walked over to the wall on my right and grasped the bar. I walked in and stood in the middle of the elevator.

"You had better grab one of the rails if you do not want to fall on your face."

"I did alright the last time I rode on this ride."

"Maybe you did but we are going down to the ground level, a straight vertical drop of almost two miles."

"You serious, this ship's two miles high?"

"Yes in fact it is a little over two miles; however, we at the present are a thousand feet shy of two miles."

"What is taking this elevator so long?"

"At the speed we will be traveling, the ship has no time to open all the necessary hatches so they are opened before the drop starts. I seriously recommend you hold on to one of the rails. You will have a few minutes wait. Once I have placed the destination."

"Ground level," she yelled into the room.

I did as she recommended and walked over to the rail and grabbed the rail with my remaining hand. Five minutes went by when out of the blue the elevator dropped and quickly picked up speed and continued to pick up speed. The force of our drop forced my feet off the lift's floor. I felt myself getting lighter as the force on my body grew as we continued to pick up speed. I looked around and Mallowon was standing straight up with her hands gripped tightly around the rail. Her feet were set hard on the floor. Her face had a look of strain and concentration. I could feel my arm growing numb and my hand starting to slip off the rail. I focused on my grip and squeezed as hard as I could through the numbing of my arm. The palm of my hand grew sweaty and started to burn with pain; blood squeezed out from underneath my hand.

We began to slow after five minutes of falling; the drop in the speed was subtle. I just barely noticed the change in speed. We continued to slow, a minute went by, and the force that had kept my feet off the floor started to dissipate. As the effects of gravity returned I fell, face first to the lift's floor. We came to a stop; Mallowon walked towards me and helped me to my feet. I looked at the rail I had left finger impressions on the rail and there was a trickle of blood running down the side.

"Alex, come on there are a lot of people on the survival list."

The doors opened into a large room with dozens of pillars (two feet in diameter and ten feet high). We stepped into what looked like a large lobby with a second level that circled three of the four walls of the room and extended halfway into the room. The walls to our right and left had staircases stretching towards the middle of the room. The room was white lit by wall mounted light fixtures and a large chandler hanging in the middle of the room. There were five doors on the wall across from us on the lower level and three on the upper level. Both the right and left wall had two doors a piece, the lower level had two large double glass sliding doors on both sides. The center of the room had a large monitor displaying a list of words.

Mallowon turned to her right, walked towards the double glass doors and moved off to her left a few feet. She reached behind one of the light fixtures and pushed a button on the base of the light fixture. Three feet from the light fixture, part of the wall moved back into the wall and slid up, opening a hidden room. She walked over to the hidden opening and motioned for me to follow. Once I was through the opening, the door behind me slid down closing the hidden room. We now stood in a hall that had a wide opening that reached from the floor to the ceiling and to either end of the hall leaving only two feet of the left side wall. There was a second door across from where we now stood. The hall was poorly light; lit by only two blue lights, stationed at either end of the hall just above the doors. Mallowon walked through the wide opening in the hall.

I followed her into the room only about twenty feet wide and ten feet long. The room was also lit by blue lights which were mounted a foot below the ceiling. The room was also lit by the white glow of eight computer monitors which were stationed on desks. Each desk had a Talin sitting in front of the monitors working on their respective computers. A female Talin, one of the Talins closest to us, glanced up at Mallowon then glanced over at me. The Talin slid her chair back stood up walked past us turned to her left and walked through the door. Mallowon walked over to the now vacant computer station and sat down; I walked over to her and looked upon the monitor. I watched as she opened file after file on the computer when after her ninth file a window with a list appeared on the screen.

"What are your friends' and families' names?"

I told her the names of my parents and my friends; she typed their names into the computer then pushed enter on a keyboard that resembles a human keyboard. After a few seconds the list went blank and reappeared with only the names of the ones we were looking for. She saved the information of where my friends and parents were located. A second later a data pad rose from the desk's surface; Mallowon grasped the data pad with her right hand and returned the computer to its original screen. She slid the chair back, stood up and walked towards the hallway.

"Come with me, Alex," she said as she moved towards the hall.

I followed her as she turned to her left walked through the door and came to a stop in a small room; only ten feet to each of the four walls. In the center of the room was metal table surrounded by metal chairs. The wall on the right had two odd machines mounted against the wall. The wall on the left had a few monitors resting on a bottomless countertop. On the table were a few books, some plates of food, and a few empty glasses. The room was almost completely vacant; only Mallowon, the female Talin that gave up her computer and me were there. The female Talin had her back turned towards us with a data pad in her hands.

"Alex, you stay here while I find your friends and family. Have some food, something to drink or read a book. I will be back as soon as I find everyone."

Mallowon turned around, left the lounge leaving me with a Talin so immersed in what she was reading to notice anything. I walked past her, over to the two machines mounted on the right wall and looked them over. The machine closest to the door had a video screen cycling through pictures of foods. The second machine also had a video screen; however, this one had pictures of drinks and desserts cycling. I hadn't realized it until I looked back at the first machine that I was in fact hungry. I looked the first machine over again, there didn't appear to be a keypad or any way to use the machine.

"Just tell it what you want and if it is in its memory it will provide the food to you," said the female Talin, looking up from her data pad.

"Thank you."

I looked back upon the machine. The screen was cycling through a small selection of human food (hot dogs, pizza, hamburgers/ cheeseburgers, and a small verity of food from other nations). I ordered a slice of cheese pizza. After two seconds a door slid up and a slice of pizza slid out. I retrieved my food, walked over to the table, sat down opposite from the Talin and started to eat my pizza. I finished eating my pizza, looked around the room once more, and decided to look at one of the data pads left on the table. The data pad was written in a foreign style that I did not recognize. I put the data pad back down, sat back in the metal chair, and tried to get comfortable. I gave up and took out the data pad I had saved my earlier thoughts on and began to read them. As I read the events kept replaying in my head and the detail of the events grew. I was unable to add or edit any of the text on the data pad. I was only allowed to read its contents.

I read through my data pad a few times; each time coming up with more things I wanted to add. I pocketed my thoughts after having read it a dozen times; my mind buzzed with the new thoughts I wished to add. I was getting inpatient. I was growing bored with every passing minute and then a few seconds later the door opened and Mallowon walked through followed by my friends. Crystal, David, and Mike had some cuts and scraps on their faces and arms but nothing life threatening. They paused behind the female Talin and looked towards me then started to move over towards me. I stood up and started to walk over towards them, as soon as I stood up, they stopped in shock.

"Dude, your arm, what happened?" asked Mike as he moved closer.

"I've told you once I've have told you twice leave the demolitions to me," David said, walking around the table and stopping to my right with a small smile on his face.

"Alex, come on tell us what happened," Crystal said as she passed Mike.

"Which would you like, the long version or the short version?"

"You probably should go with the short seeing as Zar has something for you," said Mallowon.

"Alright the short is I got attacked by one of the enemy, the wound on my arm got badly infected, and to save my life my arm had to be removed."

"We need to get back to the medical level, if the three of you would like to come with us, you can talk some more with Alex after he has met with Zar."

"Thank you, we would love to join you," said Crystal.

Mallowon turned and led us out of the lounge and back through the small computer room, back through the hidden door and back into the room with the elevator. We walked over to the elevator. Mallowon once again placed her hand on the wall to her right. A few minutes later the doors opened and two Talins and one person from one of the other species walked out and passed us. We entered the lift; Mallowon and I walked over to the bar on our left and took hold. Mike, Crystal, and David, like I had done on my first ride on this lift, stood in the center. The door closed, the lift started up slowly then without warning we took off. We quickly picked up speed growing faster by the second. My body grew heavy, from the looks of it so did Crystal's, Mike's, and David's bodies as they were on their knees with their hands on the floor.

I couldn't keep myself standing any longer, I was forced to let go of the bar and forced to the floor. I could feel my arm slowly giving out under my increased weight and the increasing pressure on my body. The pressure stopped rising and remained at its maximum for a short time. I then noticed the pressure over my body lessening at the same time my weight started decreasing. I was once again able to hold myself up with my left arm but was still unable to get to my feet. My friends were lying on their chests just barely able to take a breath. The lift suddenly dropped in speed, the pressure holding me on my hand and knees dissipated. I reached up, grasped the bar, and pulled myself back to my feet. Crystal, and David had gotten to their knees and Mike was still lying on his chest.

The speed dropped again and with it the reaming pressure dissipated. Crystal and David got to their feet; however, Mike remained on the lift floor breathing slowly. Mallowon let go of the bar, walked over to Mike and rolled him over onto his back. Other than his breathing, he remained motionless. Mallowon dropped down to her knees and began checking his pulse and responses.

"One of you, help me get him to his feet!" Mallowon said, looking towards David and Crystal.

David walked over and kneeled next to Mike opposite of Mallowon. Mallowon and David wrapped Mike's arms around theirs and lifted Mike off the lift floor. The lift stopped, the doors behind them opened and they walked out of the lift. Crystal and I followed them into the hallway that Mallowon and I had been in a few hours before. Mallowon and David turned left and began walking down the hall with Mike in tow. Crystal and I followed them to the end of the hall and then into the medical facilities on my left. The facility was still filled with Talins moving quickly around the room trying to treat all the wounded that were lying on the many beds and tables.

Mallowon and David walked through the chaos of the triage room, to the door that I had been tricked into going through. We followed them through the door and into the room where I was forced unconscious. The room was unoccupied, aside from Crystal and me. The room had been cleaned, even the bloodstained wall off to my right had been scrubbed clean. There was medical supplies lining the countertops and hanging out of the cabinet doors. Crystal walled across to the other door. The door slid open and Crystal walked through. I soon followed her through the door. The new room was identical to the room filled with wounded people except there was less wounded. Mallowon and David had walked over to a vacant bed and laid Mike down flat on his back.

David left Mallowon, walked across the room, joined Crystal and I at the door and the three of us watched as Mallowon began passing medical instruments over Mike. She continued her scans for a few minutes, then turned, walked back across the room towards us, and stopped in front of us. The floor beneath our feet began to vibrate.

"Your friend will be fine. He passed out from the pressure forced on to his body. He should wake up at anytime however. For right now, Alex, you have to come with me to see Zar. While we are gone you two can stay with your friend," said Mallowon as she looked back at Mike.

"How long will you be?" asked Crystal.

"I will be back shortly. Zar wishes to see Alex so it will be awhile before he comes back," Mallowon said.

"Okay, see you later, Alex," said David.

"See you later."

Mallowon opened the door held it open for me. I walked through the door and Mallowon followed me through the door. We walked across the small operating room and back into the triage room. She turned to our right, walked to the back of the room and placed her hand on the wall as she has done before. Part of the wall (the size of a door) moved an inch into the wall then slid up into the wall. Mallowon removed her hand from the wall and stepped through the doorway. I followed her through the doorway and into an overly light room with large medical equipment scattered around the room. Zar, James, Gupp, and an alien from one of the other species were in the center of the room engaged in conversation. Mallowon moved past some of the machinery, walked over to the four of them and joined in on the conversation.

"Alex, don't be shy, come over here, we have something for you," James said a few seconds later.

I followed Mallowon's path past the same machinery that she had passed and walked to where they were gathered. They were sitting around a rectangular table. On the table there were circuits, motors, and a few things I didn't recognize, but looked complex. There also appeared to be some equipment lying on the tables behind them and before them. Gupp was in the process of merging a circuit and one of the complex objects on the table.

"Alex, come here, and sit," Zar said as he spotted me.

I walked over to the table and sat down in a vacant chair across from Gupp and James. The alien sat off to my left, Mallowon sat to my right, and Zar was seated to my left in a chair at the end of the rectangular table. Zar stood up, walked away from the table and deeper into the room. He made a commotion in the room for a few seconds before he came back with a bundle of clothes. He walked past the table, sat back down in his chair and set the package on the table.

"I would first like to apologize again for how we went about removing your arm. For what you did to help us and for what you did to cheer up Queen Paloween, we all owe you and your friends a debt that we may never fully pay. However, the gift I am about to give you was authorized by Queen Paloween and approved by Hamole for what you did for them. After we removed your arm I took measurements of your removed arm and with the help of Gupp, Whaloa, Herban, James, Mallowon, Casune, and me, we constructed this."

He unwrapped the cloth, removed a metal arm and set it on the table. The arm was completely metal from the tips of the fingers continuing past the elbow. Past the elbow were the metal ended and clusters of fibers stuck out of the metal.

"If you would like to have this prosthetic attached, we will begin the surgery when you are ready. This prosthetic will work better than your old arm and will be stronger, that's the extent of how much detail I can tell you because this is a top secret prosthetic. If you go through the surgery I will tell you more about what this arm is capable of."

"Well it will take me time to get used to not having my right arm and I would rather have a functioning prosthetic arm then no arm at all. So when does the surgery start."

"We can start in a few minutes. We have to prepare the room first. The same room we operated on your dying arm. You can wait here with James until Mallowon comes for you."

Zar, Gupp, Mallowon, and Casune stood up and pushed their chairs in. Zar picked up the arm and the four of them left the room leaving James and me alone.

"Do you have any idea why that prosthetic is top secret?"

"I have no idea why it is; even if I did I was sworn to secrecy."

"Is there anything you can tell me about it?"

"Sorry I know as much as you do. I was asked to assist only because I am a brain surgeon or at least I was."

"Any clue on how long of a wait I have?"

"It shouldn't be long from what Zar said, he was anticipating you going along with the surgery."

I looked around the room briefly from my seat as silence fell onto the room. I began to wonder what the prosthetic could do, and how it would feel attached. Roughly five minutes passed when Mallowon reentered the room.

"The room is all set, Alex. If you and James will follow me, we can begin."

She turned around, the door opened for her, she stepped through, and the door closed behind her. James and I stood up, walked around the machinery, and walked through the door. We turned to our left and passed through the door, entering into a somewhat familiar room. The room had changed greatly in the short time since Mallowon and I had crossed it. All but a foot of countertop was covered in medical equipment. Surrounding what was once a bed now a table was eight small rectangular tables. The large table had a headrest surrounded by three tables and there were four tables circling the right side of the table. Zar, Gupp, Mallowon, and Casune were joined by Whaloa. The five of them were around the table working on monitoring equipment.

"Alex, lie down on the table and then we can begin," said Zar.

I walked over to the table, climbed on to the metal surface, and lay back on the table. After less than a minute Zar walked to the right of the table and set some equipment on the closest table. He picked up a device the size of a small bottle and moved closer to me.

"Alex, I have to give you this drug. It will put you in a deep sleep for a long period of time. It should be long enough for us to attach your prosthetic."

"Go ahead."

I lay back on the table and immediately my head grew heavy and my eyes closed. The room became black and busy with the sounds of movement. I began to see many colors (oranges, yellows, greens, reds, blues, purples, and grays). After a short time the colors separated and I found myself on my back staring at a sky with an aerial battle taking place. The image seemed familiar. The sounds from the surgical room faded and were replaced with familiar battle sounds.

I rolled over onto a dead Talin. I quickly looked at my surroundings. I was in a crater nearly filled with dead Talins. I moved towards the edge of the crater and peered over the ridge. I was in a mountain range that once had what looked like a forest that had been present.

The forest had been cleared all but a few broken trees and rows of stumps. Talins, another alien species that resembled the Talins, and a third species unlike any of the species I had seen were at war with one another. The three of them were hard at war with one another; neither of the species had taken sides. The dirt ground was covered in two different colors of blood: a dark red and a bright green.

There were numerous large tanks (three different designs) that surrounded the battlefield. They did not move nor did they fire into the battlefields. They remained still with their guns fixed on the other tanks. The battlefield went quiet. Then a brilliant bright light from above blanketed the battlefield. Everything went dark, the sounds of screams echoed through the dark. The battlefield returned. There were now only two species left. The third species, the one that I had not seen before was lying on the ground chard and motionless. The second species was twice the size of the dead species and was covered in black tar identical to the Shadow creatures.

Neither the Talins nor the species that looked a lot like them were to be seen. All fighting including the fighting above stopped, ships from the third species fell out of the sky exploding on impact. All the other ships had changed course and now headed away from the battle. Shadows on the ground were in a dead run for the stationary tanks. The battlefield cleared out, and then the tanks started to move in many directions.

The ground started to shake; my ears were filled with the sound of ground being crushed. There was nothing close enough to be making the crushing sound. The sound continued to grow louder and louder, the ground's shaking grew stronger with every passing second. I looked behind me, a tank was passing over the crater and me. The light from the outside went black; a hatch on the under side of the tank opened and a Shadow creature stepped out. I raised my hand. I didn't want to but I was no longer in control of my body. The Shadow creature reached down, grasped my arm, and pulled me to my feet. I moved forward. I did not want to go into the tank. I was no longer in control of my legs.

I looked down at my hands. They were covered in the black tar that was covering the shadows. I was scared and yet I was not afraid of anything, I was pumped and ready to go. I walked to the bridge of the tank and sat down in a vacant chair in front of a computer console and I began to work on the console without so much as a word of instruction.

Everything went black again. I was now in a structure walking back and forth.

Coming from outside was the sound of a distant battle. After twenty minutes the sound of the battle grew louder, heavier, and closer. I was not alone there were numerous Shadows all around me. Some of the surrounding Shadows were walking back and forth, waiting for the approaching battle. I wasn't scared, I was pumped and ready for battle, and somehow I knew my comrades were just as eager and pumped as I was. I was unarmed and yet I had the confidence of an army. I was sure that I would come out of the approaching battle alive.

There was an explosion nearby. The structure shook and dust and rock fell to the floor. Four of the surrounding Shadows stumbled to their knees and quickly stood back up. Dust clung to their knees briefly before the dust and part of the floor dissolved with a simmer and a puff of smoke rose from both their knees and where their knees rested briefly. There was a second explosion, closer this time, more powerful and more destructive. A wall behind me erupted into the structure sending chunks of rubble across the room slamming into six of the Shadows. When the ruble hit the six Shadows, there was a simmer as the debris slammed into them and slamming two of the Shadows into nearby walls.

There was a loud scream from outside the structure followed by dozens upon thousand of loud screams. Someone outside screamed "attack" and milliseconds later weapons were being fired and soon were joined by small explosions. A second later a howl was realized from somewhere outside the surrounding walls. At the sound of the howl I suddenly had the urge to run outside and confront my enemies. However, I refrained from my urge to attack and instead I readied myself for battle. I could hear moans and screams from outside the walls, some sounded familiar like the sounds I heard elsewhere, and others were unfamiliar.

I suddenly lunged forward. I didn't really want to move but the urge to come to the aid of my comrades was overwhelming. I wasn't the only one as a large majority of the Shadows charged through the opening that had been created by the progressing battle. The others and I charged through hallway after hallway until we reached the battlefield (a large lobby looking room) then we charged into the battle. We jumped from the second story and landed on top of Talins and the two other species I saw previously. As we dropped part of me felt guilty and a desire to attack my comrades, both of which quickly subsided. The Talins and the other two species were no longer fighting instead they were busy attacking more of my comrades on the lower level.

My falling comrades and I landed on top of a pile of the enemies. I felt a surge of power as I swung my right arm then my hand or claw slammed into my target's face (my target a Talin resembled Shaurha). The force of the blow sent the Talin flying through the air into other enemies. I watched as the Talin's face grew black and spread across the Talin's body. We wiped the enemies out of the lobby at the same time replenishing some of our numbers, by converting some of the Talins and some of their cousins. We waited for something, I didn't know what; however, I was now even more eager to attack now that I had tasted battle.

After what seemed like an eternity in the lobby were joined by more of our enemies. All of us lunged forward, charging into battle, we were fired upon; however, their weapons had little effect on us. I felt a small tingling on my chest as their weapons fire made contact. The others and I pushed forward into the enemy. A few of my comrades were killed by small explosions caused by some of the Talin cousins. Immediately our targets changed and we were now charging the enemies with the explosives. The third species jumped in our way forcing us to attack them. Although they were outnumbered they put up a fight. With a simple hit they sent a handful of my comrades to the floor. Although they knocked us down, we got back to our feet quickly.

As much of a fight as they put up they soon were overwhelmed and were sent bleeding to the floor and across the room. We pushed through the remaining of the enemies and their remains. Once again we replenished some of our ranks bringing more brothers/comrades to life. We charged through the hall our enemy entered from, meeting no resistant we continued outside. Our party was now pushing fifty stronger or larger. We charged out into a field full of craters surrounded by dirt and a massive army. An army consisting of all three species looked to be five times larger than the force than that of the last battle. Even greatly outnumbered I was still not terrified instead I was still pumped and eager to battle my enemy.

We charged against an overwhelming enemy and a large portion of our enemies, mainly the third species charged at us. As they moved closer they kicked up dust which blocked the view of the rest of our enemy's army. After a few minutes of running we engaged the enemy. We clashed and were soon *getting our asses handed to us. For every one of us there were five of them. We fought hard taking as many of them out as we could before we were all killed. We were almost wiped out when suddenly there was an explosion from above and suddenly a bright flash of white light fell over the field. I felt warm and rejuvenated as the light faded and the battlefield had changed for the better and worse. The third species was frozen stiff. They were no longer attacking what was left of my party. They turned towards the horizon, which had changed considerably.*

The horizon was now black and was at war with the third species making very quick work of them. Those of us that still remained in our party took the opportunity to do as much damage to our surrounding enemy as we could. We moved quick and hard, not giving them enough time to gather their thoughts or realize what we were doing. We dropped close to forty before we were once again battling what remained of our enemy's forces.

Chapter Thirteen
A Debt Paid (Part 2)

I awoke in a familiar room, my head hurt, my right side tingled, and burned slightly. Was it just a dream? It seemed so real, the smells the sounds and how everything felt seemed real. It felt like I was there participating in the battle even though there was no way I could have been there. I never left the *Colonizer*, let alone earth. It suddenly hit me why I was back in one of the medical rooms. Zar had performed surgery on my right arm, attaching a prosthetic arm to my shoulder. I looked at my arm; my flesh had been melded to the metal of the prosthesis. There were small black veins under my flesh that extended from the prosthetic up my arm before disappearing deeper into my shoulder.

I closed my prosthetic hand, forming a fist then opened my hand back up. I could see my hand close and open but I could not feel it. I stretched my arm out towards the door and moved my wrist in no particular way. When I bent my wrist down, part of my forearm rose up. A second later a projectile lunched across the room and struck the door. There was an explosion which pushed the door out of its frame sending the door across the hall, slamming into the far wall of the hallway. The explosion sent sparks in all directions and a black cloud of smoke rose from the door. The wall surrounding the doorframe was black with soot and the floor and the ceiling in the hall directly in front of my room was also black with soot.

Seconds after the explosion, the room was filled with the sound of alarms blaring. I moved my wrist back up and the part of my arm closed. I sat there on the bed and looked at my arm. Above where my forearm had opened, there was a rectangle cut in the metal. I brought my prosthetic closer to my face examining my prosthesis closely.

"Alex, is everything alright in there? Is it safe for me to come in?" Mallowon's voice asked from the hall.

"Yes, as far as I can tell."

She took a quick glance around the doorframe on my right before she moved into the room. She walked across the room, came to a stop on my right and sat on the bed.

"Let me see your prosthetic?" asked Mallowon, sitting down.

She sat facing the doorway and me. I raised my prosthetic to her, she took the prosthetic in her hands. She ran her hands up the prosthetic until she reached the small rectangular cut in my arm. She pushed down on the rectangular panel causing it to move into my forearm. She moved her finger away from the panel. The panel rose up out of my forearm and folded up revealing a small monitor on the panel and a small panel with various buttons in the inside of my arm. Mallowon took a small parcel out of one of her pockets in her uniform. She unfolded the parcel, and then removed two pen-like tools from one of its folds.

One of the two tools was shorter than the other and had a very fine metal tip. She took the longer of the two tools and pushed down on the lower farthest right corner. The panel with the buttons rose out of my prosthetic. Mallowon lifted the panel out of the prosthetic, setting it down on the bed in front of us. Mallowon then moved her head closer to my prosthetic. In her right hand she had the longer tool and her left hand had the shorter and finer tipped tool. Using both tools she began to move the tools in and out of the prosthesis. There were small ticking and hissing sounds every time she moved the smaller tool into the forearm; at the same time the prosthetic fingers would twitch. After a minute of her probing the prosthesis, the lower part of the prosthetic forearm opened.

This time nothing happened when the launcher rose from its hiding place. Mallowon tinkered on the inside of my prosthesis for a few minutes and then my wrist fired again. This time the blast passed through the doorway and struck the door while it lay on the wall across from us. The force of the explosion sent the door to the floor and increased the soot on the surrounding hall.

"What in hell is going on in there?" asked Hamole's voice from the hall.

"What is that kid doing to my ship?" asked another voice from the hall.

"This one was my fault, Captain Movork. I am in the process of correcting a malfunction in Alex's prototype prosthesis. I accidentally tripped the firing mechanism for the rockets. I should have the problem fixed in a minute. I recommend you two stay there until I am finished just in case."

"Very well, Mallowon," replied Captain Movork.

Mallowon continued to work inside my prosthetic. After a few minutes she removed the two tools. Then she placed the panel back into the prosthetic and once again used the larger of the two tools to push the corner of the panel down. The panel settled back into my prosthetic and then Mallowon closed the panel with the small screen. A second after the panel closed I felt a tingling running through the remainder of my shoulder stopping in the middle of my back.

"Do what you did before. This time there should be no problems."

I rotated my wrist as I did before. This time the launcher did not come out nor was there any explosion.

"Good that's one bug found and fixed."

"Is it safe to come in now, Mallowon?" asked Captain Movork.

"Yes it is, Captain."

A second later a large husky old looking Talin walked around the doorframe. His skin was a dark gray. His face had many scars cutting across his skin. Some of the scars were deeper than others especially the one that cut across both of his eyes. Captain Movork was followed in the room by Hamole and one other Talin. The other Talin and Hamole were both carrying the same kind of rifles Hamole and his soldiers had.

"If everything is fine can I cancel the alert, Captain Movork?" Hamole asked, steeping further into the room.

"Yes go ahead. In fact you can return to your duties."

"Thank you, Captain. Alex, it is good to see you're awake. I hope you make good use of your prosthetic," said Hamole before he and the other Talin left.

"Mallowon, in the future before any prototype prosthetics are given to someone on this ship make sure there are no bugs involving the firing mechanism. We do not need any unwanted holes in this ship."

"In the future I will, Captain."

"I have one more question before I return to the bridge. Who authorized this kid to receive a prosthetic let alone an experimental military prosthetic anyways?"

"Zar, Gupp, Whaloa, Casune, a human brain surgeon by the name of James, and I were authorized to give Alex a prosthetic by Queen Paloween. Hamole made a request to the queen to authorize us to give Alex the full military version. Queen Paloween approved Hamole's request. We had to make a prosthetic specifically for Alex because of certain circumstances. If either of you would like to know what those circumstances are you have to talk to Zar he knows everything about Alex's circumstances."

"I see. I will do just that thank you, Mallowon. If you will excuse me I have other matters to attend to."

"Mallowon, I would like to know what my circumstances are."

"You have to speak with Zar."

"Fine, take me to him."

"Okay."

Mallowon stood up and walked to the entrance of my room. I stood up and followed her as she turned to the right. We walked down the familiar hallway to the double door which I hadn't noticed until then was marked with the words medical ward. We passed through the door and stepped back into a room that had been busy with Talins running from patient to patient. Now there was no chaos. All the beds and tables were still full of patients but none seemed to be in any dire distress. Mallowon walked across the room stopping in front of the wall opposite of me. I watched as she placed her hand on part of the wall. Beneath her hand the wall was glowing in a faint hazy blue. The door pushed into the wall then slid up into the ceiling. The door slid back down and locked in place.

I walked across the room and stopped in front of the wall. Off to my left was the small glowing part of the wall Mallowon placed her hand. I raised my right hand and placed it on the panel. The door slid back into the wall before it slid up into the ceiling. I walked through the doorway. I walked around the various machinery until I reached the rectangle table where Zar and Mallowon were sitting across from each other. Zar was staring down at a data pad and Mallowon had picked up a circuit and was examining it.

"Have a seat, Alex," instructed Zar, peering up from his data pad.

I walked over and sat down at the end of the table closest to the door.

"What can I do for you, Alex?" asked Zar while he put down his data pad on the table.

"Why did I have a prosthetic specifically made for me and what are my circumstances?"

"Like I told you before your physiology is different from Talins and all the other species we have encountered. Although your immune system can fend off the enemy's infection, it appears that the infection has altered your physiology a little."

"How has it changed me?"

"Mallowon and Hamole have observed you having and increase in strength. In the lift Hamole noticed that your balance has been increased. The fact that you were able to access this room proves that your vision has increased. I wouldn't be surprised if the rest of your senses and abilities are increased or will increase over time."

"When did Hamole and Mallowon observe an increase in my strength?"

"After you and Hamole crashed Hamole found out that the controls of the fighter had welded together and that you broke the bond welding had made. When you and Mallowon went to the lower levels of this ship you held on to the rail, while under extreme forces. She noticed that on the way back up in the lift that while your friends were forced to the floor of the lift you were able to stay standing longer. We have noticed that other humans have remained standing longer than your friends; however, they were forced to the floor sooner than you were and some of them were more physically fit than you are. Because of these unique differences we had to make a prosthesis that was compatible with your physiology. If you notice anything else unusual tell Mallowon or me. Even the smallest thing could help us."

"While I was in the lift with Mallowon it was as though I could feel and hear the slightest change in the lift's speed."

"Anything else?"

"It could be nothing. While I was knocked out I had a dream. A dream that was as clear and real as we are talking now. The dream was about a war between three different species. One of the species was Talin. Another looked as though they were cousins of the Talins and the other species I don't remember what they looked like. Towards the end of the battle there was a bright flash of light, a second later the battle was over and the battlefield was crawling with Shadows. The third species was lying dead on the ground and both the Talins and what appeared to be your cousins became the Shadows. I watched as the battle ended and after the flash I was one of the Shadows."

"That's some dream. It probably is your mind trying to deal with everything that has happened to you in the past eight days."

"The second time I was knocked out I had the same dream only this time I had a continuation of the ending, plus a second battle. After the first battle I found myself in a structure unlike anything on earth. I was surrounded by Shadows. I was one of them. There was a battle being waged off in the distance that grew close quickly. We charged into battle once the battle moved into the structure. Around twenty-five or thirty Shadows jumped to the first floor of a large room. We landed on a mix of the three species from the first dream. The three species had been fighting another party of Shadows, and had almost won when we dropped in.

"After the battle there were only a few Talins and your cousins dead. The rest had been turned into Shadows and the third species were lying on the floor bleeding to death. After a minute we charged back into battle to only be stopped a few feet from the structure's exit. We cleared out the enemy, replenished the ranks before we charged outside to greet the enemy. By this time our part had grown to fifty Shadows. When we reached the outside we were greeted with a battle of two hundred and fifty of the third species. Being that the third species could not be turned into Shadows, they were sent in to kill as many in the part as they could before we killed them. We battle, the Shadows were down to our last six, and our enemy still had eighty strong. There was a bright light like before, I felt stronger and rejuvenated. When the light faded the horizon was black. All but the third species had been turned to Shadows.

"Seizing the opportunity the remaining five of us attacked the only remaining enemy. They had moved their focus away from us long enough for us to kill every last one of the eighty. Then I woke back up in A-16."

"Maybe this is more than your mind trying to deal with everything. There may be nothing to these dreams but nevertheless I will have the battles you described looked into. I hope they are only dreams and not real. Anything else?"

"I don't know if there is anything else."

"Mallowon, take Alex and his friends to the lower levels and see if you can find his parents. While you're gone James and I will prepare the last surprise we have for you, Alex."

I stood up and walked back over to the closed door. As I grew closer to the door around a few feet the door opened. I walked through the door shortly followed by Mallowon.

"The last I knew your friends were still in the rec room. We shall check there first."

Mallowon led the way out of the medical facility down the hall, stopping at the door to the rec room.

"Attention all personal, prepare for lift off. Once the engines have heated up we will be leaving earth's atmosphere. The transport ships will be making one final trip before we leave orbit they will rendezvous with us in orbit. At this time I would like all personal to report to your stations and prepare for a rough exit. All of our guests that would like to help us with our escape. Speak to any Talin for further instructions. That is all," said Movork's voice on the intercom.

Mallowon walked through the rec room doors. I followed her once again through the rec room doors and into the rec room. The rec room was much busier than it had been on my last visits. Both of the couches were completely occupied with Talins, a few of the other species and two humans (a man and a woman). All of the chess-like games were occupied by two people heavily involved in their games. David and Mike were sitting in front of computers and Crystal was to my left involved in the virtual game. The *Colonizer* began to shake. The people sitting at the chess games fell out of their seats. Everyone sitting in front of the computers held on to the tables for support.

Crystal lost her footing and fell to the floor and from the looks of it the virtual game ended. Crystal stumbled to her feet and exited the game. She looked around the room a few times before she saw me.

"Alex, you're awake! Were you woken by the alarms going off?" yelled Crystal.

"No, I caused the alarms to go off."

"How did you do that?" asked Crystal, looking at my prosthesis.

"My prosthesis malfunctioned."

I raised my arm showing off my prosthesis to her.

"How?" she asked with eyes even more focused on my new arm.

"I will tell you later."

"Alex, your new room is A-90; it's at the end of the hallway we just came through. It will be on your right. A change of clothes will be brought down to your room shortly. When you and your friends have finished here all of you should return to your room and talk. It's best to talk about stressful things. I have to leave now and return to my duties," said Mallowon.

Mallowon turned walked back through the doorway and turned left before the doors closed behind her. I turned back to face Crystal, she had walked over to David and Mike. Both of them were still sitting in front of computers. I walked into the rec room further and looked around. Most of the people there were human, all of which had bandages somewhere on their bodies. There were a few wounded Talins reading data pads and a few were playing the chess game. There were two aliens working on some of the computers near David and Mike. David and Mike turned around to face Crystal. They spoke briefly then walked across the rec room towards me.

"Alex, welcome back to the world of the two handed," said David as he approached.

"How is your arm?" Mike asked, coming to a stop a few feet in front of me.

"Don't really know yet."

"Seeing you with a metal arm is going to take some time to get used to," said David.

"No kidding. Let's go to my room and talk in quiet."

"Why?" asked Mike.

"There are a few things I need to tell you and I want to know what happened to you three during the battle."

"Alright let's go to your room."

I turned around and the three of us walked out the rec room. I turned right and led them down the hall. Six feet from the rec room door was a door to a bedroom six feet after that and another door. The left wall had doors separated by six feet; each of the doors on the left side was positioned in between the doors on the right. As I went I looked at a few of the doors for their room numbers. We walked for at least ten minutes when the end of the hall came into sight. The rooms' numbers grew in value as we came closer to the end of the hall and the front of the *Colonizer*. I began looking only at the right side of the hall for my room. We reached my room and as we approached, the door opened for us. We walked across the threshold of my new room. Aside from the fact that everything was on the opposite side, everything in my new room was identical to my previous room (minus a few blast marks and a broken door).

I sat down on the bed. Crystal sat on my right. Mike sat on my left and David sat down on the floor facing us. None of us spoke. David's and Mike's eyes were focused on my metal arm and Crystal's eyes moved from Mike, to David, then to me and back to Mike. Crystal looked uneasy and inpatient as if she had something on her mind. I could tell that she did not want to be the first to talk. She looked as though she was waiting for one of us to speak. David, Mike, and I traded glances. I could see that they too had something on their mind but they looked like they could not find the words. At that time I figured that they too had stories they didn't want to talk about. After five minutes of quiet I finally found the courage to speak.

"I don't know about you three, but I can't stand the silence any more. What happened to you all during the battle?"

"I was one of the few lucky ones that returned to the hanger bay with my fighter in one piece except as I began my return one of the few remaining fighters killed my gunner," said Crystal, looking down at the floor.

Later I found out that all the fighters that made it back to the hanger bay had logs taken. Through Shaurha and Queen Paloween, I was allowed to view the logs. Crystal and the other pilots that returned their fighter to the hanger bay were indeed lucky. Out of one million fighters from the United States only one thousand fighters made it back to any of the hanger bays still in flying conditions. Once I reached Crystal's log I understood why she did not want to speak. When her gunner was killed a majority of his remains was sent to the front of the cockpit. She had flown with her gunners remains surrounding her and covering her for more than an hour.

"You were definitely lucky, Crystal. My pilot crashed our fighter ten yards away from the bunker above the hanger bay doors," said David with a little cheer in his voice.

There were pretty much logs about every fighter that returned with survivors. Out of the one million fighters launched in the U.S. there were close to one hundred thousand logs taken. My name was nowhere mentioned in any of the logs. As for David he was lucky too but I don't think he knows it or he does not wish to talk about it. From the reports of the soldiers in the bunker his fighter just barely missed the wall of the hanger bay and the outside of the bunker.

"So Mike what happened to you?"

"I don't want to talk about what happened," said Mike as he spoke he averted his eyes away from us to the door.

It turns out that Mike was not mentioned anywhere in any log, report, or file. I tracked down the pilot of Mike's fighter. He told me that they crashed and were separated forcing my curiosity to a close for the moment.

"Alex, what about you? You said there was a long version, so what happened?" asked David.

"My gunner and I killed a few fighters before the transports began their descent. We destroyed one transport with rockets and then after a few more fighters we got hit pretty badly. Most of our weapons were dead and we were going to crash so we decided to fly our fighter into a transport. Once we got close enough we ejected and began our rough descent. My gunner was killed causing the air to whip around the capsule and then I crashed into some ruins and then..."

The door opened and Shaurha walked into my room. In her arms was a pile of clothes.

"Hello, everyone. Alex, it's good to see you're awake. I brought you a change of clothes. And I have a message for you from Captain Movork. He hopes you enjoy the new room and he wants you to be more careful with this one. He also wishes to see you after you change. All of you can follow me to the command level. When you have changed join us outside your room." She handed me the clothes and left the room followed by Mike and David.

Once Crystal and I were alone she gave me a kiss and whispered in my ear, "I'm glad you're alive." Then she left the room, leavening me alone in my room. I changed my clothes quickly and joined the others in front of my room.

"Alright follow me." She turned to my right and began walking down what remained of the hall.

She led us down the remainder of the hall. At the end of the hall, was a glowing panel very similar to those that I have previously seen.

"There is nothing here," said David.

"There is a blue panel on the wall, can't you see it?"

"Alex, David is right, there is nothing there," said Mike.

Shaurha and Crystal did not say anything. Shaurha walked took a few steps and placed her hand on the panel. The wall slid back in on itself and rose into the ceiling revealing a circular elevator about eight feet in diameter. I looked at David. He had a look of stupidity on him. Mike carried the same expression. The elevator had a circular carpet and the walls were black with lights mounted inside the walls. We all filed into the elevator one at a time due to the fact the door to the lift was big enough for only one person to pass through at a time. Shaurha moved to the side of the lift as we piled in. Once the four of us were in she pushed a button to close the door. The door to the lift closed and we began to climb higher up the ship. The lift began to pick up speed quickly, but was nowhere near as fast as the larger lift that ran through the whole *Colonizer*.

After four minutes we began to slow. A minute later we came to a stop. The door opened and Shaurha walked out. We followed her out of the lift. We now stood in a room that looked to be the largest room ever constructed, this one room stretched from the front where we stood to the back of the ship. This one room was almost as wide and as long as the entire ship. The room was mostly white. Portions of the right and left walls were extremely colorful. In between the pillars were whitish tan tables and chairs. Both the right and left walls had machines identical to the one I used earlier. Every couple of feet there were metal pillars about five feet on each side and about eleven feet high. In front of us about two three hundred feet was a wall with three doors evenly spaced.

She walked forward a few feet turned to her right and walked toward the right wall. We followed her as she moved about the cafeteria. She then turned left after walking about seventy feet and walked forward into the vast room. We walked past dozens of rows of tables, chairs, and the large support beams. Shaurha turned once again and walked down a path in between a row of tables and the wall in the center of the room. It was more than one wall in the center of the room housing three doors. There were in fact three other walls that housed the three doors. She turned to her right and faced the wall with the three doors. She placed her hand on the wall and the door slid open. She walked across the threshold of the door; we followed her through the door. We were now once again in an elevator.

This elevator was roughly the same size as the lift we just left and looked pretty much identical to the last. The elevator door closed behind Crystal, Shaurha once again pushed a button on the elevator's wall. After a minute we began to move even higher into the *Colonizer*. After another ten minutes we began to slow until we came to a stop after two additional minutes. The door ahead of us opened and Shaurha exited the lift. We followed her out of the lift. The room we were now in was colored black and was dimly lit. The walls, ceiling, and the floor were all black. The walls and the floors had lights mounted into them. The lights were evenly spaced about four feet on all four walls. In between the lights looked to be a door about two and half feet wide and three to four feet high. A few of the doors had been left open.

The open doors concealed a black chair sitting in front of black dual controls. Off to my right was a staircase that had a path going underneath it; the path led to the other side of the room.

"This way," said Shaurha, walking along the side of the staircase.

We followed her to the front of the staircase; she then turned and started to climb the stairs. At the top of the staircase was a large gray metal door that was a foot higher than the ceiling. The door cut the staircase off from the next level. Shaurha stopped about halfway up the staircase and walked over to the staircases left. She bent down and pushed a few buttons on the next step. The door above us started clicking and whining and after a minute the door slowly began to open. The light from the next level shined through the small opening lighting the staircase slightly. After about ten minutes, the door opened completely and then the five of us continued up the staircase about another eight steps.

At the top of the staircase were three doors: one to my right, one to my left and one in front of the staircase. Shaurha walked to her left the door, slid into the right wall and then she passed through the doorway. We followed her into the next room. This room was full of Talins, humans, and a handful of people from other races. Everyone was scattered about working on various computer stations. All the different species were intermingling with one another. This room was a bit smaller than the room below us and was much brighter as well. What wall there was, was a pale white the floor was a gray carpet and the ceiling was the same color as the walls. The room was lit by six three feet long lights and one four foot long light that hung from the ceiling. The wall in front of me had a large screen that almost expanded the entire length of the wall. The screen had a picture of the sky outside the ship. Half the screen was black from the smoke and the rest showed part of the sky below the smoke cloud. The screen slowly moved across the surface of earth. Under the cloud of smoke I was able to see ruins moving closer to us.

Shaurha walked into the room further. We followed her into the room. As we moved into the room I recognized some of the people in the room. Movork, Hamole, and President Clark were talking to a large party of humans. There was a handful of children clinging to some of the adults' legs.

"Captain Movork, I brought Alex and his friends as requested," said Shaurha as we approached them.

"Thank you, Commander Shaurha. From what Hamole and President Clark told me you have done quite a bit to help the survivors of the *Kento*. Alex, you deserve a special thanks to you for saving my son. I would have expected him to be the one doing the saving; however, I suppose everyone needs to be saved now and then," Movork said, patting Hamole on his shoulder.

"To be fair he saved me from being Shadow food."

"Regardless, thank you."

"Captain, the evacuation is almost complete. The last twenty-two transports are en route. They should be docking shortly."

"Thank you, Tatone," said Captain Movork.

The screen changed from the half view of the smoke cloud to a fuller view earth's surface and a small portion of the screen showed a portion of the *Colonizer*. After a few minutes six transports came into view. The first three transports flew into the lower hanger bays, the remaining three fighters slowly moved closer to us. After about a minute the three transports were only a few thousand feet from us; when suddenly an explosion came from the middle transport. The hall of the transport caught on fire and burned. Gray smoke poured from the burning transport. The middle transport began falling out of the sky. The fighter fell quickly, and then it crashed into some ruins and then exploded sending fire and smoke into the air. The last fighter began to close the gap when a Shadow fighter dropped from the sky and attacked the transport.

The enemy's fighter dropped down further and continued its assault on the transport ship. A minute later the alarms on the bridge began to blare and the ceiling lights turned red. The screen pulled back and once again showed the view of the smoke cloud and earth's devastated surface. The smoke cloud started to move further down the screen and began to glow a bright violet. The enemy separated from the cloud. A few enemies broke away from the pack and began attacking the two transports.

"This is your captain speaking. Everyone to your battle stations. We are engaging the enemy," Movork said, putting down a very small microphone.

Three minutes later and fighters began to leave the *Colonizer*.

"Come with me, Mike, Crystal, David, Alex, those fighters are going to need as much help as possible."

"Wait for me, Shaurha. I want a piece of them," said Hamole.

Shaurha led us out of the bridge, back down the staircase and back into the black room. A second after we reached the floor the door at the top of the staircase opened and around thirty Talins came running down the stairs. The thirty Talins spread out around the room; each one stood in front of a door. The doors slid open and the Talins climbed into the chairs and put on a small flimsy headset.

"Come on there is no time to waste, Alex," said Hamole as he climbed into a chair.

While I was watching the thirty Talins my friends and Shaurha had already climbed into a gun. I climbed into a vacant turret and slid the headset on. The door closed behind me, and then the chair slid even further into the turret. The controls turned on and the walls around me slid back into the ship. The surrounding glass shined what light there was outside upon me. I looked to my left, I could see David in his turret. I glanced to my right and Hamole was already taking aim with his gun.

The controls consisted of three monitors and two joysticks. The joysticks had two triggers on them; one was on the inside of the joystick and the other on top of the joystick. The monitor in front of me displayed a few stats and the monitor on the right displayed what looked like radar. The monitor on the left displayed a lot of the Talin language. "The left screen was completely useless I could not read any of it."

"All you have got to do is push the triggers down on the joysticks, the guns will do the rest. Be careful the guns can overheat so watch the monitor in front of you. If they overheat the gun will need a few minutes to cool," said Shaurha over the headset.

A minute went by and the enemy's forces grew larger and closer. One of the fighters began to fire on the *Colonizer*. The black excretions from the enemy's ships dissolved on an electric shield that protected the *Colonizer*. As the excretions hit the shield sparks rained down the shield. The fighters flew closer, a few seconds later the enemy was engaged by Talin and hybrid ships. The mass of enemies scattered and began firing upon the Talin and hybrid ships. The turrets to my right began firing at the enemy. I began firing at the enemy a second later. I could not distinguish the good from the bad fighters.

The battle began to spread out around the ship; as the battle scattered out it became easier to distinguish between them. The enemy continued to fire upon us every time they flew towards us. Seven fighters flew towards us focusing their excretions on one section of the shield. A small handful of turrets and I began firing upon the seven fighters. Two of the turrets focused upon one of the fighters for a few minutes. I continued to shoot on the closest fighter. The last turret was firing upon one of the lower fighters of the seven.

The fighter being fired upon by the two turrets burst into flames and then fell out of the sky. One of the other fighters began getting fired upon by one of the turrets. A few seconds later the fighter was fired upon by the second turret.

The two fighters being shot from the other two turrets exploded. One of the fighters flew off course and crashed into another fighter. A few seconds later the fighter I was firing upon erupted into flames. I continued to fire upon it as the fighter fell to the earth. A few seconds later it exploded sending the debris to the earth's surface. A few seconds later another fighter erupted into flames and fell as the two turrets continued to focus their fire. There were only two fighters left out of the seven and they had grown much closer to us. The five of us began to focus our attention to the two remaining fighters as they rapidly approached. The fighter being shot by me and two other turrets burst into flames and crashed into the shield. The fighter dissolved as it hit the shield and sparks rained down from where the fighter crashed. The second fighter had come at us at an angle from the left as all five of us focused on the last fighter. It too burst into flames and crashed into the *Colonizer's* shield in roughly the same spot as the last fighter.

This fighter like the last dissolved into the shield when it hit; however, this time a large portion of the ship passed through the shield. What remained of the ship flew past Hamole's turret and slammed into the side of the *Colonizer*. I could see out of the corner of my right eye as fire roared out the side of the *Colonizer*. I brought my attention back to the battle before me. Our enemy was scattered about before me. The majority was engaged in a firefight with our ships. There were explosions everywhere in the sky too many to count and from the distance I was at I had no idea which fighters were being destroyed. We continued to fire at any fighter that flew past me or came in range of my turrets. One of the enemy fighters began to fly straight at me. I changed the direction of my fire to the fighter that was now heading for me. I could see just about every shot I made hit the fighter. The fighter continued to fly towards me for a minute. Then my guns stopped firing, and no matter how many times I pulled the triggers on the joysticks the barrels of my turret would not move.

The enemy ship grew closer by every passing second and still my turret's barrels would not fire. The fighter was getting too close and

I had no way to stop it from crashing into the shield. Only yards away from crashing when a Talin fighter dropped out of nowhere and began firing upon the enemy fighter. After a minute the enemy ship exploded. The Talin fighter flew through the enemy's explosion and pulled a tail of fire behind it. Some of the debris from the fighter slammed into the *Colonizer's* shield. The debris dissolved as it came in contact with the shield. Another fighter flew past; I pulled the triggers and the barrels fired upon the enemy target. The fighter moved too fast for me to destroy it. I only hit it a few times on its back side. As it passed other turrets fired upon it. From what I could see the other turret only hit the fighter a few times.

Out of the corner of my left eye, I saw a fighter break through the shield and crash into one of the turrets a number of levels below. Fire poured out of the turret after the fighter crashed. After forty minutes the battled thinned out quite a bit; however, there were still enough fighters to keep those of us operating the turrets and those in the fighters occupied. After forty-five minutes the number of turrets on the *Colonizer* had lessened a bit. We continued to fire on any enemy fighter that flew past or came in range. The enemy fighters were soon joined by a large number of Talin fighters that descended from the mass of smoke and opened fire upon the enemy fighters. The Talin reinforcements made quick work of the enemy fighters. The enemy ships were quickly destroyed. Only a few managed to escape from the fighters that now greatly outnumbered the enemy. The Talin reinforcements ascended back up into the cloud of smoke and the other Talin and hybrid fighters returned to the *Colonizer*. There didn't appear to be very many ships returning to the *Colonizer*.

The walls surrounding the turret closed, the door behind me slid open, and the chair slid back. I removed my headset and climbed out of the chair. The majority of the doors in the room had opened and the occupants within were also climbing out of the turrets. There were forty-five doors around the room; only around thirty doors had reopened. Hamole, Shaurha, Crystal, David, and Mike all survived the battle. I looked past Hamole, the two closest turrets on his turret's right were still closed. I looked to my right; the two doors making up the corner of the room were still closed and the door on the right wall was dented into the room a foot. There was no smoke, no air, and no sound coming from behind any of the sealed doors. Shaurha and

Hamole walked forward into the room; they both looked around the room surveying the number of survivors and how many turrets had been lost.

"I am going to have to ask you four to return to your rooms on the medical level. Alex, you should be able to open the lift doors with your prosthesis. It will be some time before Zar will be able to talk to you again so you have some time to kill. To return to the dining hall it is the fourth button from the top one. For the other elevator it is the sixth button down," said Shaurha.

"Alright, see you later."

The four of us walked over to the elevator door. I raised my right hand to the bluish panel next to the door. The door to the lift opened and we filed into the elevator, then I pushed the fourth button down next to the elevator door. The door closed, and then we began to descend back down deeper into the ship. After a few minutes the elevator slowed down to a stop. The door opened and we walked out of the lift. The dining hall was as we had left it; there was no sign of battle anywhere. The lift door across from us opened and six Talins walked out of the lift. The door closed behind them; we began walking around the tables and chairs like before. About halfway back to the lift the four of us passed the six Talins. Each of the six had their hands full of equipment and tools; all six were moving as fast as they were able to with their arms full of equipment.

A quarter of the way to the lift, the elevator doors opened again, and another six Talins emptied out of the lift. These six had their hands full of equipment and tools as well; we passed them a few minutes later. We reached the lift door I placed my hand on the bluish panel; the door didn't open. We stood there for a few minutes waiting for the lift to return to the dining hall. About five minutes went by before the lift doors opened and another six Talins exited the lift. Three out of the six Talins had their arms wrapped around an arm full of stretchers. We took the opportunity to board the lift before we were forced to wait for it to return.

I pushed the sixth button down. The door closed and we began to descend further into the *Colonizer*. After about two minutes the door opened again. The hall in front of us was full of Talins and a few of the other species. Zar and Mallowon were behind the mass of people ahead of us. We slipped out of the elevator quickly and then six more

Talins boarded the lift. The door closed and six more Talins ascended higher into the ship. We walked single file through the mass of people.

"It is good that you four survived. There isn't anytime to talk now. Alex, when I have finished with my duties I will send for you," said Zar as we passed him and Mallowon.

We continued down the hall; we passed my room and came to a stop at the doors to the rec room. We stopped just before the door.

"What should we do?"

"David and I were in a middle of a computer game and since we have the time we want to finish our game," said Mike.

"I was thinking about exploring this ship a little bit."

"That sounds like a good idea, do you mind if I tag along?" asked Crystal.

"No I don't mind. We will be back in a few hours."

Crystal and I continued down the hall a little while until we reached the elevator's doors. I placed my hand on the panel on the door's right. The doors slid open and Crystal and I entered the lift. We both walked over to one of the rails and grabbed the rail. I heard a voice coming from somewhere in the lift.

"What floor would you like to go to?"

"Ground level."

"Why go there?" asked Crystal.

"It was the only thing I could think of."

Chapter Fourteen
An Unwanted Party

The elevator doors closed and then the lift began to move. A few minutes later we began picking up speed. The pressure applied to my body never changed. I looked over at Crystal who wasn't having any trouble standing. We continued to pick up speed. The lights in the shaft formed a solid white line along the corners of the lift. The lift kept picking up speed for nearly five minutes. Until it came to a steady speed for a few seconds and then the lift began to slow down. The change in the elevator's speed was subtle, just barely noticeable. The lift made a sudden rather noticeable drop in speed. The lift shook a little bit when our speed dropped.

The lift continued to drop suddenly in speed and with it the lift continued to shake harder. For nine minutes the lift continued to drop in speed and shook until we slammed to a stop. The shaft outside the lift had thick black smoke pouring from below the rails. I looked up at the shaft, it appeared as though the lift had rammed through some of the hatches. The sides of the shaft had sparks spraying out of the metal walls. A few of the hatches were trying to move into the walls but the damage prevented them from moving into the walls. Some shards of metal fell from higher up the shaft and slammed into the top of the elevator. The roof of the lift cracked and a few pieces of glass fell from the roof.

Slowly the lift doors opened, as they moved they dug into the metal at the door's base. The doors opened only part of the way about two feet wide before they came to a halt. We climbed through the stuck doors and into the large two-story lobby we had previously been in. I looked back at the lift after we had walked into the room a few feet; the panel next to the door was no longer blue. Now the panel was a dark shade of black and had burnt marks on the panel itself and on the wall surrounding it.

"How are we supposed to get back up?" asked Crystal while she looked back at the elevator.

"I don't have a clue. I guess we should continue without the original plan and explore some more of this ship."

"I am curious if Marissa is still alive. I want to know."

"We can go and look for her in the same place Mallowon found you, David and Mike."

"That won't work. There are too many people in there."

"How did Mallowon find you three in the first place?"

"It was as if she already knew where to look for us. David asked how she was able to find us so easily. She said that as everyone was brought on board the ship we were divided into groups. Each group was assigned an area of the ship and while the groups were being formed we were asked for our names. I guess they have everyone's names in a data bank or file as well as what group we're in."

"That makes sense. Just before she left to look for you she used computer for a few minutes in a hidden computer room."

"Maybe we could use the computer to find Marissa?"

"I doubt it everything on the screen was in their handwriting. However, maybe we could get a Talin to help find her for us."

"And while we are at it we can see if our parents made it on board."

I didn't say anything to her nor could I look into her eyes. I didn't have the guts to tell her that her parents were dead. I know I should have but I just couldn't tell her. I know she will hate me if she ever found out that I knew and did not tell her. I felt that it was not my place to tell her, the truth.

"So, Alex, where is this computer room?"

"It's over there on the other side of that wall," I said, pointing to the wall on the elevator's right. "The computer room is just behind the wall. I am surprised that you did not see it when you walked past it earlier."

"I must have had my head turned," Crystal said, walking over to the wall. "So open the door already," she said, standing next to the wall.

I joined her next to the wall, smiled at her and placed my hand behind her head on the wall. The door opened like before. We crossed the threshold of the door and entered the hall lit dimly by blue lights. I walked out a few feet, turned to my left and entered into the computer room. Crystal followed me into the computer room. There were a few Talins like before working on some of the computers. There was also another person from another species immersed in its computer. None of the occupants of the room paid any attention to our arrival. We stood there scanning the room looking for a free computer. Crystal found a vacant computer in the back on the room.

We slowly and quietly walked to the back of the room. Once or twice as we went past, one of the occupants of the room would look up at us but would revert to their work seconds later. We reached the computer. There was only one chair to sit in so I let Crystal have it. Or should I say Crystal helped herself to it. We both looked upon the screen everything looked like gibberish; there were hundreds of symbols lines and shapes across the screen. I had no idea what any of the gibberish was. We stared at the screen for five to ten minutes when a hand fell upon my shoulder.

"How did you two get into this room? The control panel to this room is hidden from your people like most of panels. You should not have been able to have gotten in here without help. What was the name of the person who let you in here?" asked a female voice.

"Come on give me their names."

"No one let us in here," said Crystal.

"Really, then how did you get in then?"

"It's a long story, but the short of it is I can see the panels and apparently the prosthesis I was given here on this ship works on these bluish panels," I said while turning to face a horribly scarred Talin.

She reached down, grabbed my fake arm, and held it close to her face. She studied it for a few minutes and then let my arm go.

"What are you two doing in here anyways?"

"We wanted to find a friend and our parents."

"Well you came to the right place. How did you know to look here?"

"Doctor Mallowon brought me in here once before and then left to find Crystal and my other friends."

"So have you found who you are looking for?"

"No we can't read your written language."

"That would make it difficult, wouldn't it? Allow me to help you with your search."

"Thank you," said Crystal.

"I am not doing it for you, girl, I want my computer back and the sooner you are out of my way the sooner I can get back to work. What are their names?"

"My parents' names are Janis and Frank Cox."

"Sorry, little girl, they're not among the living," she said a minute after looking up their names.

"My parents' names are Jeff and Lorain Track."

"Sorry they did not make it either," she said a minute later.

"What about Marissa Harris, did she survive?"

"Yes she and her aunt survived." She then began to tell us how to find them.

"Could you give us a printout of where she is or a data pad with directions or maybe a map?"

"Do we have to do everything for you people...? Here take this data pad the directions are in you written language so you can find your way. There is also a map of the ship just in case you monkeys get lost. Now leave me to my work because of you monkeys, I am probably way behind schedule."

We left her to her work, and then we left the computer room. Crystal handed me the data pad. The screen read "Stupid Monkeys" across it.

"God...she is a nasty old hag...isn't she?" asked Crystal.

"Yes she is."

"She gave us a useless data pad, didn't she!"

"Maybe not, the screen has changed to a map. I guess she did give us what she said she would."

"She is still...a nasty old hag!"

"There is no doubt about that."

The data pad was now displaying the room we were standing in. The screen it appeared to have a flashing violet light with a sign saying "current position" in English. Surrounding the flashing light was a flat layout of the lobby indicated by white lines. There was a yellow line coming out of the light leading across the room past the broken elevator and through a double door. The screen displayed nothing beyond that point.

"Where...does it say to go?"

"Straight through those doors, that's all the map shows."

"Let's get going."

"Okay."

We began walking across the lobby. I glanced down at the data pad as we approached the doors. The flashing light didn't move from its position until the doors ahead of us opened and we passed through. The hallway in front of us was long and had doors on both walls about every five feet. The overall design of the hall was virtually identical to the rest of the hallways I have previously seen on this ship. The smooth chrome-like floor, was dull and had signs of damage and wear. There were a few signs that the floor had been polished; an extremely shinny spot here and there. There were specs of blood and dirt on the floor and also the walls. The walls mainly had bloody handprints stained on them.

We walked further into the hall; I glanced down at the data pad. The violet line extending from the flashing light continued deeper into the hall. We continued into the hall as well. As we progressed further in, the line on the data pad continued to move. The line changed directions after what seemed like forever. The line came to a stop turned to its left and continued through a door. We continued through the door and followed the map down another hallway identical to the previous hallway. We walked for close to ten minutes when the hall changed its directions and continued to our left. We continued to follow the map and the hall. We were led to the end of the hallway and another door. The door opened and there were thousands upon thousands of people walking about a large open room with a structure in the center.

The room had three levels. The four walls had three beds stacked atop of each other. The upper two levels had additional walls; the additional walls formed a path in between the wall of the room and the wall of the level. The additional walls had brakes every fourteen feet. The structure in the center of the room looked like large boxes; which were stacked to the ceiling of the room. Each one of the boxes was about fifteen feet high and each had windows. The top level had a few doors on the outer walls. There were about eight boxes in total; all of their sides appeared to the same length. While the boxes were fifteen feet high they appeared to be about twenty-five feet wide. All the boxes were about hundred feet from the walls of the upper two levels. There were a few bridges that were attached from the ceiling that connected the upper levels to the structure in the center of the room.

There were also ladders that reached from the upper levels all the way to the first level. The upper levels went out into the room about ten to twelve feet. The room had numerous kinds of lighting fixtures. Some of the lights were mounted on the walls others were hanging from the ceiling or embedded in the floor. From what I could see there were thousands of lights scattered throughout the room. On the first level there were some unusual plants growing in beds of grass surrounding the structure. The leaves were purple with a light green glow. The plants had small trucks that had cone shaped branches that extended two feet from the truck. The Talins don't actually designate planets with an individual name. The majority of the refugees referred to them as Conediy. There was a path from where we stood separating two of the Conediy beds to a door on the outside structure.

"Where now?" asked Crystal while looking around the room.

I looked at the data pad.

"We have to go through that door," I said, pointing to a door at the base of the closest box.

We walked across the room and passed through the door. On the other side of the door people were walking about the room gathering food and something to drink from the food and drink dispensers and then sitting down at one of the many tables available. The inside of the box looked a lot like the exterior of the box. The room was lit by four wall mounted lights about eight feet off the floor. Across from us was another door and off to our left there was another door. I looked at the map on the data pad. The line passed through the door ahead of us. A minute after I checked the map, Crystal and I walked across the room and passed through the door. This room was sectioned off. There were five sections in this room. Each section was cut off from the rest of the room by a thin wood wall.

Four of the five sections were positioned in the corners of the room. The fifth section was in the middle of the room. There was only a three-foot path that connected the cubicles. The length of the outside walls for each section was eleven feet. The two interior walls of the section were only eight foot. The walls of the center section were six feet on all sides. Both of the walls were eight feet long and were connected to a three-foot wall that possessed a door. The section in the middle of the room had a door on the wall on our right side.

I walked forward into the sectioned off room a little. I glanced at the data pad once again. The line led to the section in the middle of the room.

"Do you suppose she is in one of these rooms?" asked Crystal.

"I don't know, the map says to go into the center room."

We walked forward, turned to our right when we reached the wall of the center room. Then we walked forward a few feet then turned around and faced the door.

We walked through the door. In the center of the six-by-six-foot room was a ladder going to the box stacked above us.

"Ladies first," I said while bowing to her.

"Ah, ah, ah, a gentleman, how rare," Crystal said, climbing the ladder.

"I am positive you had other motives for me climbing the ladder first," she said while climbing.

"What can I say? I like the view. Ha-ha," I said as I started climbing.

"I bet you do," she said, stepping off the ladder and onto the floor of the next box.

"How could I not like your ass?" I said, stepping off the ladder.

"I thought as much, no gentleman here. Enough talk about my ass. Now where does the map say we have to go?"

We now stood in a room mostly identical to the room below us except there was no room in the middle and the three out of the four rooms in the corners were a little longer on the exterior walls. Aside from the four doors one to each room there were two doors one door ahead of us and the other door off to our left. The path behind us and off to our right was gone replaced by the walls of the rooms. This room was lit by lights mounted in the ceiling.

"Come on, where do we have to go now?" Crystal said, moving in front of me.

I looked once again at the data pad; the light was now flashing above the smallest of the four rooms.

"It looks as though they are in this room," I said, walking over to the smallest room.

Crystal walked over to the smallest room, knocked on the door three times and then stepped back. She waited a few minutes, no response and then knocked again. This time she knocked four times and a little harder. She stepped back again and waited for a few minutes. Then she stepped back up to the door and then started to knock as the door opened. A little girl named Marissa dressed in pajamas opened the door; standing behind the girl was an older looking woman maybe in her late forties.

"Hello, Alex. Hi, Crystal. Where have you been?"

"I am glad you and Marissa made it out of the military facility," said Crystal.

"I am glad you are alive but could you give us a few minutes to change and then we can talk."

"No problem, Laura."

The door closed and Crystal stepped back a little. We stood in the path for a short time; near ten minutes at least. The door opened and one tired child and one exhausted adult emerged.

"Since we're up we can get something to eat. Would you two like to join us? After how kind you were to my niece and how you helped her, the least I can do now is share a meal and conversation with the two of you," said Laura.

"Okay sounds like a great idea," said Crystal.

Laura walked over to the ladder and started to climb down followed by Marissa, Crystal and then me. We followed them out of the five cubical rooms and into the small cafeteria. Laura and Marissa walked over to one of the food dispensers, ordered some food and sat at a nearby empty table. Crystal and I got some food to eat, and then joined Laura and Marissa at the table. We began eating our food and as we ate Marissa kept asking questions about where we went and how we are doing. In between Marissa's questions Laura asked us how we survived the battle and if we knew anything. We finished our food and finished telling our stories when over the intercom Captain Movork spoke.

"Attention, we will be lifting off in a few minutes I want everyone at the ready it is likely we will be attacked again. All personnel to your stations and prepare to leave this planet's atmosphere."

"We should probably get back to the medical level as soon as we can."

"Alex, what happened to your arm?"

"Marissa."

"I'm sorry, Aunt Laura, I was just curious."

"It's okay, Marissa. I will tell you later but for now Crystal and I have to be getting back."

"I will come back down to see you again, Marissa. There is a lot we got to catch up on," said Crystal as she stood up from the table.

Crystal and I walked over to the door, turned and waved goodbye to the two of them. We passed through the door and began to walking on the path that passed in between two grassy gardens. The ship began to shake hard, harder than before. I could see that people who were up and about were having trouble staying on their feet. I looked over at Crystal who was having trouble remaining on her feet. The plants in the gardens swayed back and forth; the bridges connecting the upper levels rattled as they swayed. I walked over to Crystal. I wrapped my right arm around her and helped her regain her footing. We stumbled over to the door ahead of us. She used my weight to help hold her up. As we approached the door rattled as it opened for us.

The ship continued to shake; Crystal's weight forced us off balance, which sent us to the wall on our left. We continued further into the hall. Crystal now used the left wall for support as we walked. We made our way down the hall slowly. We followed the hallway to the end then passed through the door at the end of the hall. The alarms went off about three minutes later, turning the hallway red. A few of the doors ahead of us erupted with Talins, humans, and people from the other species. All were carrying guns. A very small number of them had swords strapped to their backs. Everyone ran in different directions. Most of the humans had a hard time running with all the turbulence. Some ran further down the hall others ran towards the lobby. Quite a few of them took places along the hall and had their weapons ready for combat. We walked down the hall back towards the lobby.

We passed dozens of soldiers along the way a small portion of them had a hard time standing still. They looked more nervous than anything. We reached the double door at the end of the hallway. We passed through the doors to the lobby. There were soldiers standing around the lobby. Some were positioned on the second level. Everyone aside from Crystal and I had a gun in hand. There were a few pieces of equipment laying up against the wall to our right. Some of the equipment was partly inside of the elevator. The damage to the lift appeared not to have been repaired. Crystal and I walked slowly across the hall making our way back to the entrance of the computer room. I opened the door like before. We passed through the entrance and then walked into the computer room. The room was no longer blue. The room was very well lit by bright white lights and we could clearly see everything in the room.

We walked a little further into the room. There were many Talins in the room; some were sitting in chairs in front of computers, others were standing behind the people sitting at the computers. The people standing were looking upon some of the computers. Others were standing at the back wall looking at a screen that took up the entire back wall. The screen displayed a map of the entire ship (every floor, every room, every hallway and every compartment). There were a few Talins that I did recognize in the room. The first was Hamole and the second was Whaloa. Whaloa was standing behind one of the operators observing the work being done on the computer. Hamole was at the back wall looking the map of the *Colonizer* over. We walked forward into the room further. Just about everyone was too busy to pay any attention to us moving into the computer room.

"Hey you two. What are you two doing back in here?" asked a nasty and familiar voice. "You humans are not allowed in here, now get out. Or you will be sent back to the surface of your planet."

"Shut up. These two have earned the right to be in here and since this is their planet being attacked they have the right to know what is happening. Besides, we need all the help we can get. Now get back to work or it is you that will be left on their planet. Do you understand?"

"Yes, Admiral Hamole!"

The nasty old hag walked back to the same computer she found us on earlier and sat down. Although she was ordered to go back to work her eyes were focused on us. I could feel her eyes trying to burn Crystal and me to a crisp. "She definitely had no love for humans."

"What are you two doing down here? I thought you and your friends were still on the medical level," asked Hamole.

"We wanted to come down to see if Marissa survived and we also wanted to see if our parents were alive."

"You picked a bad time to do that. How did you get down here anyways the elevator is extremely damaged?"

"About that, we were actually the last to use the lift and that was about forty minutes or more ago. Wait a minute, how did you get down here? We left before you and we were the last to us the elevator."

"There are elevators that go all the way down the ship from the command level down to the ground floors. These elevators hold three people only and they have possible stops at every level of this ship. These elevators are slower but at the moment are the only ways to get from the top of the ship to the lower levels. You two are very lucky to have survived the crash of the main lift. Due to the damage we received from the last battle some of the systems on this ship have been acting up. The lift's speed controls was one of those systems instead of a controlled rate of drop the lift continued to pick up speed erratically. It turns out that some of the hatches were also affected because they did not open when you began your descent. So like I said you are extremely lucky."

"What is happening now Hamole?" asked Crystal.

"We have left earth's atmosphere and are now in space engaging the Shadows' forces. But there is a likely chance that they will try to board us. So any and every one that can fight have been asked to fight."

"Is there anything we can do to help?" asked Crystal.

"Yes there is, but it puts you two in danger. We have a warship rendezvousing with us shortly. What we need is as many people armed and willing to fight for their survival. We need to hold off the enemy until the *Franchasno*, the ship en route, gets here."

"We don't have any weapons with us," said Crystal.

"Crystal, that's not entirely true my prosthesis has weapons built into its case."

"As for you, Crystal, we have a few weapons in this room in case we ever needed them. Alex, go talk to Whaloa; she will reactivate your arm's weapons and instruct you on how to best use them. Crystal, come with me so you can pick out a weapon."

I walked across the room over to Whaloa. She was still observing a Talin working on the computer in front of her. Crystal went with Hamole over to the back wall, turned and walked to the right and passed through a door that was pretty well hidden.

"Excuse me, Whaloa."

"Hello, Alex. I heard everything Hamole said. Let me see your arm."

I raised my arm to her. She looked at my prosthesis then pushed on the forearm. The small hidden computer rose out of my arm. Whaloa began pushing on a few buttons with her fingers.

"All you have to do to get your arm to fire is to think about shooting your prosthesis and it will fire on your thought. Be careful. To shoot your rockets, bend your wrist down and they will fire. Be careful not to overuse your prosthesis's weapons; it can get very hot, possibly too hot for you to handle."

"Thank you, Whaloa."

"No need to thank me. I am doing my job. I recommend you get your hands onto a gun to be even more careful. One last thing the weapons will not fire unless opened. All you got to do is bend your wrist once to open it and a second time switches your prosthesis into the rocket mode."

"Thank you again."

I left Whaloa to her work. What she suggested was a good idea. I walked over to the hidden door. Crystal and Hamole were still in the room looking through the weapons they had in stock. I walked through the doorway. The room had many guns, swords, and one or two shields. Crystal was looking through the guns trying to find something that fit her and was comfortable to use.

"Is it alright if I have a gun too?"

"It is fine. The more I thought about it the more sense it made for you to have one. Go ahead choose whatever you want just make it fast. The enemy could break through our fighters at any time."

I walked around the room looking at as many of the guns as I could. I saw a few things that I wanted to use but decided not to take everything. I came across a gun that was lightweight and smaller than the hybrid rifle that I had. Crystal found herself a gun perfect for her, roughly the same length as the one I picked but wider. We left the small armory and returned to the computer room. As we left the room there was a loud crash from outside the room. The lights of the computer room darkened and the room shook. The lights came back on the map, to our right was flashing in several spots across the *Colonizer*.

"Not good, seven enemy transports have breached our shields and hull. We have to remove the enemy before they can do anymore damage," said Hamole.

"Where is the closest one?"

"Not good, not good at all. The closest transport is right outside this room in the lobby."

"Shouldn't the soldiers in the lobby be able to handle the enemy?"

"If any of them survived the crash, they were most likely either killed or turned. In any case we are going to have to try and deal with them ourselves."

"Hamole, we are going to need more firepower than what we have on us."

"Alex, you're right. We need more weapons; back into the armory."

We picked up the shields, strapped the swords to our backs. We put on some armor, a few additional guns, and we pocketed a few grenades. If the three of us were going to die clearing the lobby, we were going to take as many of the enemy down as we could.

"Whaloa, bring up the cameras in the lobby. We need to know where the enemies are."

"Here you are, Hamole."

The screen in the back changed from a map of the ship to a few cameras' points of view of the lobby. A few of the cameras were no longer working. The lobby was trashed, where the large monitor once stood was now a large black cone ship which had dug deep into the floor. The room was no longer filled with light there was black everywhere. There looked to be some of the hounds and a few of the two-legged creatures scattered about. The closest enemy was ten feet away from us and faced in the opposite direction.

"The rest of them must have gone through the doors in the lobby. Hopefully none of them decides to come back any time soon. Come on let's go, Alex and Crystal. We have to deal with these foul beasts in the lobby first."

Hamole walked to the door to the lobby we followed. I was getting nervous now.

The door opened and we stepped into the lobby. The lobby was truly trashed and dark. Luckily there was still enough light to see. From what I could see there was only twenty of the enemy forces in the lobby. We were greatly outnumbered, but for some reason I was no longer afraid of the enemy. I looked around the room there was debris and rubble everywhere. We walked slowly along the lobby's elevator wall. We walked as tight to the wall as we could. Hamole led us over to the double doors. One of the doors had been ripped out of the wall and now lay on the floor. A portion of the wall also had been removed along with the door.

"Get a grenade out of one of your pockets. We are going to draw them into the hallway. Wait until I say to throw," said Hamole quietly.

We stepped onto the door and crossed the threshold of the doorway. There were black bodies both of the enemy and of burnt soldiers. The floor and the walls were scorched and the lights sent sparks raining down to the floor. The sparks provided very poor lighting to see; only providing brief orange flashes of light which hardly penetrated the darkness.

"From here I can only see two Shadow hounds. They both are on the second level. That is all we need to get their full attention."

Hamole took aim with his gun and shoot across the room. He hit his target on its side; the hound howled and fell to the floor of the second level. The second hound looked up at its comrade's cry when Hamole shot again. The blast from his gun flew across what was left of the lobby. Hamole's second shot hit its mark as well. The hound's head was taken right off the dog's shoulders. The head had exploded when Hamole's shot hit sending the remains of the head up against the back wall. The room roared with what sounded like an anger mob screaming.

"Move further back and arm those grenades," Hamole said, backing up into the hall.

We joined in his retreat into the hall. We had to step over a few of the bodies on the floor as we moved deeper into the hall. What light there was left in the lobby was darkened as a mass of blackness descended upon the entrance of the hallway. The entrance of the hall howled and then moved into the room.

"Throw now," Hamole yelled with a trace of fear in his voice.

Crystal and I threw the grenades at the mass of black. Weapons fire flew down the hall and struck a couple of the enemy. We joined Hamole and shot upon the enemy. Our weapons fire hit two different humanoid enemies. I hit one on the leg separating the leg from its owner. Crystal's struck the chest of an enemy, forcing a hole right through its abdomen. We continued firing upon the mass of enemies. A few seconds later came a loud pop, and then the entrance of the hall was filled with the black mass turning to a bright shiny orange. The air grew hot and dry very quickly. The mass of black matter was replaced by a hot orange fireball. The fireball consumed the whole mass of enemies and branched out further into the hall while growing in brightness. The fire crawled along the walls floor and ceiling for a few seconds before the fireball began to slow. After a few seconds the fire clasped in upon itself.

The fireball faded away, all that was left of the enemy was burnt statues. We stared at the burnt figures before us hoping the blaze of fire killed all the intruders. After a few minutes Hamole turned and started to walk down the hall once more. Crystal and I began to follow him down the hallway. "RROAAR!" A roar came from behind us. The three of us turned back to the entrance of the hallway when a red hound charged through the burnt statues. The statues crumbled into dust as the hound forced its way through. We raised our guns when the hound lunged over Crystal and me. Hamole was forced to the ground by the red hound. The hound snarled into Hamole's face, its claws were pushing down upon Hamole's shoulders. The hound snapped its jaws shut biting down on Hamole's gun.

"Don't fire upon the hound. You could hit me."

"Then what are we supposed to do?"

"The black substance around its body is gone we could try and pull the hound off or one of you could use your swords and kill this blasted thing."

I set my shield down and then pulled out my sword and swung as hard as I could. I struck it dead in the back of the neck. A few trickles of blood ran down its neck from the small cut left by my sword. The hound paid no attention to my attack and continued to snap at Hamole. I swung again at its neck; more trickles of blood ran down the sides of its neck. I removed my blade from the cuts on its neck and stabbed the point of my blade into its neck as hard as I could. The tip dug into its flesh a few inches. The hound moved back a few inches snapping the tip of my sword, leaving the tip in its neck. The hound returned to its attacks upon Hamole.

"Come on, do something. I don't know how long my gun can take this kind of punishment."

Crystal and I looked at each other and then grabbed the hound by its back legs and pulled with every fiber of our beings. The hound didn't move an inch; we continued to pull.

"SSTOP WHAT YOU'RE DOINGGGG! TRY SOMETHING ELESSSSS!" Hamole yelled as the hound removed its claws from Hamole's gun and dug into his sides.

We let go of its legs and the hound returned to its attacks upon Hamole.

Running out of ideas, I reached under the dog's razor sharp neck and grabbed its neck with my right hand. I squeezed as hard as I could I couldn't tell if I was doing any damage to it or not so I just kept applying pressure on its neck. But still the hound continued its attacks. If only I could shoot the damn beast we would be rid of this foul creature. I felt a surge of force from under the hound's neck. The hound twitched a little then fell to its side and went limp.

"Thank you, but I told you not to shoot the hound," Hamole's said, standing up with a face covered in the hound's darkish red blood.

Hamole spat some of the blood out of his mouth and then wiped his face on his uniform. He looked at his gun and tossed it to the floor. Almost the entire width of the gun had been eaten. There were large teeth marks cutting through the remaining inches of the gun. There was about a nine-inch gap in the length of Hamole's gun. Hamole removed a gun from his right side; the gun was covered in Hamole's blood. Both of his sides were wet from where the hound had clawed him. I could see that he had to be in pain although his face didn't show it.

"We should make sure there are no more of the enemy in the transport and lobby," Hamole said, walking over to the reddish hound and kicked it in its side.

I looked at the hound's neck, or what was left of its neck, and the lower portion of its mouth, both were gone replaced with blood. There didn't appear to be any bone left in its neck. Hamole kicked the beast once more then walked towards the lobby door and poked his head into the lobby.

"The lobby looks empty; let's have a look at the transport," Hamole said, walking into the lobby.

Crystal and I walked over to the lobby entrance and walked through the doorway. Along the outside of the doorway there were a few of the enemy bodies and a few had been reduced to ash. The side of the door facing the lobby was mostly clean, only burnt marks on the doorframe. There didn't appear to be anything other than us alive in the lobby. We slowly moved closer to the transport ship paying close attention to the ship's details for signs of life. We moved even closer to the ship. Its exterior had a shinny black coating on its surface. The shinny coating looked similar to the substance covering the skin of the enemy. The substance began to move slowly down the exterior of the transport ship and fell to the floor with a splat.

Judging from the floor it appeared that the substance had crawled along the transport ship's hall and fell to the floor many times before. We observed the substance movements for a few minutes then Hamole slowly moved closer to the ship. He looked closer at the ship and slowly he began to walk around its exterior. After he went almost three thirds of the way around, he moved in even closer then stepped up onto a pile of debris that circled the nose of the transport. He chose his footing carefully to keep from losing his balance and falling face first into the substance on the transport. He took a grenade from one of his pocket and tossed it into the transport ship. He quickly moved away from the transport and motioned for us to do the same.

The section where Hamole tossed the grenade lit up quickly. A second later a bubble of fire emerged from the ship's side. The bubble of fire stretched thirteen feet from the transports side. It reached one of the upper level's walls; the wall was instantaneously blackened.

The enemy transport ship sizzled and moaned as the fire crawled throughout the ship. The fire went out and all that was left was streams of smoke rising from the transports opening. The black substance stopped moving and then became dry and stiff.

"Admiral, our forces need help in cargo bay four," Whaloa said, walking out of the computer room.

"Thank you, Whaloa. Alex, Crystal, would you lend me your assistance."

"I'm in."

"We really have no choice but to help, don't we?"

Chapter Fifteen
A Debt Paid (Part 3)

Hamole led us across the lobby back through the doorway and down the hallway. As we walked at the ready, down the hall we had to step over numerous bodies lying dead and bleeding on the floor. We continued deeper into the hallway; the bodies began to thin the deeper we went. It seemed like we walked for an hour or more. I reached into my right pocket and removed the data pad with the map on it. After walking a ways down the hallway; we came upon a hole in the right wall. Chunks of the wall lay on the floor ahead of us along side what remained of the door. The door had been ripped from the wall and thrown to the opposite wall. The hole in the wall was nine feet in width and was over nine feet in height. Whatever caused the hole dug into the ceiling a few feet; in places I could see very small holes leading to a next level.

Hamole stepped through the hole and over a mound of debris. Some of the debris shifted a bit as he crossed the threshold of the hole. Crystal and I joined Hamole on the other side of the hole. The hall ahead of us was in shambles. There were bodies (mostly Talins and humans) lying on the floor or sitting against the walls bleeding with their torsos ripped in half or with claw marks dug deep into their flesh. There was blood everywhere; pools of blood clotting on the chrome floor, streaks of blood stretched along the walls darkening the red paint and there were a few blood marks on the ceiling. There were few bodies of the enemy anywhere in the hall. I counted about ten bodies in total. Aside from the blood and all the bodies there were claw marks on the walls, ceiling, and the floor. Like the hallway before this one there were a few blackened spots in the hall. There were a few doors in this hallway only two of the six doors had been ripped from its hinges. One of the doors was the first hole we crossed over and the second was the second door on our left.

Like the first door, the second door had been thrown across the hall and now lay a few feet further into the passageway. Beyond the door there didn't appear to be any battle damage of any kind. The hole ripped in the left wall was slightly smaller than the one behind us, close to five feet wide and only as high as the ceiling about seven feet. The hole in the wall led to a small hallway with only two doors on the right. The remains of a doorway lay on the hallway's floor. This hall was twenty feet long and had the same design as the halls before it. There were also bodies lying on the floor and against the walls. The door to the hole in front of us lay on the floor on top of a dead Talin. The Talin under the door looked like she had been crushed. Only her head, an arm, and a few inches of her chest weren't under the door. The rest of her was under the door and was greatly flatter; the door was only slightly off balance.

"We are here," said Hamole.

On the other side of the hole of the smaller hall was a large room that was at least the size of a football field close to a hundred yards from where we stood to the wall ahead of us; the room was close to fifty feet wide. We walked into the room. The room had obvious signs that a battle had taken place. In the center of the room there was five men still alive and standing tall. Two of the five men I recognized. Stan and Jack were standing with their weapons at the ready and aimed towards us. After a few seconds they lowered their guns. Bodies from both sides surrounded them. Half of the bodies were Talin and human and the other half was of the enemy forces.

Black blast marks covered the floor in front of us; and the hole we just passed through. The room had boxes and fuel tanks off to our right and left; there were also boxes along the far wall and a few boxes lined up in the center of the room. There were a few bodies lying over some of the boxes; their hands still clung to their weapons. Boxes stacked up top of each other lined both the right and left walls. Burn marks and blood painted the walls of boxes. There was a door left open across from us on the opposite wall.

We started to walk into the room. As we walked into the room we had to step over the countless bodies that covered the cargo bay floor. We walked to the center of the room joining the five of them.

"Were you the ones that called for help?" asked Hamole.

"No we responded to the sounds of the enemy. We arrived just a few minutes ago."

"What is your name?"

"Captain Markus Hasse and these four are what's left of my squad."

"Have you surveyed the room for survivors?"

"No we haven't."

"That is what we should do now."

"And who are you to give orders?" asked Markus.

"I am Admiral Hamole of the Talin military force."

"My apologies, sir. You heard the man, start surveying the bodies for survivors," said Markus.

"If you find any survivors call me over. If you find an enemy alive kill it, do not let it live," said Hamole as he started his task.

We slowly walked around the room surveying the bodies on the ground. We found dead body after dead body; there was practically no sign of life anywhere in the room. The eight of us spread out over cargo bay four's floor. Hamole began to look through the dead bodies in the center of the cargo bay. Crystal walked over to the right side of the cargo bay and looked along the wall. I did the same thing Crystal did except on the opposite wall. The others looked around the room in various spots. I walked over to the left side and looked at the bodies lying around on the floor. I walked through one continuous pool of blood my shoes left ripples in their wake. Some of the bodies were too badly injured, to still have been alive. Some large cuts starting an inch blow the neck to a few inches above the waist. Some of those cuts had forced some organs outside of the body.

Some of the other victims of the battle had had their heads removed or some of their limbs; other bodies had been cut into two different pieces (either across the waist or from head to toe). There didn't appear to be anyone left alive in the room just the remnants of a battle. I reached the end of cargo bay four and I didn't find a person alive. Hamole had cleared a path by moving the victims' remains closer to the right and left walls. He left the remains of the Shadow hounds and Shadow soldiers (the two legged creatures) where they lay.

"Hamole, I found a few survivors over here," Crystal yelled from across the room.

Hamole set the last body down and carefully walked through the field of remains. He had to leap over a few of the bodies a few times before he was able to continue. I started making my way across the room; as I went I looked upon some of the victims on the floor. The victims were too badly injured, to be alive so I didn't stop to check for a pulse. Every corpse that I saw had fatal wounds somewhere on them. The enemies lying dead of the floor had holes shot through their sides or a hole blown into their head. A few of the remains on the cargo bay floor twitched once or twice when I walked past.

I joined Hamole and Crystal on the right side of cargo bay four. The others joined us a few seconds later. There were three survivors, one Talin and the other two were human. The Talin was lying on the floor; he had cuts deep into his limbs and a few on his torso. One of the humans was sitting with her back against the wall holding her right side and her chin resting on her chest. The second human was lying on his right side; his back was up against one of the boxes along the wall. He had a pool of blood surrounding his abdomen. I didn't see any wounds on his left side. All three of the survivors were still breathing; however, they were taking long and slow breaths. Hamole walked over to the Talin; kneeled next to him and looked at his wounds. Hamole ripped off one of the survivor's sleeves and gazed at the injured limb. Hamole stood up, pulled his weapon and without hesitation or a second thought, Hamole pulled the trigger on his weapon and shot the injured Talin in the head.

Hamole walked over to the closer of the two remaining survivors. Closest to Hamole was the male soldier lying on his side. Hamole knelt next to the soldier and started to roll the man onto his back. As Hamole moved the man; his blood began to pour out from his sides; a few trashed organs fell out of him and onto the floor. After that the man didn't live much longer only three minutes maximum. Hamole rolled the man back onto his side stood back up and walked the remaining distance to the female soldier. Once again he knelt down. Hamole looked upon the female soldier, and then at her injury.

"You will live, won't you?" Hamole asked her.

"Yes," she said, looking up at Hamole.

"What is your name?"

"Jessica."

She looked to be close to Crystal's and my age. She had long filthy, dirty blond hair. Her face was covered with her long hair. Hamole helped her to her feet and asked for a better look at her wound. She winced with pain as she pulled her shirt high enough for Hamole to see the wound. She pulled her left side of her shirt up; she had a fist size black and blue mark surrounded by a light red circle.

"You don't look like you were too badly injured," Hamole said, stepping back a few inches.

"Well I was hit…"

"Not now; I need to know how many are left and which way they went."

"I don't know exactly how many are left; however, I would say anywhere from fifteen to thirty and I didn't exactly see which way they went."

"Since we didn't see any of them on our way here, they must have gone through the open door. Grab some of the guns on the floor and come with us we are going to rid this ship of those horrid beast."

"You're kidding? They made short work of us. Just look around you they tore through us in a few minutes. We had over a hundred soldiers and the enemies you see dead are from a few grenades. There is no way that the nine of us will be able to eliminate the enemy. They are too powerful."

"We may be outnumbered but we have to try anyways. If we could lure the enemy back into this room, we could use the explosive containers to even the playing field. We can't move the containers because they are far too heavy to move and the enemy may notice that it's a trap. The six of you go through the open door and look for the enemy slowly. If you find any large groups of the enemy, retreat to this room. If you find any stray Shadows, kill them before they kill you or worse. After you have found the enemy and have returned to this room, run across the room and through the broken doorway. The three of us will be at the end of the hall with the trigger to some explosives. I will have a camera in the room to see where the enemy is in relation to you. After you hear the explosion, continue running or you will be cooked alive. Alex, before you leave can I have a word with you."

"Stan, Jack, Adam, go with them they will need as much help as possible," said Markus as soon as Hamole had finished.

I walked over to Hamole. We both walked a little on the path he had made.

"Alex, use your right arm; it will do more damage to the enemies. Don't forget your arm has two ways of firing; use both if you have to but try to be careful."

"I will."

"Alright; the six of you get going," Hamole said, coming to a stop.

The six of us walk along the remainder of Hamole's path and passed through the open doorway. We entered into another hallway. The walls had claw marks dug deep in their surfaces. The tar-like ooze was smeared along the surface of the chrome floor. In amongst the black ooze were pools of blood; however, there was no corpses anywhere in the hall. There were doors on both sides of the hall all of which were closed tight and had no damage a side from the claw marks left in the doors' surface. We walked further into the hall for ten maybe fifteen minutes before we came to a change in the direction of the enemy. A door on our left side had been beaten from the wall and lay on the floor surrounded by debris. The surface of the door had claw marks running across numerous dents. We cautiously passed through the opening in the wall. The six of us had our weapons armed, ready to fire and aimed down the hall just in case we were attacked.

We passed through two living quarters three more halls and a second lobby before we found anything alive. We came to a stop when we found some Talins alive in a hallway. This hall was covered in blood and had signs that a massacre took place. Only four Talins had survived the encounter. The hallway had bodies ripped apart lying scattered about on the floor. Two of the Talins were only five to six feet from us both of whom had their weapons aimed through the doorway in front of them. One of the other two Talins was only three feet from the first two and had his weapon aimed toward the last Talin. The last Talin was at the end of the hall with her weapon aimed down another hallway. We began to walk further into the hallway when the Talin at the end of the hall screamed and a second later stopped.

We focused on her. She had dropped her gun; her hands were now wrapped around something that pierced her torso. I tried to see what she was holding; however, my view was cut short as the third Talin crossed in front of my view and opened fire on the last Talin. The two Talins turned from their positions in front of the doorway and aimed past the third Talin and began firing down the hall. The three of them filled the width of the hall making it so I was unable to see what they were firing upon. A few seconds later the firing stopped. As the first two Talins started to turn back towards the door, both of their backs exploded sending blood and organs onto the walls. Coming out of their backs was a translucent hand covered in blood and remnants of organs. A second later they were ripped in half. Their torsos fell to the ground in one direction and their legs went in another. The enemies' right hand was covered in the remnants of the two Talins.

Crystal, Jessica, Stan, Jack, Adam, and I raised our weapons and fired upon the two near invisible enemies. As our fire flew down the hall both of the enemies moved back through the doorway. Our fire flew past them and struck the third Talin on his chest and his right arm. One of our shots struck a third translucent enemy in the head. A second after our shots hit the Talin and the enemy, the Talin's chest exploded into the hall and then they both fell to the ground.

"Keep...firing!" said the third Talin before he died.

We immediately understood why he said that and began to fire down the hall as we slowly backed up through the smashed door. We slowly passed through what was left of the doorway to provide cover for our party. We were all through the doorway except for Adam. He was further in the hall still firing upon the enemy. Jack and I fired past him while he slowly backed up. Suddenly out of the blue Adam was thrown to the left of the hall with such force that he crashed through the wall. His neck and spine snapped on impact causing him to bend in half. We turned and ran as fast as we could through the hallway. We had made it to the second lobby and just ran across the floor to the hallway we had come from. As we reached the doorway the door opposite us erupted with Shadows of all kinds.

We continued to fire behind us while we ran down the hallway. A few seconds later we came upon the entrance to the first of the two living quarters. We turned to our left and ran through the ravaged room. As we passed through the room we threw our guns to the floor, pulled out our last guns and fired upon the enemy. We ran down another hallway and turned left again passing through the second living quarters. The whole time that we ran we shot blindly back at the mass of enemies. We knew that we were outnumbered and outgunned and the only reason we fired upon the mass of charging Shadows is that we slowed them down a little with every shot. We left the living quarters quickly as we did we discarded our empty guns to the floor.

We just ran down the hallway until we reach the first smashed hallway. The girls were now in front of Jack and Stan and they were in front of me as we ran through the doorway. I felt a drag on my right side as my arm bounced off some of the debris still attached to the wall and then it hit me. I stopped, turned quickly to face down the previous hall and a second later my wrist separated. Two sections came out of my wrist one on top of my wrist and the other was below my wrist. Immediately missiles lunched from the top section of my wrist followed by shots from the lower side of the prosthesis. The missiles exploded on impact sending a small portion of the mob to the floor, the blasts from the lower section struck a few of the Shadows sending them also to the floor.

Although I did damage to the mob they did not slow to attend to their fallen comrades. Instead they moved over their comrades' bodies. I fired again and then turned and ran down the hall. As I ran down the hall I would partially turn towards the mob and fire another set of missiles upon them. There was still too many for me to make much of a difference but I had to try, if anything it slowed them down a little bit. I came in view of the cargo bay, fired another set of missiles, and ran even harder. I passed through the door and ran along Hamole's path. I didn't dare fire another set of missiles this close to the explosive containers. I crossed through the ripped open doorway and into the hallway. Hamole, Crystal, and Jessica were at the end of the hall. Stan and Jack were just making it to them.

Both the girls were motioning for us to hurry up. I saw Hamole look down for a second then he looked up and pushed down upon a small box in front of him. He and the girls disappeared behind the walls of the doorway. Stan and Jack leaped over a small barricade Hamole, Markus and the other solider had built. I heard a loud pop and then a thunderous explosion that shook the floor beneath my feet rushed over me. I kept my balance and continued to run down the hall as the temperature of the air rapidly grew hot as fire crawled along the floor, walls, and ceiling. The horrendous force from the explosion quickly caught up to me forced me to the floor. I could feel the extreme heat of the hot air as it washed over me. I felt pain across my forehead as my head bounced off the floor and then everything went dark. I awoke running out of a familiar structure; my blood was hot, pumping fast, and hard. I was eager to fight and ready to die if it came to that. I was nowhere near scared. The pain on my hands and face had grown. I was surrounded by Shadows; however, I felt nothing towards them. No anger, no hatred, no love and no friendship, nothing at all.

We charged through the hall our enemy entered from, meeting no resistance we continued outside. Our party was now pushing fifty stronger or larger. We charged out into a field full of craters surrounded by dirt and a massive army. An army consisting of all three species looked to be five times larger than the force of the last battle. Even greatly outnumbered I was still not terrified instead I was still pumped and eager to battle my enemy.

We charged against an overwhelming enemy and a large portion of our enemies mainly the third species charged at us. As they moved closer, they kicked up dust which blocked the view of the rest of our enemy's army. After a few minutes of running we engaged the enemy. We clashed and were soon getting our asses handed to us. For every one of us, there were five of them. We fought hard taking as many of them out as we could before we were all killed. We were almost wiped out when suddenly there was explosion from above and suddenly a bright flash of white light fell over the field. I felt warm and rejuvenated as the light faded and the battlefield had changed for the better and worse. The third species was frozen stiff. They were no longer attacking what was left of my party. They turned towards the horizon, which had changed considerably.

The horizon was now black and was at war with the third species making very quick work of them. Those of us that still remained in our party took the opportunity to do as much damage to our surrounding enemy as we could. We moved quick and hard, not giving them enough time to gather their thoughts or realize what we were doing. We dropped close to forty of the enemy before we were once again battling the remains of our enemy's force. The last enemy fell; its blood and the blood of its comrades soaked into the brown dirt which covered the surface of the land.

My head moved from side to side, there was no more enemy forces in sight only new soldiers all with the same drive to win I had. We turned back towards the structure and began to walk back inside.

Everything went dark again. I opened my eyes. I wasn't back home at my house, I wasn't on the *Colonizer* and I wasn't outside walking back inside the structure. Instead I was in a city. The buildings looked organic like they were living, breathing structures.

I moved my head around looking at everything there was to see in the city. I was standing in the middle of a road surrounded by my brothers and the organic city. My comrades in front of me began to move along the road. The Shadows on the outside of our group were looking into the thin glass-like membrane of the buildings. Some of my comrades broke from the group, jumped through the thin membrane, and slaughtered the inhabitants of the buildings. Only two of the inhabitants survived only now they were on our side and saw as we saw.

Our two new comrades were bug-like creatures with wings on their back which allowed them to fly. The flying bugs circled our party at a fast speed. Now even they wanted to kill or convert their former species. A small part of me felt guilty and sorry for them briefly. We moved further down the road passing organic structure after organic structure. Every once in a while some of my brothers would charge through the thin clear membrane and slaughter some of this planet's inhabitants. On a few occasions my brothers would return with converters.

We had walked to the end of the road. In front of us was a large white structure with organic looking walls. The structure was large; the top of the structure was a long cylinder. The top had massive doors folded down to its side. At the base of the structure there were large doors around forty feet wide and twenty feet high. Each one had metal bars going down to the ground in between the metal bars was more of the thin clear membrane. The Shadow soldiers ahead of me lunged into the doors. When they came in contact with the doors they fell down to the ground. They got to their feet and charged at the door again and once again they fell to the floor again.

They continued to charge the doors and fell to the ground. I could hear my fellow comrades' frustration in the form of loud grunts and screams. No matter how much my comrades slammed into the membrane their attempts failed. Above the doors a handful of the inhabitants had quickly gathered and was excreting a dark green fluid from their hands on top of some of our group. I could only see half of the group of inhabitants. Their waists were hidden from my view by a part of a wall.

These natives were different from the bug-like natives. These didn't look as tall as we were and had spikes coming off of their hands and arms. Their chest was protected with a bone-like plate. They had large eyes that went around their heads. Their torso was connected to a small neck maybe only inches thick and black. Along the sides of their torso were small limbs that seemed to be useless. These inhabitants reminded me of an ant and in a lot of ways they looked like it too. I couldn't tell what it was that they were excreting from their hands; however, whatever it was had little effect on us.

In the sky our new comrades flew through the air and attacked the group above. Immediately the group above us retaliated to our air attack. The group's attack moved to our brothers in the sky. Their excretions flew across the sky; coming in contact with my brothers. A few of the excretions landed square on the head of the Shadow bugs above. My brothers in the sky flew through the heavy bombardment of enemy attacks and swooped down upon the enemy above. I watched as blood of the enemy rained down on my comrades. A dark green blood covered my brothers charging the door.

The ground began horrendously shaking. I looked around at our surroundings. There was nothing in the vicinity that could be causing the tremors. The sounds of my comrades charging the doors were drowned out by a thunderous bang. The upper parts of the structure dropped a couple about twenty feet towards the ground and then recoiled back up. When the upper parts reached the top, a large mass of rock was hurled out of the structure and was lunched into the sky. I watched as the mass of rock climbed into the air and vanished from view. A few seconds later there was a flash of light above followed by an explosion. The mass of rock came in contact with one of our warships and had destroyed it.

The group of Shadows surrounding me grew with anger and hatred. My blood boiled with the death of so many of my brothers. Some of my brothers began growing restless, so they began to attack the sides of the structure. At first the walls only cracked slightly. However, as their attacks continued the cracks turned into small holes. I slowly moved forward through the legion of my brothers until I reached the right side of the structure. I joined my brothers in their assault on the wall. Every time I slammed into the wall with my shoulders and my head, pain would rush through my body and disappear at my feet.

The wall began to crumble in front of us. After a few more minutes the wall gave way and the inside of the structure was revealed. The legion immediately began to force our way through the opening. Inside there were six groups of about a dozen or so of the ant-like enemy. As soon as we entered the structure the enemy began to excrete the fluid at us. My comrades in front of us were covered in the enemy's excretions. My comrades covered in the enemies' excretions fell to the floor as their whole body stiffened. They shattered into tiny pieces when they came crashing to the floor. This made the blood of every one of us in the structure boil even more. We charged further and faster into the room and quickly engaged the enemy.

We lunged at the enemy. I was hit a few times by the enemy's attempts to stop us. I felt their excretions stiffening my legs and arms. However, the stiffening didn't slow me down enough to stop my anger or my attacks. We charged into the closest group and after a few swipes from our hand we ripped through their bodies. Blood flew in every direction. I could feel the blood running off of the black tar-like skin that covered my body. There was blood everywhere on the floor. We continued on to the next group and began to tear them limb from limb. A small part of me felt really bad for them; however, an even larger part of me was glad they died and that part of me wanted more death by my hands.

The entrance of the structure quickly filled with my brothers. The enemy tried to retreat; however, we rushed upon them not giving them a chance to retreat. Their blood rained down onto the floor as we charged through the remaining enemies. Their screams echoed throughout the entrance for a few seconds before drifting off into silence. We continued deeper into the structure. With every corridor we entered, we met light resistance. A few of the other Shadows fell and shattered as they were consumed by the enemy's excretions. We climbed level after level, passing through hallway after hallway and room after room. The enemy's forces in the structure grew thinner the higher and deeper we climbed. After forty minutes of slaughtering we came to a room with no exit aside from the door we had passed through.

The room was large and had large organic looking controls resting on the floor and screens hanging from the ceiling and the walls. There were only seven of the enemy in the control room and they didn't look like they were paying attention to the commotion my comrades and I were making. There were two of the enemies stationed at the workstation on both the right and left wall and the other three enemies were across from us. One of them stood in the middle of the wall looking up at a large screen with their planet displayed upon it. Surrounding their planet was hundreds of Shadow warships and fighters. Some of our ships had been destroyed and were now a cloud of wreckage.

With in the wreckage there was a large cluster of rocks floating among the debris. There were also a few ships in orbit and they were engaging the Shadow ships. These ships looked strange mostly organic with a blend of technology mixed in. From the looks of the battle the enemy was winning against our space forces even though we outnumbered them three to one. These structures similar to large canons gave the enemy a large advantage. Every Shadow in the room knew we had to take control of the canons and use them on the enemy.

We ran into the room screaming and roaring as loud as we could into the room. The enemies stopped what they were doing and turned to face us. All of their faces were plastered with fear. They ducked behind the computer consoles on the floor and began excreting the fluid out of their right arms. Some of my party took the excretions to their face and continued to charge. Others were hit in their legs and arms which slowed them down; however, not enough to stop their assault. The enemy's blood poured out as we tore into their flesh. I could feel bones crumble as my hand dug through their bodies. They made no sound as they were slaughtered; they had no time to, they were dead in seconds of our attack. The console in the room were covered and dripping with the blood of their former operators.

We removed some of the corpses that lay on top of the consoles and then some of us took positions at the consoles. After a few minutes my brothers at the controls to this weapon began to roar and moan. I could tell that they were getting frustrated with the controls due to the fact they didn't know how to operate or read them. With every passing minute their frustration grew. A couple of them hit the surface of the console and walked away growling to themselves. Ten minutes went by and no progress was made forcing my remaining comrades to abandon their positions. We regrouped and started to head for the door when the door opened and our new bug-like comrades flew into the room.

They rushed past us and then took positions in front of the consoles and began to operate them. We watched them work on the controls for three, maybe four minutes when the structure began to rapidly and tremendously shake. The large screen at the back of the room focused in upon one of the enemy ships. A few seconds later a large rock ripped through the enemy ship. There was a brief white cloud surrounding the ship's wreckage seconds after the rock came in contact with the ship and seconds before the ship erupted in flames. The fire lasted for less than a minute before it was extinguished by the cold vacuum of space. The screen began to grow dark slowly followed by the rest of the room. The moans and screams of the Shadows quieted to a whisper then vanished.

The room went completely dark not a glimmer of light shined anywhere I turned my head. It was too dark to see anything including my own hands. I tried to walk forward but my legs would not move from their positions. There was no sound, nothing to touch, nothing to see, and nothing to smell. I was standing in an endless abyss of blackness with nothing but my own thoughts to accompany me. I closed my eyes for a second to blink. When I reopened my eyes I found myself in a small organic room. The walls of the room were only ten to fifteen feet long and only seven feet high. The walls were red and looked like it was made out of living muscle. Off to my left there was a grey slab of tissue extending from the ceiling to the floor. I started to walk towards the door as I did I noticed that I was no longer covered in the black substance that covered the Shadows. I was once again a pale human only wearing a pair of jeans.

I moved towards the grey slab again the tissue rolled up into the ceiling revealing an organic looking hallway. I stepped out into the hall. There were three paths: one led to my right, the second led to my left and the third was on *the opposite wall a few feet from me on my left. The walls of the hall looked identical to the walls in the room I just left. Both the walls were lit by small glowing organic orbs. The floor and the ceiling were made up of smaller muscles than the walls and had a clear glass like material covering the surface of the muscles. I could see that the muscles would flex and contract every few seconds.*

I looked down both the right and left paths for a clue as to where I was or where to go. The path to my left looked longer than the right so I decided to walk at least to the third path and have a look down. The path was smaller than the other two and at the end of the path there was another slab of grey tissue. I walked to the tissue slab once again the grey slab rolled into the ceiling. On the other side of the tissue door was a room, a little larger than the room I awoke in. Along the walls of the room were white slates of bone supported above the ground by an organic mass. Every few seconds the mass supporting the bone tables would show signs that they were alive.

I passed through the doorway and entered into the room a few feet. To my left was a thin clear membrane that separated me from another room. On the other side of the clear membrane was a single white bone table with a green scaly bloody body. His arms were hanging off the side of the table. Its hands were hanging limp showing no sign of life. Its head lay to its left side with its tongue hanging partially out. I walked up to the clear membrane and looked closer at the corpse in the opposite adjacent room. The chest of the corpse had been cut or ripped open. Its organs had been removed from the corpse and some were now lying on some small bone countertops along the back wall.

I began to hear my name being called from somewhere. I couldn't see anything in front of me and when I looked behind me I didn't see anything. The calling of my name grew louder and louder. I looked behind me again and still nothing. I looked back into the other room and as looked back at the corpse the room began to change. The wall across from me began to change from muscular looking to a white wall. The change continued to spread from the middle of the wall to both the floor and the ceiling.

The corpse vanished from on top of the table and which revealed a grey table that extended all the way to the floor. The organic look to the room slowly dissolved into a more unnatural look. The calling of my name grew even louder than before; I turned back around. The room had almost completely changed from an organic look all that was left was the organic mass that held the slabs of bone off of the floor. After a few seconds the mass of organic muscle and the slab of bone began to vanish, and were replaced by a grey table like the room behind me. As I watched the room change, the grey tissue membrane hanging from the ceiling opened and as it rolled up into the ceiling it changed from its organic look. As the room stopped its change Zar walked through the now white doorway.

"Alex, what are you doing in here? There is no reason for you to be in here let alone out of bed."

I walked over to the doorway and stuck my head out of the room. The halls were identical to the halls of the *Colonizer*. I stepped back into the room.

"Alex, is there something wrong?"

"I don't know maybe. When I woke up everything looked different."

"How so?"

"The walls floor and ceiling of my room the hallways and these two rooms looked like organic muscles. And they looked like they were alive. Also before I was standing over there looking into the other room and there was a green bloody scaly corpse cut open on the table."

"Tell me did you have another dream like the two times before?"

"Yes, except it was different."

"It appears that when you got hit in the head for some reason you were thrown into another one of those dreams. I originally suspected that our medication caused the dreams. However, from the number of times that you have had these dreams, although this is only the third, I suspect that when you are in really deep sleep that you experience memories of the Shadows. We will have to keep an eye on you the next time we have to bring you in unconscious."

"You didn't notice anything when you walked in or as you were walking in the hallways."

"No nothing out of the ordinary. Why?"

"As soon as I heard you calling my name the organic look to everything began to change into how everything looks now."

"You were probably still somewhat unconscious and everything looked the way they were due to something probably in your dreams."

"When I awoke from the dreams before I never got up and saw anything remotely like this."

"Alex, don't forget you were hit in the head by some debris in the explosion. That is what probably caused the hallucination."

"Zar, how long have I been unconscious?"

"Only two hours. While you were unconscious I took the liberty of attaching the artificial skin on your prosthesis. It allows you to feel with your right arm. It has also has a greater protection against heat and cold."

Chapter Sixteen
Futility of War

"Two hours isn't bad and thank you, Zar, for the artificial skin...Zar, how is everyone; did they all survive the explosion?"

"Yes they survived; only they suffered minor burns and inhaled some toxic gasses. They will be okay. The levels of toxic gases weren't high enough to cause them any long-term harm. They should be up and about in a few hours."

"Wait a minute. I was closer to the explosion than any of them. How did I not inhale toxic gases or receive any burns?"

"As I told you before the trace amounts of the Shadow's substance in your system has had some unusual effect on you. It is possible that your lungs are able to breathe more hazardous gases. It also appears that your skin has increased its tolerance to heat. Or at least that is what it appears. I think that you should go back to your room and get some more rest."

"Maybe you're right I am a little tired."

Zar walked over to the doorway. The door slid up into the wall and he passed through the doorway. I followed him out of the room and into one of the *Colonizer's* hallways. Zar turned to his left and began to walk down the hall. He continued past the doorway I thought was my room and continued to walk to the end of the hallway. In front of Zar and me was a doorway similar to the others except for the blue glowing panel next to it.

"I thought my room was back there."

"No your room is a floor up. You came down here the same way we are about to go back up."

"How is that possible I don't remember using the elevator?"

"Alex, you were hit in the head. That can mess with your mind not to mention your circumstances," Zar said as the lift door opened and he stepped in.

I nodded and joined him inside the lift. The door closed. Zar said "medical level" and the lift started up. We rose for a minute or two then the doors opened and we exited the elevator. We walked down the hall for a minute then stopped at my room. I approached the door and passed through as the door slid into the ceiling. After a few seconds Zar followed me into the room.

"Alex, I just remembered that Captain Movork wished to see anyone of your party as soon as someone woke up. So we have to go up to the command deck."

"Why does he want to see one of us?"

"He wants to know what happened to his son mostly."

"Alright let's go then."

We left my room, turned to the right, and walked back to the elevator. Zar placed his hand on the blue panel. The door to the lift opened and then the two of us climbed in. The door closed and then we began to move. After two to three minutes the lift came to a stop and we climbed out into the large cafeteria. Some of the tables had been turned over and others had been broken. There was some blood on the pearly white floor and chairs. At the moment there were a few Talins, a few humans and a large variety of aliens eating at untouched tables. Zar and I walked across the bloody floor of the cafeteria. We passed the occupied tables and walked over to the elevators in the middle of the room. Once again Zar placed his hand on a blue panel next to the lift's door.

The door opened a few minutes later, then we entered the lift, the door closed, and we rose higher into the *Colonizer*. I could hear a hum from outside the lift as we ascended higher and higher into the *Colonizer*. After close to three minutes we came to a stop, the door opened, and we climbed out of the lift. We entered into the room of turrets. There was more damage than there had been three hours before. More of the turrets were closed and a few had their doors dented into the room. There were a few Talins working on the doors.

They looked like they were trying to repair or replace the doors or at very least reinforce the existing one.

A few of the doors had been reinforced with a metal pipe attached to two metal plates. The pipe was fastened to the floor in a thirty degree angle. One or two of the other doors had been welded shut. There were only four or five doors closed that had not been sealed or repaired. There looked to be a large number of the turrets still in working condition.

Zar walked along the staircase turned to his right as he reached the end of the staircase's wall. I quickened my pace as to catch up to him. He began to climb the staircase followed by me a few seconds later. As we reached the door at the top of the staircase Zar moved to his right and like Shaurha, he pushed a few buttons on the next step. The doors slowly began to separate and after a few seconds the doors had opened completely up. Zar continued up the staircase. Once we reached the top of the staircase Zar turned to his right walked to the end of the hall. The door to the bridge opened and we walked through the door. The bridge had received no damage of any kind.

There were eight Talins aside from Movork and Zar stationed around the room. Aside from me there were no other humans on the bridge. The screen off to my left displayed a global view of earth. Earth no longer looked as it had more than a week ago. Earth was no longer a blue-green gem. Now earth was a swirling mix of black, brown, red and orange. In orbit, there were wrecked ships from both sides. The hulls of the ships surrounded earth as a black and red ring.

"Hello, Alex, thanks for coming up here. Did Zar inform you as to why I wished to see you?"

"Yes he did."

"Alright both of you follow me."

Movork walked in between Zar and myself and passed through the bridge door behind us. Zar followed him out of the bridge followed by myself. As I exited the bridge Movork was passing through the door in front of the staircase. A few seconds later Zar and I joined Movork on the other side of the door. On the other side of the door was a long hallway looking to be about hundred feet long. The hallway was eight feet wide and about nine feet high. The base of the floor and the walls had lights stretching the length of the hall. On both the right and left walls were ten doors separated by less than ten feet of wall. On the far wall there was only one solid metal door.

Zar and I followed Movork to the opposite side of the hall. As we approached Movork the door in front of Movork opened and he passed through. The door closed behind him only seconds before we reached the door. On the opposite side of the door was a long room. From where I stood to the back of the room looked to be fifty to a hundred feet. In the center of the room stood a table almost as long and wide as the room itself. Surrounding the table stood dozens of gold colored metal chairs with black pads on both the seat and the back. Six lamps sat on top of the table evenly apart. Each lamp had two light sources aiming down at the table. Each of the light sources had a wide mouth close to a foot wide.

Movork had walked further into the room drew a chair back and had sat down in the chair closest to us. Zar walked past Movork and sat down on Movork's right. I walked past Movork and sat down in the closest seat on his left.

"Alright, Alex, tell me what happened on the ground level."

I spent the next three hours telling Movork about Crystal's, Hamole's, Jessica's, and my experience hours before. He was most concerned when I told him about his son getting attacked by a hound. His face definitely showed his feelings towards his son. Not only did he reveal strong concern for his son but respect and how proud he was of Hamole. When I approached the end of our experience he began to show concern for all eight of us. When I reached the end of our experience Zar began to speak.

"I will continue from here, Alex," said Zar.

"Okay, Zar."

"Whaloa and two of the computers technicians set out from the security room after receiving no response from Whaloa's call. After they left the security room the slowly made their way to the cargo bay; double checking the lobby for safety. The lobby had sustained extreme damage to its infrastructure mostly on the second floor. The particle fields sealed the transport into the *Colonizer's* hull preventing very much atmosphere from escaping. They made a quick walk through of the lobby and then moved into the same hallway as Alex, Crystal, and Hamole. When they reached the entrance to the cargo bay Whaloa and the two technicians found Hamole, Jessica, Stan, Jack, and Crystal behind barricade of debris.

"The two female humans looked like they passed out from exhaustion. Hamole had received major wounds to his torso and passed out due to the tremendous pain he must have been in. Stan and Jack had hit their heads when they leaped over the barricade. Markus and the other solider were still conscious and trying to attend to the others when Whaloa and his party arrived. Alex was found in the hall in front of the cargo bay. He was also unconscious. He had sustained a blow to the back of the head in the explosion as well as some burns on his back and legs. Whaloa and the technicians made sure that everything in the vicinity was dead before they even approached any of them. Once they felt that they were safe they got on the intercom and called for medical aid. When some of the medical staff reached them they brought everyone to the medical ward for treatment. All of them will live. I was able to heal all of their wounds."

"It's good to know that you three survived the intrusion by the Shadows. Alex, I see Zar grafted the artificial skin to your skin. When did you find the time for Zar to do the grafting?"

"I grafted the skin while I was treating his wounds. I saw no reason that he should undergo another surgery when I was already treating him."

"Zar, one last question before you can go and return to your duties. How long will my son be unconscious?"

"I would say another few hours."

"Alex, thank you for once again saving my son. You and your friends have been a tremendous help."

"You're welcome, Captain Movork."

"I don't know about you two but I have to be getting back to my duties on the bridge. From the look on Alex I would say he could stand some more rest, Zar."

"You are right, Captain, he does look exhausted. Captain, I will see you later. Alex, come with me I will escort you back to your room," Zar said, standing up from his chair and then moving to the door.

I stood up and joined Zar a few feet in front of the door. After a second, Zar moved towards the door. The door opened like before. After it opened Zar and I passed through the opening. I followed Zar back to my room. Once alone I wasted no time going to sleep. Thankfully my sleep was undisturbed and peaceful. I woke hours later to a knock on my room's door. I got out of bed, opened my dresser, and threw on a shirt. I walked over to the door. The door opened as I approached. Standing outside my door was Crystal, Jessica, Stan, Jack and Mallowon. The five of them were standing on the opposite side of the hall talking amongst themselves. The noise of the door opening alerted them to me. They stopped their conversation and looked at me for a second. After a second Crystal quickly walked over to me and aggressively wrapped he arms around me. She was far too happy to hide her feelings towards me.

"After I saw you get hit in the back of your head I thought you were done for. Then when the fire covered your body my heart broke." As she spoke, tears ran down her checks.

She released me from her hug after two minutes then turned to face Mallowon and Jessica.

"Would you not say anything to David or Mike about how I feel about Alex. The four of us have been friends for a long time and we all agreed that the four of us would be only friends. I know that both David and Mike also have feelings towards me but I don't share the same feelings. If they knew about Alex and me, our friendship would most likely be over."

"Your secret is safe with me. It's the least I can do," said Jessica.

"I don't like keeping secrets, but for two heroes I will make an exception. Just don't go abusing my secrecy," Mallowon said while looking uneasy.

"Yes what Jessica said," said Stan.

"I won't say a word."

"Thank you both for this. It means a lot to Alex and me."

"Yes thank you both."

"You both are welcome," said Jessica.

"Now tell me, why are the five of you here outside my room?"

"I wanted to see you of course," said Crystal.

"I wanted to say thank you for saving my life earlier."

"We really have nothing else to do. Since Captain Hasse gave us permission to come with you."

"And Zar asked me to check in on you. Since you appear to be fine,

I will leave now and return to my duties. If any of you need to get something to eat, Alex can activate the lift to the cafeteria with his arm," said Mallowon before walking down the hall to my left.

"I don't know about the two of you but I haven't eaten in awhile."

"Now that you mention it I haven't either."

"Come to think of it neither have we," said Jack.

"Nor have I."

"Before we go we should find David and Mike. Knowing them, they are most likely in the rec room still playing on those computers," said Crystal before she started to walk down the hall.

Jessica, Stan, Jack, and I soon followed Crystal. We walked to the entrance of the rec room and then passed through the doorway. The rec room was mostly deserted. There were only four living things in the room. An unknown species was lying on the longer of the two couches reading a data pad. A Talin was heavily immersed in one of the chess games against the computer opponent. And David and Mike were of course sitting in front of the computers playing one of the games. When we entered the room none of the four paid us any attention.

We walked over to David and Mike. Crystal began calling to them when she was only a few feet from them. Neither of them responded to their names being called. Crystal, Jessica, and I stopped behind them. Stan and Jack joined us behind David and Mike a minute later. I looked at the computer in front of Mike. His character was battling countless monsters at any given time. The game looked familiar but I couldn't remember what the game was called or what it was. I watched for a minute as Mike eliminated his character's enemies. Crystal placed her right hand on Mike's left shoulder and her left hand on David's right shoulder. Both of them immediately almost completely jumped out of their seats.

"Holy shit, why did you do that?" Mike said as he stopped his game.

"Yah and where have you two been for the past ten hours?" asked David as he too stopped his game.

"Alex and I went looking for someone when we were invaded."

"Invaded, what are you talking about? When did we get invaded?"

"Eight to nine hours ago. You two didn't know. The Shadow invaded the *Colonizer*. Hamole and the five of us stopped one of the groups of Shadows."

"How could you two not know?"

"We have been here playing on the computers."

"You two probably haven't eaten in a while. Am I right?"

"Come to think of it you're right. I haven't eaten in a while," said Mike, closing his game.

"Me neither," said David as he also closed his game.

"We haven't either, so we were going up to the cafeteria to get some food. Crystal and I figure neither of you have eaten anything for a few days. So we figured we should ask you to join us."

"Come on, at least get something to eat then," Jessica said, moving closer to the four of us.

"Who are you three?"

"Stan."

"Jack."

"And my name is Jessica and while you two were playing games we were helping deal with the invaders!"

"Calm down, let's go," said David.

The seven of us left the rec room turned to our right and walked to the end of the hall. Once we reached the lift I opened its door and then David, Mike, Stan, and Crystal climbed into the lift. The door closed and they rose to the cafeteria. I placed my hand on the panel next to the door again and waited for the door to open. The door opened after three near eight minutes. Jessica Jack and I climbed into the lift. The door closed behind Jessica.

After a few seconds the lift began its ascent and after a few minutes the lift stopped; the door opened and we climbed out of the lift. The cafeteria had all the tables repaired and straightened up. All but a few tables in the cafeteria were occupied by mostly Talins. David Mike Stan and Crystal were standing off to our right waiting for us to join them. From what I could see there was a few small groups of people from the other species. Only four tables were left unoccupied. Two were in the middle of this side of the cafeteria and were surrounded by the other tables. One of the four tables was at the back of the room. The last table was in the third row and was the fourth table in. Each row of tables had enough space for people to walk through without any problems.

After a few seconds of looking into the mass of people we began walking towards the closest food dispensers. There was no line, for that matter there was no one at any of the dispensers. The seven of us each got our food and drinks then took a seat at the closest vacant table. We began eating our food. I ate quickly and while I did I looked at the various Talins around us taking in their differences. The majority of them had some form of battle scars somewhere on their bodies. I finished my food and drink in thirty minutes, the others finished minutes later. David and Mike began asking the three of us about the invasion. The five of us told them everything that happened after Crystal and I left them at the rec room hours before. We didn't get very far into our ordeal when we were interrupted by Nozad and Flito. The two of them came over and sat down next to Crystal and Mike.

"Hey it's good to see you two alive," said Nozad.

"What can we do for you two?"

"Captain Movork, Shaurha, and Hamole would like you and your friends to come to the bridge."

"Did they say why?" asked Crystal.

"No they didn't say why. Just that they wanted for you to join them on the bridge," replied Flito.

"All right, let us go," said Mike, standing up from his seat.

"Before we do the seven of you need to take care of your trays," Flito said, standing up.

"And how do we do that?" asked David, standing up with his plate in hand.

"Just put it into a dispenser."

The rest of us stood up then picked up our trays and then walked over to one of the food dispensers. We each placed our trays and cups into similar dispensers. After we finished with the dispensers the nine of us walked over to the elevator in the middle of the room. Nozad placed his hand on the blue pane next to the middle door. The door opened and Nozad walked into the lift.

"There is not enough space in there for all of us," said Mike.

"You are right, that's why four of you are going to have to wait a few minutes while the rest of you use the lift. I have to stay here so the rest of you can get into the lift when it returns," said Flito.

"Mike, Crystal, and the new girl get in," said Nozad while waving them in.

Mike, Crystal, and Jessica walked into the lift. The door closed and they ascended to the bridge level. David, Flito, Stan, Jack and I waited for a few minutes for the lift to return. After close to seven minutes the lift door opened, and then we filed into the lift. The door closed behind us seconds later. We rose higher into the *Colonizer*. After more than three minutes the lift came to a stop, the doors opened and then we walked out. The door closed behind us. The others were already at the staircase in the black room. As we walked to join them they began climbing the stairs. The door above the staircase was just about finished opening when we reached them on the staircase.

Nozad led the way to the bridge. The bridge was occupied by dozens of people humans, Talins and a handful of people from other species. Most of them were facing the large screen to our left. Upon our entry into the bridge Captain Movork, Shaurha, and Hamole, walked over to us.

"Good, good, you all made it just in time. It's about to start," said Movork, looking back at the screen.

"What is about to start?" asked Crystal.

"Hold on."

"Attention. This is President Peter Clark. As you all know by now we have been attacked by a horrible alien race. At the same time we were also saved by another much friendlier alien race. As a result from the attack, we the leaders of earth have agreed that if we can't keep earth as ours then it will belong to no one else. So in ten minutes all of the nuclear missiles will be launched if they are still capable. Even if the missiles do not launch then all the missiles will detonate as the enemy makes its descent into our planet.

"Hopefully the radiation from the nuclear detonation will keep them from stripping our planet long enough for us to regroup and grow strong enough to fight back and win. We as humans did not win this battle. We may have survived to fight another day but we lost our home. The Talin race has kindly supplied us with a place to seek refuge. Some of you might be asking why the Talins couldn't stop the

Shadows from invading. The truth is they are spread too thin. They are engaged in heated battles on many planets and in many solar systems. They are trying to save themselves and anyone in need and that as many of our nations have learned in the past can take its toll. Now fellow humans and our new friends join me in watching as we stick it to the Shadows," President Clark's voice stopped speaking over the intercom.

We turned to the screen and looked upon it for a few minutes. There were signs of movement above earth. Dozens of Shadow ships of many different sizes began their descent into earth's atmosphere. All the ships vanished into the cloud of smoke that surrounded the surface of earth. A minute went by and the cloud began to reveal a detonation and then a second a second later. Then four at once, six more hundreds upon hundreds of blast quickly tore the cloud surrounding earth apart. Then too many nukes were detonating for me to keep track.

I could see rings of red and black clouds spreading around the globe. The blasts collided with one another making the clouds fall to the surface and rise higher in the atmosphere. There was no sign of the Shadow ships. The ruins of civilizations that had been there for centuries and millennia had been completely wiped from the surface of the planet. Each of the detonations allowed a small and brief glimpse of fire burning earth's sky.

"This is Captain Movork. To all of you humans I am sorry for your loss. I would love to say we could have done something to stop the Shadows from invading but as President Clark said our forces are stretched thin. I know everyone on this ship has been through hell in the last few days but we still have to get out of this solar system. The next thing we have to do is pass through the asteroid belt before we can go to ultra light speed. We will be getting an escort from the ship *Franchasno*. It has been waiting close to the belt for us to arrive. While they waited they made as many repairs to the ship as they could.

"The *Franchasno* will be flying in front of us providing cover and destroying the asteroids that the fighters can not. I ask anyone that has and is capable of flying a fighter let it be hybrid or Talin report to any of the hanger bays to be designated a fighter. Your job is to destroy any meteor, small asteroids, and an enemy fighter that makes an appearance. That is all for now," Movork's voice left the intercom.

"Alex, I know you and your friends have flown fighters in the past few days. I also know that all of you have been through a lot; however, I have to ask you to help defend this ship again. If the seven of you could go back downstairs and man a turret when we enter the belt it would be a great help. Nozad, Flito, go with Alex and his friends.

"Alright we will do it, Captain Movork."

We left the bridge, walked to the staircase and had to wait as Flito opened the door. We then climbed down the staircase and waited for the doors to the turrets to open. We only had to wait two minutes for the doors to open. The number of turrets had greatly dropped. Less than one half of the turrets surrounding us looked to be in working conditions. After a few more seconds the elevator's door opened and out walked five Talins. The door above the staircase reopened and out walked a large number of Talins. Nozad, Flito, my friends, and I climbed into turrets that were close together.

The door closed after I sat down in the chair. I put on the headset and waited to be slid further into the turret. After a few minutes the walls of the turret opened and then I was slid further into the turret. After a few seconds swarms of fighters left the *Colonizer* and flew past us. I watched as the distance from the asteroid belt grew closer and closer. After fifteen minutes the *Franchasno* came into view. The damage the *Franchasno* received became more visible. There were blasted makes all over its hull. Without a doubt the *Franchasno* was smaller than the *Colonizer* and designed for one purpose: battle. This ship had large mass cannons positioned all around the ship. From the looks of it the cannons combined could fire in a full 360 degrees. There also appeared to be a few smaller guns scattered about the ship. A lot of the smaller guns had been destroyed. A large portion of the destroyed guns still glowed due to fire.

The *Franchasno's* engines started and began to move to face the asteroid belt. A few minutes later hundreds of fighters lunched from the *Franchasno's* hanger bays. The space in front of the *Franchasno* began to light up as many fighters began to fire upon the asteroid belt. After a few seconds the cannons fired upon large asteroids. The asteroids crumbled under the power of the cannons. There was no fire, no smoke, and no coals, the asteroids just fell apart when they were hit. I watched as the debris from the large asteroids was fired upon by the countless fighters in front of the *Franchasno*. The firing on the asteroids slowly came to a stop and became more chaotic.

Through my headset I heard that the enemy engaged our fighters and that they were approaching the *Colonizer*. I couldn't see the enemy forces; however, I could see our forces returning to the *Colonizer*. As they returned to the *Colonizer* they began getting fired upon by the enemy. Our fighters' speed increased and within a few minutes they were flying around the *Colonizer*. The enemy forces immediately focused their fire upon the hull of the *Colonizer*. Luckily all of their fire was stopped by the shield. We only began firing when they were close enough for any of the turrets to do damage to the enemy ships. Turrets all over the *Colonizer* began firing upon the enemy with bright red laser beams. Each of the turrets fired many laser bolts very quickly. I began firing when the enemy fighters flew past my view and disappeared in the blackness of space. The enemy fighters were virtually invisible. I could only see them when they were a short distance away.

"Give the computers a few more minutes to switch to infrared. The enemy fighters should be indicated in red and our fighters should be in blue. Be careful when you choose your targets. The enemy fighters are faster than our fighters in space," said a voice through my headset.

After the voice cleared off of the headset the metal walls slid back over the turret. Then all of the walls began showing red and dark blue lights. The detail of the fighters was poor. Only the basic outlines of the fighters were lit. The rest of the walls were as black as space itself. There were quite a few fighters from both sides. Too many to count and the computer was unable to display the fighters furthest away. The infrared scans appeared to have a range equal to the turrets' firing range. I chose my target and began firing upon the red silhouette of an enemy fighter. I could see the blast from the barrels of my turret flying through space and hitting the enemy. I couldn't see any of the enemy's fire, nor could I see fire from any of the other turrets or ally fighters.

My target's light indication grew in intensity before it disappeared into the dark abyss of space. I began firing upon a different target. The enemy fighter started moving erratically trying to dodge my shots. I could see that some of my shots struck the back of the fighter. I could see a small explosion forming out of the back of the fighter. The fighter's signal dimmed as it flew out of my firing range before it disappeared. A few seconds later another fighter flew past me. His heat signal covered most of the walls. The red glow lit my turret in a bright reddish orange glow witch lasted for only milliseconds as the fighter passed. A few seconds later the inside of my turret turned to a dark blue as an ally fighter whipped past me. A few seconds later and another enemy fighter flew past in a heated chase with the ally fighter.

My view of the battle returned. I waited to fire for a few seconds just in case there was any more ally fighters flying to close. After a minute I chose a target and began firing upon it. Like before the fighter grew brighter then disappeared into darkness. I found another enemy fighter and began firing upon it almost immediately the enemy disappeared into the darkness. This went on for two hours it seemed. The enemy's fighters dwindled to nothing. We lost a large portion of our fighters in the battle from what I could see. I couldn't really tell how many ally fighters were left.

"We are done here. The turrets will not be effective in the asteroid belt. If you have flown a fighter, report to one of the hanger bays. We lost a great number of fighters in the battle," said Movork through my headset.

The dark blue lights of the ally fighters went dark, followed by my controls. The door behind me opened and then I slid back. I climbed out of my turret. I looked around the room, as far as I could tell none of the turrets had been destroyed. Nozad, Flito, and all of my friends climbed out of their turrets.

"Come on we need to get to hanger bay B. It's the closet one," said Nozad.

"Why do we need to go anywhere?" asked David.

"Because we are pilots and that is what is being called for," replied Flito.

"We will stay here where it is safe," said David.

"If you wish to stay alive then you should come with us and clear a path through the belt!" replied Flito as he walked over to the lift.

"We need to defend both ships and clear a path otherwise we will not make it through the belt!" said Nozad, as he too walked over to the lift.

"If any of you are going to help then you need to come with us now. If not then you will not be able to come down later," said Flito.

Jessica and Mike walked over to Nozad and Flito. Stan, Jack, and I joined the four of them seconds later then followed by Crystal and a reluctant David. Nozad placed his hand on the blue panel next to the lift door. The door opened and he stepped into the lift Jessica, Mike, Stan and I followed him into the lift a second later. The door closed behind us and we began our three minute descent into the *Colonizer*. We came to a stop and the door opened into the cafeteria. We exited the lift and sat down at a vacant table for a few minutes. Seven minutes later the door of the lift opened and out walked Crystal, Jack David, and Flito. Crystal, Jack and David walked over to us and stood at the end of the table. When Nozad saw the three of them he stood up and joined Flito in front of the lift.

The two of them split up and walked over to the doors on either side of the lift. Nozad was on the lift's left and Flito stood on its right. They both placed their hands on the doors and then stepped away from the both door. Both of them walked back over to us and stood to my right at the end of the table.

"We have a few minutes to wait. Most likely both the lifts are on one of the lower levels," said Flito.

"How far down is hanger bay B?" asked Mike.

"The hanger bay is ten floors blow us," replied Flito.

After eight minutes the left lift opened, Nozad stood up and walked over to the opened door. He stepped partly into the lift.

"Some of you come with me, these elevators can't hold all of us," said Nozad.

I stood up and walked over to the lift. I walked into the lift and waited. A few seconds later I was joined by Mike, Jessica, and David in the elevator. Nozad stepped into the lift. The door closed behind him and a second later we began to descend deeper into the *Colonizer*. Our descent lasted anywhere from ten to twenty minutes before we came to a stop and then the door opened. The five of us stepped out of the lift into a wide and long hallway. The hall was fifteen feet wide and looked longer than the first half of the cafeteria. Off to our left was a second lift doorway. On the right and left walls there were very few doors in sight. This hallway looked similar to all the other hallways on the *Colonizer*.

We walked into the hall a few feet and waited for the others to arrive. We waited for a few minutes and then the door of the other lift opened. The others walked out of the lift and joined us in the hallway. Led by Nozad and Flito we walked deeper into the hallway, then turned to the right, and walked down a connecting hallway. We walked down the hallway for a few minutes until we reached the end. In front of us there was a large metal door and on either side of the door was a long pane of glass. Through the glass I could see the room on the other side of the door.

Chapter Seventeen
A Lucky Escape

We passed through the doorway and entered into a large grey and silver room. The room had numerous crashed fighters lying on the floor. Two large metal claws were moving around the room picking up a wrecked ship and then disappearing through the metal wall to my right. When the claws reached the wall two different doors opened allowing them passage. Below the two doors at the base of the wall was a third doorway.

The third doorway was smaller than the two larger doors. To our left was a wall that was open to space. Every few seconds there was a yellowish orange glimmer of the particle shield across the opening.

On the other side of the room were multiple levels. Every odd numbered level was enclosed with a multiple windows. Each even numbered level had dozens of people walking about. A large number of the people were positioned at computer consoles along the edges. Everyone was busy moving around on the levels to pay attention to the movement of the claws. The room began to get filled with the sound of metal grinding together. The sound of metal grinding grew louder as the wall off to our right began to split apart. The center of the wall slowly began to open as the two pieces of the wall disappeared into the wall in front of us and behind us. Two minutes after the wall had started to open Nozad and Flito started to walk into the hanger bay. The two of them moved in towards the opening wall. The rest of us followed both of them seconds later.

We walked through the opening. On the other side was a larger room than the first half of the hanger bay. The room looked to be double the length of the first section of the hanger bay. The ceiling of the section of the hanger bay was higher. The walls had thousands of rows of fighters lining the right, left, and back walls. Each wall was stacked almost to the ceiling with fighters. Every row of fighters had staircases going to the ceiling. Each row consisted of ten fighters. The center of the room had a large party of people standing in a group around a single person. The group of people was a mix of humans, Talins, and a large handful of people from the other species. The nine of us started to walk over to the party of people. As we approached the party disbanded. The members of the party separated and walked over to the rows of fighters. Nozad, Flito and the rest of us came to a stop in the center of the room.

Nozad and Flito walked forward to the person that had been surrounded by the group and then they talked with him briefly. After a brief moment he waved at us then turned and walked towards the rows of fighters along the right wall. The ten of us walked over to the right wall. When the man reached the first rows of fighters he started to climb the staircase in between two rows of fighters. He climbed to the tenth column of fighters and came to a stop. He then directed us to walk to the next fighter in the column. All of the fighters looked to be of Talin origin.

The Talin fighters were more rounded and smother than the hybrid fighters. The wings were shorter and narrower and there was only room for the pilot in the cockpit. The cockpit was mostly enclosed with a two and half foot windshield. The rest of the ship had solid metal plating covering its frame. Gun turrets similar to those mounted around the *Colonizer* were attached on the under side of the fighter's wings. These turrets were smaller and looked like they had an even smaller range of fire then their larger counterparts. The engines were eleven feet from the cockpit and looked like they could produce tremendous speed. All the fighters had a golden yellow sandy look. In a few spots of the fighter there appeared to be small black dots.

"Everyone, get into your fighter and start your launch sequence. If you have flown one of the hybrids before then you should have no trouble piloting these ships," yelled the male Talin into the hanger bay seconds before he sat down in his fighter.

Nozad and Flito took the first two fighters after the male Talins fighter. Crystal took the next fighter, then David and then I was next. As I came closer to my fighter the cockpit slid forward and down. I climbed into the fighter. As I sat the controls and consoles lit up. The controls greatly resembled those found in the hybrid fighters. I looked out the open cockpit a millisecond before Jessica reached her fighter. As Mike reached his fighter Jessica had already climbed into her fighter. Stan and Jack walked out of my view seconds later. After a second the cockpit closed then I felt the pressure inside the fighter change as I was sealed from the outside atmosphere. The lights from the controls and the consoles lit the fighter up in a mix of colors. The lights dimmed as I looked over the consoles. I looked around the cockpit for a few seconds before I found a small and flimsy headset with the microphone and speaker on the left side. I put on the headset and looked over my controls once more while I waited for orders.

"Attention, everyone, this is your squad leader. In a few minutes the auto launch program will start. When you leave the hanger bay you and only you will be in control of your fighter. As soon as you are in control of your fighter fly straight towards the belt. Our objectives are to clear a path through the asteroid belt, destroy any enemy ship possible and defend both the *Colonizer* and the *Franchasno*. If you get too badly damaged then report back to one of the hanger bays on the *Colonizer* or the *Franchasno*. Not all of you will make it back to either the *Colonizer* or the *Franchasno*. If you die here today then I want you to know that you died in order to save another race from our enemy. Now let us get out there and do our job."

My fighter and I began to shake and rattle as the engines started up. Through the windshield I saw the various fighters opposite of me lifting off. The fighters hovered in midair for five to ten minutes before the closest fighter to the open wall took off, followed milliseconds later by another fighter and then another. Until the right wall of the *Colonizer* was completely empty of fighters. I was surprised that fighters on the back wall flew past a minute later. After close to five minutes I felt a jerk as my fighter flew out into the hanger bay then turned left and accelerated out of the hanger bay. The engines shot off and I drifted through space for a few seconds before I took control.

I reactivated the engines and flew towards the asteroid belt and the *Franchasno*. I was surrounded by thousands of fighters all with the same destination as me. After four minutes we reached the back of the *Franchasno*. A few seconds after we reached the *Franchasno* one of its cannons began to fire. A few seconds later the cannon fired upon a large asteroid. Two green bolts of energy flew through space and struck the asteroid in its center. A millisecond after getting struck the energy bolts appeared out of the asteroid's backside. The asteroid crumbled as the bolts forced their way through the asteroid's surface and core. There was no fire nor was there any smoke just dust and small chunks of asteroid. As the remains of the asteroid drifted apart they were immediately fired upon by the massive horde of Talin fighters. The asteroids were fired upon until they were left the size of basketballs, baseballs, and small boulders.

The horde of fighters moved away from the asteroid debris and began their assault upon other smaller asteroids. The *Franchasno* fired its cannons fifteen minutes or so. Every time fighters would consume the debris field until there was very little left. Dozens of fighters including me flew along the outside of the *Franchasno's* hull. From my view the *Franchasno* looked as though it had received tremendous damage. In quite a few places its hull had been punctured. The hull had been so damaged in spots that I could see into some of the *Franchasno's* levels. Bodies and debris floated in between its particle shield and its hull in the badly damaged sections.

We passed the nose of the *Franchasno* and in doing so we entered into the asteroid belt. As the fighter ahead of me grew close to the various size asteroids drifting in the belt they opened fire upon them. Like the fighters before them they reduced the asteroid to next to nothing. The cannons on top of the *Franchasno* continued to fire up the belt all the while moving very slowly into the belt. The majority of the fighters had moved deeper into the belt clearing as much as they possible could. The fighter closest to me began firing their turrets upon a chuck of rock. The bolts from his turret drilled into the surface of the rock. As the bolts hit the rock it moved with each strike from the fighter. Immediately the fighters surrounding me scattered as we grew deeper into the asteroid belt.

251

I and a few other fighters flew straight into the belt in search of targets. I began firing upon asteroid after asteroid. I moved onto another rock when the one I was working on was dwindled down to next to nothing. Every fighter worked as I did moving deeper into the belt slowly removing the obstacles in our way. After twenty minutes of flying into the belt and destroying rocks I turned around and began to fly back towards the two Talin ships. In twenty minutes I and the other fighters had grown quite a distance away from our allies. Both of the ships looked like I could reach out and hold them in my hands.

As I flew back to the two Talin rescue ships I cleared myself a path to fly. Once I reached the two vessels I immediately began firing upon the obstacles in their path. The number of fighters in flight around the two vessels was well in the tens of thousands. All of us worked for a few hours clearing a path through the belt. The *Colonizer* had completely entered the asteroid belt and was joining in the task of clearing asteroids. Out of the abyss of space and the asteroid belt the enemy began to attack any and every ship they could. The enemy ships were as black as the space that they were flying through and were faster than anything I have ever seen. Even though they were faster and impossible to see, they weren't very agile. With the number of asteroids still lingering around the enemy found it hard to fly at high speeds.

After a few minutes of colliding with the obstacles of space they dropped their speed down to what we were flying at. I was only able to see the enemy fighters due to the fact that the windshield of my fighter highlighted the enemy fighters within its scanning range. They began firing upon us and both the *Colonizer* and the *Franchasno*.

"Stop destroying the blasted rocks and fire upon the enemy ships whatever you do, do not let them get away or they will bring in reinforcements," said our squad leader through my headset.

Just about everyone stopped firing upon the belt and turned our attention upon the enemy force attacking other fighters the *Colonizer* and the *Franchasno*. A small portion of the Talin fighters kept on firing upon the asteroid belt. Those were the main target of our enemy, they didn't want us to clear a path. On occasion they would aid us in our task by destroying the rocks in their way. We engaged the enemy fighters as best as we could. After we polished off the enemy and began to return to our prior task my fighter identified a fighter trying to escape. It appeared that my fighter was the only one to spot the enemy so I went in pursuit of the escapee. He flew quickly through the mine field of rocks. I accelerated to keep up with him as best as I could. The enemy moved quickly through the belt and once I saw open space I slowed to a near crawl. Resting outside the asteroid belt were five Shadow warships waiting for sight of us. I started to turn my fighter around. As I began my flight back to the Talin vessels some of the larger asteroids around me crumbled under enemy fire.

The concussion from the enemy fire tore through the masses of rock sending debris varying in size in all directions. The enemy fired again and continued their attacks fortunately only hitting the asteroids around me. The asteroid's debris struck the hull of my fighter causing my fighter to shake horribly. I struggled to regain control of my fighter as additional debris collided with me. Chucks of rock crossed my path as I drifted through the mine field. I could hear rocks smashing into all sides of my ship and other rocks. The cockpit grew a bright red followed by alarms blaring. No voice came on telling me what was going on, nor what was damaged. My fighter's engines repeatedly shut down as I flew back. Every time the engines shut down I had to turn them back on. I had trouble reigniting my fighter's engines. Quite often it took multiple attempts to reignite my fighter's engines.

After reigniting my engines more than ten times I came in sight of the two Talin vessels. As I grew closer to the Talin vessels my ears were filled with static through my headset. I continued having trouble with my engines as I came in sight of the other fighters. As I neared the cleared path my engines quit. I tried reigniting them but had no success. I drifted past dozens of rocks; occasionally I collided with asteroids. With each collision I was pushed in a different direction. I had no control over my fighter. I was; however, still able to fire my turrets upon the smaller asteroids only when I was able.

With each collision my speed was reduced.

I cleared the asteroids and drifted into the cleared portion of the asteroid belt. The static grew louder as I grew closer to the *Franchasno*. After a few minutes of drifting I began to hear some conversations through the overwhelming static. I was unable to understand a single word involved in any of the conversations. Due to the static I was unable to distinguish anything that was said. Drifting through space,

I started broadcasting my distress, my location and a warning about a trap waiting for us. I broadcasted on every frequency I could. As I repeated the message I listened through my headset for the slightest indication that my message was received. I repeated my message on nineteen different frequencies before I reached through to someone.

"This is a private frequency that is kept open for Captain Movork and me. Who is using this frequency?"

"Sorry, but I need to get a message to Captain Movork or the captain of the *Franchasno*."

"I heard your message already, it said nothing that would concern either captain. Now back to my first question: who are you and why are you really on this frequency?"

"This is the only frequency I was able to reach anyone. I need you to tell Captain Movork that Alex Track has news about the enemy and our plan to escape."

"Alex, hmm tell me what your news is and maybe I will give him the message."

I had to tell him what I saw in hopes that he would relay my message. I finished five minutes later by that time I had grown dangerously close to the hull of the *Franchasno*.

"Now if that pleases you I would really like some help out here I am a few meters from the *Franchasno's* hull. And I am unable to reignite my engines."

"Well that, Alex, is all I need. I will not send your message along to Movork just yet. First I will get you back to the *Colonizer*. I am ordering some of the fighters closest to you to give you a tow to one of the *Colonizer's* hanger bays. Then I will send your message."

"Thank you, Captain."

There was no response.

I continued to drift meters from the massive hull of the *Franchasno*. The static drowning my ears went silent. Minutes later the alarms shut down followed by the lights illuminating the controls a few seconds later. The only source of light came from the lights along the hull of the *Franchasno*. I drifted in complete near darkness for quite a while. It seemed like an hour had passed when another Talin fighter flew over my head and stopped meters in front of me and above. The fighter hovered far enough for me to see it through my windshield. I felt a slight jerk from my right and then I slowly started to move away from the *Franchasno*. After a few minutes of being towed I regained my view of the *Colonizer*. Seconds later I felt another jerk but from the left side. I looked through the windshield again and saw three different fighters above me.

Two of the fighters had fired their tow cables. The middle fighter was flying further ahead of the other two fighters. The closet fighter to me was on my right. As they flew they grew further away from me. I felt my fighter suddenly jerk forward. My speed increased quickly. The three fighters guided me through the cleared path in the asteroid belt. The size of the *Colonizer* grew rapidly as we approached bringing the six open hanger bays into view. The left and the right fighter began to pull me towards one of the lower two hanger bays. The center fighter pulled up and left the two remaining fighters to guide me into the hanger bay. Seconds later I felt a slight jerk from behind then my speed and the speed of my two towers began to drop.

The first two fighters passed through the particle field followed by me two seconds later. Once I entered the *Colonizer* I felt my speed drop very quickly and abruptly. As we flew through the hanger bay the two ships in front of me began to descend bringing me along with them. The hanger bay looked identical to hanger bay B aside from the door with the long glass windows was on the left side of the hanger bay. I was guided through the large open wall and then was brought to a stop. The two fighters also came to a stop and hovered above the bay floor. I slowly began to descend to the bay floor. A second later my left wing landed followed by my right wing and the back of my fighter. The two moved forward and then landed about forty feet from me.

I saw the two fighters' cockpits open. A Talin, someone from one of the other species on board, climbed out. Both of them put their headsets back into their fighters and walked to the wall on my right. They had lowered me closer to the left side of the ship then the right. I pushed the button to open the hatch but had no response. I looked around the cockpit for the manual release with no results. The little light that the hanger bay provided me with was not helpful. I continued to search for the release as the two pilots walked the forty feet over to my fighter. I began running my hands along the base of the hatch feeling for the release. On both the right ad left side I found a small handle. The left handle moved slightly as I ran my right hand over it.

I gripped the handle as best as I could and began testing it for functionality. After a few seconds of trying I found that the handle turned forward towards the nose of the fighter. I continued to turn the handle, as I turned I got heavy resistance. After ten seconds the hatch let out a whine and the pressure changed within the cockpit. I reached over and began turning the right handle as fast as I could with my left hand. Once I hit the resistance I had to switch hands and let my prosthesis do the work. Once again after ten seconds of resistance the hatch whined, then the pressure changed again followed by the hatch sliding down the noise of the fighter. I removed my headset and dropped it in the chair of the fighter. I walked a few feet from my fighter. Seconds later I was joined by the two pilots that towed my fighter and me.

"What did you do to your fighter?" asked the Talin.

"I didn't do anything to it."

"Then how do you explain that?" asked the other pilot.

I looked back at my fighter. The engines had been battered, nearly ripped from the back of the fighter. The wings had been dented in upon themselves. The turrets were barely attached to the underside of the wings and looked like they shouldn't have worked as long as they had. I was surprised that the engines worked at all with all the damage they had sustained. The engines looked like they had been hit by the enemy's blasts. The engines looked like they had been plugged and the metal surrounding them just blew away from the engines. The insides of the engines had rocks from the belt embedded in the metal.

"Boy, you are without a doubt lucky," said a female to my left.

I turned to see a human female walking past my fighter.

"How did that happen?" asked the female as she joined me.

"I think I was shot by a Shadow warship. Then I crashed into some smaller asteroids."

"You really are lucky to be alive; if you were hit by a bolt from a Shadow warship," said the Talin.

"Thank you all for saving my ass."

"You're welcome...Hey what is your name?" asked the female.

"Alex, what are your names?"

"Amanda Pinafore," replied the female human.

"My name is Aldam Kech. I'm from the former planet known as Frostise."

Aldam was about six feet tall. He had purplish blue eyes which resembled cat eyes. He had ridges above his forehead. All of the ridges looked like they had scales covering them. There were a few holes in the side of his face that had small pipes covered by skin coming from the holes. His skin was dark brown and had a wood grain texture.

"And I am called Halado."

"Attention, clear the hanger bay floor now. We have damaged incoming vessels," said a voice over the hanger bay intercom.

"We should leave the bay floor quickly," said Halado.

The rest of us agreed and then the four of us started to walk towards the left wall when three fighters flew through the entrance of the hanger bay. All three of the fighters were heavily smoking from their engines. The fighter in the middle moved toward the right wall forcing the fighter next to the middle fighter to crash into the upper two levels of the hanger bay. The fighter tore into the levels creating a long cut in almost as long as the first half of the hanger bay. The fighter came to a stop imbedded in the upper two levels. At the same time the center fighter moved to the right and collided with the fighter on its right. The right fighter slammed into the right wall and bounced off and was forced into a spin. The fighter slammed into the hanger bay floor and flipped repeatedly before it was flung into the air then slammed down onto the cockpit.

The cockpit was crushed under the force of the slam. The fighter continued to slid on the floor; further crushing the cockpit. The sounds produced from both the right and left fighters drowned out any screams that may have been present. The fighter in the center was forced down by the right fighter. The fighter came right at the three of us. The others moved out of the way just as the fighter flew past my right side. As the fighter passed I was spun to my right. I watched as the fighter slammed into the floor and scrapped along the floor until it came to a rest a hundred or so feet from me. The floor behind the fighter had a three-foot wide cut dug through the metal surface. The cockpit to the fighter opened a few seconds after it came to a stop. The pilot climbed out of her fighter and ran away from it. She ran along the cut her fighter dug in the metal floor. She came to as stop a few feet from me and put her hands to her mouth. She ran the rest of the way to me.

"I'm so sorry, your arm. I broke your arm," said the human female.

"No you didn't."

"Yes I did look at it."

I raised my right arm. My prosthesis was bent slightly at the elbow in the opposite direction. The motion of moving my arm caused from the elbow down to swing back and forth. Some of the artificial skin had been torn and hung from the elbow. There wasn't enough of the skin torn to show the metal surface under the skin. Small drops of blood ran down along the tears in the artificial skin.

"At this time everyone please clear the hanger bay floor. There are still more inbound fighters," said the same voice over the intercom.

"My arm is fine. Now come on we have to leave the hanger bay floor."

"But your arm, doesn't it hurt?" asked the female after she nodded her head.

"No, not at all, now come on."

She nodded again then started to walk the remainder of the way to the right wall of the hanger bay. Aldam, Halado, and Amanda caught up to us a few minutes after we reached the right wall.

"You must be in tremendous pain?" asked Aldam.

"No I'm not."

"Your arm has been shattered. How can you not be in any pain?" asked Halado.

"Here I will show you."

I raised my prosthesis up. As raised my arm the lower portion of my arm swung back and forth like before. With my left hand I grabbed the torn skin and pulled it down my forearm of the prosthesis. My arm burned with pain as I tore more of the artificial skin. Some blood ran down the surface of the prosthesis and built up along the crease of skin I had created.

"Now that hurt."

"I understand now. You have a prosthesis," said Halado.

"See you didn't break my arm."

"No, but I broke your prosthesis," said the female beginning to cry into her hands.

"Stop crying ah...What is your name?"

"Samantha."

"Hi my names Alex and don't worry about my arm. I am sure it can be fixed."

"Alex, who gave you your prosthesis?" asked Amanda.

"A hand full of people authorized the operation. One of those people was the top Talin doctor Zar and another was Admiral Hamole."

"Why did they authorize the surgery?" asked Aldam.

"They said that they owed me a debt and that Princess Paloween gave the order for me to have the surgery immediately."

"Why would the queen do something like that?" asked Halado.

"I have no clue. If I see her again I was planning on asking."

"How do you know the queen?" asked Aldam.

"I will tell you later first I think I should return to the medical level and get my prosthesis fixed."

"There is no need to go back to the medical level. The doctors on the other side of the hanger bay should be able to repair your prosthesis," said Halado.

"The four of you should get to some fighters and help clear that path."

"There is no need...before we entered the hanger bay an order was given for all fighters to return to *Colonizer*. Something was said that the enemy was waiting for us to clear the asteroid belt. The captains of both vessels were working on a plan to clear the remainder of the path and deal with the enemy in waiting," said Samantha.

"It's good to know that my message reached Captain Movork."

"Can we go and get your arm fixed it's freaking me out?" asked Amanda.

"We are going to have to run across the hanger bay. Fighters could enter the hanger bay at any time," said Halado.

We waited a few minutes then started to run across the hanger bay. After running halfway across the hanger bay; two fighters flew in and landed past the open wall. The two fighters were immediately picked up by the claws after the pilots had climbed out. Another fighter entered the hanger bay as we reached the left side.

"This way," said Halado while turning to his right.

We walked along the left wall for about a minute and a half. Halado turned to his left and passed through a grey metal door. We followed him through the door. On the other side of the door was a hallway. The hallway went off to my left for a couple hundred feet before the hall ended. On my left the hall went on for what seemed like a thousand feet maybe more. The wall we passed through had small lights mounted on the wall separated by thirty feet. On the other side of the hall there were a dozen doors separated by less than hundred feet. Halado turned to our left and started walking down the hall. We walked past two of the doors before Halado stopped and turned through a door.

We walked through the third door on the left side of the hall and entered into a room with two tables, each three feet long resting in the center of the room and a five-foot long desk towards the back of the room. There were racks filled with data pads along both the right and left wall of the room. The two tables were covered with loose data pads. There was on other person in the room. A Talin was sitting behind the desk working on a computer in front of him. Behind the Talin were rows of equipment tools and medical instruments. We walked into the room further. Then Halado and the other three stopped in front of the two tables. I walked forward, stopping a foot or two from the desk.

Chapter Eighteen
Lazarus Protocol

"Excuse me...Doctor."

"My name is Mozet. What can I help you with?"

"My name is..."

"I don't care about your name! What is your problem?"

"Are you able to fix my prosthesis?"

"Let me see your primitive appendage."

I raised my arm up like I would shake his hand and the forearm dropped and dangled in front of Mozet.

"Bring it closer."

"This isn't primitive at all. This prosthesis was made by Talins and only one has been currently made for a human. That means you're Alex."

"Yes, how did you know?"

"Zar contacted all the medical staff and told us about your particular case."

"Well, can you fix it?"

"No, not here; this is just an office. The equipment needed is down the hall."

"Mozet, do you know what Captain Movork and the captain of the *Franchasno* are planning?"

"No, I do not know. They haven't informed anyone of their plan. Whatever it is they are planning involves the complete evacuation of the *Franchasno*."

"Thank you."

"Enough of that; let's get your arm fixed and get you on your way," Mozet said, standing up from behind his desk.

He walked around his desk, passed me and proceeded past Halado, Aldam, Amanda and Samantha. I joined the four of them and then we followed Mozet out of his office. After passing through the doorway, he turned to his right and started to walk down the hallway. We followed him down the hallway. He walked past two doors and when he reached the third door, he turned and passed through the door. We followed him through the door and entered into a light gray room. Beds extended from the right and left side wall. The beds extended five to six feet from the walls and were about two and half feet wide. Small two-foot wide tables rested at the end of every bed in the room. Eight beds lined the walls. In the back of the room there were metal shelves separated by a skinny door. The door separating the racks was one and half feet to two feet wide and was as high as the ceiling (about eight feet high).

There were small computer monitors, computer consoles, and display screens in between each of the beds. The grey floor had a few one and half foot bloodstains stretching past the first table on both sides of the room. Pools of blood rested on the surface of the next table on both sides. The next four tables were covered with cloth and medical instruments. Lights about two feet long rested above the head of each bed. Each light was less than a foot and half away from the head of the beds. We walked halfway into the room. As he passed the beds Mozet looked down at the two bloody beds and shook his head.

We stopped at the back of the room. The door between the racks slid into the ceiling revealing a smaller room. The room on the other side of the doorway was packed full to the ceiling with racks full of medical supplies and other equipment. There was a small path that led through the mass of equipment. The far wall had metal crates staked to the ceiling. Each one of the crates had Talin markings across the front. Mozet walked along the path and after a second he disappeared behind a wall of equipment. After a few more seconds he reappeared at the back of the room. He walked along the back wall and came to a stop in front a few stacks of crates from the right wall. He pulled one of the metal crates out of the third to last stack, opened it, examined its contents, closed the crate, and started walking along the back wall of crates again. He disappeared again only to reappear a few seconds later ahead of us carrying two crates.

"Come on out of my way. We will do this back at my office," Mozet said as he approached us.

We stepped to either side of the door and let him pass. After passing us he walked past the eight tables and then left the room. We followed him out of the room seconds later and back to his office. By the time we had returned to his office he was standing behind his desk, he already had the two crates open and was in the process of removing their contents and setting them on his desk. We walked into the room and then walked towards Mozet's desk.

"Hold it! Everyone, that needs a prosthesis fixed may continue; everyone, else stay behind those tables!" said Mozet, raising his voice.

Halado, Amanda, Samantha, and Aldam stopped walking and stayed near the tables while I walked towards his desk. I stopped a few inches away from his desk and placed my prosthesis in front of him. Mozet picked up my broken limb and looked it over again. Then he pressed down on the computer screen compartment and waited for it to open. After two minutes of waiting he picked up one of the devices that had been stored in one of the crates. He placed the device under the elbow then placed my prosthesis down on the device, and then he pushed some buttons on its sides. The devices lit up and wrapped around the prosthesis's elbow. I heard ticking and drilling sounds coming from the device as it worked.

After five or six minutes the device stopped working and unwrapped itself from my prosthesis. Mozet reached forward and pulled the forearm of the prosthesis. Immediately the forearm separated from the upper portion of the prosthesis. As he pulled the forearm, a bundle of wires an inch and an half in diameter and five inches long followed the forearm. The bundle of wires was the only thing connecting the two pieces of the prosthesis. The bundle of wires consisted of many different colors. Some of the wires had small clamps attaching them to another wire. Mozet moved his head inches above the bundle of wires and looked upon the wires while he used his hands to separate each wire. He continued to look through the wires for a few minutes.

Mozet then reached to his right with his right hand and retrieved one of the devices on his desk. With his left hand he held the wires apart and with his right hand he placed the device into the opening and pushed down on the back of the device. After a second a small grey jet of smoke rose from within the bundle of wires. He removed the device after a few more seconds and returned to his search through the bundle of wires. He moved some of the wires around then after a second he picked up the device again and placed it back into the bundle of wires. Once again a jet of smoke rose from out of the wire bundle and vanished into the air. Mozet removed the device from within the bundle of wires and placed it down on top of the desk. He continued to look through the wires for another couple of minutes then he let go of the bundle of wires.

Mozet then pushed my prosthesis's forearm towards the elbow with his right arm and with his left he guided the bundle of wires back into both parts of the prosthesis. After a minute he stopped an inch away from the upper arm and placed the forearm down onto the device under the prosthesis's elbow. Then Mozet pushed a button next to the one he had pushed before. The device turned on and wrapped itself around the forearm and the upper arm. The device began to work. After a few minutes the device stopped working and unwrapped itself from around the prosthesis. Both parts of the prosthesis had been reconnected and the wires had been concealed inside the prosthesis. Mozet pulled the device from under my prosthesis and placed it back into the closet crate. Then he picked up the other device and placed it into one of the crates.

"Your prosthesis is fixed. As for the artificial skin you will have to get that repaired the next time you see Zar," Mozet said, standing up from behind his desk.

"Why can't you mend the skin?"

"First of all the equipment I would need, I just don't have down here. Even if I did the solution used to make your particular skin is too new and would only be on the medical level."

"Thank you for repairing my prosthesis."

"Yes whatever; I have a lot of work to do so if you could go on about your business and leave me be."

"Alright."

I turned and started to walk across his office. When I reached Halado, Aldam, Amanda, and Samantha, Mozet spoke.

"Hold on; did Zar give you a FX-19 when he grafted your artificial skin?"

"No; what is a FX-19?"

"This device heals small tears in the artificial skin. It should also be able to heal your normal flesh."

"Why couldn't you use the FX-19 to mend the artificial skin?"

"As I said it only heals small cuts, the amount of damage your skin received was too severe for it to heal," Mozet said as his desk started beeping.

"Here take this FX-19. I am surprised that you weren't given one when the skin was grafted. Although with the amount of work they have it's not unexpected. Be careful with that arm of yours."

"I will try."

The five of us walked to the door and passed through after it had opened. We turned to our left and started to walk down the hallway. Just as we reached the door that led to the hanger bay, Mozet called my name.

"Alex; wait you have been requested on the bridge immediately."

"How am I supposed to get to the bridge? The main lift is not working."

"Yes, I know; that's why you will have to take the maintenance lift."

"Where is the maintenance lift?"

"You wouldn't be able to find the lift. It is hidden, so unauthorized people wouldn't be able to access."

"Then how are we supposed to us the lift."

"I will lead you to the lift. After the lift has come to a stop you should be able to find your way to the bridge."

"Alright, then where do we go?"

"First I have to find out if the hanger bay is safe for us to cross."

"Alright."

Mozet turned around, walked back to the door of his office and passed through the door. After a few minutes he returned from his office.

"Let's go," he said as he passed us and continued through the door and into the hanger bay.

The five of us walked through the door following Mozet into the hanger. The hanger bay had a few more crashes than when we left a short time ago. Five fighters had crashed; three of the fighters had crashed on their undersides and had a tail of fire following them about ten feet long about three feet wide. The flames were varying in sizes anywhere from a foot to three. The flames were also of different colors. Orange flames covered the majority of the tail. The other two fighters were lying on there top with the cockpit crushed due to the fighter's weight. Both of the fighters had thick and heavy smoke pouring out of the entire fighter. As the smoke rose it was immediately being drawn through vents at the top of the hanger bay. Above one of the two smoking fighters, one of the claws dangled about forty feet from the fighter and sixty feet from the ceiling with sparks spraying out of each of the claw's fingers.

Small jets of white smoke rose from the fingers and vanished into the air. Medical crews had already gotten to the three fighters on their bellies and were working on getting the pilots out of their fighters. There were crews attempting to get to the other two fighters and rescue the pilots but the smoke was too thick and too strong. Mozet turned to our left after a few seconds of looking the room over. We joined him and walked along the wall separating the hanger bay and the hallway for ten feet then we turned to our right and walked around the trails of fire. After walking across the hanger bay, we turned right again until we reached the double hanger bay door then we passed through the door and entered into another hallway.

The hall looked identical to any other hallway on the *Colonizer* in the overall scheme. There were signs of blood on the chrome floor and there were deep cuts dug into the floor and the walls. Both walls had doors separated by eight feet for as far as my eyes could make out. Mozet turned to the right and began to walk along the hall. We followed him down the hall. As we walked some of the ceiling mounted lights flickered on and off. After twenty minutes we walked past the doors of the main elevator. After about an additional fifteen minutes, we came to a stop in front of a section of the wall that shined in a bright and magnificent shade of green. A few inches from the glowing section of the wall was a glowing blue panel which was hardly noticeable due to the over whelming shine of the wall.

Mozet definitely had no trouble seeing the blue panel as he walked right up to it and placed his hand on the panel. A second later the wall rose into the ceiling revealing a small and narrow passageway. The passageway wasn't completed; both the walls were unfinished showing the metal beams that held the walls together and the many wires that passed through the entire ship. The ceiling was also unfinished; you could plainly see every part of all the lights. There were a few rafters connecting across the width of the hall. The wall across from us had a door and was also unfinished. Next to the door about three four inches was a blue glowing panel. You could see all the circuits that made the panel function with the outside layer of the wall not in place. The door stood with a heavy looking metal frame about six inches wide and stood nine feet. The frame were the door met the panel was a maximum of four inches wide. The floor wasn't chrome like all of the other halls. The floor to this hall was dual flat and had no shine to it. However, in a few small places the floor looked like it was chrome. Even though the hallway was not finished everything in the hallway was in working order.

Mozet walked across the hall and placed his hand on the glowing panel and steeped back seconds later the door opened revealing another room. The room was large and appeared to be quite busy with life. This room had four levels each level could be seen through the metal grates that made up the floor of the upper three levels. All four of the floors were connected my metal staircases. Off to our right there was another door. The wall across from us looked to be a couple thousand of feet away. The wall was too far away to see any detail of any kind. The holes in the metal grate were to fine to be able to see completely to the next level. However, due to the design of each level I was able to see the last level.

Mozet turned to his left and walked to the other door. As he approached the door slid into its right wall. Mozet passed through the door and waited in the doorframe for us to join him. We walked along the wall until we reached Mozet.

"This is where we part."

"Why?"

"Because, there is work I have to due here; if you recall correctly."

"Alright."

"Once you are in the lift just push the glowing blue button above the hundred other buttons on the lift's right wall. After pushing the button the lift will take you a few levels below the bridge."

He then steeped out of the lift, then he let us slide into the lift. Once we were all in the lift the door started to close.

"The top button is the one you need to press," he said as the door closed behind us.

"Alex, you're the closest to the buttons. The blue button is..." Halado said as I pushed the glowing blue button and stopped when he discovered I was able to see the hidden button. "How did you know where the button was?"

"All of my natural abilities and my senses have been enhanced."

"How?" asked Aldam.

"There is trace amounts of the substance that covers the Shadows in my blood."

"Everyone, back away from Alex and do not touch him," Halado said, backing up into the lift's back wall.

"There isn't enough of the substance in my system to make me one of them, nor kill me. The reason I have the prosthesis is that Zar and Hamole had to remove my arm in order to stop the substance from spreading any further. Also it appears that humans have a high resistance against the substance. And this resistance is what keeps the substance from growing."

"Did Zar say all of this to you?"

"Yes he did, is that good enough for you, Halado?"

"I am still keeping an eye on you."

"Fine, what about the rest of you? Do you have any problems with me?"

"I am keeping an eye on you too. I have seen too many people turn into Shadows in my life I have come to know the signs. Halado, if I see any signs I will kill him where he stands."

"Regardless of what is in your blood I will accompany you. It is the least I can do after breaking your prosthesis," Samantha said, looking at the others.

"What about you, Amanda?"

"I was ordered to see you to safety and until I receive new orders I will follow my last order."

"I take it the four of you will be accompanying me to the bridge."

"Yes we are," said Aldam.

"If that is what you all want to do there is nothing I can do to stop you."

The lift fell silent as we continued our ascent higher into the ship. No one spoke the remainder of our ascent. After an hour and a half we came to a stop. The wall on our right side opened into an unfinished hallway. This hallway looked like the last hallway that we encountered except this hallway was two times longer. We exited the maintenance lift and walked the length of the hall. As we approached the door ahead of us opened allowing passage through. We now stood in a hallway; to my right the hall looked like it went on for as far as my eyes could see. The left side looked like it went on for a couple of hundred feet before the hall stopped.

"Halado, how are we supposed to get to the bridge from here?" asked Amanda.

"Just because I am a Talin doesn't mean that I know my way around our ship."

"I'm sorry. I just thought that you might have been here before."

"Sorry, I haven't."

"Aldam, do you have a clue of where to go?"

"No. Like Halado, I haven't been this high in the *Colonizer* before. If we had a map we could probably find our way."

"Wait I have a map," I said, taking the data pad out of my right pocket.

"Let me see," Halado said, sticking his left hand out to receive the data pad.

I went to place the data pad in his hand as my hand approached his, he withdrew his hand a few inches.

"Sorry but I can't take any chances. Just drop the data pad into my hands."

"Fine, here you go," I said as I dropped the data pad an inch into his left hand.

He took the data pad and looked upon its screen. Then he pushed down on some of the buttons on the data pad. For ten minutes he worked on the data pad then he broke out laughing.

"What is so funny?"

"Stupid monkeys," he said as he continued to work on the data pad.

"What was that, Halado?" asked Amanda.

"It's just a message that has been programmed into the data pad. The message 'stupid monkeys' flashes across the screen every time I put a destination into the data pad."

"Where did you get your map?" asked Aldam.

"From an ugly old hag when I and one of my friends were down in the security room on the ground level."

"What were you doing there?" Samantha asked, walking down the left side of the hall a few feet.

"My friend and I were looking for a few people that we lost contact with after the battles."

"Did you find them?" asked Amanda.

"No, we didn't find all of them."

"Sorry to hear that," said Samantha.

"If you don't mind me asking; who were you looking for?" asked Amanda.

"I don't mind. We were looking for our parents and someone we met back on earth."

"Did you find your parents?" asked Samantha.

"No, we didn't find them."

"Did your friend find their parents?" asked Samantha.

"No her parents died in the meteor storm."

"Do you know what happened to your parents?" asked Amanda.

"No I don't know what happened to them."

"You don't seem to be at all concerned about them?" asked Amanda.

"That's because I don't remember them. The only thing I know is that they are my parents."

"I'm finished. This data pad will now lead us to the bridge," Halado said, handing the data pad carefully to me.

"Alright; then let us continue," I said while I glanced down at the data pad.

The yellow line indicated for us to turn to the left and walk down the hall.

"We have to go to the left."

I started to walk down the hall. Samantha walked on my right and Amanda walked on my left. Halado and Aldam walked a few feet behind us. Every few minutes I would glance down at the data pad.

The line on the data pad continued on down the hallway. After fifteen minutes the line veered off to the left and passed through a door. I turned when the line passed through the door and followed it through. We were led into a long hallway that cut across the entire ship. The hall looked to be a couple of thousand feet long. We started to walk down the hallway after a minute of looking down the hall. There was no end in sight to the hallway.

We followed the line on the data pad down the hallway. After twenty minutes the yellow line turned to the right and passed through a door with a glowing blue panel next to it. Halado walked up to the panel and placed his hand on the panel. After a few seconds the panel shined a dark red.

"What is wrong?"

"I don't have clearance to use this lift."

"What are we supposed to do now?" asked Amanda.

"We should look for another way to get to the bridge," Samantha asked, starting to walk back down the hall.

"Hold on, let me try?"

"Why?" questioned Halado.

"I have been able to use my prosthesis to open every door I have come upon."

"Go ahead I doubt it will work."

I walked over to the panel and placed my prosthesis upon the panel and stepped back a few seconds later. We waited for five minutes; Samantha and Aldam started to walk back down the hall when the door opened revealing a lift with two Talins inside. Both of the Talins looked to be completely exhausted and ready to fall asleep where they stood. They both walked out of the lift and turned to the left and started to walk down the hallway. When the lift door opened both Samantha and Aldam stopped walking and turned around and joined us at the lift entrance. We filed into the lift. Once we were into the lift a voice from within the walls spoke.

"Where would you like to go?"

"Halado, do you know where this lift will take us?"

"It is supposed to end at the main cafeteria?"

The lift started up as he finished his last word. We rose higher into the *Colonizer* climbing level after level. We climbed for almost twenty minutes before we stopped and the door opened into the large

271

cafeteria. We stepped out. I looked to my right then my left trying to figure out where we came out. We were a hundred feet away from the door my friends and I had used before. There was another door on my left about the same distance from the door on my right. I continued into the room and walked around the rows of tables. I reached the middle section in the room and placed my hand on the glowing panel next to the middle door. I stepped back and waited for the lift doors to open. When the door opened I stepped inside and immediately noticed that the others were still standing in front of the lift door.

"Are you four coming with me or would you like to stay here?" I asked, yelling across the room.

I stepped into the doorway and held the door open as they started to walk across the room. After a minute the door tried to close but I pushed it open and held it in place as they crossed the cafeteria. After another minute they joined me and filed in to the elevator while I held it open. Once they were all in the lift I slipped in as I did the door immediately closed. The lift started and we began our seven minute ascent to the black turret room.

"Alex, have you seen the cafeteria before?" asked Aldam.

"Yes several times before actually. Every time I come to see Movork, Shaurha, and our president. I have also operated some of the turrets in the next room."

"How did you become so popular?" asked Aldam.

"My friend Crystal and I were the humans that led Shaurha and what remained of the *Kento's* crew to safety. I also saved Hamole's life a few times while we were fighting the Shadows. In one of my battles against the Shadows I was attacked and my right arm was bit by one of the hounds. Once we were on board the *Colonizer* my arm was removed in the medical facility."

The door to the lift opened. The turret room was brightly lit by many lights in the ceiling. The walls of the turret were still black but now there was light shining upon the walls. All of the turrets in the room were closed. The majority of the doors in the room had horizontal red lines crossing them. A few of those doors had been dented into the room a few inches and had been welded shut. Some of the doors had been removed and had the old damaged door lying against the new doors. There were a few Talins working on sealing a few of the doors.

I walked along the wall of the staircase, turned and started to walk up the staircase. Halado, Aldam, Amanda, and Samantha followed me up the staircase. When I reached the end of the staircase I walked over to the right and searched for the button Shaurha and Zar pushed previously. After a few seconds I found the button, then I pushed it down and the door above us separated revealing the door in front of the staircase. After the doors had opened enough for us to pass through we climbed the remaining stairs. Once I reached the top I turned to my right and walked through the door. The bridge was fully manned. All of the computer consoles had Talins operating them. Movork was sitting in the center of the room with a data pad in his hands and was looking upon the large display screen. I walked towards Movork slowly.

"Excuse me, Captain. One of your guests has arrived," said a Talin facing the display screen.

"He has; where?" Movork said, moving his head from right to left and then coming to a stop upon me only a few feet away from him."

"It is without a doubt good to see you well, Alex. After that transmission I thought you didn't survive your return."

"I'm glad too that I made it back alive."

"I see you made some new friends."

"Yeah, it is the least I could do. They're the ones who towed me back to the *Colonizer*."

"Alex, you should go to the conference room and we will join you in a short while. There is no need for you to join him, you four can wait in the cafeteria. If you have trouble using the lift, ask one of the engineers there to call the lift."

We left the bridge. I opened the door across the staircase for my new friends then I turned right and passed through the door above the staircase while they made their way to the turret room. I started walking towards the door on the back wall. After walking into the hall a few feet I heard a high-pitched screech coming from the second door on my left. The door was open a few inches. As I approached the door, I heard President Clark talking to someone. I looked through the crack of the door. President Clark was standing in front of a large screen. The screen was dark and had a grey silhouette of a man. There were no distinguishable details on the image being displayed.

"Hello, President Clark."

"What do you want? I was hoping I would not get another call from you. What are you doing calling? Someone could overhear us."

"You messed up, Mr. President."

"Yeah and you told me that no one would be hurt!"

"I can't help it that when the Shadows attack; that there are always fatalities. I thought you would have figured that out by now, Mister President!"

"You lied to me!"

"Yeah so. I told you not to do anything that might risk the ancient ruins!"

"I had no choice if I didn't activate the United States atomic warheads then I would be a suspect. Then I couldn't help you with your plans!"

"You have better hope that your stupidity didn't destroy what I am looking for. If it was destroyed it won't be your life that I will be coming for it will be your children's. The upside to your stupidity is the Shadows will abandon your planet allowing me and my forces to find the ancient ruins."

"Mister President, have you taken the steps necessary to control your people."

"Yes I have the Lazarus Protocol is in affect. It is working properly. No matter what happens, the people of earth will not get in our way."

"HA-HA-HA good, Mister President and with the Shadows out of our way finding the ruins will be easy."

"What about the radiation from the warheads."

"That is nothing to worry about. My forces will be prepared. Tell me, Mister President, what is the Lazarus protocol?"

"We put subliminal messages in all broadcasts that when activated the Lazarus Protocol alters everyone's will of self-preservation."

"Good we don't need any reason for your people to get suspicious. President Clark, you will be hearing from me if the ruins are gone."

The screen went black taking the black face with it. The room was now near completely dark. Only a small amount of light came from the various lights in the room. After a few seconds a silhouette walked out of the shadows and stopped next to President Clark.

"Mr. President, are you sure using the Lazarus Protocol is a good idea?"

"No, my friend; I am not sure, but it is too late to do anything now, the damage has already been done."

"Can we trust him, sir?"

"No we can't, but the alternative is much worse and that we couldn't afford."

"What do you mean?"

"If I didn't assist him with his plan; he would have killed us all in search for his relics. As it is he could still come and kill us all."

"How could he do such a thing while we are under the protection of the Talins?"

"Do you think that a vessel trying to evacuate a planet and got destroyed by the Shadows would raise any suspicions?"

"He could reach us here."

"If he has a large enough army then yes he could."

"What are we to do then?"

"Nothing, we go about as though we know nothing about him."

"And if he does come?"

"Then we have no choice but to tell Movork and hope he understands. For now, my friend, I have a meeting to attend to."

"What is the meeting for?"

"Movork and Captain Almiss have come up with a plan to get us out of this asteroid belt safely."

"Do you know what his plan is?"

"No that is what the meeting is for to inform everyone of interest of the current problems."

"I will leave you to your meeting then, Mr. President."

"My friend, see to it my daughters are protected. Take any of my protection if you need to."

"I will. I will see you later, Mr. President."

"Goodbye, my friend, and take care," President Clark said as the silhouette passed through a door and disappeared from view.

President Clark's silhouette moved towards me. Immediately I moved away from the door and quickly walked to the conference room. The door to the conference room opened as I approached. I walked through the door and took a seat on the right side of the table. I had only been sitting in my seat for two or three minutes when the door opened and President Clark walked through and took a seat across from me.

"Hello, Alex, what are you doing here?"

"I don't know. I was asked to come up here by Movork. Mr. President, do you have any idea what we are doing here?"

"No I don't. It looks like we both will find out when Movork joins us."

The room fell silent. President Clark and I traded glances every so often then looked around the room. We sat there in near dead silence for a while as we waited for Movork to arrive. After ten minutes the door opened and four men walked past President Clark and sat down next to him. Two of the men sat down on his right and the other two sat down on his left. The four new men looked upon me with faces full of questions. After a few more minutes the door opened and Movork, Zar, Hamole, and Shaurha passed through the door. The four of them took seats at the table. Movork sat at the head of the table in front of the door. Shaurha sat on my left, Zar, and Hamole sat on my right. Zar sat in the seat closest to me.

"Alex, what happened to your prosthesis?" asked Zar.

"I got in a fight with a fighter."

"Yeah and who won?" asked Movork.

"The fighter won by a wing. But I left my mark on it."

"Ha-ha-ha-ha-ha-ha," Movork laughed out loud.

"Captain Movork, why are we here and why is this boy here?"

"You are all here to be informed as to what has happened and as to what we are going to do."

"What about this boy, why is he here?"

"Alex is here because he knows more about what he saw than any of us. We need to know what he knows. If you have any more questions save them until we are done with this meeting and then ask. You may just find out some of the answers to your questions."

No one spoke for a few minutes.

"Alright then we will begin. You have all been asked to this meeting so alternative plans can be made. The plan Almiss and I have come up with is not the best one and it carries a high risk that we will not make it alive. First you need to know what the problem is. Alex, tell everyone what you said in your message and what you saw outside the belt."

"I spotted a stray Shadow fighter trying to escape. I followed him through the asteroid belt keeping close to him trying to get a lock on him. He cleared the asteroid belt and when I approached the belt's edge I spotted five large Shadow ships. The five ships are positioned not far from where our path will come out. The five ships are waiting for us to finish the path. There could be more than the five ships, the five ships are all that I had time to see. After I spotted the ships I turned my fighter around and fired up the engines and tried to escape as they fired upon me."

"How did you get back?" asked one of the men on President Clark's right.

"The enemy's fire missed my fighter for the most part. However, my fighter was damaged enough so I ended up being towed back to one of the hanger bays."

"Thank you, Alex. These five ships and possibly more are waiting for us, if we continue with our current plan we will not survive. Captain Almiss and I have come up with a plan that has a better chance of working. We don't want to do this plan, but after looking our current situation over, we have decided that this is our only chance. You are here to hear our plan and give feedback and try to come up with a plan that will increase our chances," Movork said, standing up and walking to the back of the room and pushing a button on the back wall.

"What is your plan?" asked the man on President Clark's left.

"Well, Duke, we are planning to destroy the *Franchasno* near enough to destroy and disable the enemy ships."

"Movork explain more of your plan?"

"Captain Almiss and a very small number of Talins are rigging the *Franchasno* with explosives. As soon as she comes in view of the enemy they will open fire upon her. We are going to remotely control her weapons and engines. When she is destroyed either by us or by them the explosion will be huge. When it is destroyed, two Talin warships that are in waiting will come to our aid but no sooner."

"Can't we call for more ships?"

"We have already lost four warships and besides the nearest ships would take four days to reach us."

"Why not call for reinforcements and wait the four days for them to arrive."

"Long range communication is being jammed for the entire system."

"What of the asteroid belt, if we continue to clear the path as we have, they will attack our fighters then us."

"Yes we have already thought about that, Commodore. We plan on using the weapons on the *Franchasno* to clear as much of the asteroid belt, at the same time we plan on using the *Franchasno* to plow the way for the *Colonizer*. If everything goes as planned we are in good shape, if not we will not survive. Take a few minutes and think upon what I have said and talk with everyone here and bounce ideas off of us."

Movork sat down in his seat and watched as every thought upon what we said. After twenty minutes President Clark spoke. I sat there listening to everyone discussing as to what to do for an hour. Then the conference room fell silent again. After twenty minutes Movork spoke.

"Oh, Alex, if you would like to leave you can there isn't really any need for you to be here any longer. You look like you are about to fall asleep, why don't you return to your room and get some rest especially after the day you have had."

"You are probably right, Captain Movork. I do feel tired. Thank you."

Chapter Nineteen
Unimaginable Disaster

I stood up, walked past Zar and Hamole and left the conference room. I walked down the hallway and passed through the door at the end. The staircase was still open. I walked down the staircase, turned right and walked to the lift. I placed my hand on the door and waited for the lift door to open. After seven minutes the lift door opened. I passed through the doorway and turned to face the turret room. Seconds after entering the lift the door closed followed by the lift starting its descent. After seven minutes the lift stopped and the door opened. I exited the lift and walked into the cafeteria. Halado and Aldam weren't anywhere in the cafeteria. Amanda and Samantha were sitting to my right only two rows from me.

I walked along the rows of tables until I reached the end of the row. I walked over two of the closest food dispensers and ordered some fried chicken. I then turned around and walked over to Amanda and Samantha and sat down next to Samantha on her right. Amanda was sitting across from Samantha. Both of them had gotten some food and something to drink and were in the process of eating their food. As I sat they both looked up from their trays.

"What did Mowvick want?" asked Samantha.

"His name is Movork. He just wanted me to tell the president what I saw in space."

"What did you see?" asked Amanda.

"I don't think you want to know."

"Come on tell us what you saw," Samantha said, putting down her fork and looking me in the eyes.

"I saw five Shadow warships waiting for us to leave the belt."

"You saw five warships?" asked Amanda.

"Yes and there may be more than just the five."

"What do you mean may be more?" asked Amanda.

"That's all I could see in the amount of time I had."

"Do you know what Movork's plan is?"

"Yes but it isn't very promising."

"What is his plan?"

"He and the captain of the *Franchasno* are going to plow the *Franchasno* the rest of the way through the belt clearing us a path and then blowing her up when the enemy gets close. They hope the blast destroys all five ships or at least disables them. However, if there are many more than five warships; the outlook probably won't be good."

"Can't they call for more help?" asked Samantha.

"There are two ships waiting to assist us after the explosion and long range communications are being jammed," I said before taking a mouth full of food.

"That doesn't sound like a very good plan," Amanda said, before taking a bite of food.

"Neither captain wants to go through with this plan but it has the highest chance of working. That is why they called the meeting to see if another plan could be made that might have a better outcome."

"Why are you down here?" asked Amanda.

"They no longer needed me. Where did Halado and Aldam go?"

"We ran into one of their commanding officers and they were ordered to return to the hanger bay," Samantha said after swallowing some food.

"They didn't get into any trouble, did they?"

"No, they simply said that they were finishing their last orders and were returning to the hanger bay for their next orders."

"That's good."

"What are we supposed to do now?" asked Amanda.

"Are you two supposed to find your commanding officer and get new orders?"

"I was a civilian and was only asked to help evacuate earth and fight the enemy on earth. So I have no commander. I help when I can and where I am needed," said Amanda before taking another mouth full of food.

"Same goes for me," said Samantha.

"What about you, Alex?" asked Amanda.

"I am not completely sure where I stand."

"Why?" asked Samantha.

"Like you I volunteered, but I also said that I would fight the Shadows when I was given the option of getting the prosthesis. So far all I have done is as I was asked. Have both of you done just about everything that has been asked of you lately since this whole thing started."

Both of them put their forks down and stared off into the cafeteria for a minute while they thought.

"I haven't thought about it before now, but yes whenever I have been asked to help defend this ship or fight the Shadows, I volunteered," said Amanda.

"Now that you mention it I have volunteered also," said Samantha.

"Doesn't it seem strange that every person that was old enough to fight volunteered? I have even see people who were physically incapable of fighting showing up to volunteer."

"Maybe a little," said Samantha.

"Why do you think everyone volunteering is strange?" asked Samantha.

"I have my reasons."

"Tell us your reasons?" asked Amanda.

"Another time I want to speak with a few people at the meeting first."

"Alright," said Amanda before finishing her tray of food and then finishing her drink.

"I don't know about the two of you ladies but I have had a long day."

"What are you implying?" asked Amanda with an angry look on her face.

"Not on the first date and not with an audience, only participants," Samantha said, flashing me a wink with her left eye.

"I didn't mean anything by it."

"Really, then why don't I believe you?" asked Amanda.

"I was just letting you know that I was exhausted."

"Aha, sure you were."

"That is alright with me if you don't believe me. Regardless I am going to my room and get some sleep. I was going to ask if you wanted me to help you and Samantha back downstairs so you could get some rest too but maybe I won't."

"I'm sorry, Alex. I get a little jumpy when it comes to things like that and I take it the wrong way."

"Alex, where is your room?" asked Samantha.

"A few floors down."

"Lucky, you only have a few floors to go to your room. Our rooms are on the bottom floor and we have to share it with many people," said Amanda.

"There may be a few rooms available up here. I could ask one of the doctors if you would like to accompany me a little further."

"How many people sleep in the room?" asked Amanda.

"There is only one person per room."

"I'm in. I haven't had a decent sleep since before the meteor shower," Amanda said, standing up.

"I was in as soon as you asked," Samantha said, joining Amanda.

Both of them walked over to the dispensers and placed them inside and then walked back over to the table. They both sat down and waited for me to finish my food. The whole time they talked amongst themselves. After ten minutes I stood up, walked over to one of the dispensers and placed my try down inside. Both Samantha and Amanda had followed me over to the dispenser and were standing a few feet away from me smiling.

"I take it you really want to get a good night's rest?"

"You have no idea how badly," said Amanda.

"I wouldn't mind some quiet while I sleep," said Samantha.

"Alright then follow me and we will see if there are any rooms available."

I led them through the cafeteria and brought them face to face with the lift to the medical level. I placed my prosthesis on the blue panel and we waited for the door to open. The three of us filed into the lift seconds before the door closed and then we began our descent to the medical level. The lift came to a stop a few minutes later and then the doors opened. We filed out of the lift and then I led them down the hallway past my room, past the rec room and past the main lift doors. I led them all the way to the end of the hallway then we turned into the door now marked in English medical facilities. The room was deserted not a single person on any of the beds nor was there any medical personal in the room. We walked to the back of the room. I placed my hand on the glowing blue panel. The wall opened revealing the hidden room.

We passed through the doorway. The room was void of life aside from Amanda Samantha and my self. A lot of the equipment that had been in the room was now gone. The room looked quite bare from the last time I was there.

"There is no one here," said Amanda.

"There may be someone on the other side."

We turned around and walked back through the hidden door. I turned to my left and passed through the surgical room's door. There also was no one there. We continued on through the door across from us. The second medical room had only one person other than the three of us there. Mallowon was in the back of the room moving some of the equipment around. I walked though the room coming to a stop a few feet from her. She looked up as I approached her.

"Alex, what happened to your arm?"

"I was in a small incident in the lower left side hanger bay."

"What happened?"

"My prosthesis was hit by the wing of a crashing fighter."

"I see that it is working."

"Yes, I asked one of the hanger bay's doctors if he could fix it. And obviously Mozet was able to fix the prosthesis itself, but he couldn't fix the artificial skin."

"Luckily Zar made more of the solution for your skin type."

"That's good but that is not why I am currently here."

"Then what is your reason?"

"I was wondering if there were any rooms available in any of the medical rooms."

"Yes a few opened up a while ago, but they are reserved for medical purposes."

"Is there any way the two of them could get at least a night's sleep in the rooms?"

"They could only get the rooms if they had a medical reason for needing the rooms."

"What about being so exhausted that it could be mentally damaging? Neither of them have had anywhere near a good night's sleep."

"I see, alright they can have the rooms until we run out of space and need the rooms. The same goes for your other friends. There isn't anyone in need other than your two new friends so they can use the rooms."

"They haven't."

"No not yet. In fact no one has returned yet."

"Where is everyone anyways?"

"Since the lift is broken all the medical staff is at the hangers trying to take care of the wounded. And none of the wounded can be brought up here until the lift is fixed so I have nothing to do. I figured that I would move some of the equipment around and try to make it more efficient."

"I see the more efficient your environment, the better you can perform your job. Mallowen, where are the rooms?"

"Oh I'm sorry they are a level below us only a few rooms away from the lift's door. You will need the room card keys in order to use the rooms. Give me a few minutes. I will be back with two keys for your friends," Mallowon said as she walked past me then passed Samantha and Amanda.

Mallowon passed through the door and walked into the surgical room. Amanda and Samantha walked along the path in between the tables. Then they both came to a stop in front of me.

"Well, are there any rooms available?" asked Amanda, stopping a few feet in front of me.

"Yes. There were a few available rooms."

"Where did the Talin go?" asked Samantha.

"She went to go get card keys to your rooms. She should be back in a few minutes."

"Thank you for getting us our own rooms," said Samantha.

"Could you tell us about your friends?" asked Amanda.

"I don't remember much about them only a few things."

"Why don't you remember anything?" asked Amanda.

I started to tell them about how I lost my memory when Mallowon walked back through the door to the surgical room. Mallowen walked across along the path and joined us at the end of the room.

"Here are two keys for your friends."

"Mallowon, I have another favor to ask. Could you take Amanda and Samantha to their rooms? I need to get some rest before I pass out."

"You're lucky, I have nothing else to do at the moment."

"Thank you, Mallowon."

"Alright come along."

We followed Mallowon back through the surgical room and out of the medical facility. Then we began walking down the hallway. We passed the main lift then the rec room and then came to a stop in front of my room. We stopped a few feet away from the door to my room in order to prevent the door from opening.

"Goodbye, I will see you both later."

"Goodnight to you, Alex," said Amanda.

"Thank you, Alex," said Samantha.

"You both are welcome and again thank you, Mallowon, for getting the rooms and taking them to them."

"You're welcome, Alex, now get some rest."

I walked forward and passed through the door to my room as it fully opened. After walking into the room a few feet the door closed behind me. I walked over to the dresser and opened one of its compartments and placed the data pad and my card key on top of my other data pad. I closed the compartment and opened up another. The inside was bare. I closed the first and opened another. In the second compartment was another uniform like the one I currently was wearing. I closed the compartment and lay back on my bed and thought about the Lazarus Protocol. I must have fallen asleep while I thought about what the Lazarus Protocol was, because the next thing I knew I was lying on my left side in a black and silent hallway with small amounts of illumination barely illuminating the walls.

The hallway was too dark to see any detail on the walls or anything surrounding me. In front of me a flicker of light some distance away caught my eye. I raised my right arm and felt along the surface of my arm. I felt a tear in my skin, then the cold metal of my prosthesis, and then more torn flesh. I started to walk down the hall towards the flickering light when after ten steps I heard my surroundings set off a long loud nerve-racking moan. Once the moan had passed I continued along into the hallway. After another twenty steps a cold chill fell upon the hall. I felt cold rush over my body soaking through my cloths, my flesh, all the way to my bones. I continued into the hall slowly trying to push through the freezing air. Then just as fast as the freeze fell upon the hall it vanished and was replaced with a growing heat wave. I felt my temperature rising very quickly. I could feel my body producing sweat by the quart.

My clothes grew heavy as my sweat soaked into my cloths. As I grew closer to the flickering light, I raised my right arm and aimed it down the hallway. I kept my thoughts away from wanting either form of my prosthesis's weapons from coming out. I didn't know what was going on nor where I was for that matter how I got here nor did I know who I would run into (friend or foe). I continued along the hallway walking through the eerie dark and hot hall. As I walked the flickering light got brighter larger and more defined.

The lack of light the change intemperate and lack of sound was making the hairs on the back of my neck stand on end as I approached the flickering light. After walking twenty minutes I came upon the source of the flickering light. The light was coming from sparks spraying out of wires hanging out of part of the right wall. The sparks light up the immediate hallway showing the walls floor and ceiling in an orange glow. The floor was covered in debris from a hole in the right wall. The sparks were spraying into the hole casing the passageway on the other side of the wall to glow. I moved closer to the hole walking on debris as I approached the hole. I looked down into the passage. There was no light no sound the air was dry hot and cold.

I couldn't hear a thing besides my own breathing in the hallway nor coming from the passage. In the growing heat I forced myself to look into the passage. As I stepped into the wall debris beneath my feet slid out from under me. With my right hand I placed my hand on top of the wire spraying sparks. The area was no longer quiet. The sound of the debris that I had knocked loose colliding with metal and other debris ricocheted through the hallway. The endless darkness of both the hall and passage echoed the debris's fall. The air from within the passage roared as a cold wave of air rushed over my face and body. The air grew violent and strong forcing me back into the hallway. I left the hole in the wall and continued along down the hallway with a violent wind growing on my back. As the wind increased I fought to keep on my feet.

As I walked a sudden surge of wind whipped past my ears with a howl (like a pack of wolves during a full moon) and then sent me to the ground. I landed on something soft. I felt around on the floor beneath my feet with my left hand I used my right to support my weight. I felt my weight shift as my right hand sank into the mass beneath me. The mass beneath my knees was wet slick and thick. I could feel my hand move through a liquid trapped in an inch basin of flesh. Floating in the liquid was meaty chunks of matter. My kneecaps were soaking in the liquid of the moist mass of flesh. I felt around some more and found a round shaped object. I felt the object trying to identify what it was.

There was another surge of wind. The force from the wind through me off balance and forced me to fall face first in to the pool of liquid. Immediately I pulled my face from within the basin of the liquid the liquid was warm and slowly ran down my face and onto my shirt. I shook my head back and forth throwing the liquid on to my surroundings. I then used my left hand to wipe the remaining liquid from my face. I tried to get to my feet but the force of the wind kept me on my knees hunch over the mass beneath me. After a few minutes I gave up trying to get up and let the wind hold me down. I used both hands to support my weight and the weight of the wind. The wind behind me grew in power forcing the mass and me to slide forward.

Inches from the floor and the mass of flesh a horrible smell of rotting and digested meat filled the air. The smell was poring from the mass inches from my face. I started to crawl over the mass of flesh in front of me. The wind didn't let up and grew more powerful as time passed. The wind grew too much I could no longer support the weight of the wind and my own. I started to collapse to the floor when my body started to slide freely and quickly down the hall. The force of the wind pushed me off of my knees and lifted me into the air. I began spinning and flipping through the length of the hallway. I tried to reach the floor with my hands and feet but was unable to find any thing to grab onto or brace my weight on. The wind continued to grow and with it my speed quickly grew.

After fifteen minutes I started to see a bright flick of light piercing the surrounding blackness. The source of the light grew upon me very quickly. Within minutes the source of the light became defined. The hallway ended and continued out in to space. As I neared the edge of the hallway a bright flash from outside the hall from somewhere in space poured into the hall drowning the darkness with a yellowish orange light. The wind stopped dead dropping me half a foot from the end of the hall. I landed on my back with a thud. My prosthesis slammed into the floor with a bang and bounced off the floor's surface. I slowly sat up and looked out the end of the hallway.

I turned over onto my stomach and inched my way forward to the edge of the hall. I hung my head out the hallway into space and looked into the cold abyss. Inches from my head was an orange yellow field that wrapped around the vessel that housed me. Hulls of wrecked ships floated in the dead of space yards beyond the field. The hulls had been ripped from other parts. I got to my feet and looked more into the ship gave yard. Some of the hulls were big enough to see what they were from. The majority of the hulls in the graveyard was black as space and had small flickers of fire on their surface. The rest of the hulls were slightly tan with black scorch marks along the edges.

I could see along the outside of the hull. The floors below me had been cut off from the rest of the floors. About fifty yards from me drifting away on my left looked to be the missing portion of the levels. I stepped back into the hallway away from the edge and started walking back down the mysterious hall. As I walked back along the hall I met with no resistance. I reached the hole in the wall and looked through again. The other side of the hole was now dimly lit allowing me to see small amounts of the area. A hole about three feet wide and two foot long nearly covered the entire floor. A four-inch ledge surrounded the entire hole. In some spots the ledge was larger than four inches. A cross from me was a passage that was poorly lit and looked like it led across the ship.

I cleared the debris from around the opening of the edge and started to walk along the ledge. As I carefully walked along the ledge my feet kicked some of the debris into the hole. After a minute I reached the passageway, then looked back at the hole, and continued further in the passage. I started to walk further into the hall and as I walked the ground changed from hard to mostly soft. I looked down at my feet. The darkness of the hall was still too powerful for the light to reach the floor. As I walked I could hear the snapping of something like twigs. Halfway down the hallway the entire passageway was lit up. Covering the floor was dead bodies of Talin, Shadow, human, and some of the other species. All of the corpses except the Shadows had been ripped apart and were bleeding onto the floor.

I continued to walk on top of the bodies. The walls of the hall were running with the blood of the people lying dead in the passage. The ceiling was dripping wet with a mix of blood. I walked down the rest of the hall I came upon a door lying on the floor into another hallway. The door had been pushed out of the wall and down to the floor. I stepped into the hallway and looked to both my right and left side. The left side looked the same as the hallway before. The hall on my right ended with a large door ten feet wide and ten feet high. The trail of bodies continued up to the large door. A body was trapped underneath the large metal door causing the door to open and close a few inches. I turned right and walked to the door and walked up to the door. As I approached the door opened completely allowing me access.

Once the door opened I walked across its threshold. As I passed through I removed the body from under the door. On the other side of the door was a large room maybe a thousand feet high from the lowest point to the highest. In the center of the room was a large cylinder glowing in the brightest bluish white light I have ever seen. The walls of the room were shinny like they were made of gold or silver. Large bolts of the white light was flying across the room, striking one of the large hundred feet high thirty-foot wide panels and discharging large white teardrops on to a platform. The tear drops slid into a pipe then was guided into a small cylinder about fifteen feet high and had a diameter of ten feet. One of the drops filled the container halfway. As the container was filled a large claw swung from behind the cylinder in the center of the room.

The claw grabbed the smaller cylinder, then rose to the top of the room and dropped the cylinder onto a conveyer belt. The claw moved off as another cylinder was filled. The cylinder disappeared into the wall. More claws dropped from the ceiling as more white bolts lunged out of the cylinder and struck the panels around the room. To my right was a doorway. Across from me on the other side of the room was a large lift. I walked over to the doorway as I approached the door opened and I walked though. On the other side of the door was a long hallway with the right wall consisting of computers and circuits and a few windows every twenty feet.

I walked further into the hall. As I moved I looked out the windows upon the action going on, on the other side. The room had grown quite busy in just a few seconds. There were many more claws and they were all moving around the room at an incredible speed. The number of bolts coming from the cylinder had grown and were making the room glow in a near solid white. Only the black of the claws broke the white light coming from the room next to me. The light was growing too bright for me to look upon it any longer. So I continued to walk along the hallway and kept my head turned to the left as I passed the windows. The light cast large white boxes on the left walls.

After twenty minutes I reached a door and walked through it as it opened. I stepped into a lift and waited for the lift to start. There were no buttons on either side of the door nor did a voice ask me what floor. The lift after five minutes started up and I began to rise. After three minutes the door opened and I walked out into a hall that looked like the last except there were a few doors on the wall opposite the thousand foot high room. I walked to the first door and looked through the doorway. The room was full of computers and circuits scattered about the room on desks and tables. The right and left walls had large tubes running through disappearing into the back wall. I walked into the room and looked at the computers and the circuits on the tables.

After a few minutes I found nothing of interest so I left the room and moved to the next door in the hall. The door refused to open so I continued to the last door on my right. As I approached the door it opened into the ceiling allowing me to pass through to the other side. The room had large equipment stacked on top of each other and was stacked a few feet from the ceiling. There was barely enough space to enter the room. I didn't bother looking at anything I just turned around and walked to the last door in the hall. As I approached the door opened and out stepped a wounded Talin. Blood covered his chest and right shoulder.

"Another survivor, good come with me," he said, guiding me through the door and into a lift.

"What happened? I don't remember anything."

"Our plan failed horrible. We were outnumbered. Some human got the number of Shadow ships in waiting wrong. There were twenty warships and one mother ship. Eight of the warships were destroyed in the destruction of the *Franchasno*. Four warships were disabled and the rest including the mother ship were left undamaged. They began firing upon us. After a few minutes they had our shields down. Then they lunched transport and fighter ships. We were immediately boarded. The Shadows moved through the *Colonizer* quickly killing everything in their path. They did spare a lot of humans and took them back to their transports. Then the mother ship fired its cutting beams at the bridge separating the bridge level from the rest of the *Colonizer*. Then they cut off the front of the *Colonizer* destroying the hanger bays.

Two of the warships destroyed our super cannons and then the hanger bays in the back of the *Colonizer*. By this time we lost almost all power." He finished as the lift stopped.

"Are there other survivors?"

"I don't know. You are the first person I have seen from outside the power chamber."

"How did you survive?" he said, stepping out of the lift and into another hallway like the last three.

"I was able to make it back into the power chamber. This whole chamber is designed to take a pounding. So the enemy was unable to open any of the doors once I was able to get in here that is. How did you survive?"

"I don't remember. I just found myself a short distance from here."

"You know those Shadows must have been either been really pissed off or they really wanted your planet."

"Why do you say that?"

"The Shadows never risk one of their mother ships, never. Why do you think they took humans instead of killing them?"

"I think they want to overcome the resistance to the Shadow substance that my people have."

"I didn't know your people had such a resistance. Where are we going?"

"We are going to the power chamber's command room."

"Shouldn't we get off of this ship?"

"In what? The hanger bays are destroyed at the moment."

"What do you mean at the moment?"

"This power chamber is capable of more than just powering the whole ship, it also has the ability to regenerate as long as enough of the ship is intact. The first thing we have to do is retrieve the bridge level and the nose before they get out of range," said the Talin as we walked down the hall.

"How are you going to retrieve the bridge level and the nose?" I asked as the door at the end of the hall came into view.

"This ship has a tractor laser that can pull the bridge level back in place and can hold it there. The same goes for the nose. Luckily the Shadows didn't destroy our engines."

"How long will the regenerating take?"

"Awhile; it could take days to reattach both the bridge level and the nose. That's why we are going to tractor both pieces at once and start the regeneration at the same time. If the power chamber can take it then we will be able to get out of here in a day and half if not then well you can imagine."

"Is there anything I can do?"

"No there isn't," he said as we walked to the end of the hall.

"How long ago did the plan fail?"

"It has been at least a day because that's how long it took us to repair the power chamber."

"Over a day, how did I survive?"

"That is a good question. We are here," he said as we walked the remaining three feet to the door.

The door opened and we walked through. We were in a room about seven hundred feet from the floor of the power chamber and over looked the claws moving about around the center cylinder. The light coming from the chamber was dulled down by really tinted windows that expanded the entire front of the room. Below the windows were consoles about two feet off of the ground. Standing in front of the consoles were five Talins. Behind them about ten feet were four-foot high computers with many circuits sticking out the back. All the circuits were glowing in a greenish white. Another five feet and six computers hovering above six desks were being worked on by three Talins one Frostise and two people from one of the other species.

"We are about ready to power up both tractor lasers now," said the Talin closest to my right.

"Keep your eyes on the power reading. If they get too high then cut the tractors we don't need to burn out the laser," said the Talin, looking upon the power chamber.

"Bring up the display screens."

The room grew dark as the windows were covered by large monitors. One of the screens was still black the other two were displaying the graveyard surrounding us. Both of the screens focused in on the parts. The closest screen displayed the nose of the ship and the middle screen displayed the bridge level.

"Fire both lasers when they are fully charged."

After a few minutes both screens grew bright red as the beams fired. The beams hit both targets without doing any damage. Slowly the two sections moved towards us.

"Shut them off that is all we need at the moment. Let space do the rest until they reach the particle field."

Both sections of the *Colonizer* drifted through space and after ten minutes passed through the particle field. The beams fired and began to turn both targets as the beams slowed them both. The power chamber shook as both parts collided with the rest of the *Colonizer*.

"Get ready to activate the regeneration process and keep watch over the core temperature."

"Engaging the regeneration process now, sir."

"We have to shut down the regeneration; the core is overheating."

"Then shut it down."

"It won't shut down we are locked in both regenerations process."

"Kill the power then."

"We can't, the regeneration process won't allow shut down.

"Close the display screens."

The display screens rose into the ceiling. The outside was glowing brighter than before. The bolts of energy were missing the panels and striking anything in their path. The ship began to shake throwing everyone off of our feet. As I got to my feet everything grew scorching hot. The sound of glass shattering and screams of people rippled through the room before getting overwhelmed by thunder.

Chapter Twenty
A Ring of Pearls

I awoke back in my room screaming covered in sweat. It was all a dream but seemed so real. I was sitting upright with the covers of my bed on the floor. I grabbed a change of clothes and my data pads and carried them under my right arm. I left my room and walked to the rec room. I walked through the rec room doors and walked the length of the room and passed through the doors to the bathrooms. The entire room was made of metal. I walked around the bathroom looking everything over. There were no showers nor were there any baths that I could see. There were sinks along the wall opposite the door to the rec room. To my right there were four small platforms. Each one of the platforms was big enough for only two people to squeeze onto. There were no curtains around any of the platforms.

On the wall next to each one of the platforms was some controls for the platforms. Beneath each one of the controls was a piece of paper and a bench. There were five stalls on the door's left. The platforms were on the right. I walked over to the platforms and read the note above the bench. The note said that the platforms were clothes-less frequency showers and gave instructions on how to use the controls of the showers. To operate the controls I had to push the top button out of three. Each one of the buttons was for a different setting for different species. I placed my change of clothes on the bench, removed my clothes placing them on the bench next to my change of clothes and climbed into the shower. I followed the instructions. I pushed the top button and waited for the shower to start up.

The shower started by covering my entire body in bright green and blue lights. Both of the lights circled above me. After a few seconds blue white rings dropped from the ceiling of the platform and vanished into the base of the platform. The rings were separated by a second. After a few seconds soft music started coming from the shower. The music was odd like nothing I heard since I lost my memory. The music had a relaxing effect to it. I felt more at peace, freer, and calmer. As the music played I could hear a quite high-pitched whine hidden within the music. After five minutes the shower shut off. I stepped off the platform retrieved my change of clothes and got dressed. As I turned I noticed a can with another sign. The sign said to put used clothes in the can.

As I walked I put my old clothes into the can and walked across to the other side of the bathroom. I finished in the bathroom and reentered the rec room. There was still no one anywhere in the room. I walked across the room and left the rec room. I turned right and walked back to my room where I decided to get something to eat and drink. I was also getting curious if a decision had been reached. I continued past my room down to the left at the end of the hall. I opened the lift door and walked into the lift. After a few seconds the lift started, after ascending higher into the *Colonizer* for a few minutes the lift came to a stop, and the door opened. I left the lift and walked across the cafeteria floor. I decided to wait on the food and something to drink until after I found out what was going on. I walked over to the middle section of the cafeteria and placed my hand on the panel next to the middle door.

After seven minutes the door opened. I climbed into the lift, after the door closed I rose to the turret room. The door opened, I climbed out of the lift and walked to the end of the wall housing the staircase. I walked to the top of the staircase and opened the door above my head. After the door had opened enough for me to pass through I continued up the rest of the staircase. At the top of the staircase I turned to my left and passed through the door entering the bridge. The bridge was packed full of people. Everyone was looking upon the view screen. The *Franchasno* displayed across the entire bridge wall.

There were a few ships leaving the *Franchasno's* hanger bays. The ships flew at us with great speed.

"Floto, once they are on board start firing the cannons and moving the *Franchasno* through the belt," said Movork, standing in front of his seat.

"Yes, sir," said one of the many people in the bridge.

"Sir, they have landed in hanger bay D," said another person five minutes later.

"Firing, Captain," said the same person as before.

The cannons on the *Franchasno* glowed as they charged for the attack on the belt. After a minute of charging they fired into what remained of the asteroids in the asteroid belt. The cannons fired quite fast and only shot the largest of asteroids. The surrounding space surrounding the *Franchasno* was lit up with the cannons fire. Asteroids crumbled under the cannons strength sending smaller chunks of asteroids ricocheting off of the hull of the *Franchasno* and surrounding asteroids. The cannons didn't take any time to cool they didn't even take the time to recharge fully before they fired again. The *Franchasno* slowly moved in faster than it had moved before, but was slow enough to clear a path big enough to pass the *Colonizer* through.

After eighteen minutes the space surrounding the *Franchasno* received a flash of green light. The light continued to flash as the *Franchasno* pushed further into the belt. As the *Franchasno* moved, it grew smaller and smaller; however, it still took up most of the screen. After a few minutes a ripple in the *Franchasno's* shield washed over the entire ship's shield.

"Captain, the *Franchasno* is taking enemy fire."

"Continue with the plan, Floto," said Movork.

The cannons on the *Franchasno* continued to fire as the ship increased its speed. More ripples emerged across the *Franchasno's* shields. The ripples grew in frequency and became larger. The *Franchasno's* front two cannons began firing upon the enemy ships ahead of it. After a few minutes all four guns were firing at the enemy ships. The *Franchasno* pushed closer to the enemy ships. As the cannons hit the enemy ships the outside of the enemy ships began to glow reddish orange.

"Captain, the shields have failed. The enemy is now attacking the cannons."

"Floto, how many ships are there?" asked Movork.

"The *Franchasno* is reading seven warships. But there still could be more."

"Movork, how much longer can the *Franchasno* last against that many ships?" asked President Clark.

"We will soon find out, Mr. President."

The shields had collapsed and the hull and cannons of the *Franchasno* were taking heavy punishment. The *Franchasno* cleared the asteroid belt and as it passed its edge the front two cannons erupted in fire. The fire lasted only for a few seconds as the cold vacuum of space squashed the fire. The hull of the *Franchasno* started to get shot off of its frame. A few seconds later the back cannons exploded.

"Now, Floto," said Movork.

"Yes, Captain."

After three minutes the hull of the *Franchasno* began to swell and then a second later the ship exploded into flames. A bubble of force expanded from the center of the *Franchasno* and grew very quickly through space. Eventually the bubble had completely covered the *Franchasno* and was moving in all directions. The bubble suddenly grew even larger as the enemy ships were consumed by the bubble. With each ship that was consumed the bubble grew larger and expanded even faster.

"Floto, reverse the engines immediately, that explosion may be too much for the *Colonizer* to withstand," ordered Movork.

"Reversing engines now, Captain."

The image on the screen remained the same. The bubble grew again and so did its speed. As we retreated the bubble rapidly gained on us. After a few minutes the bubble started to slow and its growth also slowed. The bubble broke sending a wave in all directions. The wave consumed everything it came in contact with. The matter caught in its path was immediately broke down to dust. The ripples grew closer and closer to us. We continued to back up. You could see the asteroids in the belt moving past us only to be disintegrating minutes later. The growth of the wave slowed, but not before it overran the *Colonizer*. The *Colonizer* began to shake tremendously. Everyone that was standing reached to their neighbors for support as they were about to lose their footing. I was the only one that was able to keep their footing as the tremor continued.

The screen was filled with the glow from the shield taking the force of the wave. The *Colonizer* groaned as the tremors continued. After five minutes the tremors started to lessen. Another four minutes and the tremors had nearly ceased. For the next minute and half a tremor would run through the ship.

"Floto, what is our status?" asked Movork.

"Shields...fifty percent and holding, weapons are fully operational, our hull is seventy-five percent, and in some places it is fluctuating and our engines are undamaged."

"There is no way, we would have survived the full explosion not with that much power. Floto, take us in slowly and everyone keep your eyes on the scans. We may be able to survive one warship but no more."

"Captain Movork, when are the two ships coming to our aid?" asked President Clark.

"As soon as we have cleared the asteroid belt, President Clark," replied Movork.

We began to move back through the asteroid belt. The belt had been greatly cleared from the wave's power. On either side of the *Colonizer* there appeared to be couple thousand feet to the wall of the asteroid belt. After a few minutes, we exited the path in the asteroid belt. It appeared there was nothing left of the enemy ships as we moved further away from the belt. We continued through space, moving slowly as we advanced. There was no sign of the enemy ships anywhere around us.

"Floto, get the engines charged for light speed then ultra," said Movork.

"Engines charging, Captain."

As we passed Jupiter we saw large chunks of hulls floating above the planet. Some of the chunks were falling to Jupiter's surface getting crushed by the building pressure. The hulls looked to be that of Talin design. Among the hulls of the Talin vessels were hulls from Shadow vessels. Floating with the hulls looked to be the remains of enough cannons to make two Talin warships.

"It looks like we won't be receiving any assistance after all. So many good people lost. They should have retreated when they had the chance. We mustn't make their deaths meaning less. Floto, as soon as the engines have been fully charged, make the jump to light speed."

"Yes, Captain."

"Engines are charged and preparing to jump to light speed," Floto said ten minutes later.

"G..." said Movork as the *Colonizer* jolted to the left throwing everyone off their feet including me.

The *Colonizer* was hit again on the right side.

"Prepare for battle we must fight them off," said Movork as he picked himself off the floor.

"No, run! We are outgunned and outnumbered."

"Alex, how do you know this?"

"I have seen it."

"You said there were only five ships earlier?"

"Trust me, we will lose if we stay and fight. It is not worth our lives to battle at the moment."

"How do you know we will lose?" asked someone else in the room.

"I just know. Captain, the engines are charged, retreat while we can."

"Floto, jump to light speed."

"We are jumping to light speed now," said Floto.

The large screen was now projecting the space ahead of us which began to glow in many colors. Rings and streams began to move around in front of the *Colonizer*. The rings and streams were of many different colors mixed together with bright white light. Reds, bright violet, neon blue, orange, golden yellow, grass green, and a large number of other colors made up the rings and streams. The variety of colors and spectrum of light filled the room as the rotation of the rings and the colors grew in frequency. The barrage of colors rushed past filling the room through the screen in a rainbow of light. I could feel the *Colonizer* pulling me forward along with it. After a few seconds we lunged forward as the light coming through the screen became solid.

"Take us to ultra light speed."

"Yes, Captain."

The screen grew dark. The rainbow of lights was replaced with a cloud full of small dots varying in color. The cloud remained the same never moving.

"We should reach Tallinea in a few days. Everyone should return to their rooms or stations for the time being. Alex, Zar, follow me to the conference room now," Movork said as he walked across the bridge then past me through the door.

Zar walked out from within the crowd and walked across the bridge. He continued through the door; I followed him out of the room a second later. I followed both of them to the conference room and took a seat around the large table. Movork once again sat down in the chair in front of the door. Zar sat on his right and I sat in the chair on his left.

"Spill, Alex; tell me what you saw and when?"

I spent the next few hours telling them about the nightmare I had not that long ago. The whole experience was fresh in my mind therefore I remembered just about everything that had happened. As I talked both of them paid close attention to every word that I said. A few of the things I described caught their attention. At times they looked at each other for a second then looked back at me.

"Have you been to the power chamber before, Alex?" asked Movork.

"NO! There is actually a power chamber?"

"Yes in fact every Talin ship has one. That is what caused such a large blast with the *Franchasno*," said Zar.

"Does this ship have the ability to regenerate?"

"*Colonizers* used to, but that technology was lost over five centuries ago.

"Alex, you said you were told that the *Colonizer* was carved up by a Shadow mother ship. Were you told what the ship looked like anything at all?" asked Movork.

"No, why?"

"The existence of Shadow mother ships are things of rumor and myth. There have been no reports that Shadow ships as powerful as what you described have ever been seen."

"Is it possible that my nightmare was just that, a nightmare?"

"If I didn't know about you I would have said yes, but I'm not so sure. Some of what you have said sounds too real and other parts of your nightmare as you call it are real. It is impossible that you could know about them," said Zar.

"Zar, what are you thinking?" asked Movork.

"I am not entirely sure, but I think that Alex is in contact with the Shadows on some level. Whenever Alex has been in a deep sleep he has had bizarre dreams of being a Shadow. Each one of these dreams he has described things that have happened and there is no way he should know about them. The first two of these dreams he described an ancient war between Talins, our extinct cousins the Maltans and the believed to be extinct Hob. The last of the three dreams was of a Shadow invasion on to a planet full of bugs. All three of these dreams I suspect are memories of the past. This last dream; however, is different. It is possible that he saw the Shadows' plans and his subconscious interpreted their plan as a dream. So it is possible that there was a mother ship waiting for us. And if that is the case then he may have just saved every life on this ship."

"Zar, what do you know of the Hob?" asked Shaurha as she walked through the conference room door.

"I know as much as you do, Shaurha."

"I highly doubt that. There are only a few people that know the truth of the ancient Talin wars. And I am one of those few who know the truth."

"If you have something to share with us, Shaurha, then please share."

"I'm sorry I am under orders not to say a word of what I know."

"Shaurha, I order you to tell us what you know."

"I am sorry, Captain Movork, I can't."

"I am the captain of this ship you will obey my orders!"

"My orders come from Prince Palarise."

"The prince is dead. Your orders are lifted when he died unless, unless he is still alive!"

"As of this minute, you three are under orders not to say a word about this!"

"Unacceptable, you may be the commander of the entire military. But this is my ship and you will do as I say, do you understand me. Now I want to speak with the prince now, or you will be arrested for treason and placed in the brig!"

"You can't do that!"

"Can't I? Your orders supposedly come from someone that's believed to be dead. Therefore without verification that that person is alive, your orders don't mean anything!"

"Movork, you need verification, fine. When we reached the Tallinea's defense network, I will take you to him!"

"That is not good enough! Shaurha, you will call the prince now!"

"Fine, you have left me with no other choice," Shaurha said, walking to the back of the room.

He stepped in front of the controls on the back wall. After a few minutes the screen in the middle of the table descended from the ceiling. The black screen went from a blank black screen to a screen filled with white and gray static. After a few minutes the screen changed to display a young looking Talin.

"Shaurha, the *Colonizer* escaped the Shadow's trap that is good. Why did you contact me?"

"I had no choice, Captain Movork forced me to call you."

"Has he now?"

"Yes I did, Prince Palarise. I have to know how you survived and why you have not come forward with your survival."

"It is because of my father."

"The king, what does your father have to do with your survival being a secret?"

"Everything, more than any of you know."

"He is not the king he appeared to be. If he is alive and he finds out that I am still alive, he will try to take his revenge on me his own son."

"What revenge? And how dare you talk about the king that way."

"I tried to kill him before he kills anymore people in his delusional campaign."

"Explain, Prince Palarise," demanded Movork.

"My father is trying to find a weapon of the Hob. The weapon dates back to the Ancient Wars. The text that my father learned about the weapon from says that it can bring unimaginable power and destructive force. He believes that the last piece of the weapon was on the Hob's home planet buried in among the ruins of their dead race."

"The Hob's planet was lost in the Ancient Wars, no one knows where it is."

"My father believes that the planet earth, the humans' home, was the Hob's home planet and the last battle grounds of the ancient wars.

My father informed the Shadows of earth's many resources in order to make his invasion of earth easier. My father believes that humans are descendants of the ancient Hob warriors."

"I think President Clark knows someone who is looking for the ruins."

"Alex, President Clark has done nothing but help with the evacuation and he agreed to the detonation of earth's atomic bombs," said Shaurha.

"I saw him talking to someone a few doors down back in the hallway. The other person's face was displayed on a large screen. This person said that the relic in the ancient ruins he was searching for had better not have been damaged. The person then asked if measures were in place to keep all humans from causing any trouble was in effect. President Clark said that the Lazarus Protocol was in effect. Maybe President Clark was talking to your king."

"I guess it is possible but why would President Clark do such a thing?" asked Zar.

"He said the alternative would have been complete annihilation. This way the human race continues on."

"Alex, when did you see all this?"

"Before the last meeting we had in here."

"Prince, I believe your father is right that humans are descendants of the Hob race. I don't know if Shaurha has said anything about Alex or not, but through Alex I believe that humans and the Hob are related," said Zar.

"Shaurha has told me about Alex and his unique situation."

"In fact, Prince, he is the only reason we are talking to you at the moment if he had not told us to run we most likely would not have survived."

"More than you know, Movork, I assure you."

"How was your father planning on invading earth?"

"Every prisoner that has been sent to prisons or sentenced to death has been put on remote planets to build him an army. An army that he can command outside the laws of Talin rule. His army also is reinforced with pirates and mercenaries; making his army large and very powerful. My father has been informing the Shadows of planets with high resource value for decades. Each one of the races lost, my father believes, have had one of the fragments of the weapon."

"Do you know why your father is searching for the weapon?"

"He is using the Shadows not only to help him in his search, but also to help wipe the Shadows out for good. However, I am afraid that my father will use the weapon to take control of the entire Talin civilization."

"Why would he do that? He is already king."

"He may be the king, but he like your president doesn't have complete control over his people and that is something I fear he wants."

"Prince, what would you have us do?" asked Movork.

"There is nothing that you can do, but wait while I get enough evidence to unite our civilization against my father. If I can't then my father could gather more followers. Until you hear from me, I order the three of you to remain quiet about what you know. Only call me if there is something new to report. Alex, I can't order you to remain quiet, I can only ask that you do. I must go; I will contact you, Shaurha, when I need to. Goodbye for now."

The screen went dark and rose back into the ceiling.

"Zar, Shaurha, would you make sure Alex gets back to his room. I have to think about all this. Alex, your species is something very different from any of the races we have met with yet. Descendants of the ancient Hob warriors, who would have thought the Hob survived the last battle? Shaurha and Zar, we will talk later."

"Yes, Captain."

Shaurha, Zar and I left the conference room and returned to the medical level. The whole way down to the medical level not a word was spoken. They left me at my room and walked back to the lift door and began their trip back up to the bridge level. I walked to the rec room and passed through the door. There were a few Talins reading off of data pads the back wall was loaded with humans working on computers. Only two of the humans I recognized. One was Amanda and the other was Samantha. I walked over and sat down in front of a free computer and loaded my thoughts I had saved on a data pad into the computer and began to work on them.

For the next three days I worked on my notes as often as I wanted to. I would periodically use the maintenance lifts to go to the many levels of the *Colonizer*. I looked for my friends in every place I could but had no results. After the battle people were scattered around the ship and without Talin help they were unable to go from level to level. As Movork had said previously there had been a lot of casualties. The number of Talins on board had been greatly reduced making it hard for me to get any information about anyone.

The first day Amanda, Samantha, and I visited Marissa and her aunt. The rest of the day I spent looking for my friends. The second day I was able to find Mike and Jessica. Both of them had been injured in the space battle and were in a makeshift medical bay. Later that day around midnight the main lift was brought back on line. By three o'clock testing of the lift had been finished and was cleared for us by Whaloa and Gupp. A lot of the systems had been stripped away in order to get the lift to work again. Twelve in the afternoon on the second day the makeshift medical bays had been dissolved and all occupants were transformed to the real medical level. Thousands of people were treated and sent on their way or back to their duties. Over two thousand people lost their lives in the medical level and an unknown number of people were lost in the space battle.

Later that night Crystal made her way to the medical level with the assistance of a Talin. She had received some injuries but nothing that Zar, Mallowon, and the rest of the medical staff was unable to heal. Her left arm had been cut badly and she had a bandage on her right side. She had some small bandages on the right side of her face. The rest of the night we talked about what happened to her. Then as it got late she fell asleep in my arms. The next day Crystal rarely left my side; her arms were always wrapped around mine. We kissed and hugged each other in front of the others forgetting all about Mike's feels towards Crystal. She didn't care any longer about keeping Mike in the dark about our relationship. I told him the truth as our actions had already told him the whole story.

He wasn't happy a first mainly because we didn't trust him enough to tell him. The rest of the day he sulked around trying to avoid us if he could. By the end of the night he gave up and accepted our apologies. He also warned us that David probably wouldn't be so forgiving if he lived. The fourth day I was woken early in the morning by a knock on my door. I threw on some clothes and exited my room. As I stepped through the door I was pulled out into the corridor by Flito.

"What gives?"

"Movork thought you and your friends would like to see Tallinea as we approach. Come on, there isn't much time."

"Where is Nozad?"

"He is getting your friends they will join us on the bridge shortly."

We walked to the end of the hall and entered the lift. A few minutes later we came to a stop and then we walked across the cafeteria over to the other lift doors. I placed my hand on the blue panel and waited for the door to open.

"Alex, what happened to your arm? It looks like your artificial skin has been nearly ripped off."

I looked at my arm the skin had indeed been nearly ripped off all that was left was an inch of my wrist and the skin covering the hand of my prosthesis.

"Look at that, guess you're right."

"Why haven't you talked to Zar to get it repaired?" Flito said, stepping into the lift.

"I don't know. I just haven't gotten around to it yet," I said as I joined Flito in the lift.

"It's not like you haven't had the time, you know."

"I know. I just. You know, I don't know why I haven't."

We exited the lift three and half minutes later. We walked along the wall of the staircase and then climbed up the stairs. Flito opened the door and we climbed the rest of the stairs. Once we were in the bridge Movork motioned for Flito and me to join him in front of his chair. The screen to my left still had the same cloud of dots of light.

"Alex."

I turned to face Movork.

"We are about to come out of ultra light speed then we have a few minutes in normal light speed before we will drop to normal speed," Movork said as the ship jolted backward.

The screen in front of me returned to the variety of colors it had been four days before. The bridge immediately caught the assault of light as it shined through the screen. The colors were as marvelous as they had been before. After a seven-minute wait Crystal, Amanda, Samantha, Jessica, Mike, and Nozad walked through the right door.

"You all are just in time we are about to exit light speed."

"Wow...that is..." said Samantha, walking towards the screen.

"Beautiful," said Crystal, following Samantha.

"Sorry, ladies, but we are coming out of light speed in five, four, three, two, one…"

The assault of colors on the screen disappeared returning the screen to a view of space. As the colors vanished we were all pulled forward towards the large screen. No one fell, they just had to catch their footing quickly. The screen began to glow yellow with the rays of a large planet. The rays vanished from view a few seconds later as we passed the planet. We passed another planet smaller than the last. As we past the second planet a tiny bright spec blinked in the screen.

"There it is Tallinea, home," said Movork, stepping forward a few feet.

"Where is it? All I see is stars," said Jessica.

"There is no need to worry it is there we are just not close enough for you to really see it."

As we moved through space the spec grew larger and large. After a minute the spec was the size of a quarter five minutes later the spec had grown to the size of a football. Twenty minutes went by the image on the screen was of a large space station. The station looked to be the size of an entire planet. The station looked like Saturn. The largest part of the station was a giant sphere. Surrounding the sphere were smaller sphere-like moons. There looked to be more than twenty moons all connected to another moon and to the larger station. The surface of the center sphere was covered by large cannons and smaller turrets. Each one of the moons had larger cannons then the station mounted on them.

"This is Tallinea?" asked Mike.

"No this is the orbital defense network. Tallinea is concealed within the armor station," replied Movork.

"We have had to make sacrifices a long time ago in order to protect our home. And one of those sacrifices is what you see before you."

The station continued to grow as we continued to close in on the surface of the Talin home world. After a few minutes we were joined by dozens of small ships varying in size. Two were as large as the *Franchasno* others were half the *Franchasno* or smaller.

"Floto, take us into the nearest available dock for a ship of this size."

"Yes, Captain."

Chapter Twenty-One
Tallinea

The station was massive in comparison to the *Colonizer*. All that we could see was a metal wall to our left and space on the right. After circling more than halfway around the orbital network we started to dock with the station. We flew along the station until we came upon a massive platform. Small bridges extended from the wall of the station as we approached the platform. The bridges looked like they went from the ground floor to the bridge level. Among the smaller bridges was a larger bridge about five times the size as the other bridges. The bridges came in contact with the left side of the *Colonizer* sending a moan throughout the ship. A few seconds later Movork pushed a button next to his seat and spoke.

"Everyone, please remain calm, we have arrived at Tallinea. I'll personal escort everyone to the hatches. Everyone, make your way onto the station. As soon as everyone is off the *Colonizer* that shouldn't be here. We are taking this ship in for repairs," said Movork across the intercom.

"Alex, would you like to stay on board and see Tallinea for real? Of course your friends can come with us."

"Give me a minute to talk it over with my friends."

"Alright we have the time."

I walked over to my friends.

"Movork has asked if we would like to see Tallinea. Would you all like to see Tallinea?"

"Why not; it's not like we have anywhere else to go," said Mike.

"Anywhere you go I go love," said Samantha, winking at me.

"You didn't need to ask me, Alex, I'm yours and I will remain by your side," said Crystal as she wrapped her arms around my neck after she gave an evil look to Samantha.

"I think I can speak for the rest of us when I say we want to see Tallinea," said Jessica.

"Alright then, I will let Movork know our answer…Crystal, could you let go so I can tell Movork?"

"Alright," she said as she released me.

I walked back over to Movork.

"Have you and your friends made a decision?"

"Yes we would like to see Tallinea."

"We have an hour to wait, why don't you and your friends have a seat."

"Where should we sit? Everything is full."

"Seats will come out of the wall behind your friends," he said as he pushed a button next to his chair.

I looked past my friends. A few feet above the floor a bench extended out from the wall about a foot and a half. The bench stretched the entire length of the bridge.

"Thank you," I said as I walked back over to my friends.

"What is up?" asked Mike.

"Did he change his mind and wants us off the ship?" asked Jessica.

"Nothing is wrong, he just said that we could have a seat while we waited for the *Colonizer* to empty."

"Where can we sit? There doesn't appear to be any seats available."

"We are going to sit behind you five," I pointed in between Mike and Jessica as I finished.

We all slowly sat down on the bench. Crystal sat on my right with her arms wrapped around my right. Samantha was on my left sitting next to Mike. Jessica sat on Mike's left. After an hour the *Colonizer* moaned again. After a few more minutes the *Colonizer* began to move forward. We flew above the wall of the station for twenty minutes when two massive metal doors came into view in front of us. As we approached the doors they opened for us. We passed through the more than two mile high one mile wide doors. We flew through a passageway of maybe a thousand or more feet before we came upon the ending of the passage. We slowly turned as the wall on our left ended. We were now inside a large metal bubble that had been constructed by the Talin people. The entire inside of the bubble was lit by the station wall.

In the center of the station was Tallinea. Tallinea didn't look vary much bigger than earth even though it was by a few miles in diameter. The planet was completely enclosed by the station surrounding it. The planet shined bright green from the sunlight the station provided for Tallinea. Tallinea looked to be miles away from the station walls. There were six extremely large pillars constructed on Tallinea's equator that connected the planet to the station concealing it from space. The pillars connected to a ring that wrapped around the station. As the planet slowly rotated so did the pillars and the ring. Each one of the pillars looked to be miles high miles a mile wide and a mile long. There was a large gap miles wide in between all the pillars.

Massive metal scaffolding extended out of the station's inner wall almost half a mile. Floating opposite from the scaffolding looked to be a smaller station. There were many of these stations throughout the interior of the station. The smaller stations varied in size some were a little larger than the warships and there were a few that were a little larger than the *Colonizer*. Some of the stations had warships that had been in battle. Some of these ships were smoking and on fire. Some were just receiving miner repairs to their hulls. A few of the other stations had warships and *Colonizers* under construction. There were some platforms throughout the sphere that had fighters being constructed upon them. As the fighters were built they were loaded onto a large vessel and transported to some of the warships and *Colonizers* being repaired and constructed.

There were four *Colonizer* ships and five warships resting above Tallinea. The nine ships started to move towards two doors much larger than the doors we had passed through. As they approached, the doors opened revealing an orange particle field on the other side. After the ships passed the doors they passed through the particle shield. The particle shield hugged the surface of the Talin vessels as they past through. Seconds after the last vessel past through the doorway, the massive doors closed. We moved a couple of thousand feet above the stations wall. After ten minutes we began to descend lower in the bubble. We fell through the opening in between two of the eight massive structures. The glow of the planet shined through the screen as we past through the opening.

After we stopped we then began to move forward. We circled the entire planet once. As we approached our starting position we moved to the left and came in line with one of the stations. We flew in between the scaffolding and the larger of the stations. As we approached, the scaffolding raised high in the air. The station looked to be as long as the *Colonizer* about three miles in length. When we came to a stop the station and the scaffolding lowered around us. The scaffolding morphed to the shape of the *Colonizer* as it came in contact with its hull. The right side of the *Colonizer* shook a little then the left side shook. The shaking stopped.

"The *Colonizer* will be under repair for long while we might as well leave and get some rest. Everyone on board, shut down all unnecessary systems and report to the transport bays. Everyone on board has three hours before we leave the *Colonizer* then you will have to wait for the repair teams to come on board," Movork said over the intercom throughout the entire ship.

"Alright let us go," Movork said, standing up from his chair.

After a few seconds everyone in the room stood up and walked out of the room and walked to the staircase. Fifty people left the bridge. The first Talins to reach the staircase opened the door and were already going through the turret room. Everyone gathered in the turret room from the upper level. The lift in the turret was packed to the maximum capacity. After ten, seven minute trips, the room had been whittled down to four more groups of six. My friends and I filed in to the lift and began our descent after the doors closed. Once the doors opened in the cafeteria the six of us filed out of the lift. We then walked across the cafeteria. Both the right and left lift had a line twenty feet from the door.

After twenty minutes both lines had been whittled down three groups each leaving three groups waiting and two groups in the process of going to the medical level. After another twenty-five minutes the cafeteria had been completely emptied. Amanda, Crystal, Samantha, Mike, Jessica, and I walked to the main lift. I placed my hand on the blue panel next to the lift. We waited for the lift to return to the medical level. While we waited Shaurha, President Clark, two humans in black suits, and two Talins joined us. After another twenty minutes the lift door opened and we entered the lift. As we entered the lift so did the people on the right side of the medical bay. Twenty-four people piled into the lift everyone took positions around the lift and grasped the railing. As we waited the shaft made the appropriate preparations for our descent.

Like the times before we dropped at an incredible speed. All the humans in the lift were having trouble keeping their feet on the ground. The force from our descent was still too great for us. However, it was quite different from the first few trips I had taken to the ground floor. Our feet were lifted only an inch or two off the ground during our whole descent. The door to the lobby opened. The wrecked Shadow transport still remained embedded in the floor of the lobby. We turned to the left and walked through the open doorway. We continued down the hall for ten minutes before we turned and passed through a door. We entered into another hallway and after another twenty minutes we reached a large room that looked like it expanded the entire base of the *Colonizer*. The room housed large vessels about forty of these ships made up the entire room. There was only one vessel from where we stood to the wall across from us.

Each one of the vessels had a large number of Talins standing in front of them. As we walked towards the vessel a large door opened on the right side of the vessel facing us. Half the door rose higher into the room while another portion of the door lowered itself to the floor making a ramp. Everyone in the room began to file into the vessels. Movork was the last one to climb into our vessel. He stood out side the vessel for a few minutes looking to both his right and left.

"If there is still anyone on board you have twenty minutes before we are leaving," he said as he walked onto our vessel.

He walked into the ship a few feet then turned to the right and walked through a door that rested in between two rows of four seats.

"Give the order to start the vessels. On my word tell everyone to close the doors. Then depart. Understand?"

"Yes, Captain."

Twenty-five minutes went by before Movork said anything. The door closed to our vessel then the wall of the room opened. We dropped a few feet after the *Colonizer* released our vessel. The wall of the whole base level opened up, dropping over a hundred of the vessels. Each one of the vessels looked like they could hold over two hundred people pulse a load of cargo. The engines kicked in and then we began to move toward the southern side of Tallinea.

"How would you all like to see Tallinea before we take you to your new homes?"

Every human nodded in response to Movork's question.

"Take us down, Flito. Let's show them Tallinea's beauty."

As we entered the atmosphere of the Tallinea the inside of our vessel grew a little hotter. After a few minutes the heat dissipated and the air returned to normal. All the clouds in Tallinea were light green. Every few minutes the cloud would shimmer with a different color. The water surrounding the land masses was huge and had an emerald color to it. What land there was had sparkling shiny grass and other plants covering just about every inch of dirt. However, most of the ground had large sky scrapers stretching into the sky. In some cases the structures rose straight to the station wall. The surface of Tallinea was made up of mostly cities. Each of the cities rose miles above the ground. The sky was full of small crafts flying around the globe. In the distance there were ruined structures. Surrounding the small structures were many vessels. A lot of the vessels were on the ground.

"Floto, take us to the palace."

"Yes, Captain; may I ask why?"

"You will see when we get there."

We flew along the open vessel free sea towards the ruins of the palace. After five minutes we landed. The palace in the distance looked small in comparison to the cities but up close was a different story. It looked to be thousands of square feet and the entire estate took up a vast amount of land two miles from the center of the palace. The palace looked like it had been hit by a bomb. Every building had their roofs caved in and the majority of the walls knocked over. In front of what looked like the main doors to the palace a crowed had gathered and were standing in front of a large staircase. Above the crowed were three Talins. All three of them looked a little familiar, but from the distance I was at, I couldn't see who they were.

"Come on, you all need to see what is going on."

313

We left the vessel and walked a hundred yards to the crowd. As we moved closer Shaurha picked up her pace. The middle Talin on the staircase started to walk down them, as we grew close. I began to recognize the Talin approaching Shaurha as we grew closer. The two of them spoke to each other then Shaurha handed the Talin a data pad. I was able to recognize all three of them once we had gone only a yard away from them. At that point we couldn't go any further as Talin guards blocked everyone's path. The Talin that spoke to Shaurha was Prince Palarise the other two Talins were Orrea and Queen Paloween.

As we were stopped Prince Palarise walked back to the top of the staircase joining his sister in front of us. He then walked over to a computer that had been brought with one of three.

"I didn't come forward about my survival sooner because of my father. He has done many things that are against what Tallinea stands for or should I say what Tallinea used to stand for. I have here in my hands proof of my father's actions and of his followers and their actions. I have evidence of corruption in the consul. The actions of my father are not that of a king but of an emperor. So like my sister I am taking my rightful place as king of Tallinea and our entire race. My sister and I have ordered that no more *Colonizer* vessels to be produced; the ones in production will be finished. In their place we are going to design new ships. Because we no longer have one enemy we have to worry about but now we have two: my father's army and the Shadows. If any of you have doubts as to what I have said and what I am accusing my father of just look at the evidence against him." As he finished he pushed some of the controls on the computer.

Large screens rose off of the ground and came to a stop, facing the crowd. There were four eight feet long, five feet wide, monitors surrounding the crowd the screens then turned to a picture of earth. Earth's surface was as it had been days ago. As the evidence continued the screens were filled with Shadow warships and one mother ship. After a few minutes the Shadow vessels were greeted by a large fleet of small ships and a mother ship. The Shadows were immediately engaged as the fleet of small ships moved into a position above earth. The vessels in the fleet were quite fast and maneuverable when you compare them to the warships. The number of these vessels in the fleet ranged any were from one thousand to five

314

thousand of the vessels. As the battle progressed the Shadow's vessels began to dwindle.

As the Shadow's vessels were nearly wiped out they began to retreat. As they moved they were greeted by more of the vessels and another warship. The increase in vessels made it much easier to destroy the warships. As the last warship was destroyed all the vessels focused their attacks on the Shadow mother ship. All the vessels in the fleet including the two mother ships attacked the Shadow mother ship. After a few minutes the Shadow mother ship started to brake apart. The largest piece of the mother ship flew straight at us.

"What you saw was a battle that took place above the human's planet. My father's fleet completely destroyed the enemy with what looked like zero casualties. What you are about to see took place a few minutes after the battle finished."

He pushed another button and the screens switched to static. After a minute the static vanished and was replaced with two pictures of different Talins. As the crowd watched the two Talins talk to each other, they began to talk amongst themselves. I could hear anger growing in some of the crowd's voices. They weren't very pleased about the conversation involving their king.

"As you can see my father like me survived and he takes claim over the fleet above earth. From what he has said I feel that he might attack his own people and with that kind of fleet within his control it would be devastating to our society. In order to defend against his eventual attack on Tallinea we are going to ask everyone we have rescued to help defend Tallinea. We are also going to manufacture new ships similar to the vessels used by my father. We are also going to try to improve our current turrets and targeting protocols. I also wish to inform you that the palace will be reconstructed with some small changes. For instance there will be a memorial in which everyone can come and pay respect to all of my lost family and those lost in the palace's destruction. Now my sister and I must leave you so I can be crowned king," he said, removing the evidence and then walking to his sister's right side before he and his sister walked up the staircase.

After a few minutes a ship rose from the palace ruins. The ship rose into the air and past over our heads then moved in the direction of one of the cities. The crowd began to break up after five minutes. Everyone that was in the crowd climbed on board different vessels and after a minute rose into the yellowish green sky. All the vessels moved away from the palace and towards the closest city.

"Alright, back on board the transport, everyone," said Movork as he walked past me and started to walk back to the vessel.

As we slowly walked back to the transport the Talins in our party looked like they were going to be ill. They had a look on their faces of loss, the loss of their heroes due to the fact that their heroes had turned out to be frauds. Every Talin except Zar, Movork, and Shaurha looked to be in a bad mood. The news about their king's actions must have shocked and hurt them on many levels. We walked back to the transport and piled back inside. After the last person took their seat the door closed. Then we started to lift off the ground. We slowly rose into the sky. After climbing for a few minutes we began to move forward into more of the sky.

We rose into the sky and after a few minutes we passed through Tallinea's atmosphere back into the bubble surrounding the planet. Everything was as it had been forty minutes ago. After ten minutes we began to climb higher into the bubble. After a few more minutes we past through the opening in between two of the six structures and continued to rise. After an additional ten minutes we grew feet from the surface of the station. We flew feet from the wall for fifteen minutes then we began to rotate to our right. We stopped moving and hovered above the stations surface. Then after five minutes the entire transport shook for a few seconds. The right and left walls of the transport then opened. As the doors opened a cool wind rushed though the transport. Movork then stood up.

"Everyone, out of the transport we will take you to your rooms now," Movork said as he stood from his seat and walked over to the right side doorway.

All the Talins stood up from their seats and walked to either side and stepped off the transport onto the surface of the station wall. All of us humans were a little uneasy as we stepped off the transport. The surface of the station wasn't as flat as it appeared from overhead. There were large structures (a couple of levels high) covering the surface of the entire station. As I stepped off the transport I felt lighter then normal. My feet remained on the metal surface beneath me. I could just barely walk along the metal surface. I looked around. Some of my friends were having similar problems as I was or worse. Some of the other humans were having just as hard of time walking as my friends and I were. There were a few humans that were having very little trouble walking on the surface.

"Everyone, grab a human's arm and help them walk. It didn't occur to me that none of the humans have gravity plating compatible footwear," said Movork as he walked to the closet human and wrapped his arm around the human's arm.

"Every one of you have been wearing those shoes this whole time?"

"Yes is there something wrong with that?"

"No but it does explain why none of you have any trouble with the main lift on the *Colonizer*."

A lot of the Talins walked over to us humans and helped guide us over the surface of the gravity plated floor. Most of the humans just glided across the floor while we were guided further away from the transport. After a few minutes we came to a large doorway facing us. Once we reached the doorway Movork walked over to the door and walked to the right side of the door and pushed an orange panel. A second later the door started to open and after a minute the door had opened enough for us to pass through. We all passed through the doorway and into an enclosure. Once inside Movork walked to the right wall and Shaurha walked to the left and then some of the other Talins walked to the back of the room.

They all pulled pairs of shoes from compartments in the walls. Then they walked over and handed out the pairs of shoes to us humans. All the humans were given a pair of the gravity shoes. All of the shoes looked like they wouldn't fit any of us. The shoes were extremely large (about five sizes too large for the biggest foot among us).

"The shoes will fit. They will morph to the size of your foot making it a perfect fit. When any of you want to take the shoes off, all you have to do is push the button on the right side of the right shoe," said Shaurha, showing where the button on one of the extra pairs of the shoes was.

A few of the humans slid on the shoes. Immediately the shoes shrunk to the size of its wearer. After the first few people put the shoes on, everyone followed them with their example. Once everyone had their feet covered by the shoes we were immediately pulled to the floor of the enclosure. Movork walked towards the left wall with his head down towards the floor as though he was looking for something.

"Excuse me, Mike, could you step to your right a few feet?" asked Movork, raising his head to face Mike.

"Okay, Movork."

Movork squatted and then placed his hand on another orange panel. After he pushed the panel everyone began to float. After a minute the floor below us opened into a long wide corridor. The floor, ceiling, and both walls were the same length apart from each other (about fifteen to twenty feet apart). The wall that would normally be in front of us was nowhere in sight. After the floor opened fully some of the Talins pushed off from the back walls a little and glided through the doorway beneath us. Once they were on the other side of the door they pulled their feet towards them. Then they were pulled to one of the four walls. After a minute a few more Talins passed through the doorway in the same fashion as the Talins before them and fell to different walls.

All of them landed on their feet and started to walk down the corridor. The walls of the corridor were packed with many different species; more species than I had seen on the *Colonizer*. Thousands upon thousands of different species mingling, trading goods and working to help one another covered the four walls. All of us did as the Talins before had done. Most of us landed on the same wall. Movork, Shaurha, Jessica, Amanda, and a few other humans landed on different walls. Crystal, Mike, Samantha, myself and a large party of Talins and humans started to walk down the corridor.

The others above us and to our right kept pace with us. After twenty minutes we came to a stop in front of small cuts in the floor, walls, and the wall above us. The Talins on our right started to climb using the cuts on our floor to pull them away from their floor once they were a few feet above their floor they stood up and joined us. The others above us had already climbed to our left wall then after a minute they started climbing our floor. Like the group before after a few feet from the left wall they stood up rejoining us.

"What is up with this hallway?" asked Mike as Jessica joined us.

"All the walls on this station have gravity plating running through them. We decided it would require too much of our resource to produce gravity field generators large enough to sustain this entire station and the energy consumption would be too high. So instead these foot gears were built and the plating in the floor was built along with them. We use space's own weightlessness to move about the station easily and to move cargo easier. We can also fit more into one area than we could with normal gravity," Movork said as we walked along the corridor.

As we moved deeper into the corridor the crowd of people surrounding us grew thicker and thicker. It was getting harder to see through the ever growing crowd of people. I lost sight of Movork and Shaurha. I didn't stop mainly because there was nowhere they could have turned off and if they were to climb to another level I would be able to see them. After a few minutes I spotted them. They had come to a stop in front of another doorway. The doorway was on my right, next to the doorway was more of the cuts in the wall. Like before the cuts circled the room. Next to the door on the door's left was another orange panel. There were a few of the Talins and humans waiting in front of the door. A few steps after I broke free from the thick mass of people; dozens of humans and Talins walked out from within the crowd.

After we joined Movork and the others in front of the door we waited for a few more minutes then Movork placed his hand on the panel. The door opened revealing another enclosure. We past through the door and stepped onto a solid floor. Once everyone was inside the room Movork removed his hand from the door and slipped inside as the doors started to close. Then Shaurha walked to the wall opposite the doorway and climbed up cuts in the wall. Like before after a few feet she was able to stand on the wall and walk. She walked towards the door above us and after a minute or two she placed her hand on another orange panel. Our feet lifted off the floor as we started to float once again.

Everyone did as before and propelled themselves through the doorway and landed on different walls of the corridor above us. I joined our party in the second corridor. After five minutes everyone had made it through the doorway and was in the process of regrouping with everyone. The corridor in front of us was a little less packed and was shorter than the previous. The wall in front of us had another door with an orange panel glowing next on it. We walked to the end of the hall and passed through the door after Movork placed his hand on the panel. The room on the other side of the doorway was quiet different then the previous rooms. This room was shaped like a giant cylinder that reached hundreds upon thousands of feet high. The shaft was too long to see any sign of an end. The cylinder was a few thousand feet wide.

The entire cylinder had small vessels raising and descending to other levels. There were people walking on the wall of the cylinder. The floor where we were was crowded with people of many species. All of them were busy moving around the station to pay attention to a new race among them. Off to our right was a small booth resting on the cylinder's wall. The operator of the booth was sitting on an eight legged chair. Four legs were on the floor and the other four were attached to the wall. We walked over to the booth then Movork spoke with the operator. After a few minutes Movork returned then after another minute a vessel descended a few feet from us.

"All of you come along; the rest of your race is at the top of the shaft."

We all climbed onto one of the vessels and a few seconds started to head up the shaft. After hour we slowed to a mere crawl. We then began to move forward towards the cylinder wall. We came upon a ledge. We closed in upon the ledge, after a few minutes we landed a ways in on the ledge. There were a few booths scattered around the ledge and large crowds of people near the booths. In front of us there was a large corridor roughly the same shape and size as the shaft. There were a few vessels flying through the corridor.

"Okay, everyone, out of the transport. We have to walk the remainder of the way," said Movork, stepping out of the transport.

We climbed out of the transport and started walking toward the corridor. As we walked the transport lifted off of the ground and started its way back down the shaft. We spread out covering more of the corridor as we started to walk towards the corridor. After a few minutes a vessel in the corridor crashed into another sending the first of the two vessels slamming into the corridor floor. A few seconds later the second vessel crashed in front of the first vessel and started to slide straight down the corridor. My friends and the crowds on the ledge ran to the right and left sides. I had no time to move in any direction except backwards. I ran back down the corridor; the vessel continued to slide across the floor. The only thing I could think of was to run straight and hope the vessel came to a stop.

I watched as the edge of the shaft grew closer and closer. The vessel was too close now there was no way to avoid the inevitable. The edge was only few feet away from me so as I closed in on the edge I decided to jump what the hell I was dead anyway. With only a few inches left I put all my strength into my lunge.

Chapter Twenty-Two
The Truth

Everyone believes me to be dead, and that is how my sister (Queen Paloween) and all but a few people must believe me to be until the treachery has been brought to an end. I will start with my name: Prince Palarise Credity. I was set to inherit the throne when I found out that my father had been the cause of numerous invasions. That includes the planet earth. You see my father had two faces. To our people he was a kind king coming to the aid of other races. However, a very few Talins including myself saw his true side; his evil side. To the rest of my family and everyone else our vacation of exploring the outer planets of earth's solar system was just that, but my father had other plans.

He had a secret scientific station built on one of the moons of the planet the humans call Jupiter. Everyone on the station was either a criminal or species unfriendly to Talins. In the past my father has leaked information to the Shadows of where Talin military bases were and what planets had an abundance of minerals. These leaks weren't always true; however, it got the Shadows to attack the targets in question. Then the Talin fleet would come in and fight off the Shadows long enough to evacuate any possible survivors. Before the Shadows had a chance to construct a strong hold, my father's secret army would wipe the Shadows out with a large enough force to keep the targets in questions from other attacks.

To our people they believe that those planets are owned by the Shadows. I recently found out that my father strip-mined the planets he conquered. My father's last plans of invasion were thwarted by the Shadows. What my father has done is unforgivable and he needed to be stopped. I knew that if my father survived his crash, his plans would go through for the planet earth and he would continue his invasions. After we were hit I began my search for my father. A little while after Shaurha gave the order to evacuate the *Kento,* I found my father and mother about to climb into an escape pod. I couldn't let him continue with his plans; so I drew my side arm and pointed it at my father.

"Dad, don't you move, I can not let you continue with your plans." My father and mother turned.

"Son, what are you talking about? We have to get off this ship."

"Sorry, Mother, but Dad and I are not going anywhere."

"Why?"

"Because Father is the one behind the Shadows invasions of so many races. Isn't it true, Father, you have leaked information about other species to the Shadows?"

"No, it's not true, son."

"You lie. I know the truth and I have the proof and so do others. Isn't it true, Father? Aren't you behind the invasions?"

"No, I am not behind the invasions!"

"Dad, I know about your army of criminals. I know what you have them do."

My mother looked at my father. My father said nothing. He just stared at me as his temper grew and an evil grin grew across his face.

"What are you talking about, son? Why are you accusing your father of such absurd things?" asked my mother.

"Because I know everything, Father."

There was an explosion from somewhere within the *Kento.* The explosion threw me off balance and then my father took the opportunity to lunge at me. He grabbed a hold of my hand holding my firearm. We fought each other for the right to hold the gun when his attempts caused my finger to pull the trigger. My mother screamed and fell to the floor of the *Kento* with a burn in her chest. I fought my father off and raced to her side. She had died almost instantly. My father took the time to run to an escape pod. As the door closed I managed to get one shot into the escape pod. I saw my father fall to the floor as the pod was jettisoned. I rushed over to one of the remaining escape pods, climbed in and sat down in the pilot's seat.

I watched on one of the monitors as the front half of the *Kento* broke free of the back. The back half exploded; the force from the explosion forced me to land on earth's moon. I watched as what remand of the *Kento* entered earth's atmosphere and fell to earth's surface as a mass of fire. I took refuge in the human's communication station on their moon and waited for Talin ships to enter the solar system before I would make contact. For five days I waited when finally I picked up a transmission coming from Shaurha on earth's surface. I listened in on the conversation she had with Fleet Commander Orrea. When Shaurha ended the conversation, I opened one with Orrea and asked her for a lift when she came to pick up my sister. She wanted to send a ship just for me but I knew that if my father had survived; I knew I was safer dead and me being believed to be dead could come in handy so I ordered her to remain quiet about my survival.

A day later a ship came for my sister; just as the ship reached orbit a shuttle was lunched in secret. I set up my escape pod and the station to send video feed back to my com single so I could watch what happened on a computer. I greeted Orrea at her ship. We then returned to the rescue ship. Once on board the ship Orrea and I vanished to one of the vacant quarters.

"It is good to see you, Orrea."

"It's good to see me? Ha-ha you're the one presumed dead; it's more like it is I that is glad to see you prince."

"As I said before, the fewer people that know about my survival the better. I can't afford the public finding out just yet."

"Tell me why I most keep this secret?"

"Fine but you have to promise to listen to everything I have to tell. And at the end I have a favor to ask."

She agreed; I then began telling her about everything my father had done and why I wanted my survival to remain quiet. She was uneasy and horrified that my father the king of our civilization was behind everything the humans and so many other species had gone through. She couldn't accept it that my father was evil nor that my mother was killed accidentally by me and that I tried to end my father's life. But she agreed not to tell a soul, and then I asked her for a favor. I asked her to request live video feed of the humans' battle and their evacuation; I also asked her to leave a probe on earth's moon to capture all transmissions and recorded whatever happened after the planet had been abandoned. She agreed to do these favors then she left me alone in the now not so vacant room.

The room I was in was small, possessing a single bed, a dresser, and a desk with a computer hovering above it. I walked over to the computer, sat down on the chair provided by the floor, and began to type on the keyboard. After a little bit of work I managed to bring up a video feed of the humans' planet earth. I watched as their home burned. The sky was black from smoke red and orange from the fires strong enough to penetrate through the thick smoke. My sister's rescue ship broke through the cloud of smoke ten minutes later causing a ripple in the thick mass of smoke. Her ship docked with us and after a few minutes we began our long safe journey over the human's asteroid belt then home.

A day later one of our evacuation ships (a *Colonizer* class vessel) landed on the surface of earth, leaving five Talin warships in earth's orbit. I listened to the conversations Hamole had with his father and to the conversations Commander Shaurha and Captain Movork shared with the human President Clark. They began making preparations for a battle they could not win no matter how prepared they were. A day later some more Talin vessels arrived above the human's planet. Two days later the invasion began as a large Shadow force joined the space over earth. The space battle was bad to both sides worse thankfully to the Shadows.

Six Shadow warships approached the five Talin warships that were in the planet's orbit. As the battle began the humans unleashed a devastation weapon from their planet's moon. Cannons bigger than anything I have ever seen rose out of the moon. The cannons fired upon one of the Shadow warships. The blast ripped right through the warship, causing it to be destroyed immediately. After ten minutes the cannons fired again destroying another Shadow warship. Another ten minutes went by the cannons fired sticking another warship towards its back. The warship moved itself straight towards the moon and flew straight into the cannons. The surface of the moon exploded. A ball of fire and rock erupted out in to space seconds after the crash.

The other three Shadow warships immediately began to attack the five Talin warships. Both sides lunched fighters. While the warships fought the Talin fighters were hard at work preventing the enemy from entering the human's planet. The efforts of my people paid off destroying the enemy warships with the loss of three Talin ships. The remaining two Talin ships had received some damage but nothing too bad. The next day, two more Shadow warships arrived in orbit. As a battle broke out above earth the humans were getting prepared for a battle. One of the Shadow's ships erupted into flames and burnt up in earth's atmosphere a few minutes later both Talin warships exploded. All the Shadow fighters descended into the atmosphere disappearing in the cloud covering earth. The remainder of the Talin fleet decided to go after the enemy's fighters. Minutes after the last Talin warship exploded another Shadow warship took a position in orbit. Thirty minutes later two more Talin warships arrived above earth and immediately engaged the enemy warships.

The more damaged of the two warships exploded and its remains fell through the atmosphere. The fresher enemy warship retreated but not before it destroyed one of the Talin warships. The Shadow warship had sustained massive amounts of damage and went into hiding somewhere close to earth. The remaining Talin warship the *Franchasno* stayed close to earth's orbit long enough for the evacuation of the humans to finish. The next day I intercepted a message between my sister and Shaurha, Whaloa, Gupp, and Hamole. They were informing her about a human called Alex. She ordered a prosthetic to be given to Alex as thanks for what he had done for her and the four of them. Later that day Captain Movork contacted Amiss and had him move his ship closer to the asteroid belt while the *Colonizer* rose out from under the massive cloud of smoke. Amiss agreed and a little over a half-hour later the *Colonizer* rose out of the thick cloud. As they moved through space toward the asteroid belt they were attacked by a swarm of Shadow fighters and transport ships.

While they were fighting the swarm of ships, another vessel was attacking the Shadow warship that had come out of hiding. The vessel was nothing like any ship in the Talin arsenal. The vessel moved very fast around the Shadow vessel. The vessel easily avoiding the blasts from the warship's weapons due to the vessels speed. There were no Shadow fighters attacking the vessel; however, there were small fighters belonging to the vessel attacking the Shadow warship. As the battle between the two vessels continued the swarm of ships was mostly destroyed. Some of the transports had crashed through the particle field and dug into the *Colonizer*. After an hour the Shadow warship had been destroyed and the vessel that destroyed it had vanished.

After twelve hours more Shadow vessels had showed up and quickly began to make their descent through earth's atmosphere. As they began to make their descent earth began to fight back as thousands upon thousand of explosions ripped the cloud and the atmosphere apart burning everything. "I knew my father was not going to like that if he lived." The enemy ships were all lost in the chain of explosions, detonating across the globe. Immediately Shadow fighters broke from the asteroid belt in response to the chain of explosions and attacked the *Colonizer*. The men and women of every species on the *Colonizer* fought long and hard against a near in visible and extremely fast enemy. As I watched small explosions went off all around the *Colonizer* from the many fighters that swarmed around its particle field.

After a while the Talin fighters flew back into the hangers of the *Colonizer*. After a few more minutes the *Franchasno* began to turn toward the asteroid belt. Fighters were lunched from the *Franchasno* followed by thousands from the *Colonizer*. The *Franchasno* began to fire upon the asteroids of the asteroid belt. As the cannons fired the fighters also fired upon the belt. While the many ships worked on clearing a path, I picked up a transmission to Orrea from Shaurha. I listened in on the conversation for a while listening if Orrea said anything about my survival. One of the things Shaurha said brought my attention to the conversation even more. After Shaurha finished talking I opened up communications with both of them.

"Shaurha, what is so important about this human, Alex?"

"Who is this? Why are you intruding on our conversation?" asked Shaurha.

"Prince Palarise; and I want to know why this kid is important."

"Prince Palarise is dead. He died on the *Kento*. I ask again who is this?" asked Shaurha.

"Shaurha, that is the Prince; he escaped the *Kento's* destruction," said Orrea.

"How do you know, Orrea?"

"Because I have seen him alive and well right before Queen Paloween and I left earth. He has been on board my ship this whole time."

"You have known this whole time and you haven't told anyone?"

"Yes Prince Palarise ordered me to secrecy."

"As the commander of the military I should have known about these things. Prince Palarise, why have you not revealed yourself?"

I spent the next hour telling Shaurha everything about what my father had done and what I have done to stop him.

"My prince, I already knew about the things your father has done."

"You did?"

"Yes I am one of the few people that have been gathering evidence against him."

"That's good, now tell me about this human Alex?"

Shaurha told me everything that Alex and his friends went through and everything that Alex had told to Zar, Mallowen, Hamole, Movork, and herself. She then told me about her and Zar's suspicions about Alex. As they told me everything I began to piece things together.

"Thank you, Shaurha. I have a few things to look into if anything else arises call Orrea and he will transfer you to my room. Orrea, keep your com open for Shaurha's calls."

I shut off the com and went back to watching the *Colonizer's* progress. The progression of the path had been brought to dead stop. I switched to one of the probes left by the *Kento*. The computer showed two Talin warships waiting behind the largest planet in human's system. As I watched the two vessels were forced into a battle by three Shadow warships. One of the Shadow warships left the battle and the other two were destroyed by the two Talin ships. As the two Talin vessels began to make repairs a large blast cut right through one of the two ships. Then the second was cut in half. The blasts continued to carve the Talin ships up. The firing stopped as I took control of the probe and moved it toward the source of the blasts.

Leaving orbit of the large planet was twenty-four warships and one really large Shadow ship. The large ship looked like it toppled the *Colonizer* in size and certainly in firepower. The twenty-five ships moved toward the asteroid belt spreading out around the belt a little. What looked to be a Shadow mother ship had eight of the warships surrounding it. A few of the warships fired into the asteroid belt striking some of the asteroids and grazing a Talin fighter. As I looked upon the trap waiting for the *Franchasno* and the *Colonizer* the image began to turn to static. I could no longer bring up transmissions from either probe. I walked to my bed and got some sleep for I had been awake for five days straight. I awoke a few hours later to my computer buzzing. I got up and walked over to my computer and turned it on after a minute Shaurha, Movork, Zar, and Alex were displayed.

We shared every piece of information we had found out with Alex, Zar, and Movork and they shard information with Shaurha and me. After we finished our chat I decided to see if the probes were still operational or if they had been discovered and destroyed. Both probes had been over looked and were transmitting again. I brought up the feed from the *Kento's* probe first. A large path had been made from the destruction of the *Franchasno* making a path for the remaining Shadow fleet to pass through the asteroid belt safely. There was no sign of any of the Shadow vessels near the asteroid belt so I brought up the feed from the probe on the moon. I looked on as a massive war was being wagged between the Shadows and another party.

Both sides had a massive fleet of ships fighting in and around earth's orbit. The Shadow mother ship had survived and so did thirteen warships. The other party consisted of small vessels larger than fighters and transports but definitely smaller than warships and the mother ship and one ship equal to the size of the mother ship. The vessels moved fast around the Shadow ships. The entire space was swarming with fighters from both sides and Shadow transports moved towards the third parties mother ship. The small vessels looked like they could be made for battle as they had many guns and could take tremendous fire. Both of the mother ships were engaged in a heated battle trying to carve the other up. However, both of their shields were holding under the enemy's fire.

From the number of battleships that were attacking the Shadow ships, I would say that they were winning the battle. After ten minutes of me observing one of the warships was destroyed followed by another and then another. The Shadow warships were being destroyed right and left. Every time the battleships moved onto another warship focusing their fire on certain areas. Only ten warships left and the Shadow started to turn and run from the battle but they were cut off by more battleships and another mother ship coming through the path in the asteroid belt. With the additional ships the party made quick work out of the Shadow warships. Then every vessel weather it be fighter battle ship or the two mother ships opened fire on the enemy mother ship. The extreme amount of fire that was put on the enemy quickly destroyed the mother ship sending the largest portion of its debris into the moon.

I lost my signal from the moon. I switched to *Kento's* probe and watched and listened for something.

"Emperor Jatrit Credity, we have cleared the enemy out of the system. The Hob's home world awaits you, Emperor."

"Thank you, my favorite son. Your brother was a fool and that is why he is dead. When the weapon is reassembled we will have no trouble getting complete control over the entire galaxy. No the universe," said my father, laughing.

"A brother? We have a brother?" I said to myself as I turned off my computer and walked back to my bed.

I lay back and pondered the thought that I may have to kill a brother I only just found out about. Worse than that, my father has a larger army than I thought and they are more destructive than the Shadows ever were. The battleships I had never seen but liked the idea of a ship that was fast, maneuverable and powerful enough to destroy a warship with as little as a scratch on them. The thought of mother ships on both sides that had never been seen made my gut turn. As I thought about it, if we were ever going to stand against my father in battle the Talin fleet would need something just like those vessels and turrets that would be able to fire upon those ships.

I had down loaded all the transmissions that were sent from both probes. I had my evidence against my father now. I knew if I were going to stop him in his campaign the Talin race would need to move in a new direction and needed a new king. I didn't want to be king but I knew I was not up to me it was something I inherited like my sister and was something that I had to do. She was queen and I was king and we were going to have to raise an army bigger than anything Tallinea has ever seen to stop the Shadows once and for all and prevent my father from reassembling the ancient Hob weapon. I got to my feet went over to the computer and contacted Orrea.

"Orrea, where is my sister's room?"

"Her room is on the command level in one of the private quarters."

"I want you and my sister waiting for my outside her room. I will explain everything when I arrive."

"Yes, Prince."

I closed the transmission and then shut my computer off and removed the memory cell then left my room. I turned to my left and walked along the hallway until I came in front of the main lift. As I walked I passed dozens of people all of who looked surprised and glad to see me. I entered the lift and ordered for the command level. The door to the lift closed and I then began to rise higher in Orrea's ship. After twenty minutes the door opened and I exited the lift. As I stepped outside the lift I was greeted by my sister.

"Palarise, you're alive. How did you get here?"

"I am sorry, Paloween. I have been here almost as long as you."

"You have been here alive this whole time and didn't tell me. You have left me thinking that you were dead this whole time. How could you?"

"I am sorry, Paloween. I had to. I have my reasons and that is why I am here."

"What reasons?"

"I can't tell you here. I will tell you in your quarters."

"Orrea, you knew my brother was alive this whole time, didn't you?"

"Yes I did."

"Why didn't you tell me?"

"Your brother ordered me not to."

"Palarise, I order you to tell me why now."

"You can't order me around."

"Yes I can. I was crowed queen a day ago."

"If you want to know then I will tell you but not unless we are in the privacy of your quarters."

"Fine, but you had better tell the truth."

"Don't worry, I will."

I followed Orrea and my sister Queen Paloween her room. After I was in the room I found her computer and placed a call to the *Colonizer*. I received Captain Movork on the other side and asked him to get Shaurha and Zar and report to the conference room.

"Palarise, explain yourself now."

I began telling her about Alex and how he had been having dreams of the Shadows' past conquests and origins. I then continued to tell her about a rumor about the ancient weapon that I heard from our father when I was younger. I then told her what our father was planning to do with the weapon if he ever finds it and about everything he has done to find the fragment of the weapon. She looked as though she didn't believe me. The next words I didn't expect from her.

"You still haven't told me about how you survived?" she said with tears in her eyes.

I told her about the conflict our father and I had on the *Kento* and how our mother was a casualty of our battle.

"Lies, all lies. How could you kill Mother then say such bad things about our father?"

"Prince Palarise, I have gathered Zar and Shaurha as requested," said Movork through the computer.

"Paloween, I have evidence against our father. Here take a look."

I plugged the memory cell into the computer and opened the last two transmissions. All of us looked on as the battle played out as my father's army made quick work of the Shadow warships and one of their mother ships.

"So there are mother ships. Alex was right about the incident."

"If we had stayed and fought we wouldn't have survived."

"You are correct Zar, Movork. What is worse is my father has two of them with the same kind of power and possibly more."

"This could be anyone's army," said my sister.

"That's what I was hoping as I watched but when I heard and saw this next transmission there was no denying that army is our father's," I said as I brought up the last transmission.

"How could Father do this? How could he? He could have saved Alex and all of his people from leaving their homes. His actions are disgraceful. He must be stopped."

"That is what I have been trying to do ever since I found out about our father's actions. I think we need to make a few changes to our current military strategy. From the way the battle looked I would say that the Shadows are starting to lose and if we let my father do the winning then we are all doomed."

"What should we do, brother?" asked my sister.

"First we have to unite our people and those we protect against our father. We have to show the battle and the conversation to everyone. Then we need to start building more ships, ships like what my father is using. We need to increase the efficiency of the turrets on all the warships and we have to build our own mother ships. We need to get everyone that we protect to help fight both of our enemies, otherwise we will not have enough manpower. It will take my father awhile to realize he is still missing one fragment of the weapon and when he learns his son has it he will return to Tallinea full force."

"Palarise, where did this weapon come from?"

"It came from the ancient wars. It was created by the Hob as a final attack only."

"Only the weapon was designed wrong. It could kill the Hob but it caused both the Talin and Maltans to mutate into the Shadows," said Shaurha.

"Then why does our father want such a weapon?" my sister asked.

"He doesn't know what the weapon really does. He only found out about the weapon from a piece of scripture written by the Hob a millennium ago."

"How do all of you know then?"

"Alex has seen the memories from one of the Talins that was turned in the Ancient Wars. His experiences in these dreams have been to close to the truth not to be real. The detail of our cousins and the Hob were completely correct."

"When we reach Tallinea, I will reveal my survival and the evidence against our father. Paloween, you and I will have to meet with the consul to discuss what to do."

"Before you do that you should arrest certain members of the consul for treason. I have all the evidence you will need to arrest them. When we arrive I will hand the evidence to you. Until then arrest them and hold them with no privileges and I mean none. I'm transmitting the list of the corrupted consul members to you now," said Shaurha while she walked to the computer in the conference room.

"Thank you, Shaurha. I didn't know my father's followers went that high."

"No need to thank me. I was only going to do something about them when I was able to do something about your father."

"Is this everything?" my sister asked.

"Yes you know now as much as we do."

"Thank you, Movork, for getting Zar and Shaurha. I will get in touch with you all when the time is right. Shaurha, I will meet you when you dock with the orbital defense network."

"Okay, future King Credity of Tallinea."

The screen then went dark; leaving my sister, Orrea, and me in my sister's room. A few hours later we arrived in Tallinea space. Orrea's ship docked with the station and then Orrea my sister and I made our way down to the consul chambers. While we made our descent I contacted what was left of the royal guard and our private police force. I ordered the police and royal guard to meet us when we landed outside the consul chambers. After an hour we landed outside the consul chambers, both our private police and the royal guard were waiting by the structure's door. Orrea, my sister and I walked into the men and women waiting for us.

"Prince Palarise, Queen Paloween, it is good that you're alive. Although we thought, Prince Palarise, that you were dead."

"I know. I will explain everything at a later date but first there are a few matters that must be dealt with inside," I said as I handed each of them a copy of the list Commander Shaurha gave me.

"What are they accused of?"

"They are accused of treason of the highest degree. They are to be taken to the most secure prison facility where they will wait trial by their peers. They are not to see a single person that includes counsel. They are to be given small rations of food and are not to have access to any computers at all they are to remain in their cells until their trials. They aren't allowed any personal effects of any kind and a full body scan will be done to make sure they have nothing on them other than their prison clothing. I want a guard watching each one of them constantly. Now let's get these traitors before they have a chance to run."

We walked through the door entering into the lobby. We then turned to our right and walked into a hallway. We reached a set of lifts and we all filed into the two lifts and raised forty floors higher into the structure. The door opened and we walked out into another hallway. We walked to our right the light coming through the windows cast shadows of us as we walked. After a few minutes we came upon the door to the consul chamber. My sister opened the door and walked into the chamber with the royal guard following.

"Queen Paloween, you are finally back and unharmed. That is good news."

"We were afraid that something had happened to you on your way back."

"Don't worry about your family's memorials. We have already made the decisions for you. And if you would like, we could make more decisions while you take time to mourn your loss."

"That is enough; I order everyone to be quiet. My family hasn't been dead less than two weeks and you already want to take control over everything."

"Don't be ridiculous. We just want to help you during these awful times."

"Now who's being ridiculous."

"Prince Credity, we thought you were dead."

"Officers, you may proceed with the arrests."

"Arrests, what arrests, and on what grounds?"

"You and a third of the consul are under arrest on the grounds of high treason. You are to be taken to a maxim security facility."

"You can't do, this we have done nothing wrong."

"We have the evidence of your actions."

"As a member of the consul, I demand to see the evidence against my fellow members."

"As Queen of Tallinea, I hereby open a full investigation into the consul's actions thereby temporarily removing everyone from their position as member. All of you that have not been arrested, take heed, the new consul will be watched over extensively. Also you will be kept informed of how the investigation is going. I now suggest you call it a night and go home."

We left the chambers and made our way to our transport. Our police took the fourteen out of thirty consol members away to a maximum security prison. And the royal guard followed us to our former home the royal palace.